D1218520

THERAPY

Books by Jonathan Kellerman

FICTION

Therapy (2004)
The Conspiracy Club (2003)
A Cold Heart (2003)
The Murder Book (2002)
Flesh and Blood (2001)
Dr. Death (2000)
Monster (1999)
Billy Straight (1998)
Survival of the Fittest (1997)
The Clinic (1997)
The Web (1996)
Self-Defense (1995)
Bad Love (1994)
Devil's Waltz (1993)
Private Eyes (1992)
Time Bomb (1990)
Silent Partner (1989)
The Butcher's Theater (1988)
Blood Test (1986)
When the Bough Breaks (1985)

NONFICTION

Savage Spawn: Reflections on Violent Children (1999)
Helping the Fearful Child (1981)
Psychological Aspects of Childhood Cancer (1980)

FOR CHILDREN, WRITTEN AND ILLUSTRATED

Jonathan Kellerman's ABC of Weird Creatures (1995)
Daddy, Daddy, Can You Touch the Sky? (1994)

THERAPY

JONATHAN KELLERMAN

THERAPY

DOUBLEDAY LARGE PRINT HOME LIBRARY EDITION

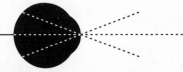

This Large Print Book carries the
Seal of Approval of N.A.V.H.

To the memory of Warren Zevon.

Special thanks to Dr. Leah Ellenberg.

THERAPY

CHAPTER

1

A few years ago a psychopath burned down my house.

The night it happened, I was out to dinner with the woman who'd designed the house and lived in it with me. We were driving up Beverly Glen when the sirens cut through the darkness, ululating, like coyote death wails.

The noise died quickly, indicating a nearby disaster, but there was no reason to assume the worst. Unless you're the worst kind of fatalist, you think: "Something lousy happened to some poor devil."

That night, I learned different.

Since then, the Klaxon of an ambulance or a fire truck in my neighborhood sets off something inside me—a crimp of shoulder, a catch of breath, an arrhythmic flutter of the plum-colored thing in my chest.

Pavlov was right.

I'm trained as a clinical psychologist, could do something about it but have chosen not to. Sometimes anxiety makes me feel alive.

◆

When the sirens shrieked, Milo and I were having dinner at an Italian place at the top of the Glen. It was ten-thirty on a cool June night. The restaurant closes at eleven, but we were the last patrons, and the waiter was looking tired. The woman I was now seeing was teaching a night course in abnormal psychology at the U., and Milo's partner, Rick Silverman, was busy at the Cedars-Sinai ER trying to salvage the five most seriously injured victims of a ten-car pileup on the Santa Monica Freeway.

Milo had just closed the file on a robbery-turned-to-multiple-homicide at a liquor store on Pico Boulevard. The solve had taken more persistence than brainwork. He was in a position to pick his cases, and no new ones had crossed his desk.

I'd finally finished testifying at the seemingly endless child-custody hearings waged by a famous director and his famous actress wife. I'd begun the consult with some optimism. The director had once been an actor, and both he and his ex knew how to perform. Now, three years later, two kids who'd started out in pretty good shape were basket cases living in France.

Milo and I chewed our way through focaccia and baby artichoke salad, orrechiati stuffed with spinach, veal pounded to paper. Neither of us felt like talking. A bottle of decent white wine smoothed the silence. Both of us were strangely content; life wasn't fair, but we'd done our jobs well.

When sirens came, I kept my eyes on my plate. Milo stopped eating. The napkin he'd tucked in his shirt collar was spotted with spinach and olive oil.

"Don't worry," he said. "Not a fire."

"Who's worrying?"

He pushed hair off his forehead, picked up his fork and knife, speared, chewed, swallowed.

I said, "How can you tell?"

"That it's not a big-red? Trust me, Alex.

It's a black-and-white. I know the frequency."

A second cruiser wailed by. Then a third.

He pulled his tiny blue cell phone out of his pocket and punched a button. A preset number rang.

I raised my eyebrows.

"Just curious," he said. His connection went through, and he told the phone, "This is Lieutenant Sturgis. What call just went out in the vicinity of upper Beverly Glen? Yeah, near Mulholland." He waited, green eyes dimmed to near brown in the miserly light of the restaurant. Under the spotted napkin was a baby blue polo shirt that really didn't work well with his pallid complexion. His acne pits were flagrant, his jowls gravid as freshly filled wineskins. Long white sideburns frizzed his big face, a pair of skunkish stripes that seemed to sprout artificially from his black hair. He's a gay policeman and my best friend.

"That so," he said. "Any detective assigned, yet? Okay, listen, I happen to be right near there, can make it over in ten—no make that fifteen—make it twenty minutes. Yeah, yeah, sure."

He snapped the little phone shut. "Double

homicide, two bodies in a car. Being this close, I figured I should have a look. The crime scene's still being secured, and the techs haven't gotten there, so we can still have dessert. How are you with cannoli?"

◆

We split the check, and he offered to drive me home, but neither of us took that seriously.

"In that case," he said, "we'll take the Seville."

I drove quickly. The crime scene was on the west side of the intersection between the Glen and Mulholland, up a skinny, decomposed, granite road marked PRIVATE that climbed through sycamore-crowned hillside.

A police cruiser was stationed at the mouth of the road. Staked to a tree several feet up was a FOR SALE sign bearing the logo of a Westside Realtor. Milo flashed the badge to the uniform in the car, and we drove through.

At the top of the road was a house behind high, night-blackened hedges. Two more black-and-whites kept us ten yards back. We parked and continued on foot. The sky was purplish, the air still bitter with the smolder of two early-summer brush fires, one up near Camarillo, the other past Tujunga. Both had just been vanquished. One had been set by a fireman.

Behind the hedges was stout wooden fencing. Double gates had been left open. The bodies slumped in a red Mustang convertible parked on a semicircular flagstone driveway. The house behind the drive was a vacant mansion, a big neo-Spanish thing that was probably cheerful peach in the daylight. At this hour, it was putty gray.

The driveway bordered a half acre of front yard, shaded by more sycamores—giant ones. The house looked newish and was ruined by too many weird-shaped windows, but someone had been smart enough to spare the trees.

The top was down on the little red car. I stood back and watched as Milo approached, careful to stay behind the tape. He did nothing but stare. Moments later, a pair of crime-scene techs walked onto the property lugging cases on a dolly. They talked to him briefly, then slipped under the tape.

He walked back to the Seville. "Looks like gunshot wounds to both heads, a guy and a girl, young. He's in the driver's seat, she's next to him. His fly's open, and his shirt's half-unbuttoned. Her shirt's clean off, tossed in the backseat along with her bra. Below the shirt she wore black leggings. They're rolled down to her ankles, and her legs are spread."

"Lover's lane thing?" I said.

"Empty house," he said. "Good neighborhood. Probably a nice view from the backyard. Seize the night and all that? Sure."

"If they knew about the house, they could be locals."

"He looked clean-cut, well dressed. Yeah, I'd say local is also a decent bet."

"I wonder why the gate was left open."

"Or maybe it wasn't, and one of them has some connection to the house and a gate-clicker. For all we know, one of their families built the place. Crime Scene will do their thing, hopefully they'll find IDs in the pockets. The car's plates are being run right now."

I said, "Any gun in sight?"

"A murder-suicide thing? Not likely."

He rubbed his face. His hand lingered at his mouth, tugged down his lower lip and let it snap back up.

"What?" I said.

"Two head-shots plus, Alex. Someone jammed what looks to be a short spear or a crossbow bolt into the girl's torso. Here." He touched a spot under his breastbone. "From what I could see the damn thing went clear through her and is lodged in the seat. The impact jolted her body, she's lying funny."

"A spear."

"She was skewered, Alex. A bullet to the brain wasn't enough."

"Overkill," I said. "A message. Were they actually making love or were they positioned sexually?"

He flashed a frightening smile. "Now we're veering into your territory."

CHAPTER

2

The techs and the coroner gloved up and did their thing under heartless floodlights. Milo talked to the uniforms who'd arrived first on the scene, and I stood around.

He loped over to one of the big syca-mores, said something to no apparent lis-tener, and a nervous-looking Hispanic man in baggy clothes stepped from behind the trunk. The man talked with his hands and looked agitated. Milo did a lot of listening. He took out his notepad and scrawled with-out breaking eye contact. When he was fin-ished, the man was allowed to leave the scene.

The spear in the girl's chest appeared to

be a homemade weapon fashioned from a slat of wrought-iron fencing. The coroner who manipulated it free said so out loud as she carried it beyond the yellow tape perimeter and laid it on an evidence sheet.

The uniforms checked the property for similar fencing, found iron around a pool, but a different diameter.

DMV came through with the car's registration: the Mustang was one year old and registered to Jerome Allan Quick, of South Camden Drive in Beverly Hills. A wallet in the pocket of the male victim's khakis yielded a driver's license that confirmed him as Gavin Ryan Quick, two months past his twentieth birthday. A student ID card put him as a sophomore at the U., but the card was two years old. In another pocket, the techs retrieved a joint wrapped in a baggie and a foil-wrapped condom. Another condom, out of the foil but unrolled, was discovered on the floor of the Mustang.

Neither the girl's black leggings or her gold silk shirt contained pockets. No purse or handbag was found in the car or anywhere else. Blond, thin, pale, pretty, she remained unidentified. Even after the spear was removed, she lay contorted, chest thrust at the night sky, neck twisted, eyes wide-open. A spidery position no living creature would have entertained.

The coroner wouldn't commit but guessed from the arterial blood spatter that she'd been alive while being impaled.

◆

Milo and I drove to Beverly Hills. Once again, he offered to drop me off; once again, I laughed. Allison would be home by now, but we weren't living together, so there was no reason to let her know where I was. Back when Robin and I did live together, I checked in most of the time. Sometimes I was derelict. The least of my sins.

I said, "Who was the guy you interviewed?"

"Night watchman employed by the real estate company. His job is to drive around at the end of the day, check out the high-priced listings, make sure everything's secure. The brokerage gives the key out to their agents, and agents from other outfits can come by and borrow copies. Supposedly a foolproof system, but doors don't get locked, windows and gates are left open. That's probably what happened here. The house was shown today by three brokers. It was the watchman's last stop, he covers everything from San Gabriel to the beach. He's the one who found the bodies and phoned it in."

"But you'll paraffin him, anyway."

"Done. No gunshot residue. I'll also be checking the three brokers and their clients."

I crossed Santa Monica Boulevard, drove east, headed south on Rodeo Drive. Shops were closed, but storefronts were bright. A homeless man steered a shopping cart past Gucci.

"So you're taking the case," I said.

He rode half a block before answering. "Been a while since I had me a nice little whodunit, good to stay in shape."

He'd always claimed to hate whodunits, but I said nothing. The last one had closed a while back, a cold-hearted killer executing people with artistic talent. The day after Milo filed his final report, he said, "Ready for some low-IQ bar shootings, bad guys holding the smoking gun."

Now he said, "Yeah, yeah, I'm a glutton for punishment. Let's get this over with."

◆

Jerome Allan Quick lived on a pretty street a block and a half south of Wilshire. This was the middle ground of Beverly Hills, meaning pleasant houses on fifth-acre lots that ran between one and two million.

The Quick residence was a two-story white traditional, open to the street. A white minivan and a gray baby Benz shared the driveway. Lights out. Everything looked peaceful. That would change soon.

Milo phoned Beverly Hills PD to let them know he'd be making a notification call, then we got out and walked to the house. His knock elicited only silence. His doorbell ring brought footsteps and a woman's voice asking who it was.

"Police."

Lights on in the entry illuminated the peephole in the door. The door opened, and the woman said, "Police? What's going on?"

She was in her midforties, trim but wide in the hips, wore green velour sweats, glasses on a chain, and nothing on her feet. Ash-blond hair was texturized to faux careless-ness. At least four shades of blond that I

could make out in the light over the doorway, blended artfully. Her nails were painted
silver. Her skin looked tired. She squinted
and blinked. The house behind her was
silent.

There's no good way to do what Milo had
to do. She sagged and screamed and
tore at her hair and accused him of being
crazy and a goddamn liar. Then her eyes
bugged and her hand snapped across her
mouth and a retching sound forced its way
through her fingers.

I was the first to follow her into her
kitchen, where she vomited into a stainless-
steel sink. Milo hung near the doorway,
looking miserable but still taking the time to
examine the room.

As she threw up convulsively, I stood behind her but didn't touch her. When she was
finished, I got her a paper towel.

She said, "Thank you, that was very . . ."

She started to smile, then she saw me for
the stranger I was and began to shake un-
controllably.

◆

When we finally made it to the living room,
she remained on her feet and insisted we

sit. We perched on a blue brocade sofa. The room was pretty.

She stared at us. Her eyes were blood-shot. Her face had gone white.

"Can I get you coffee and cake?"

Milo said, "Don't go to any trouble, Mrs. Quick."

"Sheila." She hurried back to the kitchen. Milo clenched and unclenched his hands. My eyes ached. I stared at a Picasso print of an old guitarist, a reproduction cherrywood grandfather clock, pink silk flowers in a crystal vase, family photos. Sheila Quick, a thin, gray-haired man, a dark-haired girl about twenty, and the boy in the Mustang.

She returned with two mismatched mugs of instant coffee, a jar of powdered whitener, a plate of sugar cookies. Her lips were bloodless. "I'm so sorry. Here, maybe this will make you feel better."

Milo said, "Ma'am—"

"*Sheila.* My husband's in Atlanta."

"Business?"

"Jerry's a metals dealer. He visits scrap-yards and smelters and whatever." She fooled with her hair. "Have one, please, they're Pepperidge Farms."

Lifting a cookie from the plate, she

dropped it, tried to pick it up, crushed it to crumbs on the carpet.

"*Now* look what I did!" She threw up her hands and cried.

◆

Milo was gentle, but he probed, and he and Sheila Quick fell into a routine: short questions from him, long, rambling answers from her. She seemed hypnotized by the sound of her own voice. I didn't want to think about what it would be like when we left.

Gavin Quick was the younger of two children. A twenty-three-year-old sister named Kelly attended law school at Boston University. Gavin was a very good boy. No drugs, no bad company. His mother couldn't think of anyone who'd want to hurt him.

"It's really a pretty stupid question, Detective."

"It's just something I have to ask, ma'am."

"Well it doesn't apply here. No one would want to hurt Gavin, he's been hurt enough."

Milo waited.

She said, "He was in a terrible car crash."

"When was this, ma'am?"

"Just under a year ago. He's lucky he

wasn't—" Her voice choked. She lowered her head to her hands, and her back hunched and trembled.

It took a while for her to show her face. "Gavin was with a bunch of friends—college friends, he was just finishing his second year at the U., was studying economics. He was interested in business—not Jerry's business. Finance, real estate, big things."

"What happened?"

"What—oh the crash? Pointless, absolutely pointless, but do kids listen? They denied it, but I'm sure drinking had something to do with it."

"They?"

"The boy who was driving—his insurance company. They wanted to reduce their liability. Obviously. A kid from Whittier, Gavin knew him from school. He was killed, so we couldn't very well harass his parents, but the time it took the insurance company to compensate us for Gavin's medical was— you don't need to hear this."

She grabbed a tissue and wiped her eyes.

"What exactly happened, Mrs. Quick?"

"What happened? Six of them piled into a stupid little Toyota and were speeding way too fast on Pacific Coast Highway. They'd been to a concert in Ventura and were heading back to L.A. The driver—the boy who died, Lance Hernandez—missed a turn and plowed right into the mountainside. He and the front-seat passenger were killed instantly. The two boys in the back next to Gavin were only injured slightly. Gav was sandwiched between them; he was the skinniest, so he got the middle spot, and there was no seat belt. The Highway Patrol told us it was lucky for him he was squished so tight between them because that prevented him from flying. As is, he was thrown forward and the front of his head hit the back of the driver's seat. His shoulder was wrenched, and some small bones in his feet broke when they were bent back. The funny thing is, there was no blood, no bruising, just the smallest bump on his forehead. He wasn't in a coma or anything, but they did tell us he'd suffered a severe concussion. He had a memory loss that was pretty bad for a few days, it really took weeks for his head to clear fully. Other than that, when the bump went down, there was nothing you could see from the outside. But I'm his mother, I knew he was different."

"Different how, Mrs. Quick?"

"Quieter—does it matter? What does it have to do with this?"

"Collecting background, ma'am."

"Well, I don't see the point of it. First you come in here and tear my life to shreds, then you—I'm sorry, I'm just taking it out on you rather than kill myself." Big smile. "First my baby gets thrown against a seat, now you're telling me he was shot by some maniac—where did it happen?"

"Off of Mulholland Drive, north of Beverly Glen."

"All the way up there? Well, I wouldn't know what he'd be doing there." She looked at us with newfound skepticism, as if hoping we were wrong about everything.

"He was parked in his car with a young woman."

"A young—" Sheila Quick's hand wadded the tissue. "Blond, good figure, pretty?"

"Yes, ma'am."

"*Kayla,*" she said. "Oh my God, Gavin and Kayla, why didn't you tell me it was both of them—now I have to tell Paula and Stan— oh God how am I going to—"

"Kayla was Gavin's girlfriend?"

"Is—was. I don't know, they were something." Sheila Quick placed the tissue on the sofa cushion and sat immobile. The crushed paper began expanding, as if by its own volition, and she stared at it.

"Mrs. Quick?" said Milo.

"Gavin and Kayla were off and on," she said. "They knew each other from Beverly High. After the accident, when Gavin . . ." She shook her head. "I can't tell her parents, I'm sorry—will *you* tell them?"

"Of course. What's Kayla's last name and where do her folks live?"

"You can use my kitchen phone. I'm sure they're up, at least Stan is. He's a night person. He's a musician, composes commercials, movie scores. He's very successful. They live up in the flats."

"The last name, ma'am?"

"Bartell. Used to be Bartelli or something Italian like that. Kayla's a blondie, but she's Italian. Must be northern Italian. At least on Stan's side, I don't know what Paula is. Do you think I should call my husband in Atlanta? It's really late there, and I'm sure he's had a busy day."

◆

Milo asked a few more questions, learned nothing, got her to sip from one of the mugs of instant coffee, found out the name of her family physician, Barry Silver, and woke him up. The doctor lived in Beverly Hills and said he'd be over soon.

Milo asked to see Gavin's room and Sheila Quick took us up a maroon plush-carpeted staircase, flung the door open, flicked a light switch. The room was generous and painted pale blue and stank of body odor and rot. A queen-sized bed was unmade, rumpled clothes were piled on the floor, books and papers were strewn haphazardly, dirty dishes and fast-food cartons filled in the empty spaces. I've seen the police leave drug houses more composed after an evidence toss.

Sheila Quick said, "Gavin used to be neat. Before the accident. I tried, I gave up." She shrugged. Shame colored her face. She closed the door. "Some battles aren't worth fighting. Do you have kids?"

We shook our heads.

"Maybe you're the lucky ones."

◆

She insisted we leave before the doctor arrived, and when Milo tried to argue, she

pressed a hand to her temple and grimaced, as if he was causing her great pain.

"Let me be with my thoughts. *Please.*"

"Yes, ma'am." He got the address for
Stan and Paula Bartell. Same street, Camden Drive, but the eight hundred block, one
mile north, on the other side of the business
district.

"The Flats," Sheila Quick reiterated.
"They've got some place."

◆

When you see stock footage of Beverly
Hills in the movies, it's almost always the
Flats. Directors favor the sun-splotched,
palm-lined drives like Foothill and Beverly,
but any of the broad streets wedged between Santa Monica and Sunset will do
when the connotation is primal California af-
fluence. In the Flats, teardowns began at 2
million bucks and pumped-up piles of
stucco can fetch more than triple that
amount.

Tourists from the East usually have the
same impression of the area: so clean, so
green, such miserly lots. Houses that would
grace multiple acreage in Greenwich or
Scarsdale or Shaker Heights are shoe-

horned onto half-acre rectangles. That doesn't stop the residents from erecting thirteen-thousand-square-foot imitations of Newport mansions that elbow their neighbors.

The Bartell house was one of those, a hulking, flat-faced wedding cake set behind a pitiful front yard that was mostly circular driveway. White fencing topped with gold finials shielded the property. A security sign promising ARMED RESPONSE hung near the electric gate. Through the fence, double doors with frosted-glass panes were backlit teal green. Above them, a giant porthole showcased a white-hot chandelier. No vehicles in front; a four-car garage provided ample shelter for automotive pets.

Milo inhaled, and said, "Once more with feeling," and we got out. Cars zipped by on Sunset, but North Camden Drive was still. Beverly Hills has a thing for trees, and the ones lining Camden were magnolias that would've loved South Carolina. Here they were stunted by drought and smog, but a few were flowering, and I could smell their fragrance.

Milo punched a button on the squawk box. A man barked, "Yes?"

"Mr. Bartell?"

"Who is this?"

"Police."

"About what?"

"Could we come in please, sir?"

"What's this about?"

Milo frowned. "Your daughter, sir."

"My—hold on."

Seconds later, lights flooded the front of the house. Now I saw that the glass doors were flanked by orange trees in pots. One was failing. The doors swung open, and a tall man walked across the driveway. He stopped fifteen feet from us, shaded his eyes with his hands, took three steps more, into the floodlights, like a performer.

"What's this all about?" said a deep, hoarse voice.

Stan Bartell stepped up close. Late fifties, Palm Springs tan. A big man with powerful shoulders, a hawk nose, thin lips, a bulky chin. Waxy white hair was drawn back in a ponytail. He wore black-framed eyeglasses, a thin gold chain around his neck, and an iridescent burgundy velvet robe that brushed the ground.

Milo produced his badge, but Bartell didn't come any closer.

"What about my daughter?"

"Sir, it would really be better if we came in."

Bartell removed his glasses and studied us. His eyes were close-set, dark, analytic. "You're Beverly Hills police?"

"L.A."

"Then what are you doing here—I'm going to check you out, so if this is a scam, you've been warned." He returned to the house, closed the doors behind him.

We waited on the sidewalk. Headlights appeared at the south end of the block, followed by bass thumps as a Lincoln Navigator drove by slowly. Behind the wheel was a kid who looked no older than fifteen, baseball hat worn backwards, hip-hop music bellowing from the interior. The SUV continued to Sunset, cruising the Strip.

Five minutes passed with no word or sign from Stan Bartell.

I said, "How much detail will Beverly Hills PD give him?"

"Who knows?"

We waited another couple of minutes. Milo ran his hand along the white fence slats. Eyed the security sign. I knew what he was thinking: all the safety measures in the world.

◆

The electric gate slid open. Stan Bartell stepped out of his house and stood on his front steps and waved us in. When we got to the door, he said, "The only thing they know about LAPD being here is something called a notification on a kid my daughter knows. Let me see your badge just to be safe."

Milo showed it to him.

"You're the one," said Bartell. "So what's with Gavin Quick?"

"You know him?"

"Like I said, my daughter knows him." Bartell shoved his hands in the pockets of his robe. "Does notification mean what I think it does?"

"Gavin Quick was murdered," said Milo.

"What does my daughter have to do with it?"

"A girl was found with Gavin. Young, blond—"

"Bullshit," said Bartell. "Not Kayla."

"Where is Kayla?"

"Out. I'll call her on my cell phone. C'mon, I'll show you."

We followed him inside. The entry hall was twenty feet high, marble-floored, a lot larger than the Quick's living room. The house was an orgy of beige, except for amethyst-colored glass flowers everywhere. Huge, frameless, abstract canvases were all painted in variations upon that same noncommittal earth tone.

Wordlessly, Stan Bartell led us past several other huge rooms to a studio at the rear. Wood floors and a beamed ceiling. A couch, two folding chairs, a grand piano, an electric organ, synthesizers, mixers, tape decks, an alto sax on a stand, and a gorgeous archtop guitar that I recognized as a fifty-thousand-dollar D'Aquisto in an open case.

On the walls were framed gold records.

Bartell slumped onto the couch, pointed an accusing finger at Milo, and pulled a phone out of his pocket. He dialed, put the phone to his ear, waited.

No answer.

"Doesn't mean a thing," he said. Then his bronze face crumpled, and he broke into wracking sobs.

◆

Milo and I stood by helplessly.

Finally, Bartell said, "What did that fucking little bastard do to her?"

"Gavin?"

"I told Kaylie he was weird, stay away. Especially since the accident—you know about his fucking accident, right? Must've had some kind of brain damage the little fu—"

"His mother—"

"Her. Crazy bitch."

"You've had problems with them."

"She's nuts," said Bartell.

"In what way?"

"Just weird. Never leaves the house. The *problem* was their son going after my angel." Bartell's fists were huge. He raised his eyes to the ceiling and rocked. "Oh, Jesus, this is bad, this is so fucking *bad*!" His eyes sparked with panic. "My wife—she's in Aspen. She doesn't ski, but she goes there in the summer. For shopping, the air. Oh shit, she'll die, she'll just crumple up and fucking die."

Bartell bent and grasped his knees and rocked some more. "How could this happen?"

Milo said, "Why do you think Gavin Quick would've hurt Kayla?"

"Because he was—the kid was weird. Kaylie knew him from high school. She broke up with him a bunch of times, but he kept coming back, and she kept letting him down too easy. Little bastard would show up, sniff around even when Kaylie wasn't in. Bugging me—like kissing up to the old man would help. I work at home, I'm trying to get some work done, and the little fucker is bullshitting me about music, trying to have a conversation like he knows something. I do a lot of jingles, have deadlines, you think I want to discuss alternative punk with some stupid kid? He'd sit himself down, never want to leave. Finally, I told the maid to stop letting him in."

"Obsessive," I said.

Bartell hung his head.

"Was he more obsessive since the accident?" said Milo.

Bartell looked up. "So he did it."

"Unlikely, Mr. Bartell. No weapon was found at the scene, so my instinct is he was just a victim."

"What are you saying? What the fuck are you—"

Footsteps—light footsteps—made all three of us turn.

A pretty young girl in low-riding, skintight jeans that looked oiled and a black midriff blouse exposing a flat, tan abdomen stood in the doorway. Two belly-button pierces, one studded with turquoise. Over her shoulder was a black silk bag embroidered with silk flowers. She wore too much makeup, had a beak nose and a strong chin. Her hair was long, straight, the color of new hay. The blouse revealed luminous cleavage. A big gold *"K"* on a chain rested in the cleft.

Stan Bartell's tan faded to blotchy beige. "What the—" He slapped his hand over his heart, then reached out toward the girl with both hands. "Baby, baby!"

The girl frowned, and said, *"What,* Dad?"

Stan Bartell said, "Where the hell have you been?"

Kayla Bartell stared at her father as if he'd gone mad. "Out."

"With who?"

"Friends."

"I called your cell."

Kayla shrugged. "I switched it off. The club was loud, I couldn't have heard it anyway."

Bartell started to say something, then drew her near and hugged her. She glanced at us, as if seeking rescue.

"*Da*-ad."

"Thank God," said Bartell. "Thank almighty God."

"Who are these people, Daddy?"

Bartell let go of his daughter and glowered at us. "Leave."

Milo said, "Ms. Bartell—"

"No!" shouted Bartel. "Out. Now."

"Who *are* they, Daddy?"

"They're *no one*."

Milo said, "At some point, I'd like to talk to Kayla."

"When pigs take the Concorde."

◆

When we reached the door, Bartell stood on his front steps and jabbed a remote control. The gates began sliding, and Milo and I barely made it through before they clanged shut.

Bartell slammed his door.

Milo said, "Your friendly neighborhood policeman, making friends and spreading good cheer wherever he goes."

◆

As we drove away, he said, "Interesting how Bartell assumed Gavin had done something to Kayla. You used the word 'obsessive.' "

"Bartell's hostility could just be resentment at someone sniffing around his angel. But obsessiveness can be a side effect of head injury."

"What about that pigsty room? Kid's mother claims he used to be neat. That fits with brain damage?"

"Catch a strong blow to the frontal lobes, and there can be all sorts of changes."

"Permanent?"

"Depends on the severity of the injury. In most cases, it's temporary."

"Gavin got hurt ten months ago."

"Not a good sign," I said. "I'd like to know how he was functioning, in general. The student ID in his pocket was two years old. Assuming he dropped out, what's he been doing since then?"

"Maybe getting on the bad side of the wrong people," he said. "Getting *obsessive*. I'll have another go-round with Sheila. Bartell said she was weird. You spot anything?"

"The context we saw her in, anything less than breakdown would be weird."

"Yeah . . . I'll check the father out when he gets back from Atlanta . . . I love my job—enough for one night. Drop me back at the Glen and nighty-night."

I got onto Sunset and crossed the border into Holmby Hills. Milo said, "The big question right now is, who was the girl? And why impale her and not Gavin?"

"That and the way she was left says a sexual thing," I said. "Eliminate the male, have your way with the female."

"Think the coroner will find evidence of sexual assault?"

"If we're dealing with a sexual psychopath, the impalement might suffice."

"Surrogate penetration?"

I nodded.

"So maybe it's a twisted thing," he said. "Nothing to do with the victims, they were just a couple of kids happened to be in the wrong place at the wrong time."

"It could go that way," I said.

He laughed softly. "And I volunteered for this one."

"Who better than you?" I said.

"Meaning?"

"Meaning you'll do a good job on it."

He didn't answer. I slowed down for a couple of turns, got on a straight stretch, and glanced at him. The merest excuse for a smile wormed its way across his lips.

"What a pal," he said.

◆

The following morning I had an early breakfast with Allison Gwynn before her first patient. Her office is in Santa Monica, on Montana, east of Boutique Row, and we met at a pastry shop nearby. It was 7:40 A.M., and the place hadn't yet filled with people of leisure. Allison had on a white linen suit and white sandals that set off her long black hair. She never goes out without makeup and an assortment of serious jewelry. Today it was coral and gold, pieces we'd picked up on a recent trip to Santa Fe.

She was there when I arrived, had finished half a cup of coffee. "Good morning. Don't *you* look handsome."

I kissed her and sat down. "Morning, Gorgeous."

We'd been seeing each other for a little over six months, were still in that stage where the pulse quickened and the body flushed.

We ordered sweet rolls and set about getting into conversational gear. At first it was small things, then sexual banter, then work. Shoptalk can kill a relationship, but so far I'd enjoyed it.

She went first. Busy week, grading papers for the courses she taught, a full patient load, volunteering at a hospice. Eventually, we got around to talking about the previous night. Allison takes an interest in what I do—more than an interest. She's attracted to the ugliest aspects of human behavior, and sometimes I wonder if that isn't part of what cements us. Maybe it's life experience. She was sexually humiliated as a teenager, widowed in her twenties, carries a gun in her purse, and loves to shoot at paper human targets. I don't think much about it. Too much analysis, and there's no time to live.

I described the crime scene.

She said, "Mulholland Drive. When I went to Beverly, we used to go up there to park all the time."

"We?"

She grinned. "Me and the other alleged virgins."

"A religious experience."

"Not back then, you can be sure of that," she said. "Young boys and all that—too much enthusiasm, not enough finesse."

I laughed. "So it was a well-known make-out spot."

"That you missed out on, you poor Midwest boy. Yup, my dear, Mulholland was *the* make-out spot. Probably still is, though there's probably less lover's lane stuff going on because kids are allowed to do it in their own rooms. I'm amazed at how many of my patients go along with that. You know the rationale: Better I should know where they are."

"There are two families who probably feel that way right now."

She pushed hair behind her ear. "Tragic."

The sweet rolls arrived, coated with almond slivers, warm. She said, "A vacant house. That creative we weren't. They probably spotted the FOR SALE sign and the open gate, seized the opportunity. Poor parents. First the boy's accident, now this. You said he changed. In what way?"

"His room was a sty, and his mother claimed he'd once been neat. She didn't say much. It wasn't the time to press."

"No, of course not."

I said, "His ex-girlfriend's father described him as obsessive."

"In what way?"

"Showing up at the girl's house unexpectedly. When she wasn't home, he'd bug the father, hang around asking questions. The father also implied Gavin had been overly persistent with his daughter. His first reaction when he thought his daughter was dead was that Gavin had done something to her."

"That could be more like Protective Dad."

"Could be."

"Was there any postconcussive syndrome?" she said. "Loss of consciousness, blurred vision, disorientation?"

"Some transitory memory loss is all the mother mentioned."

"The crash was ten months ago," she said. "And the mother's still talking about him as changed."

"I know," I said. "The damage might've been permanent. But I'm not sure any of that matters, Ally. Make-out spots attract voyeurs and worse. Either Gavin and the girl were interrupted midcoitus, or they were positioned to look that way."

"A sicko." She studied her sweet roll but didn't touch it. Smiled. "To be technical."

"It's a little early in the day for technical," I said.

"Mulholland Drive," she said. "The things we do when we think we're immortal."

◆

We strolled the three blocks to her office. Allison's hand clasped my biceps. Her open-toed white shoes had generous heels, and that brought the top of her head to my bottom lip. A bit of ocean breeze lifted her hair, and soft strands brushed against my face.

She said, "Milo volunteered for this one?"

"He didn't seem to need any convincing."

"I guess it makes sense," she said. "He's been looking pretty bored."

"I hadn't noticed."

"You'd know better, but that's how it's seemed to me."

"He'll be getting plenty of stimulation on this one."

"So will you."

"If I'm needed."

She laughed. "Be good for you, too."

"I've been looking bored?"

"More like restless. All that caged animal energy."

I growled and beat my chest with my free hand and let out a low-volume Tarzan roar. Two women power-walking our way scrunched up their lips and gave us wide berth as they passed.

"You just made their day," she said.

◆

Milo, bored. He griped so much about work stress, personal stress, the state of the world, anything at hand, that I'd never considered the concept.

When had Allison seen him last . . . two weeks ago. Late-night dinner at Café Moghul, the Indian restaurant near the West L.A. station that he uses as a second office. The proprietors believe his presence ensures them peace and security and treat him like a maharajah.

That night, Allison and I, Rick, and the big guy had been treated to a gut-stretching banquet. Allison and Milo happened to sit next to each other and ended up talking for most of the evening. It's taken him a while to warm up to her. To the notion that I'm with someone new. Robin and I were together for over a decade, and he adores her. Robin had found happiness with another man. I thought I was dealing with that pretty well as she and I struggled to build a new kind of friendship. Except for when I wasn't.

I was waiting for Milo to stop acting like a kid caught in a custody dispute.

The morning after the Indian dinner, he

called me, and said, "You have your quirks, but when you settle on one, she's a keeper."

◆

The day after the murder, he phoned. "No semen on the girl, no sign of sexual assault. Unless you count the spear. The same .22 was used to shoot both of them, one bullet each, right to the forehead. Your hostile or out-of-control shooter tends to empty his weapon. Meaning this was a guy with confidence. Cool, maybe with experience."

"Confident and careful," I said. "Also, he didn't want to make a lot of noise."

"Maybe," he said. "Though given the site—the nearest house is a couple of acres away—he was probably okay on that account. Also, the gun would have gone *pop pop,* no big explosion. No exit wounds, the bullets bounced around the kids' brains, did the kind of damage you'd expect from a .22."

"Has the girl been identified?"

"Not yet. Her prints don't appear to be in the system, though I can't say for sure, because the computer's been screwing up. I've talked to our Missing Persons guys, and they're putting together some paper. I did a bit of calling around to other stations, but young blond girls aren't a rare commodity when you're talking MP. My guess is she'll turn out to be another of Gavin's Beverly Hills friends. Though if she was, you'd expect someone to miss her by now, and no one called or filed at B.H. on a missing girl."

"Sleepover," I said. "Nowadays, parents are lenient. And affluent parents are more likely to be out of town."

"Would've been nice to talk to Kayla . . . meanwhile, I got the coroner to shoot some preautopsy pictures. Just got back from picking them up, have the least scary one to show around. It almost looks as if she's sleeping. I want the Quicks to have a look at it, figure the father's back, maybe the sister, too. I put a call in to them, but no one answered, no machine."

"Grieving," I said.

"And now I'm going to interrupt the process. Care to join me? In case I need help in the sensitivity department?"

4

In the afternoon daylight the Quick residence was even prettier, well kept, the lawn clipped, the front yard ringed by beds of impatiens. Daytime parking was restricted to permit holders. Milo had placed an LAPD banner atop his dash, and he handed me one for the Seville. In his free hand was a manila envelope.

I put the banner in the car. "Now I'm official."

"Hoo-hah. Here we go again." He bent one leg and flexed his neck. Opening the envelope, he pulled out the death shot of the blond girl.

The pretty face was now a pale mask. I studied the details: ski slope nose, dimpled chin, eyebrow pierce. Lank yellow strands that the camera turned greenish. Greenish tint to the skin that was real. The bullet hole was an oversized black mole, puffy around the edges, just off center in the unlined brow. Purplish bruises had settled around the eyes—blood leaking from the brain. Bloody residue under the nose, too. Her mouth hung slightly open. Her teeth were straight and dull.

To my eye, nothing close to "almost sleeping."

I returned the picture, and we approached the Quick house.

A woman in a black pantsuit answered. Younger than Sheila Quick, she was slim and angular and brunette, with firm features and an assertive posture. Her dark hair was short, feathered in front, sprayed in place.

Her hands clamped her hips. "I'm sorry, they're resting."

Milo showed her the badge.

She said, "That doesn't change the facts."

"Ms.—"

"Eileen. I'm Sheila's sister. Here's *my* badge." She slid a cream-colored business card out of a jacket pocket. The diamond on her finger was a three-carat pear.

Eileen Paxton
Senior Vice President and
Chief Financial Officer
Digimorph Industries
Simi Valley, California

"Digimorph," said Milo.

"Ultratech computer enhancement. We do film work. On the biggest pictures."

Milo smiled at her. "Here's a picture, Ms. Paxton." He showed her the death shot.

Eileen Paxton's gaze didn't waver, but her lips worked. "She's the one who was found with Gavin?"

"Do you recognize her, ma'am?"

"No, but I wouldn't. I thought Gavin was found with his girlfriend. That little hook-nosed thing. That's what Sheila told me."

"Your sister assumed," said Milo. "A reasonable assumption, but she was mistaken. That's one of the reasons we're here."

He kept the photo in Eileen Paxton's sight. She said, "You can put that away."

"Is Mr. Quick back from Atlanta?"

"He's sleeping. They both are."

"When do you think they'll be available?"

"How would I know that? This is a terrible time for the entire family."

"Yes, it is, ma'am."

"This city," said Paxton. "This world."

"Okay then," said Milo. "We'll check back later."

We turned to leave, and Eileen Paxton began to close the door, when a male voice from inside the house said, "Who's out there, Eileen?"

Paxton was halfway inside when she said something unintelligible. The male voice retorted. Louder. Milo and I faced the house. A man emerged, his back to us, talking to the doorway. "I don't need to be protected, Eileen."

Muffled response. The man closed the door, swiveled, and stared at us. "I'm Jerry Quick. Any news on my boy's murder?"

Tall, thin, round-shouldered, he wore a navy blue crewneck sweater over khakis and white Nikes. Thinning gray hair was arranged in a careless comb-over. His face was long, deeply seamed, lantern-jawed. Bluish smudges stained the crinkled skin beneath wide-set blue eyes. His eyelids

drooped, as if he were having trouble staying awake.

We returned to the front steps. Milo held
out his hand. Quick shook it briefly, glanced
at me, said, "Do you have anything yet?"

"Afraid not. If you've got time—"

"Of course I do." Quick's lips twisted as if
he'd tasted something bad. "My executive
sister-in-law. She met Spielberg once and
thinks her shit doesn't stink—come on in.
My wife's totally out of it, our doctor gave
her Valium or something, but I'm fine. He
wanted to dose me up, too. I want to be focused."

◆

Milo and I sat on the same blue sofa, and
Jerome Quick took a Chippendale-repro
armchair. I studied the family photos again.
Wanting to imagine Gavin as something
other than the thing in the Mustang.

In life, he'd been a tall, dark-haired, pleasant-looking kid with his father's long face
and wide-set eyes. Darker eyes than his father's—gray-green. In some of the earlier
pictures he wore glasses. His fashion sense
never changed. Preppy clothes, designer
logos. Short hair, always, in either a conser-

vative crew cut or gelled and spiked cautiously. A regular kid with a tentative smile, not handsome, not ugly. Walk down any suburban street, check out a mall or a multiplex theater or a college campus, and you'd see scores just like him. His sister—the law student in Boston—was plain and serious-looking.

Quick saw me looking. "That was Gav." His voice caught. He cursed under his breath, said, "Let's get to work."

◆

Milo prepared him for the picture, then showed it to him.

Quick waved it away. "Never seen her." Quick's eyes dropped to the carpet. "Did my wife tell you about the accident?"

"Yes, sir."

"That and now this." Quick sprang up, strode to a mock-Chippendale coffee table, studied a crystal box for a while, then opened it and pulled out a cigarette and lit up with a matching lighter.

Blue smoke rose toward the ceiling. Quick inhaled deeply, sat down, and laughed harshly.

"I quit five years ago. Sheila thinks it's

gracious to leave these out for guests, even though no one smokes anymore. Like the good old days in Hollywood, all that crap. Her sister tells her about Hollywood crap . . ." He stared at the cigarette, flicked ash on the carpet, and ground it into the pile with his heel. The resulting black scorch mark seemed to give him satisfaction.

I said, "Did Gavin talk about a new girl-friend?"

"New?"

"After Kayla."

"Her," said Quick. "There's an airhead for you. No, he didn't say anything."

"Would he have told you?"

"What do you mean?"

"Was he open about his personal life?"

"Open?" said Quick. "Less so than before the accident. He tended to get confused. In the beginning, I mean. How could he not be confused, he caught a tremendous blow right here." Quick touched his forehead.

Same spot where the bullet had entered his son's skull. He didn't know yet. No reason for him to know yet.

"Confusion," I said.

"Just temporary. But he found he couldn't

concentrate on his studies, so he dropped out of school."

Quick smoked and grimaced, as if inhaling hurt.

"He got hit on the prefrontal lobes," he said. "They told us it controls personality. So obviously . . ."

"Gavin changed," I said.

"Nothing huge, but sure, there'd have to be changes. But then he got better, almost everything got better. Anyway, I'm sure Gav's accident has nothing to do with this."

Quick puffed rapidly, flicked more ash. "We need to find out whoever did this. Bastard leave any clues?"

Milo said, "We have no suspects and very little information. We haven't even been able to identify the girl."

"Well I don't know her, and I doubt Sheila does. We know the same people."

"Is there anything you can tell us about Gavin that might help?"

"Gavin was a great guy," said Quick, as if daring us to argue. "Had his head on his shoulders. Hell of a golfer. We both loved golf. I taught him, and he learned fast, leaped right over me—a seven handicap, and he was getting better. That was before the accident. Afterward, he wasn't as coordinated, but he was still good. His attention would wander . . . sometimes he'd want to take the same shot over and over—wanted to do it perfectly."

"Perfectionistic," I said.

"Yeah, but at some point you're causing a traffic jam on the green, and you have to stop. In terms of his interests, he liked business, same as me." Jerry Quick slumped. "That changed, too. He lost interest in business. Got other ideas. But I figured it was temporary."

"Other career ideas?" I said.

"More like career fantasies. All of a sudden econ was down the drain, and he was going to be a writer."

"What kind of writer?"

"He joked about working for the tabloids, getting the dirt on celebrities."

"Just a joke," I said.

Quick glared. "He laughed, and I laughed back. I told you, he couldn't concentrate. How the hell could he write for a newspaper? One time Eileen was over, and he asked her if she knew any celebrities he could get dirt on. Then he winked at me, but Eileen just about dirtied her pants. Gave some big speech about celebrities deserving their privacy. The thought of offending some big shot scared the hell out of her . . . anyway, where was I . . ." Quick's eyes glazed. He smoked.

"Gavin becoming an investigative reporter."

"Like I said, it wasn't serious."

"How did Gavin fill his time after he dropped out?"

Quick said, "By hanging around. I was ready for him to go back to school, but apparently he wasn't, so I—it was a hard time for him, I didn't want to push. I figured maybe he'd reenroll in the spring."

"Any other changes?" I said.

"He stopped picking up his room. Really let it go to seed. He'd never been the neatest kid, but he'd always been good about personal grooming. Now he sometimes had to be reminded to shower and brush his teeth and comb his hair. I hated reminding him because he got embarrassed. Never argued, never gave me attitude, just said, 'Sorry, Dad.' Like he knew something was different and felt bad about it. But that was all getting better, he was coming out of it, getting in shape—he started running again.

He was light on his feet, used to do five, six miles like it was nothing. His doctor told me he was going to be fine."

"Which doctor is that?"

"All of them. There was a neurologist, what was his name—" Quick smoked and removed the cigarette and tapped his cheek with his free hand. "Some Indian guy, Barry Silver, our family doctor, referred us to him. Indian guy, over at Saint John's . . . Singh. He wears a turban, must be one of those . . . you know. Barry is a friend as well as our doctor, I golf with him, so I trusted his referral. Singh did some tests and told us he really didn't see anything off in Gav's brain. He said Gav would take time to heal, but he couldn't say how much time. Then he sent us over to a therapist—a psychologist. To help Gav recover from the trauma."

"A neuropsychologist?" I said.

Quick said, "She's a therapist, that's all I know. Woman shrink, Koppel, she's been on TV, radio."

"Mary Lou Koppel."

"You know her?"

"I've heard of her," I said.

"At first Gav saw one of her partners, but they didn't hit it off, so he switched to her."

"What was wrong with the first partner?"

Quick shrugged. "The whole process—you pay for your kid to go in and talk to someone, it's all hush-hush, you're not allowed to know what's going on." He dragged on his cigarette. "Gavin told me he wasn't comfortable with the guy and that Koppel was going to see him. Same price. They both charged two hundred bucks an hour and didn't accept insurance."

"Was it helpful?"

"Who knows?"

"What feedback did Dr. Koppel give you?"

"Nothing. I was out of that loop—the whole therapy thing. I travel a lot. Too much, been meaning to cut back."

He smoked the cigarette down to the butt, snatched another, and chain-lit, then snuffed out the first one between his thumb and index finger. Onto the carpet.

He mumbled something.

Milo said, "Sir?"

Quick's smile was abrupt and unsettling. "I travel all the time, and it's hell. You know the airlines, disciples of the devil. Frequent business flyer? They could care less. This time, after Sheila called me about Gavin, and I told them why I needed to go home, I got treated like a king. They tag you as bereaved, and you get prioritized all the way. Upgrade to first class, no one could do enough for me."

He barked what might've been laughter. Smoked, coughed, smoked some more.

"That's what it took. That's what it took to get treated like a human being."

◆

Milo asked him about his daughter, and Quick said, "I told Kelly to stay in Boston. She's got law school, what good can it do her to come here? If you release the . . . release Gavin to us and we have a funeral, then she can come home. When will that be?"

"Hard to say, sir," said Milo.

"That seems to be your tune."

Milo smiled. "Kayla Bartell—"

"Haven't seen her around for a while. She knew Gav from high school, and they fooled around for a while."

"Fooled around?"

"Like kids do," said Quick. "Her father's some kind of composer. *Eileen* informs me he's important."

"You've never met him."

"Why would I?"

"Gavin and Kayla—"

"That was Gav's business . . . to be honest, guys, I don't get these questions," said Quick. "What happened can't have anything to do with Gav. He went up to Mulholland with some girl and a pervert—some sex fiend—took advantage, right? It's obvious, right? Isn't that what you're thinking?"

Before Milo could answer, Quick's eyes swung to the stairs. Eileen Paxton stomped down, ignored us, and hurried into the kitchen.

A kitchen faucet opened. Then, the hard clash of pans. Moments later, Sheila Quick made her way down the stairs, tentative, unsteady. She stopped on the bottom step, studied the floor, as if unwilling to commit. Her eyes were unfocused, and she gripped the banister for support. She wore a pink housecoat, had aged a decade overnight.

She saw us, said, "Hello" in a slurred voice. She noticed the cigarette in her husband's hand, and her lips turned down.

Jerome Quick smoked defiantly. "Don't stand on the bottom like that, come all the way down—be careful, you're on Valium." He made no effort to help her.

She remained in place. "Is there anything . . . new, Detective?"

Milo shook his head. "Sorry to bother you again, Mrs. Qui—"

"No, no, no, you're helping me—us. You were very . . . gracious. Last night. It can't have been easy for you. You were gracious. It wasn't easy for you *or* for me."

Jerry Quick said, "Sheila, go back to bed. You're—"

"They were nice last night, Jerry. It's only polite that I—"

"I'm sure they were great, but—"

"Jerry. I. Want. To. Be. Polite." Sheila Quick came down the stairs and sat down on a side chair. "Hello," she said, brightly.

"Ma'am," said Milo, "we have learned that the girl with Gavin wasn't Kayla Bartell."

Sheila Quick said, "You said she was blond."

Jerome Quick said, "There's a rare commodity in L.A."

"I do have a picture," said Milo. "It's not a pleasant picture, it's postmortem, but if you could look at it—if we could identify her, it might speed things along."

Sheila Quick stared at him. He showed her the death shot.

"She looks so . . . dead. Poor little thing." Shaking her head. She snatched the photo from Milo and held it closer. Her fingers trembled, and the corners flapped. "Are you showing pictures like this of Gavin to other people?"

"Sheila," said Quick.

"No, ma'am," said Milo. "We know who Gavin is."

She examined the photo. "Gavin never said he had a new girlfriend."

"Gavin was twenty," said Jerome Quick. "He didn't need to check in about his social life."

Sheila Quick continued to stare at the picture. Finally, she handed it back.

"Another one," she said.

"Ma'am?"

"Someone else's baby is gone."

CHAPTER

5

Milo received written permission to speak to Gavin's doctors, and we left. It was nearly 5 P.M., the sky was milky white and poisonous, and both of us were low and hungry. We drove to a deli on Little Santa Monica, had sandwiches and coffee. Mine was roast beef with hot mustard on pumpernickel. Milo opted for a wet, multi-decked monster layered with pastrami and coleslaw and pepperoncinis and some things I couldn't identify, all stuffed into a French roll. When he bit into it, it collapsed. That seemed to give him joy.

He swallowed, and said, "Model family."

"They're no ad for domestic life," I said,

"but the father may be right, and it doesn't matter."

"Perverted stranger kills his boy. That sure distances it from the family."

"I don't see this as a family crime," I said. "The fact that the family doesn't know the girl could mean she's the kind of girl you don't bring home to Mother. Which may lead us to her being the primary target."

"Someone with nasty friends."

"The killer impaled her and took her purse. That could've been trophy-taking, but what if he didn't want her identified quickly?"

"The primary target for sex, killing, or both?"

"Don't know," I said. "There was no sexual assault, but to me the impaling still has a sexual quality to it. Gavin was shot once—dispatched. That's consistent with the killer wanting him out of the way so he could take care of his real business."

"*If* Gavin was shot first. No way we can pinpoint that."

"Logic says he was," I said. "The girl was alive when the killer impaled her. It's unlikely Gavin would've sat by passively while that happened. Or that the killer would've taken the risk of fighting a young, healthy male. He dispatched Gavin, with a single shot, then turned his attention to the girl. Her size, her fear, and the killer's overwhelming dominance subdued her. Maybe he promised her he wouldn't hurt her if she didn't resist. Any signs she fought back?"

He shook his head.

I said, "She watched Gavin get murdered, sat there, terrified, and hoped for the best. The killer used the spear on her, then he shot her, too. To me that says big-time anger. With both kids dead, he had time to inspect his handiwork, fool with the scene. Either Gavin and the girl had already begun a sexually charged tableau, or he set one up. Either because it *was* a sex crime, or he wanted it to be seen that way."

He put his sandwich down. "You're offering me lots of choices."

"What are friends for?" I said. "Have you come across any other impalement murders?"

"Nothing yet." He picked up his sandwich, and a huge chunk disappeared in his maw. Think the condom was Gavin's, or did the killer bring it?"

"It was in his pocket, so it was probably his."

"So you think exploring Gavin's psyche is a waste of time? I was thinking his therapist might be helpful. And you know her."

"I know who she is."

"From her being on TV."

Here we go. I hid my mouth behind my coffee cup.

He said, "You make a face when you talk about her."

"She's not someone I'd refer to," I said.

"Why not?"

"I can't get into the details."

"Give me the basics."

◆

Five years ago, an otherwise thoughtful judge had asked me to evaluate a seven-year-old girl caught in a vicious divorce. Both parents were trained marriage counselors. That should have been ample warning.

The mother was a young, passive, pinch-featured, preternaturally anxious woman who'd grown up with violent, alcoholic parents and had shifted from couples work to processing hardened drug addicts at a county-financed clinic in Bellflower. Her ex-husband, twenty years older, was pompous and psychopathic, a newly minted sex therapist and guru of sorts, with an Ivy League Ph.D. and a brand-new job at a yoga institute in Santa Barbara.

The two of them hadn't spoken in over a year but each insisted upon joint physical custody. The arrangement was to be simple: three days at one home, four at the next. Neither parent saw the problem shuttling a seven-year-old girl ninety miles between her father's faux-adobe house at the ashram and the mother's sad, furnished apartment in Glendale. The alleged crux of the conflict was the calendar—who got four days, who got three, and what about holidays? After two months of raging debate, the topic switched to coordinating the conventional diet favored by the mother with the vegan regimen embraced by the father.

The real crux was mutual hatred, two hundred thousand dollars in a jointly owned investment account, and the alleged sexual rapaciousness of the father's four girlfriends.

When I do custody evaluations, I make it a point to talk to therapists, and these combatants each had one. The father's was an eighty-year-old Indian swami who spoke heavily accented English and took medication for high blood pressure. I made a trip to Santa Barbara, spent a pleasant two hours with the corpulent, bearded fellow, breathing in incense and learning nothing of substance. The father hadn't kept an appointment with his avatar in six months.

"Is that okay with you?" I asked the swami.

He shifted out of lotus position and did something impossible with his body, winked, and smiled. "What will be, will be."

"There's a song like that."

"Doris Day," he said. "Terrific singer."

◆

The mother's therapist was Mary Lou Koppel, and she refused to talk to me.

First she avoided me completely by ignoring my calls. After my fifth attempt to get through, she phoned and explained. "I'm sure you understand, Dr. Delaware. Confidentiality."

"Dr. Wetmore's given consent."

"I'm afraid it's not hers to give."

"Whose is it?"

The phone crackled. She said, "I'm speaking conceptually, not legally. Teresa

Wetmore is in an extremely vulnerable place. Thad is extremely abusive, as I'm sure you know."

"Physically?"

"Emotionally," she said. "Where it counts. Teresa and I have made progress, but it's going to take time. I can't risk unleashing the demons."

"My concerns are for the child."

"You have your priorities, I have mine."

"Dr. Koppel, what I'm after is any insight you can give me that might help me make recommendations to the court."

Silence on the line. Static.

"Dr. Koppel?"

"The only insight I can give you, Doctor," she said, "is to avoid Thad Wetmore like the plague."

"You've had troubles with him."

"I've never met him, Doctor. And I intend to keep it that way."

I wrote her a follow-up letter that was returned unopened. The custody case festered until the Wetmores ran out of money, and the lawyers quit. The judge followed my recommendations: Both parents needed extensive child-rearing education before joint custody had a chance of working. In any event, a weekly two-hundred-mile round-trip shuttle wasn't in the best interests of the child. When the judge asked if I'd like to be the educator, I said I'd supply a list of names, then I thought about who'd annoyed me recently.

Three months later, Teresa and Thaddeus Wetmore filed separate ethical complaints against me with the state psychology board. It took a while to get out from under that, but finally the charges were dismissed for no cause. Shortly after that, Dr. Mary Lou Koppel seemed to be popping up all over the airwaves.

An expert on couples communication.

◆

Milo finished his sandwich. "Sounds like a lovely person. What's her shtick for the media?"

"Anything she wants it to be."

"Self-proclaimed expert?"

"Talk shows are always hungry for filler," I said. "If you say you're a specialist, you are. My guess is Koppel hired a publicist and bought herself a nice little dog and pony show that feeds her practice."

"So young, yet so cynical."

"One out of two ain't bad."

He grinned, sopped juice from his plate with his sandwich, and finished off the soggy mess. "Is head injuries a hot media topic?"

"If you're asking whether Koppel's a qualified neuropsychologist, I don't know. Which is what Gavin needed, at least in the beginning. Someone who could find out what was really going on with his brain and make specific recommendations for rehabilitation."

"The neurologist said he couldn't find anything."

"All the more so," I said. "If I had to bet, I'd say Koppel wasn't into neuropsych. It's a small field that requires specialized training. Most neuropsych people don't do straight psychotherapy and vice versa."

His eyes half closed. "Claire Argent was into that, right?"

Dr. Claire Argent had been one of many victims of a monster we'd chased a couple of years ago. A quiet woman, cloaked in secrets, found bisected at the waist and stashed in the trunk of her car.

"She was," I said.

He breathed in deeply. Closed his eyes

and massaged the lids. "You're saying Gavin mighta been mishandled by Koppel?"

"Or I'm wrong, and he got a thorough workup."

"I was thinking it would be smart to talk to Koppel. Even if Gavin turns out not to be the primary vic, maybe he mentioned the blonde to his shrink, and I can cut through a lot of procedure."

"Don't hold your breath trying to get through. Given her high profile, I don't imagine she'd want to be associated with a murdered patient."

"I've got written consent from the parents."

"That allows her to talk," I said. "It doesn't compel her. She can be choosy about what she tells you. If she tells you anything."

"You really don't like her."

"She was obstructive when she didn't have to be. A child's welfare was at issue, and she didn't care."

He smiled. "Actually, I was thinking I could ask *you* to speak with her. One doc to another. That would free me up to do the other stuff. As in following up with Missing Persons, maybe expanding to searches up and down the state, going over the autopsy reports, ballistics records, checking out the girl's clothes. No sweat, though. I took this one on, I'll see it through."

He threw money on the table, and we left the deli.

"I'll talk to her," I said.

He stopped on the sidewalk. Beverly Hills women glided around us, in a cloud of perfume. "You're sure."

"Why not? No phone tag this time. Face-to-face, it'll be interesting."

CHAPTER

6

My house, designed for two, is set among pines and perched above a bridle path that snakes through Beverly Glen. High white walls, polished wood floors, skylights in interesting places, and not too much furniture make it look larger than it is. Realtor's hype would label it, "airy yet proportioned for intimacy." When I arrive home alone, it can be a mass of echoes and negative space.

This evening it felt cold. I walked past the mail on the dining room table and headed for my office. Booting the computer, I looked up Mary Lou Koppel in the American Psychological Association directory and ran her through a few Internet search engines.

She'd earned her Ph.D. at the same place I had, the U. A year older than I, but she'd entered grad school shortly after I'd finished. Her dissertation on breast-feeding and anxiety in new mothers had been accepted five years later, and she'd followed up with an internship at one of the university hospitals and a postdoc fellowship at a mental health clinic in San Bernardino.

Her license was bona fide, and the state board listed no disciplinary actions against her. I'd been right about her lacking any training or certification in neuropsychology.

Her name pulled up 432 hits on the computer, all excerpts from interviews she'd given on various TV and radio shows. A closer look revealed lots of repetition; it cooked down to three dozen actual references.

Mary Lou Koppel had spoken with great confidence about communication barriers between men and women, gender identity, eating disorders, weight loss strategies, corporate problem solving, midlife crisis, adoption, learning disabilities, autism, puberty, adolescent rebellion, premenstrual syndrome, menopause, panic disorder, phobias, chronic depression, posttraumatic stress, sexism, racism, ageism, sizeism.

One topic that had held her interest was prison reform. She'd given eight radio interviews last year in which she decried the shift from rehabilitation to punishment. In two of the talks, she'd been joined by a man named Albin Larsen, listed as a psychologist and human rights worker.

The photos I found showed a pleasant-looking woman with short, shagged caramel hair. Her face was round with chipmunk cheeks and terminated in a sharp little off-center chin. Her neck was graceful but starting to loosen. Crisp, dark eyes. Wide, determined mouth. Gorgeous teeth, but her smile seemed posed. In every picture she wore red.

Now I knew whom to look for.

◆

I left for her office the next morning at eleven-forty-five, figuring my best bet was to catch her during her lunch break. Her office was in Beverly Hills but not Bedford Drive's Couch Row or any of the other fashionable streets where high-priced therapists congregated.

Dr. Mary Lou Koppel plied her trade in a two-story building on Olympic Boulevard and Palm Drive—a mixed-use stretch near the glitzy city's southern border. Down the block were an auto-painting franchise and a private school housed in what had once been a residential duplex. Beyond those sat a florist and a pharmacy advertising discounts for seniors. Traffic on Olympic was nonstop and freeway-deafening.

Koppel's building had a windowless front, with brick facing painted the color of wet sand. No identifying marks other than black plastic address numerals too small to read from across the street. The front door was locked, and a sign said to enter through the rear. Behind the structures was a six-space parking lot backed by an alley. Three slots marked RESERVED were occupied by small, dark Mercedes sedans, not unlike Jerry Quick's.

I fed a meter on Palm and made my way over.

The ground floor was a long, dim, red-carpeted corridor that ran along the east side of the building and had the popcorn smell of a theater lobby. One occupant: an outfit called Charitable Planning. An arrow painted on the wall directed me to the stairway and when I got there faux-bronze letters specified what awaited me on the second story.

PACIFICA-WEST PSYCHOLOGICAL SERVICES

Upstairs was pewter-colored industrial carpeting, blue-gray walls, better lighting. Unlike the first floor, no long hallway. Progress was halted by a perpendicular wall set ten feet in. A single door was marked RECEPTION.

Inside was a large unoccupied waiting room set up with blue tweed chairs and coffee tables stacked with magazines. No reception window, just a door and three signs. FRANCO R. GULL, PH.D., MARY LOU KOPPEL, PH.D., ALBIN A. LARSEN, PH.D.

Larsen was the human rights activist with whom Koppel had shared some of her prison reform interviews. Feeding two practices for the price of one.

Next to each sign was a call button and a tiny, faceted bulb. A sign instructed patients to announce themselves with a button push. A clear light meant the doctor was free, red signified Occupied.

Gull's and Larsen's lights were red, Koppel's wasn't. I announced myself.

◆

A few moments later, the blank door opened, and Mary Lou Koppel stood there wearing a red short-sleeved cashmere top over white linen pants and red shoes. In person, her dark eyes were nearly black. Clear and bright and inquisitive, and all over me. Her hair was tinted lighter than in the photos, she'd put on a few wrinkles, her bare arms were soft, freckled, plumper than the rest of her. Yellow diamond cocktail ring on her right index finger. Big canary-colored stone, surrounded by tiny sapphires. No wedding band.

"Yes?" she said. Smooth, soft, low-pitched voice. Radio voice.

I gave her my name, handed her the card that says I sometimes consult to the police. She read the small print. "Delaware." She handed it back, looked into my eyes. "That's an unusual name . . . have we met?"

"A few years ago, but only telephonically."

"I'm afraid I don't understand."

"The Wetmore divorce case. I was assigned by the court to make custody recommendations. You were Teresa Wetmore's therapist."

She blinked. Smiled. "If I recall correctly, I wasn't very cooperative, was I?"

I shrugged.

"Unfortunate," she said. "What I couldn't tell you at the time, Dr. Delaware—what I probably still shouldn't tell you—was that Terry Wetmore tied my hands. She didn't like you one bit. Didn't trust you, forbade me to divulge anything to you. It put me in a bit of a bind."

"I can imagine."

She placed a hand on my shoulder. "The rigors of our profession." Her hand lingered, trailed my jacket sleeve, dropped. "So what brings you here today—what else can I *not* cooperate with you about?"

"Gavin Quick."

"What about Gavin?"

"He was murdered two nights ago."

"Mur—oh my God. Oh, no . . . come in."

◆

She led me through a short corridor, past a copying machine and a watercooler, to one of three doors at the rear. Her office was paneled in slabs of pale bird's-eye maple, carpeted in double-plush deep blue wool, and furnished with a glass desk on a black granite base, a Lucite desk chair, oversized, baby blue leather sofas and recliners arranged with a designer's eye. The ceilings were cork—soundproofing. Nothing was nailed to the highly figured wood walls. Her diplomas and a framed psychologists' license were propped in a glass étagère off to one side, along with crystal paperweights and what looked to be pueblo pottery. Sea-green drapes concealed what I assumed were the windows. Their placement meant a view of the parking lot and the alley. The room managed to be generous yet cozy. *Airy yet proportioned for intimacy . . .*

Mary Lou Koppel sat behind the glass desk. I took the nearest soft chair. Very soft. I sank low, was forced to look up at her.

She said, "This is horrible. I just saw Gavin last week. I just can't believe it."

I nodded.

"What happened?"

I gave her the bare details, ended with the unidentified blond girl.

She said, "That poor boy. He'd been through so much."

"The accident."

She placed her hands on the glass desk-top. Her wrists were tiny, her fingers short but thin, the nails coated by clear polish. Near her right hand was a Limoges box filled with business cards, a pair of reading glasses, and a small, silver cellular phone. "Do the police have any idea what happened?"

"No. That's why I'm here."

"I'm not clear what it is that you do for them."

"Sometimes the same goes for me," I said. "This time they've asked me to make contact with you because we're peers."

"Peers," she said. "They think I can help solve a murder?"

"We're talking to everyone."

"Well," she said, "I was Gavin's therapist, but I don't see how that can be relevant. Surely you don't think this had anything to do with Gavin's treatment."

"At this point, it's an open book, Dr. Koppel."

"Mary Lou," she said. "Well, sure, I can understand that logic . . . in the abstract." She fluffed her hair. "Before we go any further, perhaps I should see some sort of written release. I'm aware that with Gavin deceased, there's no legal confidentiality. And I certainly don't want to be seen as obstructive. Again. But ... you understand, don't you?"

"Absolutely." I gave her the release form the Quicks had signed. She glanced at it. "Can't be too careful. Okay, what would you like to know?"

"Gavin's parents implied there were personality changes following the accident. Some falling off in his personal hygiene, what sounds like obsessive behavior."

"Are you familiar with the sequelae of closed-head injuries, Dr. Delaware?"

"I'm not a neuropsychologist," I said, "but it sounds as if there was postconcussive syndrome and some personality changes."

"With closed-head, anything goes—may I call you Alex?"

"Sure."

She showed me gorgeous teeth. Switched back to serious. "This was a pre-frontal-lobe assault, Alex. You're aware of the role of the prefrontals in terms of emotional reactivity. For all we know, when Gavin's head hit the back of the seat, he received the equivalent of a minor lobotomy."

"It had been ten months," I said, "and he hadn't recovered fully."

"Yes ... I found that worrisome. Then

again, the human brain—especially the young human brain—can be wonderfully plastic. I was hopeful."

"For full recovery?"

She shrugged.

"Plasticity," I said. "You do neuropsych."

She studied me for half a second. "I keep up with the journals. There was no need for neuropsych because the organic end was being handled by a neurologist. He and I agreed there was nothing further to be gained by subjecting Gavin to yet more tests. What the patient needed was emotional support, and my job was to provide it."

I pulled out my notepad. "Dr. Singh."

"Very good man."

"Did he refer Gavin?"

She nodded.

"When?"

"Gavin's been in treatment for about three months."

"Seven months after the accident."

"It took a while for things to settle."

I pretended to read the pad. "He was referred to your group, not to you directly."

"Pardon?"

"I've been told that Gavin began with one of your partners but switched to you."

She crossed her legs. The black marble pedestal blocked most of the movement, but I could see the tip of one red shoe. "Now that you jog my memory, that's exactly what happened. Singh referred Gavin to the group and Franco—Dr. Gull—was on call. Franco saw Gavin a couple of times, then I took over."

"Problems between Gavin and Dr. Gull?"

"I wouldn't term them problems," she said. "Back then—immediately after the accident—Gavin was extremely irritable. Once again, par for the course. You know how it can be with therapists and patients. Sometimes you mesh, sometimes you don't. And Franco's patient load was already heavy."

The black eyes found mine. "Like with you and Teresa Wetmore. I'm sure most of your patients adore you and trust you. But others . . . are you with the police full-time or do you still see patients?"

"I do short-term private consults."

"No therapy?"

"Not usually."

"Private practice *can* be tough," she said. "The HMOs with their nonsense, the thin referral stream when money gets tight. I suppose working for the police can be helpful providing a nice steady income."

"I'm not employed by the police. I do short-term consults for them, too."

"Ah . . ." She smiled. "Anyway, Gavin did become my patient, and I felt we were making progress." Her legs uncrossed, and she shifted forward in her chair. "Alex, I can't think of anything I could tell you that would help a police investigation."

"What about Gavin's obsessiveness?" I said.

"I wouldn't call it that. Nothing on the level of a full-blown OCD. Gavin could be a bit persistent, that's all."

"Getting an idea in his head and not letting go?"

She smiled. "You're making it sound more pathological than it was. He could be a bit . . . enthusiastic."

"His parents said he'd switched career goals. From business to journalism."

That seemed to surprise her, and I wondered how well she'd known her patient.

"People change their minds," she said. "Young people especially. Sometimes tragedies get people to focus on what they really want to do."

"Is that what happened to Gavin?"

Noncommittal nod.

"Did he have any plans to return to college?"

"It was hard for him to stay motivated, Alex. One of my goals was helping restore a sense of meaning to his life. But it had to be gradual. Gavin was still wrestling with the changes."

"So he'd slowed down cognitively."

"Yes, but it was subtle. And, I believe, exacerbated by emotional stress. I'm curious, Alex. Why are you so interested in his personality?"

"I'm interested in his obsessiveness because the police are wondering if it could've gotten him into trouble."

"How so?"

"Angering the wrong person."

"The wrong person."

"Anyone who'd react violently."

She touched a finger to her lip. "I'd be surprised at that—Gavin consorting with violent people. He was a nice boy, a *conventional* boy. He certainly never mentioned anything like that to me."

"Was he pretty communicative?"

The black eyes rose to the ceiling. "How

shall I put this . . . like many young men, Gavin wasn't much for introspection."

"What did he talk about?"

"I was working on getting him to open up about his feelings. Anger at feeling different. Guilt, about surviving the accident. Two of his friends were killed, you know."

I nodded.

She said, "My sense was that Gavin knew he'd lost something—an edge, a sharpness—but he had trouble expressing himself about it. I suppose that could've been aphasic. Or just a postadolescent male's lack of verbal skills. Either way, I knew he was wrestling with his feelings. I couldn't push him too hard, Alex. One time, though, he did express himself in a way that I thought was extremely eloquent. This was just a few weeks ago. He came to session looking downcast. I waited him out, and finally he punched the arm of the sofa—that sofa—and shouted, 'This is fucked, Dr. K! To everyone else I look okay, everyone keeps telling me I'm okay, but I know I'm not okay.' Then he stopped, his chest was heaving and he was flushed, and the next time he spoke it was so soft I could barely hear him. What he said was, 'It's like one of those android movies. I'm not me, anymore, I'm still the box I came in, but someone's fucking with the wiring.' Then he said, 'I really miss being *me*.' And, finally, he cried. I thought it was a breakthrough, but the following week, he canceled his appointment, and the one after that. I've only seen him once, since then, and during that session it was as if nothing had happened. All he wanted to talk about was cars and sports. It was as if we were starting from square one. But that's how it goes with young men."

I said, "Did he talk about his social life?"

"Social as in dating?"

"Yes."

"There'd been a girlfriend, some girl he knew in high school. But that was over."

"Because of the accident?"

"That would be my assumption. Once again, I needed to step around personal topics."

"Gavin was guarded about his outside life."

"Very."

"Did he mention any other girls?"

She shook her head.

"Would you mind looking at a picture of

the girl who was killed with him? It is a morgue shot."

She shuddered. "I don't see the point."

"No problem."

"No, you might as well show it to me," she said. "I need to integrate all this misfortune."

I placed the death shot on the glass tabletop. She didn't attempt to touch it, just stared at it. Her mouth lost determination. A vein pulsed at her temple. Rapid pulse.

"You know her?" I said.

"I've never seen her in my life. I'm just imagining. The way it was for the two of them."

CHAPTER

7

Mary Lou Koppel walked me out of her waiting room and watched me descend the stairs. When I paused to look back, she smiled and waved her fingers.

Back home, I checked my messages. Three nuisance calls and Allison letting me know she'd had a cancellation, it had been a long time since we'd seen a movie, did I have time tonight? I phoned her exchange, said how about dinner first, I could be there by seven.

Next, I booted up the computer, logged on to my faculty MEDLINE account, and reviewed articles on closed-head prefrontal injuries. With serious brain trauma, bleeding and lesions showed up on X-rays or CAT scans. But in less dramatic instances, the damage was subtle and invisible, the result of something called *axonal shearing*—a microscopic shredding of nerve fibers. Those cases resisted neurological tests and could be best diagnosed by neuropsychological evaluation. Instruments like the Wisconsin Card Sort or the Rey-Osterreith Complex Figure test pulling up problems in attention and thought and information processing.

Patients with prefrontal injuries sometimes had temper-control problems. And they could grow impulsive and obsessive.

I printed a few articles, changed into shorts and a T-shirt and sneakers, and took a long, hard run, not wanting to think about the short sad life of Gavin Quick. I thought about it, anyway, and focused on appreciating my own life. After showering and getting back into street clothes, I tried Milo at the station. By the time I'd reached his car phone, I'd put the interview with Mary Lou Koppel in context.

She'd cooperated but really hadn't told me much. Maybe she didn't know much. Gavin had been in therapy for three months, and my guess was there'd been plenty of missed appointments. Combine that with his resistance and Koppel's avoidance of his cognitive problems, and treatment didn't amount to much.

Mary Lou Koppel's approach boiled down to what's known in the trade as "supportive therapy." Not necessarily a bad thing; sometimes all a patient needs is a yeah-saying or a shoulder to cry on. But sometimes being "supportive" is an excuse for not doing more.

"You're saying she was phoning it in?" said Milo.

"Maybe she did her best. She sat in that office with Gavin, I didn't."

"Chivalrous. But you still don't like her."

"I have nothing against her," I said.

"I must've heard wrong. You get into why she stonewalled you the first time?"

"She brought it up right away. Said the patient hated and distrusted me and forbade her to tell me anything."

"Taking a dig at you, pal?"

"The patient did file an ethical complaint against me."

"Ouch," he said.

"The charge was dismissed."

"Course it was," he said. "What, a disgruntled weirdo?"

"Something like that."

"Assholes."

Supportive therapy.

I said, "Anyway, that's about it on Gavin's emotional state."

"Not as smart as he used to be and obsessive."

"We knew that before."

"It's still interesting."

I said, "Anything new on the girl's ID?"

"Nope. Not much in terms of physical evidence, either. Gavin's prints popped up on the steering wheel but nothing on any of the door handles, not his, not the girl's. Someone did a careful wipedown. Meaning an organized mind, right? Which would fit with the stalker scenario. Plenty of tire tracks on the driveway. Unfortunately, a whole mesh of them, too much overlay, so the techies couldn't pick out a good impression. With Realtors going in and out, it's what you'd expect. None of the neighbors saw or heard anything, no reports of suspicious characters or unfamiliar cars. I'm having the Sex Crimes people look at their files, see if any scary Peeping Toms are newly out on parole."

"Any more about the sequence of death?"

"The coroner agrees with your logic about Gavin getting shot first, but he can't make a definitive statement, has no physical evidence to back it up. The blood spatter says both Gavin and the girl were sitting down when they got popped, and the blood all over the girl's chest plus almost nothing around the head wound says she was alive when that iron stick got jammed through her. I drove around looking for construction sites, see if I could find any missing wrought iron, but *nada*. I'm getting the feel of a surprise blitz. That make sense?"

"It makes perfect sense," I said. "The bad guy follows them, watches, probably parks out on Mulholland and continues onto the property on foot. He waits, sees some necking, gets aroused. If the condom was Gavin's, he and the girl would've been about to consummate. At that point, the bad guy steps out of the dark and boom."

"The element of surprise. There was no semen in or on her, even though she was topless, her leggings were still on, so that sounds right."

"Anything else on the autopsy?"

"Her last meal was half a Big Mac, a few fries, and ketchup. The estimate is six hours before she died. Gavin's stomach gave up pasta with basil and garlic bread. Mrs. Quick confirms that's what she'd cooked for dinner. She and Gavin ate together five hours before the murder. Then he spent some time in his room, and she went to hers and watched TV."

"No dinner date," I said. "Gavin and the girl ate separately, then hooked up. What time did Gavin leave his house?"

"Sheila didn't hear him leave—got defensive about that and went on about Gavin being an adult, she didn't want to hover."

"Given what he'd been through," I said.

"Yeah," he said. "I showed Blondie's picture to her again, 'cause she didn't seemed as drugged. Same answer: total stranger."

"Maybe it was a pickup," I said.

"I thought about that and assigned a D-I to comb the clubs with both their pictures. The coroner prepared blood and tissue samples for DNA processing, but unless the girl's physical data got coded in some official data bank, that's likely to dead-end. So far, she doesn't seem to be listed in any of our Missing Persons files. That could mean a runaway from another town, or the running away would've happened years ago.

The coroner's reluctant to estimate her age, but I had a close look at her and she seems slightly older than Gavin, maybe twenty-three to twenty-five. And she doesn't look like a runaway. Her clothes were good, and she was put together nicely—makeup, earrings, nail polish. Not great teeth—she's missing a few in the rear—but what shows is straight. Tint in the hair, but she's a natural blonde. Coroner said he could smell perfume on her, thought it was Armani. I didn't pick that up at the scene, and by the time I got to the morgue she was smelling of other things. But I'll buy it, Dr. Quan has a good nose."

"Too put-together for a prostitute?" I said.

"For a street girl, yes. Too conservatively dressed for your basic hooker. A higher-priced spread? Maybe. Why?"

"No dinner date," I said. "Hooking up for one purpose."

"You see a kid like Gavin knowing how to find himself a nice-looking pro like that? He was dressed like a student, it's not like he put on a Zegna suit and trolled the B.H. hotels with a wad of cash."

"But growing up in B.H. he might know

about the hotels. With enough cash in his pocket, he'd be in a position to negotiate."

"We found thirty bucks in his wallet."

"What if he'd already paid the girl, and she had the money? Her purse is missing. If so, robbery would have been icing on the cake for the bad guy."

"A call girl doing an outdoor trick with a brain-damaged kid," he said.

"That's the thing about some closed-head injuries. The problems can be subtle. Unless you knew what Gavin was like before, he wouldn't have come across brain-damaged. Just a clean-cut kid driving a cute little red convertible. We know he could be impulsive and compulsive, and maybe that's what led him to approach a pro. He'd have his needs—especially since the relationship with Kayla Bartell was over."

"Koppel say why they broke up?"

"She assumed it was due to the accident. I don't get the feeling she really knew much about Gavin."

"A pro," he said. "A young, horny guy, his girl breaks up with him, maybe his confidence slipped . . . could be."

"Something else," I said. "His talk about

digging up dirt. What if he actually followed up on his tabloid dreams? What better place to nab a celebrity than an expensive hotel?"

"He starts out trawling for movie stars and picks up a pro?"

"Youthful impulsiveness heightened by brain damage."

"Okay," he said, "I'll check out the concierges at all the Beverly Hoo-Has. Not that they're going to admit letting pros through the door. I'll also ask BHPD if they know her, as well as show her picture to our Vice guys. Meanwhile, she's just a well-dressed blonde."

"Anything traceable in her clothing?"

"The blouse was DKNY, Calvin Klein thong panties and pushup bra, no label in the leggings. Good shoes. Excellent shoes—Jimmy Choo. From what I hear, that's a serious investment. There's a Jimmy Choo store right in B.H, on Little Santa Monica, so I went over there. We're talking five, six hundred bucks for a spike and a strap. No one recognized her as a customer, but when I described the shoe, the sales-woman knew it right away. Two seasons old, coulda been bought at discount at Neiman's, Barneys, whatever."

"Expensive shoes," I said. "Well put-together. You'd think someone like that would be missed."

"Sure, but a girl living alone, it could take a while for someone to realize she's missing. It looks like this is gonna be a long, drawn-out deal. Thanks for your help, Alex. If I learn anything, I'll let you know."

◆

I picked Allison up outside her office. Her hair was loose, and she laced her fingers through mine and kissed me hard. Neither of us was hungry, and we opted for movie first, food later. An old Coen Brothers film, *Blood Simple,* was playing at the Aero, a few blocks up on Montana. Allison had never seen it. I had, but the picture merited a second look.

We left the theater shortly after nine and drove over to Hakata on Wilshire where we sat in a booth, away from the rock-star posters and the good cheer of the sushi bar, and ordered sake and salmon skin salad and steak teriyaki and mixed sashimi.

I asked Allison how she'd have treated Gavin Quick.

"When I get head injuries they've usually been through a complete neuropsych eval," she said. "If they haven't, I send them for one. If the testing pinpoints deficits, I recommend some targeted special ed. With that out of the way, I concentrate on marshaling the patient's strengths."

"Supportive therapy."

"Sometimes they need more than that. The challenge is learning to deal with a whole new world. But sure, support's a big part of it. It can be tough, Alex. Two steps backwards for every step forward, lots of mood changes, and you never know what the end result will be. Basically you've got a person who knows he's not what he used to be and feels helpless to change."

"Gavin told his therapist he missed being himself."

"Pretty eloquent."

I poured sake for both of us. "Nice light-hearted date, huh?"

She smiled and touched my wrist. "Are we still dating?" Before I could answer, she said, "Why all these questions about the

technique, honey? Is his mental status related to his murder?"

"His mental status became an issue because Milo wondered if Gavin could've
bothered the wrong person. But my guess
is that the girl was the target, and Gavin was
just unlucky."

"Unlucky again," she said.

We ate.

A moment later: "Who's the therapist?"

"A woman named Mary Lou Koppel. Her
stated goal was to open him up emotionally.
Doesn't sound as if it went too well."

She put her cup down. "Mary Lou."

"You know her?"

She nodded. "How strange."

"What is?"

"She's had a patient murdered before."

CHAPTER

8

I pushed my food aside.

Allison said, "I'd met Mary Lou a few times before. Conferences, symposia. Once we sat on a panel together. Back when I was foolish enough to sit on panels. What I remember about her most vividly are her red clothes and her smile—she always smiled, even when it didn't seem appropriate. As if she'd been prepped by a media coach. On the panel, she had lots to say but no data to back it up. Clearly, she hadn't prepared, was relying on charisma."

"You're not a fan."

"She put me off, Alex. But I wondered if I was just jealous. Because everyone knew how well she was doing professionally.

Word had it she was charging fifty percent more than the rest of us and was turning away patients. The murder was over a year ago. I was at the Western Psych Association convention in Vegas and Mary Lou was scheduled to give a talk on psychology and the media that was canceled at the last minute. I hadn't planned to attend, but one of my friends was registered to hear her—Hal Gottlieb. That night I was having dinner with Hal and some other folks and he joked that he'd lost money at the blackjack tables and that he was going to sue Mary Lou Koppel for it. Because Mary Lou's canceling her talk had given him free time and he'd ambled over to the casino. Then he told us she'd canceled because one of her patients had been murdered. There was a long silence; finally, someone made a crack about bad publicity, then someone else said for Mary Lou there was no such thing as bad publicity, she'd turn it to her advantage."

"Popular gal," I said.

"We mind-healers can be as catty as anyone. If only our patients knew."

"Do you recall any details about the murder?"

"For some reason I remember it as a woman victim. But I could be making that up, I really can't be sure, Alex."

"Over a year ago."

"Two Aprils ago—after Easter. That would make it fourteen months."

"Nothing about a murder came up when I ran Mary Lou through the search engines," I said. "But she started giving interviews about prison reform around that time, so maybe the crime sparked her interest."

"Could be."

"On some of the interviews, she was joined by one of her partners, a guy named Albin Larsen. Know him?"

She shook her head, probed her salad with a chopstick. "Two murders in one practice. I guess if the practice is large enough, it's not that outlandish."

"And Mary Lou's was large."

"That's what I heard."

"Well," I said, "at the very least, it's provocative. I'll pass it along to Milo. Thanks."

"Always happy to help." She pushed a wave of black hair off her face and nibbled her lower lip.

I leaned across the table and kissed her.

She took hold of my face with both her hands, pressed my mouth to hers, released me.

I poured more sake.

"This is good," she said.

"Premium brand," I said.

"I was referring to being here with you."

"Oh." I knuckled my brow.

She laughed and touched a diamond earring. "Despite my penchant for shiny things, I really don't need much. We're alive and our brains are working just fine—that's a good start, wouldn't you say?"

◆

The following morning, I finished a custody report and, wanting to get out of the house, drove to the West L.A. courthouse and dropped off the papers at the judge's chambers. The police station was nearby, and I walked over. The civilian clerk knew me and waved me up without clearance.

I climbed the stairs and walked past the big Robbery-Homicide room where Milo had once worked with all the other detectives, continued up the hall.

He'd spent a decade and a half in that room, never an insider because of his sexuality and his own loner tendencies. Early on there'd been plenty of hostility, mostly from uniforms and brass, but none recently and never from detectives.

Detectives are too bright and too busy for that kind of nonsense. For the last few years, Milo's high solve-rate had earned him silent respect.

A little over a year ago, his life had changed. Chasing down a vicious, twenty-year-old cold-case sex murder had led him to unearth some of the police chief's personal secrets. The chief, now deposed, had offered a solution: Milo, in return for not ruining both of them, would get promoted to lieutenant but would be spared the pencil-pushing that went with a lieutenant's position. Exiled to his own space, away from other D's, he'd be a special case: allowed to pick his cases, expected to keep a low profile. If he needed assistance, he was free to enlist junior D's. Otherwise, he'd be on his own.

Shunting and coopting. It's the kind of thing government does all the time. Milo knew he was being manipulated, and he hated the idea. He considered quitting—for a few moments. Veered away from self-destruction and convinced himself isolation could be freedom. Banking the extra salary wasn't bad either, and while the chief was in power, his job security was assured.

Now the chief was gone, and a new replacement had yet to be picked. Ten candidates had announced their intentions, including an assistant chief from Community Services who tossed his name in the ring after granting an interview to a San Francisco paper in which he came out of a thirty-year closet and named his longtime companion.

I asked Milo if that would change things in the department.

He laughed. "When Berger's name hit the list, eyes rolled so loud you could hear it in Pacoima. His chance of winning is about the same as my growing a second pancreas."

"Even so. The fact that he went public."

"Public as far as the public's concerned. Everyone in the department's known about him for years."

"Oh," I said.

"Times are different than when I started," he said. "No one looks, no one tells, no one leaves nasty stuff in my locker. But the basics—the psychodynamics—aren't ever going to change, are they? The way I see it, humans are built that way, it's in our DNA. Us-them, someone's gotta be in, someone's gotta be out. Every few years we have to beat someone up to feel good about ourselves. If most of the world was like me, straights would be stigmatized. Probably some evolutionary thing, though I can't figure it out. Got any wisdom for me?"

"Left the wisdom pills in the car."

He laughed again, in that joyless way he's perfected. "Savagery reigns. I'll never be lacking for work."

◆

The door to his office was open, and he was sitting at his desk, reading a file. The space is windowless, barely large enough for him, with nothing on the wall and a picture of Milo and Rick on the desk. Fishing, somewhere in Colorado. Both of them in plaid shirts, they looked like a couple of outdoorsmen. For most of the trip, Milo had suffered from altitude sickness.

His computer was on, and his screen saver was a shark chasing a diver. Each time the fish's rapacious jaws nudged the swimmer's fins, he got kicked in the face. A floating legend read, NO GOOD DEED GOES UN-PUNISHED.

I knocked on the doorjamb.

"Yeah," he grumbled, without looking up.

"Good day to you, too. Turns out Gavin Quick's not the first patient of Koppel's who's seen an untimely end."

He looked up, stared as if we'd never met. His eyes cleared. The file was Gavin's. He slapped it shut.

"Say what?"

I did.

◆

I sat in a spare chair. Our noses were three feet apart. None of Milo's cheap panatellas were in sight, but his clothes were ripe with stale tobacco.

He said, "Two Aprils ago."

"Allison can't be certain, but she thinks the victim was female. That's all I can tell you."

"Well, guess what? The department has finally limped into the cyberage." He tapped his computer monitor. The shark and diver dissipated, giving way to several icons, haphazardly placed. The screen was clouded and cracked in one corner. "At least, theoretically. This little sucker tends to freeze—donated by some private high school in Brentwood, because the kids couldn't use it anymore." He began typing. The machine made washing-machine noises and loaded slowly. "Here we are, m'boy. Every felonious slaying under the department's jurisdiction for the last five years listed by victim, date, division, and status. Probably no impaling, because I already searched for impaling . . . let's see what April produces . . ."

He scrolled. "I'm counting six . . . seven females. Five closed, two open. Let's start with Westside cases because Koppel's practice is on the Westside. More important, I can walk a few yards and get hold of the folders."

I scanned the screen. "Folder. Looks like only one's West L.A."

"Wouldn't that be easy."

It was.

◆

Flora Elizabeth Newsome, thirty-one years old, brown and brown, five-five, 130. A third-grade teacher at Canfield Street School, found in her Palms apartment on a

Sunday morning, stabbed and shot. She'd been dead for at least twelve hours.

Dr. Mary Lou Koppel had been interviewed by Detective II Alphonse McKinley and Detective II Lorraine Ogden on April 30. Dr. Koppel had nothing to offer other than the fact that she'd been treating Flora Newsome for "anxiety."

No Solve.

I read the autopsy report. "Stabbed and shot with a .22. Wouldn't it be interesting if the ballistics matched. And stabbing isn't that far from impaling."

Milo sat back in his desk chair. "I can always count on you to spark up my woefully dreary life."

"Think of it as therapy," I said.

Detective Alphonse McKinley had transferred to the Metro Squad at Parker Center. Detective Lorraine Ogden was down the hall, trying to make sense of the gibberish her computer was dishing out.

She was thirty-five or so, a big, square-shouldered woman with short, dark, gray-flecked hair and a determined jaw. She wore an orange-and-cream paisley blouse, brown slacks, cream-colored flats. Wedding band and half-carat diamond on one hand. High school ring on the other.

"Milo," she said, barely glancing up. Her screen filled with rows of numbers. "This thing hates me."

"I think you just broke into a Swiss bank."

"Don't think so, no swastikas. What's up?"

Milo introduced me. Lorraine Ogden said, "I've seen you around. Something psychologically amiss?"

"Always," said Milo, "but this is about business." He told her about the Mulholland murders and the similarities to Flora Newsome.

"Same shrink," she said. "I guess that's a connection."

"A .22 was used on all of them. Our vic was impaled, and yours was stabbed."

"Impaled how?"

"Iron rod through the sternum."

"Flora was cut up pretty badly. Knife jammed through the chest, too." Ogden bit down on her lower teeth, and her jaw got wider. "I never made any headway on her, wouldn't it be nice."

"I pulled the chart, but if you've got time, I wouldn't mind hearing about it, Lorraine."

Ogden glared at the computer, clicked it off. Her touch was hard, and the machine quivered. "My son tells me not to do that without going through the proper steps. Says it puts garbage into the system. But all I've been getting is garbage."

She got up. Six feet tall in flats. The three of us left the detectives' room and moved into the hallway.

"How old's your son?" I said.

"Ten. Going on thirty. Loves math and all that techie stuff. He'd know what to do with that abysmal piece of crap." To Milo: "I think Conference A's vacant. Let's play déjà vu."

CHAPTER

9

Conference A was a ten-by-twelve, low-ceilinged space set up with a folding table and chairs, so brightly lit it made me want to confess to something. Wal-Mart sales labels on the backs of the chairs. The table was cluttered with empty pizza boxes. Milo shoved them to the far end and sat at the head. Lorraine Ogden and I flanked him.

She took the Newsome file, paged through, paused at the autopsy photos, spent a lot of time on a five-by-seven glossy photo.

"Poor Flora," she said. "This was her graduation picture. Cal State L.A., she got her teaching credential there."

"She was thirty-one when she died," said Milo. "Old picture?"

"Recent picture. She took time off, worked as a secretary between college and teaching school, had just graduated a year before. She was finishing her probationary year at the school. The principal liked her, the kids liked her, she was going to be asked to stay on."

Her fingernail flicked the edge of the photo. "Her mother gave this to us, made a big point of telling us we could keep it—she kind of bonded with me and Al. Nice lady, she had faith in us, never bugged us, just called once in a while to thank us, let us know she was sure we'd solve it." Her nostrils flared. "Haven't heard from her in must be half a year. Poor Mrs. Newsome. Evelyn Newsome."

I said, "May I?" and she slid the folder across the table.

In life, Flora Newsome had been attractive in a scrubbed, unremarkable way. Broad face, clear complexion, dark hair worn to her shoulders and flipped, bright pale eyes. For her grad shot, she'd put on a fuzzy white sweater and thin gold chain with a crucifix. An inscription on the back of the picture said, *"To Mom and Dad. I finally made it!"* Blue ink, beautiful penmanship.

"Mom and Dad," I said.

"Dad died two months after Flora graduated. Mom wasn't doing too great either— serious arthritis. Sixty years old, but she looked seventy-five. After Flora got killed, she moved out of her house and checked herself into one of those board-and-care places. If that doesn't turn you old at warp speed . . ." She frowned. "So what can I tell you guys about it . . . Flora's boyfriend found her around 11:30 A.M., Sunday morning. The two of them had a date for brunch, were gonna head over to Bobby J's in the Marina." She snorted. "Funny I should remember that. We checked, the restaurant confirmed the reservation. The boyfriend shows up, knocks, no one answers. He keeps trying, finally uses his cell phone to call Flora, still nothing. He bangs on her window, tries to look through, but the drapes are blocking. So he goes and gets the manager. Who didn't want to let him in—he's seen the boyfriend around but doesn't really know him. The boyfriend makes noise about calling the cops, and the manager agrees to have a quick look.

Minute later, the manager's puking in the bushes and the boyfriend's calling 911, shouting for an ambulance. Not that there was a chance. Coroner said she'd gotten killed around midnight."

She motioned for the file. I slid it back and she skimmed it again. "Shot and stabbed. We counted thirty-four wounds—serious overkill. And yeah, here's one, right under the sternum. Coroner said the bad guy made the most of it by churning the knife. Lots of blood. Big blade, single-edged, like a butcher knife. Flora had a set of cutlery in her kitchen, one of those wood-block things with slots for each knife and the largest was missing. We figured the bad guy took it for a souvenir or just to hide the evidence."

"Our guy left the rail in the girl," said Milo.

"Charming. So what, you're thinking the shrink might be a link?"

Milo shrugged. "Two people in one practice murdered, some similarities in technique."

Lorraine Ogden said, "What, they each encountered the same nutcase in the waiting room?"

"It's not a bad screenplay, Lorraine."

Ogden played with her wedding band. "I

wish I could give you something more on Flora, but that baby was cold the day it got delivered. A victim with no kinks, everyone liked her, no known enemies. It smelled to me right away like a psycho killing. The problem was, a careful psycho. There were prints in the living room. Flora's, the boyfriend, her parents, the manager—he's an eighty-year-old geezer with cataracts, so don't go thinking in that direction. And a few of Flora's in the bedroom, in and around the closet area mostly. But nothing on or near the bed. Same for the kitchen and the bathroom. As in *wiped*. The bathroom, in particular. Not a smudge on the sink, no hair in the tub or on the soap. We had the techies check the pipes and the traps and sure enough, Flora's blood showed up, plus Luminol made the place look like a slaughterhouse, all sorts of wipe marks in the blood, coroner said a right-handed person. There was also a row of drinking glasses in the kitchen and one, in particular, had that squeaky-clean feel like it had been put through the dishwasher. Techie confirmed dishwasher crystals at the bottom."

"Bad guy does his thing, washes up, has a drink."

"Meticulous," said Ogden. "Not that there was any finesse to how he did her. He shot her after she died, but she was alive for at least some of the knife work. Lots of arterial spurt on the sheets, you saw the pictures. He left her lying on her back with her legs spread. Our theory was that she was surprised while sleeping. At least I hope so. Imagine waking up to that? Being fully aware?" She slapped the file shut.

"All that blood," said Milo, "and no footprints."

"Not a single one. Where's O.J. when we need him? This bastard was careful, guys. So much for the old transfer theory. We did find a shred of neoprene—black plastic—stuck on a corner of Flora's nightstand. Looked like a corner that got torn off a bigger piece. Al and I wondered if he'd brought garbage bags along, or some sort of tarp. Lab said it was consistent with industrial sheeting, the kind they use in construction. So maybe we're dealing with someone in the building trades. We were hoping for a print on that shred, at least a partial." She grinned. "Just like on TV."

"Zip," said Milo.

"Zip squared. I was so frustrated I even filled out one of those FBI profiling forms and sent it to Quantico. Four months later, I get an official Feebie letter. White male, organized psychopath, probably between twenty-five and forty and yeah, the building trades thing made sense, but they couldn't be sure, don't hold 'em to any of it."

"Our tax dollars working for us."

"Every day."

I said, "A wrought-iron fence rail might narrow down the building trades."

Ogden said, "Murderous ironworker. Sure, why not? Or he just picked it up at a construction site and sharpened it. In terms of the shrink"—she glanced at me—"pardon, the *therapist,* the only reason we found out Flora was seeing one was biweekly checks drawn on her account. A hundred bucks, which seemed steep for someone taking home four hundred. When we asked the mother about it, she was surprised. Flora had never told her she was being treated for anything. Al and I called Dr.— what was her name—"

"Koppel."

"Right, Dr. Koppel. We conferenced with

her by phone, she said she'd only seen Flora a few times, which synched with the checkbook. Six payments over three months. She didn't want to get into details—patient confidentiality. We told her dead people lose the privilege, and she said she knew that, but there was nothing to tell. She sounded pretty shook-up, said she'd flown in from a conference. Is there something hinky about her?"

"Not that I know," said Milo. "Like you said, the bad guy could be another one of her patients. No idea why Newsome was in therapy?"

"I think Koppel said 'adjustment issues.' Something along those lines. I know she denied there was anything weird about Flora's personality. We asked her about relationships with weirdos or bad guys, and she said Flora had never talked about that. She gave us a diagnosis—adjustment problem . . ."

"Adjustment disorder, anxious type?" I said.

"That sounds right. What it boiled down to was that Flora had been under stress—the pressure of her probationary year at the school, realizing she was going to be a teacher and all the responsibility that entailed. She was also having some financial difficulties because of the years she'd taken off from work to go back to school."

"Financial difficulties," said Milo, "but she shells out a hundred bucks every two weeks to Koppel."

"Koppel said that was a discount rate. She'd cut her fee in half and agreed to see Flora every other week instead of weekly."

"Doing Flora a favor."

"Basically, yes," said Ogden. "Koppel said once a week was usually the minimum in order to gain the benefits of therapy, but she made an exception for Flora. That true, Doctor? Is there a minimum?"

"No."

"Well," she said, "that was Koppel's way of looking at it." One of her hands rested atop the other. A big woman, but delicate, pianist's hands. "She made a big deal about that—how she'd accommodated Flora. I remember thinking she was talking mostly about herself, not Flora."

"Bit of an ego," said Milo. "She does the radio talk-show circuit."

"Does she?" said Ogden. "All I listen to is

The Wave, nice smooth jazz after a day of blood and evil. You talk to her yet?"

"Dr. Delaware has." He looked at me.

I summarized the conversation.

Ogden said, "Sounds like you got lots of nothing, too."

"Maybe all she's *got* is nothing," said Milo. "Dr. D. wonders if maybe Koppel went a little lax on our vic—therapy-lite. In any event, we're gonna have another go at her. The coincidence is too damn cute. Anything else we should know about Flora?"

"Not that I can think of."

"The boyfriend was never an issue?"

"Brian Van Dyne," said Ogden. "Teacher at the same school, couple of years older than Flora. The night of the murder he went to a Lakers game with two friends, then out to dinner, then they hit a couple of bars. Confirmation on all accounts. The friends dropped him off at his apartment in Santa Monica after 2 A.M. I never saw him as our guy, but we polygraphed him anyway and gave him a paraffin test, just to be safe. No gunshot residue on his hands, but it was invalid because too much time had passed. He passed the poly with flying colors."

"Why didn't you see him as the guy?" I said.

"He seemed devastated by Flora's death, really crushed. His friends said he'd been in a great mood at the game and later. Everyone we talked to said he and Flora got along fine. All that still wouldn't have swayed me, but with the poly? No way. Not him."

"Did he know anything about Flora's therapy?"

"Nope. Like Flora's mother, he hadn't been aware she'd been going."

"Biweekly appointments," I said. "Easy enough to conceal."

"And Flora was definitely concealing. She accounted for the appointments by telling Brian Van Dyne she was going to the gym. Which was logical. She'd joined the Sports Depot on Sepulveda. Step aerobics and whatnot. Al and I interviewed the people who worked there, wondering if she'd hooked up with some gym rat—maybe a muscle-bound bad boy to counterbalance wholesome Brian. But no, she kept to herself, just went there to sweat."

"Keeping her therapy secret," I said.

"That doesn't really surprise me, Doctor.

When one of our colleagues here gets a rec-ommendation to see a shrink, they either ig-nore it, or, if they go, they keep it tightly but-toned."

"The stigma."

"It's still there. Flora was serious about Brian Van Dyne. I can understand her not wanting him—or her boss at the school—to know she was having problems."

"How long was she dating him?"

"Half a year."

"Not exactly open communication," I said, "but you could be right. It does make me wonder, though, if the reason she went into treatment was more stigmatizing than work stress."

"Some deep, dark kink in her character? Who knows? Maybe Dr. Koppel will give it up."

Milo said, "If our case is related to yours, you coulda nailed it, Lorraine. Some lunatic seeing Koppel spotted Flora—and our boy Gavin—in the waiting room and smelled Victim."

"Male and female vics?" said Ogden. "What about the girl who died with yours?"

"No ID yet."

Ogden frowned. "Not a head patient?"

"Dr. Koppel denied knowing the girl," I said.

"For what that's worth," said Ogden.

Milo said, "You picked up a liar-vibe?"

"Nothing that strong, but it sounds like she was evasive with both of us, and the coincidence is giving off a definite scent. Let me know after you talk to her. Anything else?"

Milo said, "Lorraine, I was figuring to reinterview some of your principals, if that's okay with you. The mom, the boyfriend, the people Flora worked with."

"Talk to whoever you want, the main thing is closing Flora. You know Al McKinley."

"Good man," said Milo.

"Smart man," she said. "Real bulldog." She took a deep breath. "He and I really worked this one. Combed sex-offender records, did some cross-referencing with felons who work construction. It's scary how many bad guys are doing roofing or day labor. But it all came to nothing. I was so frustrated I found myself hoping some other DB with the same signature would show up, maybe this time there'd be some forensics to work with. Nice, huh? Wanting someone else to die. The neoprene . . . he uses her knife but comes prepared with plastic. We're talking a predator. And those guys don't just stop. Right, Doctor?"

I nodded.

Milo said, "Maybe this one didn't."

CHAPTER

10

anfield School occupied a block of Airdrome Avenue, three blocks south of Pico and east of Doheny. Through the chain-link fence, kids played against a backdrop of mural. Peace, love, harmony. Little kids, their faces shone with possibility.

The neighborhood was Baja Beverly Hills, a five-minute ride from Mary Lou Koppel's office on Olympic. If Flora Newsome had driven to therapy from her apartment in Palms, the trip would have stretched longer, but not much. Twenty minutes in bad traffic.

The vice principal was a black woman named Lavinia Robson with an Ed.D. and a pleasant demeanor.

She checked our credentials, asked the

right questions, got on her intercom and summoned Brian Van Dyne.

"Coffee?" she said.

"No, thanks."

"Flora was a sweetie, we were all saddened. Is there new evidence?"

"Sorry, no, Dr. Robson. Sometimes it helps to take a fresh look."

"That's true in education, as well—ah, here's Brian.

◆

Flora Newsome's former boyfriend was a tall, narrow-shouldered man in his midthirties with thinning blond hair and a wispy mustache the color of gruel. His complexion implied an aversion to sunshine. He wore a green shirt, khakis, a brown wool necktie, and rubber-soled walking shoes. Thick-lensed eyeglasses gave his eyes a stunned glaze. Add to that his genuine shock at our presence, and he looked like a man who'd landed on a foreign planet.

"Flora?" he said. "After all this time?" His voice was whispery, anemic.

Lavinia Robson's phone rang. "Brian, Pat's out for the day, why don't you take these gentlemen to her office?"

◆

The absent Patricia Rohatyn was the school's special ed counselor. Her office was cramped, linoleum-floored, filled with books and games. The air-conditioning vent rattled. The room smelled of rubber eraser.

Two child-sized chairs faced a cluttered desk. Brian Van Dyne said, "You guys sit," and went to fetch a third. He came back, settled opposite us in a large chair. No attempt to dominate; he slumped, trying to sink to our level.

"Your being here today is so strange," he said. "I just got engaged yesterday."

"Congratulations," said Milo.

"For a long time after Flora, I didn't feel like dating. Finally, I agreed to let my sister set me up on a blind date." His smile was wistful. "Karen—my fiancée—doesn't know the details of what happened to Flora. Just that she died."

"No need for her to know."

"Exactly," said Van Dyne. "I still have trouble with it. Remembering. I was the one who found her . . . what brings you here? Do you finally have a suspect?"

Milo crossed his legs, taking pains not to

kick over a stack of box games. "We're reviewing the case, sir. Is there anything that's occurred to you since the first detectives questioned you?"

"Reviewing," said Van Dyne, deflated. "No, nothing." He rubbed the bridge of his nose. "Why has the case been reopened?"

"It never closed, sir."

"Oh," said Van Dyne. "Sure, of course." His knees bumped together.

The small chair was cramping my back, and I stretched. It had to be agony for Milo, but he appeared fine.

He said, "One thing that came up in our review was that Ms. Newsome was seeing a psychotherapist. Detective Ogden told me that was a surprise to you."

"It was a total surprise. Flora never told me. Which was strange because *I'd* been in therapy and told *her*." Van Dyne fooled with his glasses. "I thought we had an open relationship."

"You were in therapy, too," said Milo.

Van Dyne smiled. "Nothing crazy, Lieutenant. I was married for three years, got divorced six months before I met Flora. My wife left me for some guy, and I was having a rough time. To be honest, I was pretty depressed. I saw a psychologist, and he counseled me and referred me to a psychiatrist for some short-term antidepressants. After three months, I felt a lot better and stopped the pills. Another two months of therapy, and I was ready to be on my own. That's what enabled me to be open to a relationship with Flora. So I'd be the last person to look down on therapy. I guess Flora felt differently."

"You think she was embarrassed?"

Van Dyne nodded.

Milo said, "Any idea why she sought treatment?"

"Not a clue. And believe me, I've thought about it."

"She was well adjusted."

"I thought she was."

"You have doubts now?"

"I just assume she went for help because there was some kind of problem. It would have had to be something Flora viewed as serious. She wasn't the type to talk for the sake of talking."

"Something serious."

"Serious in *her* mind."

"You two meet here at the school?" said Milo.

"First day of school. I'd just transferred from the Valley, and Flora was beginning her probationary year. She got assigned to assist another teacher, but I was the one who ended up showing her the ropes. One thing led to the other."

Milo pulled out his pad and scribbled. Keeping his eyes on the page, he said, "Any idea about who might've wanted to hurt Ms. Newsome?"

"Some nut," said Van Dyne. "No rational person would do what I saw. It was . . . stomach-churning."

"Did Flora ever talk about being afraid of anyone?" said Milo. "Someone harassing her, stalking her, that kind of thing?" Easing his big body closer to Van Dyne. Using Newsome's first name.

"Never. But given the fact that she kept her therapy a secret, I can't be sure she didn't hide something else."

"Did she ever seem scared or unduly nervous?"

"Being on probation was a little stressful. Who likes to be judged? But she was doing great, would definitely have passed. Teaching meant a lot to her, Lieutenant. She told me everything she'd done before that had just been a job, but this was her career."

"What other jobs did she have?" I said.

"Office work, mostly. She did some filing for a law firm, worked at a parole office, then she managed the office of a software company that went bust. Evenings she studied for her credential."

"The parole office downtown?" said Milo.

"She never said, only that she didn't like it there. Too many weird characters coming in and out. I thought that might be important and mentioned it to the first detectives, but they didn't seem to agree. Because Flora hadn't worked there for a while."

"Weird characters."

"Her phrase," said Van Dyne. "She didn't want to discuss it." He laced his hands across his chest, as if guarding his heart. "The thing you need to understand about Flora was she wasn't the most talkative person. Not very outgoing or passionate on the surface." He licked his lips. "She was very . . . traditional, more like someone from my mother's generation."

"Conservative."

"Very. That's why I was so surprised to find out she'd been in therapy."

"And you have no idea," said Milo, "about what was bothering her."

"She seemed happy," said Van Dyne. "She really did."

"About getting married."

"About everything. She was a reserved person, Lieutenant. An old-fashioned girl." Van Dyne's fingers separated, but he kept his hand on his chest. "Have you talked to her therapist? Dr. Mary Lou Koppel, she's one of those radio personalities. For all I know that's how Flora found her, from hearing her on the radio."

"Would Flora do something like that?" I said. "Listen to a show and call up for an appointment?"

Van Dyne thought about that. "It's not what I'd have predicted, but who knows? What did Koppel say about treating Flora?"

"Haven't spoken to her yet," said Milo.

"Maybe you'll have better luck than I did." Van Dyne's hands dropped to his lap. "I called her a few weeks after the murder, when I found out Flora had been seeing her. I'm not even sure what I wanted. Some memory of Flora, I guess. Maybe some sympathy, it was a horrendous time. But boy did I dial a wrong number. She was anything but sympathetic. Said confidentiality prevented her from speaking to me and hung up. Very curt. Not in the least bit therapeutic."

◆

Driving away from the school, Milo frowned and lit up a panatella. "Sensitive guy."

"He bug you in some way?"

"Not in the criminal sense, but I wouldn't want to hang out with him. Too delicate." He frowned. "Working at a parole office where the cons made her nervous. One reinterview and we've got info that wasn't in Lorraine's notes."

"Lorraine and McKinley weren't impressed with the parole job because a year had gone by."

"I'm more easily impressed."

◆

We returned to the station, where he accessed Flora Newsome's state employment records and located the parole branch where she'd clerked for five months. Not downtown, the North Hollywood office. A half-hour drive from the murder scene.

I said, "A con notices her, follows her home, stakes out her apartment. Breaking in wouldn't be much of a challenge for a pro."

"Ye olde failure to rehabilitate," he said. "Wonder what Dr. Koppel thinks about that." He stood, stretched, sat down hard.

I said, "There's another possibility. The con didn't follow Flora home, she already knew him. That's why there was no sign of a break-in. Why he didn't need to bring a knife. Maybe what brought Flora to therapy was more than adjustment problems."

"Nice, old-fashioned girl getting it on with a lowlife?"

"She kept her therapy from her boyfriend, could've had other secrets."

"Fooling with a con," he said. "Forbidden pleasures. Guilt took her to Koppel." He stared at me. "You do weave a web."

◆

He walked me through the station and out to the street, glanced at his Timex. "Think I'll have a go at Koppel. Solo, seeing as you two have issues."

"Issues." I smiled.

"Hey, I'm walkin' the walk, talkin' the talk."

◆

Later that evening, he called, and said, "Did you know shrinks don't have to hold on to files?"

"Koppel has no records of Flora Newsome's treatment."

"Straight into the shredder a month after Newsome died. Koppel says it's routine, any closed case gets trashed. Otherwise, she runs into a 'storage problem.' Also, she claims it helps safeguard confidentiality because no one can 'happen' upon the chart."

"Did she remember anything about Newsome?"

"Even less than she remembered for Ogden. 'I treat so many patients, Lieutenant.' "

"But this patient was murdered."

"Same difference."

"She gave you a hard time," I said.

"Not on the surface. She was superfriendly, nice smile, easy manner. Sends her regards, by the way. Says you're a real gentleman."

"I'm touched. She give you anything to work with?"

"She said she couldn't be sure, but she thought Newsome had come in for 'anxiety.' I decided to be direct and brought up the possibility of a con boyfriend. No reaction. If she was hiding something, she's Oscar quality."

"What did she have to say about two patients murdered in fourteen months?"

"She looked a little shaken when I phrased it that way, but said she'd never thought of it that way, her patient load was so huge, it really didn't mean anything. My impression is the lady's got a busy life, doesn't spend too much time focused on any single thing, including her patients. The whole interview was on the run. I caught her leaving the building and walked her to her Mercedes. She was scheduled to tape a show, and her cell phone kept ringing. One of her partners, some guy named Gull, had just parked *his* Mercedes in the lot and came over to say hi. She blew him off, and his expression said he was used to it."

"Two murders in one practice is routine?"

"I pressed her, Alex. She got irritated, pressed me back about whether the evidence pointed to any connection between Gavin and Flora. I couldn't give her any details, so I had to tell her no. She said, 'There you go. Given the size of my practice, it's a statistical quirk.' But I'm not sure she believed it. Her hands were on the steering wheel, and her knuckles were white. They got even whiter when I asked her if she was treating any known felons. She said no, of course not, her patients were all decent people. But maybe I stirred up her you-know-what—her *consciousness*—and she'll think of something. I'll have another go at her in a couple days, and I'd like you to be there."

"Issues and all."

"At this point, the more issues the better. I want to rattle her cage. First, though, I'm gonna talk to the parole folks, see what they remember about Flora. I've also got an address and number for Flora's mother, and if you could find time to see her, I'd really appreciate it. I've got to make sure I don't veer completely into Newsome and neglect Gavin and the blonde."

"I'll try for tomorrow."

"Thankee, thankee." He read off Evelyn Newsome's number and an address on

Ethel Street in Sherman Oaks. "She's not in board-and-care anymore, moved out six months ago and is living in a real house. Maybe someone came up with a miracle cure for arthritis."

"Anything in particular you want me to probe for?"

"The deep dark recesses of her daughter's state of mind before she got killed and any boyfriends Flora had prior to Van Dyne. After that, go anywhere you see fit."

"Sounds like a plan."

"Or reasonable facsimile. That show Koppel was taping, guess what the topic was?"

"Communication."

Silence. "How'd you know?"

"Lucky guess."

"You scare me."

11

I phoned Evelyn Newsome at ten the next morning. A woman with a vigilant voice answered, "Yes?" When I told her who I was, she softened.

"The police were very very nice. Is there something new?"

"I'd like to stop by to chat, Mrs. Newsome. We'll be reviewing old ground, but—"

"A psychologist?"

"We're taking a look at Flora's case from all angles."

"Oh. That's fine, sir. I can always talk about my Flora."

◆

Ethel Street just south of Magnolia was a twenty-minute ride over the Glen, past Ventura Boulevard, and into the heart of Sherman Oaks. This side of the mountains was ten degrees hotter than the city and dry enough to tickle my sinuses. The marine layer had burned off, endowing the Valley with blue skies.

Evelyn Newsome's block was lined with modest, well-kept one-story houses, most of them nailed up posthaste for returning World War II vets. Old-growth orange and apricot trees rose above redwood fences. Huge, scarred elms, top-heavy pines, and untrimmed mulberry trees shaded some of the properties. Others flaunted themselves, naked, in relentless Valley light.

Evelyn Newsome's new home was a pea green stucco bungalow with a fresh mock-shake roof. The lawn was flat, succotash-colored stubble. Birds-of-paradise flanked the front steps. A porch swing hung still in the baking, dormant air.

A screen door covered the entrance, but the wooden door had been left open, offering full view of a dark, low living room. Evelyn Newsome's daughter had been murdered two years ago, and her default phone voice was wary, but on some level she still trusted.

Before I could ring the bell, a big, white-haired man in his seventies appeared and unlatched the screen.

"Doctor? Walt McKitchen, Evelyn's out in back waiting for you." He held his shoulders high, had a florid face built around a purple cabbage nose and a tiny mouth. Despite the heat, he wore a blue-and-gray flannel shirt buttoned to the neck over triple-pleated gray wool slacks.

We shook hands. His fingers were sausages breaded with callus. When he walked me to the back of the house he limped, and I noticed that one of his shoes was bottomed by a three-inch orthopedic sole.

We passed through a tiny, neat bedroom and entered an equally small add-on den paneled in knotty pine and set up with a fuzzy green couch, prefab bookshelves full of paperbacks and a wide-screen TV. The air conditioner in the window was silent. A couple of black-and-white photos hung on the walls. Group portrait of a military battalion. A young couple, standing in front of this very house, the trees saplings, the lawn just dirt.

To the man's right was a bubble-topped thirties Plymouth. The woman held a SOLD sign.

Evelyn Newsome sat on the fuzzy couch, rotund and hunched with cold-set white hair and kind blue eyes. On the redwood burl table in front of her was a teapot swaddled in a cozy and two cups on saucers.

"Doctor," she said, half rising. "I hope you don't prefer coffee." She patted the sofa cushion to her right, and I sat down. She wore a white blouse with a Peter Pan collar over maroon stretch pants. She was top-heavy, with thin legs; more sag to the material than stretch.

"This is fine, thanks, Mrs. Newsome."

She poured. The cups were silk-screened HARRAH'S CASINO, RENO, NEVADA.

"Sugar? Lemon or milk?"

"Plain, please."

Walt McKitchen lingered near the doorway. Evelyn Newsome said, "I'm all right, hon."

McKitchen looked me over, saluted and left.

"We're honeymooners," she said, smiling. "Mr. McKitchen used to visit his wife at the board-and-care where I lived. She passed away, and we became friends."

"Congratulations," I said.

"Thank you. I never thought I'd get out of that place. Arthritis. Not osteo, which everyone gets when they reach an age. Mine's rheumatoid, it's inherited. I've been achy my whole life. After Flora was gone I had nothing but pain. Now I've got companionship and my doctor's come up with some new medication and I'm doing just fine. So it teaches you, things can get better." She flexed her fingers and brushed at her hair.

The tea was lukewarm and insipid, but she closed her eyes with pleasure. Placing the cup on the table, she said, "I'm hoping for some good news about my Flora."

"We're just starting to reexamine the case."

She patted my hand. "I know, dear. I meant in the long run. Now, how can I help you?"

"Is there anything you can think of that's occurred to you since the first detectives—"

"They weren't bad," she said. "A he and she, and he was black. They meant well. At first I had hope, then I didn't. At least they were honest. Told me they'd gotten nowhere. The reason was my Flora was so good, no bad influences. So it had to be someone she didn't know, and that makes it harder. At least that's what they said."

"You disagree?"

"Not about Flora being good, but there was something that bothered me. A while before it happened Flora had worked at a parole office. Right from the beginning, she hated it and when I asked her why she said she didn't care for the people she had to deal with. I said, 'then quit.' She said, 'Mom, it's just temporary until I get my credential, and the pay's good. Good jobs are hard to find.' I mentioned that to the detectives, and they said they'd check it out, but they doubted it was important because Flora hadn't worked there for nearly a year."

"What did Flora say about the people she had to deal with?"

"Nothing more than that, and when I asked, she changed the subject. Didn't want me to worry, I suppose. Flora was always protective of me. I've had my ups and downs, health-wise." Her blues eyes sharpened. "Do *you* think there could've been a connection to that place? Is that why you're here—" Her hand trembled. "The first detectives seemed sure it wasn't important, but you know, it did bother me."

"There's no evidence of a connection, but it's being looked into."

"So you already know about it."

"Brian Van Dyne told us."

"Brian." She smiled. She ran her finger over the Harrah's logo.

"Any problems between him and Flora?"

"Brian?" She chuckled. "The two of them seemed already married. Both of them so conservative, you know? Flora liked him just fine, and he adored her."

"Conservative in what way?" I said.

"Old for their age. Flora was always that way, she grew up fast. Then when she found Brian, I said, 'She's got her counterpart.' Flora's father was a man's man. So is Mr. McKitchen. That's my type, but Flora . . ." She shrugged. "I'm not being kind to Brian, Brian's a nice boy. My theory is that Flora went for him because he was so different from her last boyfriend. Now *that* one was masculine enough, but he had other problems. But you'd know about that."

"Why's that?"

"The first detectives looked into him after I told them about his temper. They said he was under no suspicion whatsoever."

There'd been no mention of a former

boyfriend in the file. I said, "I haven't reviewed every page, Mrs. Newsome. What kind of temper problems are we talking about?"

"Roy can be a nice young man, but he does fly off the handle. Flora used to say sometimes she had to walk on eggshells when Roy got in one of his moods. Not that he hurt Flora, there was never a whisper of that, he never even raised his voice. It was his quiet that bothered her—she told me he'd drop into these long, cold silences where she couldn't reach him."

"Moody," I said.

She said, "I don't believe Roy had anything to do with what happened to Flora. He has a temper, oh sure, but he and Flora parted on friendly terms, and I've known his family forever." She blinked. "Truth be told, Roy'd have no reason to resent Flora. He was the one who ended it. Ended up with another woman, cheap type if you ask me. Now they're getting divorced, and isn't that just a great big mess."

"You're still in touch with Roy."

"His folks were our neighbors back when we lived in Culver City. Roy and Flora grew up together, like brother and sister. Roy's folks own an aquarium—one of those fish stores. Roy doesn't likes animals, isn't that funny? Him I haven't seen for a while; it's his folks I occasionally talk to. His mother told me about the divorce. I think what she was really saying was that Roy should've been smart and stuck with Flora."

"What's Roy's full name?"

"Nichols. Roy Nichols, Jr. I told the other detectives, it should all be in the records."

"Did Flora like animals?"

She shook her head. "She and Roy saw eye to eye on that. Neat, both of them. Everything had to be tidy. With all that, you'd've thought Roy would pick a cleaner job."

"What does he do?"

"He's a carpenter, frames up houses. I suppose it's cleaner than plumbing."

"Construction," I said.

"You bet."

◆

I spent another quarter hour in the pine-paneled room, learned nothing more, thanked her, and left.

I reached Milo at his desk and told him about Roy Nichols.

"Bad temper, doesn't like animals, works construction," he said. "Something else Lorraine and Al didn't think to include."

"Evelyn Newsome said they talked to him and cleared him."

"Yeah, yeah . . . let me run him through the county data bank just in case . . . I've got a Roy Dean Nichols with a birth date that would make him the right age . . . and look at this: two priors. A DUI last year and a 415 the year before that. Two months after Flora was killed."

"Disturbing the peace can mean anything," I said. "Given the DUI, it was probably alchohol-related."

"I'm pulling up his DMV as we speak . . . here we go, an address on Harter Street. That's Culver City, not far from Flora's place in Palms. Are you on your way back to the alleged city? I can meet you at the station, and we'll pay this joker a visit."

"The Valley parole office isn't far from Evelyn Newsome's house. I was going to drive by, maybe go in and have a look."

"Don't waste your time. Flora only worked there for three days before they transferred her to a temporary branch office on Sepulveda and Venice. One of those projects funded by a federal seed grant. Small storefront offices, they opened half a dozen all over the city. Shorter distance for the cons to travel, heaven forfend we tax the poor souls. The hope was that the bad boys would be more compliant about checking in."

"You're talking in past tense," I said.

"You got it. No better compliance and a few million bucks down the drain, the offices were shut down. Flora stayed on until the funds ran out, so she didn't hate the job badly enough to quit. Didn't make much of an impression either. Her supervisor remembers her as quiet, said she mostly filed and answered the phone. He doubts she'd get involved with a con."

"Why?"

"He said she kept to herself and that not many cons came in."

"Enough came in to bother her," I said. "And Sepulveda and Venice is really close to her apartment. I'd like to know how many of the cons assigned to that office had sex-crime histories."

"Good luck. Parole's as bureaucratic as it comes. State office, everything's filtered through Sacramento, and now that the satellites have closed, the records are somewhere in outer space. But if it shakes out that way, I'll start digging. Meanwhile, Roy Nichols's place is also close by, and he has a record that says impulse control's a problem. And isn't it you guys who make a big deal about psychopaths not liking animals?"

"Cruelty to animals," I said. "Flora's mother said Nichols is a neat-freak."

"There you go, yet another quirk. Just the type to clean up a crime scene thoroughly. He's worth looking into, right? See you in—what, twenty, twenty-five?"

"Zoom zoom zoom."

Milo's unmarked idled at the curb, in front of the station. He was at the wheel, smoking and tapping his finger.

I drove up next to the driver's window. He handed me a staff permit, and I parked in the lot across the street. When I returned, the unmarked's passenger door was open. We were heading south before I closed it.

"Big hurry?"

"I pulled Roy Nichols's file. The 415 wasn't just some drunk breaking glass. Though you were right about it being booze-stoked. Nichols beat some guy up at a sports bar in Inglewood, did a real number on him, broke some bones. The report says Nichols thought the guy was leering at his date, a woman named Lisa Jenrette. They traded words, and one thing led to another. What got Nichols out of a felony assault charge was several other patrons swore the other guy had thrown the first punch and that he *had* come on to Nichols's date. One of those habitual assholes, always picking fights. Nichols compensated part of his medical bills and pleaded down to Disturbing. He served no time, promised to stay away from the bar, and took a rage control class."

He sped side streets to Olympic, turned left, headed for Sepulveda. "A severe jealousy problem could lead to the kind of overkill they found in Flora's bedroom."

"Evelyn Newsome said Nichols was the one who ended the relationship."

"So maybe he changed his mind, got possessive. Alex, I read the medical report on the guy he pounded. Shattered face bones, dislocated shoulder. One witness said Nichols was about to stomp the guy's head into pulp when they managed to pull him off."

We drove in silence for a while, then he said, "Rage control class. You think that stuff works?"

"Maybe sometimes."

"There's a hearty endorsement for you."

"I think it takes more than a few manda-
tory lectures to alter basic temperament."

"The lightbulb has to want to change."

"You bet."

"More tax dollars flushed," he said. "Like
those satellite parole offices."

"Probably."

"Well," he said, "that really pisses me off."

◆

Roy Nichols's house was a slightly larger,
pure white version of Evelyn Newsome's
bungalow that bore the signs of ambitious
but wrongheaded improvement: overly wide
black shutters that would've fit a two-story
colonial, a pair of Doric columns propping
up the tiny porch, a Spanish tile roof, the
tiles variegated and expensive and piled too
high, a three-foot sash of bouquet canyon
stone veneered to the bottom of the facade.
This lawn was lush, unblemished, the bright
green of a Saint Paddy's parade. Five-foot
sago palms flanked the steps—five hundred
dollars' worth of vegetation. Dwarf junipers
ringed the front, trimmed low to the ground
with bonsai precision.

In the driveway something hulked under a spotless black cover. Milo lifted a corner of the cover on a shiny black Ford pickup with a freshly chromed bumper. Raised suspension, custom wheels. A sticker protected by a plastic coating said: *How Am I Driving? Call 1-800-SCRU YOU.*

We walked to the front door. A security firm sticker was centered on a black lacquer door. Pushing the bell elicited chimes. *Oh-oh-say-can-you-see?*

"Hold on!" A woman opened. Tall, young, pretty but washed out, she had a heart-shaped face, wore a filmy black tank top over white terry-cloth shorts. No bra, bare feet. Great legs, a shaving nick on one glossy shin. Her hair was white-blond with no luster, bunched above her head in a careless thatch. Pink nail polish on her fingers, chipped badly. Darker polish on her toes, in even worse shape. Behind her was a room full of cardboard cartons. New cartons with crisp edges, sealed with brown tape and marked CONTENTS followed by three blank lines.

She folded her arms across big, soft breasts. "Yes?"

Milo showed her the badge. "You're Mrs. Nichols?"

"Not anymore. You here about Roy?"

"Yes, ma'am."

She sighed and waved us in. But for a few feet inside the door, the entire room was filled with the packing boxes. A child-sized mattress stood propped against a tied-off garbage bag.

"Moving?"

"Soon as I can get the movers over here. They say by tomorrow, but they've already missed one appointment. The house is already sold, I've got to vacate by next week. What did Roy do?"

"You're assuming he did something."

"You're here, right? I didn't do anything, and neither did Lorelei. My daughter. She's four years old, and if she wakes up from her nap, I'm going to kick you guys out."

"Your name, ma'am?"

"Ma'am," she said, amused. "I'm Lisa. Nichols, still. I'll probably go back to my maiden name, which is Jenrette, and I always thought was a lot prettier than Nichols. Right now I've got other things to keep me busy. So what's he done?"

"Could be nothing. We just want to talk to him."

"Then go over to his job site. He's working in Inglewood. On Manchester, near the Forum. They're fixing up an office building. I know he's making good money but try getting a penny out of him. Thank God his parents are cool. They want Lorelei to live decently, even though she's not theirs, biologically. I told 'em I'd stay in L.A. and they could see her if they make it easy for me; otherwise, I move back to Tucson, where *my* folks are."

"Roy's tight with a buck," said Milo.

"Roy's like a stingy old man except when it comes to his projects."

"What kinds of projects?"

"His truck, his single-malt collection, fixing up the house. Did you have a look at this place—he never stopped fooling with it. If there weren't so many boxes, I'd show you all the paneling he did in the back rooms. Rosewood paneling, expensive stuff, in all three bedrooms. Made it dark as a funeral parlor, but he claimed it would help the resale value. So what happens, we put the house up for sale and we get a buyer and the first thing they're going to do is rip out the paneling."

"That couldn't have made Roy happy," I said.

"Roy's not happy about anything."

"Moody."

She turned to me. "Sounds like you know him."

"Never met him."

"Lucky you."

◆

Milo asked if she'd seen Roy recently.

"Not for a month. He's living with his parents, four blocks away. You'd think he'd drop by to see Lorelei."

"Not a single visit?"

"I bring Lorelei over once a week. Sometimes Roy's there, but even if he is, he doesn't play with her. To him it *matters* that she isn't his." Her eyes misted. She shifted her weight, uncrossed her arms, looked down at the carpet. "Listen, I've got calls to make. Why won't you tell me what he's done? I mean, if he's dangerous, shouldn't I know?"

Milo said, "You see him as potentially dangerous?"

"What are you," said Lisa Nichols, "some kind of shrink? We went to one, 'cause of the divorce. The court ordered it, and he did that—the shrink. Asked questions instead of giving answers."

"Roy hasn't done anything. We just want to talk to him about a former girlfriend."

"The one who got murdered? Flora?"

"You know about her."

"Just what Roy told me." Her hand flew to her mouth. "You're not saying . . ."

"No, ma'am. We're reviewing the case and are talking to everyone who knew her."

"I've got a four-year-old," said Lisa. "You've got to be straight with me."

"You're afraid of Roy," I said.

"I'm afraid of his temper. Not that he ever did anything to me. But the way he gets— crawling into himself."

Milo said, "What did he tell you about Flora Newsome?"

"That she was . . ." She folded her upper lip between her teeth. "It's going to sound . . ."

"What, ma'am?"

"He said she was cold. In bed. Not good sexually. He said she probably came on to some guy, then wouldn't come through and that's what happened to her."

"That was his theory, huh?"

"Roy sees everything in terms of sex. If it was up to him . . ." Her head flipped away from us. "I've got to finish up packing. Lori will be up soon and my hands will be tied."

She gave us Roy Nichols's parents' address and phone number. Milo called there, spoke to the mother, lied about being a general contractor looking for framers and got the location of Nichols's current job site.

As we drove south on Sepulveda toward Inglewood, he said, "My guess is Flora wouldn't put out enough for Nichols, and that's why he dumped her. Ergo, his theory. Or, he was—what do you guys call it, when you put your own crap on someone else—"

"Projecting," I said. "No forced entry at Flora's apartment is consistent with someone she knew. The overkill fits with a lot of background rage, and the sexual posing suggests the source of the rage."

"Wrought-iron fence post. Got to be some of those lying around construction jobs. More than ever, I want to know where this bastard was the night Gavin and the blonde were killed. Speaking of which, I sent two

D's over to the fancy hotels, then they talked to BHPD, and no one knows our Jimmy Choo girl. The hotels are probably lying, but the B. H. cops do keep a file of high-priced call girls, and she's not in it. It's just a matter of time. Someone's got to miss her."

CHAPTER

13

Roy Nichols's supervisor was a compact middle-aged man named Art Rodriguez, with a graying beard and the excitability quotient of a stone Buddha. A DODGER BLUE sticker was emblazoned across his hard hat above an American flag decal. He wore an oversize Disneyland T-shirt under a chambray shirt, filthy jeans, and dusty work boots, held a folded racing form in one hand.

We stood out in the dusty sun, just inside the chain-link border of the construction site. The job was tacking a side addition onto an ugly brick-faced two-story office building. The original structure was gutted and windowless but a sign—GOLDEN AGE IN-VESTMENTS—remained atop the door hole.

The new space was in the framing stage, and Roy Nichols was one of the framers. Rodriguez pointed him out—crouching on the second floor, wielding a nail gun. The air smelled of raw wood and pesticide and sulfur.

Art Rodriguez said, "Want me to get him? Or you can put on hats and go up there yourselves."

"You can do it," said Milo. "You're not surprised we want to talk to him."

Rodriguez gave a tobacco-laced laugh. "This business? All my roofers are cons, and a whole bunch of the other trades are, too."

"Nichols isn't a con."

"Con, potential con, what's the difference? Everyone gets a second chance. It's what makes this country great."

"Nichols impress you as a potential?"

"I don't get into their personal lives," said Rodriguez. "Step one, they show up, step two, they do the freaking job. I get that from a few of them with any regularity, I'm a happy guy."

"Nichols dependable?"

"He's actually one of the good ones. Like clockwork. Here on the dot—kind of faggy, actually."

"Faggy," said Milo.

"Faggy," Rodriguez repeated. "As in picky, prissy, choosy. Everything has to be just so, he reminds me of my wife."

"Picky how?"

"He wants his lunch box kept away from dust, gets ticked when guys mess with his tools or don't show up on time. Any change in routine ticks him off. He folds his *jacket,* for chrissake."

"Perfectionist."

"What's your beef with him?"

"Nothing yet."

"Hope it stays that way," said Rodriguez. "He shows up, does the freaking job."

◆

Roy Nichols was six-three, an easy 250, with a hard, protruding belly, flour-sack arms and tree-trunk thighs. Under his hard hat was a head shaved clean. The stubble that blanketed his face was fair, and so were his eyebrows. He wore a sweat-soaked earth-colored T-shirt under blue denim overalls, had a rose tattoo on his right biceps. His face was square and sun-baked, bottomed by a double chin, scored with deep seams that made him look older than his thirty years.

Rodriguez pointed to us, and Nichols surged ahead of him and swaggered in our direction.

"Round one, ding," muttered Milo.

Nichols reached us, and said, "Police? About what?" His voice was thin and shockingly high. I bet many a phone caller had asked to speak to his mother. I bet Roy Nichols never got used to it.

Milo extended a hand.

Nichols showed us a dusty palm, muttered, "Dirty," and lowered it to his side. He rolled his neck. "What do you want?"

"To talk about Flora Newsome."

"*Now?* I'm working."

"We'd appreciate a few minutes, Mr. Nichols."

"About *what*?" A flush rose from Nichols's bull neck and made its way up his cheeks.

"We're taking a fresh look at the case and are talking to everyone who knew her."

"I knew her all right, but I don't know who killed her. I've already been through all that crap with some other cops—I'm on the job,

man, and they pay me by the hour. They're
Nazis, man. I stay too long in the bathroom,
they dock me. If it was a union job, they
couldn't do that, but it isn't, so give me a
break."

"I'll square it with Mr. Rodriguez."

"Right," said Nichols. He toed dirt, rolled
his neck some more.

"Just a few minutes."

Nichols cursed under his breath. "At least
let's get out of the fucking sun."

◆

We walked to a corner of the site shaded
by two portable toilets. The chemicals had
failed, and the stench was aggressive.

Nichols's nostrils flared. "Reeks. Perfect.
This is all bullshit."

"You get upset pretty easily," said Milo.

"You would, too, if your time was money
and someone wasted it." Nichols unsnapped the leather lid of his wristwatch
and peered at the dial. "Those first cops
spent days with me, man. What a hassle. I
could tell right away they thought I was a
suspect because of the way they played
around with me."

"Played?"

"One's nice, the other's an asshole. A he and a she. He faked being the nice one. I've seen enough TV to know the game." He ran a hand over his skinhead. "Now, you. What, you're getting overtime, trying to stretch it out?"

Milo stared at him.

Nichols said, "Didn't they tell you I had a perfect alibi for when Flora was killed? Watching the game in a sports bar, then I shot pool and played some darts and got drunk. A buddy drove me to my house just after midnight, and I threw up all over the living room couch. My wife tucked me in and didn't give me shit until she woke me up two hours later after stewing on it and then she reamed me. So I'm accounted for, okay? A whole bunch of people verified it, and your buddies know it."

Milo glanced at me. Both of us thinking the same thing: His wife hadn't mentioned that.

"You have any theories about who killed Flora?"

"No."

"None at all?"

Nichols licked his lips. "Why should I?"

"We've heard you do have a theory."

"I don't know what you're talking about."

"Flora's sex drive. Or lack thereof."

"Shit," said Nichols. "You've been talking to Lisa. What do you expect her to say? We're getting divorced, she hates my fucking guts. Didn't she tell you I was home that night? Shit, she didn't. See—she hates my guts."

"What about your theory?"

"Yeah, yeah, I told her that, but I was talking out of my butt—like you talk to your wife, you know."

Milo smiled.

"They need you to talk," said Nichols. "Females." He opened and shut his hand several times, miming chatter. "You come home after a hard day's work and just wanna chill and they want to talk. Myah myah myah. So you tell them what they want to hear."

"Lisa wanted to hear about Flora's sex drive?"

"Lisa wanted to hear that she was hot, the hottest, hotter than anyone else I ever met in my life." Nichols humphed. "That's what that was all about."

Milo stepped closer to Nichols. "You stroked Lisa by putting down Flora? Any particular reason you chose Flora as the bad example?"

Nichols edged back.

"Did Flora have sexual problems, Roy?"

"If you call not being able to do it problems," said Nichols.

"She couldn't have sex?"

"She couldn't *come*. She had no feelings down there, used to lie there like a . . . a carpet. She didn't *like* to do it. Wouldn't come out and say so, but she had a way of letting you know."

"What way was that?"

"You'd touch her, and she'd get this . . . upset look. Like she—like you hurt her."

"Doesn't sound like a fun relationship."

Nichols didn't answer.

Milo said, "Still, you went out with her for what—a year?"

"Less than that." Nichols's eyes widened. "I know what you're getting at."

"What's that, Roy?"

"That I got mad at her because she wouldn't put out, but it wasn't like that. We didn't fight, I never did anything but be cool with her. I took her out to movies, dinner, whatever. Spent money on her, man, and it wasn't like I was getting anything back."

"Uneven trade," said Milo.

"This is making me sound bad." Nichols's meaty shoulders flexed. He smiled. "Big deal how I sound, I have a total four-plus alibi, so you can think what you want."

"Did you break up with Flora because of her sexual problems, Roy?"

"That was part of it, wouldn't it be for anyone normal? But it's not like we were even really going together. We were neighbors, grew up together. Our parents hung out, we had barbecues together, whatever. Everyone kind of threw us together, know what I mean?"

"Parental matchmaking," I said.

He looked at me with gratitude. "Yeah, exactly. 'Flora's such a nice girl.' 'Flora would make a great mom.' And she dug me, she definitely did, so why not, she wasn't half–bad-looking, coulda been hot if she knew how to dress. And how to screw. But we *hung* out more than we *went* out, you know? Even so, I spent money on her, lots of lobster dinners. When we broke up everything was cool."

"She wasn't upset?"

"Sure she was, but it wasn't any big hysterical scene, know what I mean? She cried a little, I told her we'd be friends, and that was that."

I said, "Did you remain friends?"

"There was no . . . animosity."

"Did you continue to see each other?"

"No," said Nichols, regarding me with wariness now. He cupped his clean head with one big hand, scratched loose a flake of sun-baked skin. "I'd see her at my folks'. There was no bad feelings."

Milo said, "Those lobster dinners. Any particular place?"

Nichols stared at him. "I can eat lobster anywhere, but Flora liked this place in the Marina, out by the harbor."

"Bobby J's."

"That's the one. Flora liked to look at the boats. But then one time I offered to arrange a cruise around the Marina, and she said she got seasick. That was Flora. All talk."

"Flora was scheduled to go to Bobby J's for brunch the morning after she got murdered. She and her new boyfriend."

"So?"

Milo shrugged.

Nichols said, "New boyfriend? What, I'm supposed to know that? Don't make like I was the old boyfriend and she threw me over and I gave a shit because that is total *bullshit*."

"Roy," said Milo, "Flora's problems aside, I assume you and she did sleep together?"

"Tried is more like it. Flora could make like her legs were glued together. And it was always like you were hurting her. You wanna know my opinion, that *is* how she ran into trouble." Nichols's chin jutted defiantly. "What if she led some guy on, then wouldn't come through? Some dude not as understanding as me. For all I know, that boyfriend of hers snapped. He seemed like a wimp, but isn't it always the quiet ones?"

"You met him?"

"One time. Flora brought him by my folks' house. Thanksgiving, it was evening, after we finished stuffing our pie-holes. I was mellowing out on the couch, like when I eat that way don't make me *move,* man. Lisa and my mom were washing up and my dad and me were both blissed out watching the tube and *boing* goes the doorbell. In comes Flora all dressed up, arm in arm with this pale-faced wimp-ass dude with this wimp-ass mustache, and he's looking uncomfortable, like what the *fuck* am I doing *here*?

She claims she came by to visit my folks, but I know she's there to show me she's doing okay without me. That's how women are."

Nichols tapped his upper teeth on his lowers. "Like Mr. Teacher's gonna impress me. You check him out?"

"You don't think much of Van Dyne."

"I got nothing against him, I was happy he had her, maybe he could deal with her." Nichols smiled. "Or maybe he couldn't. That's your job to find out. Now can I go back and earn some bucks?"

"Where were you Monday night, say between 7 and 11 P.M.?"

"Monday? Why? What happened Monday?"

Milo stepped closer. He and Nichols were eye level, their noses inches apart. Nichols's chin continued to jut, but his eyes flickered, and he flinched.

"Answer the question please, Roy."

"Monday . . . I was at my parents'." The admission made Nichols flush again. This time the color reached his brow. "I'm living there till I find a new place."

"You're sure you were there Monday night."

"Yeah, I'm sure. I'm up every day at four-thirty in the morning so I have time to work out and shower and eat a good breakfast and be on the job at six-thirty. I work my ass off all day, come home, lift some more, eat, watch TV, go to sleep by eight-thirty. That's my swinging life, and I'm cool with it, okay? What I'm *not* cool with is you coming by and hassling me for no reason. I've got no obligation to talk to you, so now I'm going back to work."

We watched him swagger away.

I said, "And our first nominee in the Mr. Charm contest . . ."

Milo said, "On the edge."

"Teetering."

"You see him as our bad guy?"

"If his alibis don't check out, I'd definitely be interested."

"Flora was killed between midnight and two. He claims a buddy drove him home just after twelve, and his wife woke him at two. That sounds awfully cute, and I didn't see any mention of it in the file."

I said, "What if he came home a bit earlier and Lisa woke him up closer to one? She browbeat him, got everything off her chest, and hit the sack, left him furious and frustrated, unable to go back to sleep. He got out of bed, left the house, and drove over to someone else who'd frustrated him. High stress is a trigger for some sexual killers. And plenty of organized types maintain outwardly stable marriages while brutalizing other women."

"Have a tiff with the wife, take it out on the ex."

I said, "He seems under lots of stress now. A sexually charged fellow back to living with his parents."

"Gavin and the blonde," he said. "A couple about to get it on pushes his button because he's all pent up sexually."

"His alibi for Gavin and the blonde is even flimsier because he and his parents don't share a room. He could've easily sneaked out without their knowing. Even if they claim otherwise, they're his parents."

Nichols continued toward the framework without looking back. We watched him climb up to the second floor, strap on his tool belt, stretch, and pick up his nail gun. He took another stretch—aiming for casual before pressing the gun to a crossbeam.

Snap snap snap.

Milo said, "Let's get outta here," and we

returned to the car. He got back on Sepulveda and drove north, toward L.A. The boulevard was crammed and slow. The air—hot, unyielding—seemed to press upon the sides of the unmarked. Lots of stares. Everyone knew it was an unmarked. Even if we'd been in a VW, Milo's restless eyes would have given him away.

He said, "What *I'd* like to know is why Lorraine and Al didn't bother putting Nichols in the murder book."

"You going to ask her?"

"That's my way, bub. Open, honest, sincere."

"That should be fun."

"Hey," he said, "I'll be sensitive."

He flipped on the police radio, listened to felony calls for a few moments, muttered, "I love this city," and squelched the volume.

I said, "Even if Nichols is innocent, he gave us useful information."

"Flora's sexual problems?"

"Maybe the reason she went for therapy. That would explain her not telling Van Dyne. Now that I think about it, he also described her as not very passionate on the surface. The timing fits: She began treatment after getting dumped by Nichols and before meeting Van Dyne. Nichols claims he was gentlemanly, but I'm sure he was brutally clear about why he was ending the relationship."

"Mr. Tactful," he said. " 'Hey, bitch, unglue your legs or I'm outta here.' "

"Once Flora got over the hurt, maybe she decided she did have a problem. Seeking a woman therapist for a sexual issue makes sense."

"Koppel does sex therapy, too?"

"There seems to be very little she doesn't do."

The light turned red, and he rolled to a stop. A jumbo jet swooped down low on its approach to LAX. When the noise cleared, I said, "Assuming Nichols's alibis do check out, do you have the stomach for another theory?"

"At this point, I'll take astrology."

"As part of treatment, Koppel enouraged Flora to be more assertive and adventurous, and she began taking risks. It's standard operating procedure in cases like hers."

"What kind of risks?"

"Striking up conversations with strangers, maybe even getting picked up. And she picked up the wrong guy. Which could lead us right back to the parole office. What if Flora connected with a con? Someone aggressive and hypermacho—someone like Roy Nichols but with no boy-next-door history to rein him in. The murder could've been a sexual escapade taken too far. Or Flora changed her mind and paid for it horribly."

"A Mr. Goodbar thing," he said. "That girl was a teacher, too . . . but she was single, had a secret life. Flora was engaged to Van Dyne. And she was dating Van Dyne when she got killed. You saying Ms. Prim stepped out on her fiancé with a felon?"

"If it was a felon, she met him before she began with Van Dyne. I'm saying she could've kept another man on the side."

"Secret lives."

"Or perhaps Flora broke off with the con after she met Van Dyne, but he wasn't willing to accept that. There was no sign of forced entry. That could mean someone Flora knew, or an experienced burglar. Or both."

"Flora told her mother and Van Dyne she hated the job at the parole office because of the lowlifes. You think she was lying?"

"People compartmentalize their lives."

The light turned green, and we rolled along with the traffic sludge. The sky was brown at the horizon, bleeding to dishwater where the sun struggled through. He fooled with the radio dial again, listened to more police calls, lowered the volume.

"Cheating on Van Dyne with Mr. Bad Boy," he said. "Or maybe Van Dyne found out something he shouldn't have and went ballistic. Hell, for all we know, Van Dyne's not as innocent as he comes across."

I thought about that. "Flora's mother implied that Van Dyne was less than manly. That could've come from Flora. And his alibi turned out to be no better than Roy's."

"So maybe the sexual problems weren't limited to her. What if Ol' Brian can't cut the mustard? That could get a quiet boy plenty frustrated." He turned up the volume, seemed to be lulled by the nonstop patter of the dispatcher. The traffic swell pitched us forward a few more yards, and he switched abruptly to AM. Tuning in a talk show, he listened to the host berate a caller for admiring the president, lowered the volume yet again.

"Ogden and Al McKinley didn't include Nichols in the file, but they spent two days questioning him. Sweet old Brian didn't even get that . . . but what the hell, it's not even my case. Unless it ties in to Gavin and the blonde."

He returned to the talk show. The host was berating a caller for not taking personal responsibility for her obesity. He cut her off and on came a commercial for an herbal weight-loss concoction.

He said, "What do you think of these shows?"

"The exuberance of free speech," I said. "And bad manners. You a fan?"

"Nah, I get enough nastiness on the job, but according to today's paper, our girl Mary Lou's scheduled to be on in an hour."

"Really," I said. "You going to listen?"

"I believe in continuing education."

Milo went to talk to Lorraine Ogden while I sat at his desk and reviewed the Gavin Quick murder book. Nothing new. I turned to the Flora Newsome file.

No progress there, either. Milo returned five minutes letter, red-faced, shaking his head.

I relinquished his chair, but he perched on the desk edge, stretched his legs, loosened his tie. "My sensitivity failed. I brought up Nichols and she told me she'd worked the hell out of the case and I had no business second-guessing her. She said I should stick to my own case, the more she thought about it, they weren't that similar after all, keep her out of it. Then she shoved this in my face."

He handed me a crumpled piece of paper that I smoothed. Ballistics report from the crime lab, stamped PRIORITY and initialed by Detective L. L. Ogden. Comparisons between the .22 used to kill Gavin and the blonde and the gun that had terminated Flora's life. A tech named Nishiyama had signed off on the test.

Similar weapons, probably cheap, imported semiautomatics, but no match.

"With a cheapie," I said, "you could use one, toss it, get another."

"Anything's possible, but a match would've been a helluva lot nicer. Now I've pissed off a colleague and gotten no closer to a solve."

"She's a D-II, you're a lieutenant. I thought the lines of authority were clearer."

"In title only. My lack of administrative duties cuts both ways, everyone knows I've got no juice." He rifled though his messages. "Looks like no luck yet on the blonde . . ." His eyes shifted to his Timex. "Koppel's on the air."

He switched on his desk radio and tuned in the talk station. Another host, same level of derision. A rant about racial profiling; this guy hated it.

Milo said, "Sure, let's inspect Grandma's shoes at the airport while Mr. Hamas waltzes through."

The host said, "Okay, folks, this is Tom Curlie at the top of the hour, and we've got a hot guest coming any minute. Dr. Mary Lou Koppel, noted psychiatrist, and anyone who listens to the show knows she's been on before and knows she's smart . . . and anyone who doesn't listen, who the hell needs you heh-heh . . . today we'll be talking about . . . what's that . . . my engineer, the ever-charismatic Gary is informing me that Dr. Mary Lou Koppel is running late . . . better do something about the punctuality, Doc. Maybe see a psychiatrist heh-heh-heh . . . meanwhile let's talk about car insurance. Have you ever been rear-ended by one of those lunatics who seem to be everywhere like invaders from outer space? You know what I'm talking about: space-outs, cell-phone freaks, and just plain lousy dri-vers. Has one of them bendered your fender? Or worse? Then you know the value of good insurance, and Low-Ball Insurance is the best value around . . ."

Milo said, "Koppel's a psychologist, not a psychiatrist."

"Why let facts get in the way?"

Tom Curlie finished his spiel and segued to a prerecorded commercial for do-it-your-self legal forms. Then a woman with a sultry voice reported on the weather and freeway traffic.

Another commercial came on—Tom Curlie rhapsodizing about something called a Divine Mochalicious that could be had at any branch of CafeCafe, then he said, "The enigmatic yet pedestrian Gary is informing me that Dr. Mary Lou Koppel, our psychiatric guest, has still not arrived at the studio and that said headshrinker cannot be reached on her cell phone. *Tsk, tsk,* Mary Lou. You are now officially off the privileged roster that makes up guests on the Tom Curlie show because Tom Curlie stands for punctuality and personal responsibility and all the other virtues that have made this country great. Even though this country, in a lapse of judgment, elected a president who don't talk good . . . okay, who needs her, folks? Let's talk about psychiatrists and why they're so doggone nuts themselves. I mean, is that just my imagination, or are they all just a little bit off? So what's that all about, gang? Someone becoming a headshrinker because her own head's too dog-gone big for her own good? Or is it a matter of a rotten childhood heh-heh-heh? How do you guys feel about that, c'mon, call and let me know at 1 888 TOM CURLIE. Here we go, those lines are lighting up and my first call is Fred from Downey. Hey, Fred. Had *your* head shrunk lately?"

"Hey, Tom. First of all I wanna tell you that I listen to you every day, and that you're really coo—"

"Excellent judgment, Fred, but what about those psychiatrists—those head docs, those voodoo incantators, those *shrinks*? Think they're rowing with one paddle, blinking with one eye, suffering from brain freeze, dancing with shadows in the hall of mirrors? Is that what it boils down to, Fred? They become shrinks because they need to get shrunk?"

"Well, Tom, as a matter of fact, Tom, I know about those people. It was just about twelve years ago that I was sitting out under the stars minding my own business and they abducted me and implanted these electrodes in my—"

Milo flicked off the radio.

"Civilization and its discontents," I said.

"Malcontents is more like it. Maybe

Lorraine's right, and I should keep focused on Gavin. I'm gonna call the kids who were in the crash with him, see what that dredges up. Also, see if I can have a go with the girl-friend—Kayla Bartell—without her old man hovering."

"Still planning to reinterview Koppel?"

"That, too." He settled in his chair. "She's obviously not in her office, or that idiot could've contacted her. Let me make some calls first, then how about we drop by in two hours? Or later, if that cramps your style."

"Two's fine. Want me to try to talk to Kayla?"

"If you saw her on the street, I'd say fine," he said. "But what with it being B.H. and the father so uptight, we'd better stick to proto-col."

"Visits limited to an official police pres-ence."

"Such as it is."

◆

I drove home listening to Tom Curlie. Mary Lou Koppel never showed up, and Curlie didn't mention her again. He alternated be-tween commercials and call-ins from sad, angry listeners, then brought on his next

guest—a personal injury lawyer who specialized in suing fast-food chains for racial
discrimination and brewing their coffee too
hot.

Curlie said, "I don't know about all that,
Bill, but as far as I'm concerned, you can jail
'em for just plain lousy food."

◆

Instead of heading home, I continued on
to Beverly Hills and drove past the Quick
house. The same white minivan occupied
the driveway, but the baby Benz was gone.
The drapes were closed, and the day's mail
had collected on the front step. A gardener
pruned a hedge. An anorexic woman
walked by with a black Chow on leash. The
dog looked drugged. A block and a half up,
traffic zipped by on Wilshire. A family had
been torn apart, but the world kept spin-
ning.

I turned the Seville around, aimed it north
through the business district, entered the
Flats, cruised by the Bartell mansion. In
daylight, the house was even more out-
sized, square and white as a fresh bar of
soap. The fencing looked like a prison bar-
rier. The four-car garage doors were closed

but a red Jeep Grand Cherokee idled just inside the electric gates.

I parked and watched from across the street as the gates opened and Kayla Bartell sped through. She was on her cell phone and turned right without checking for cross traffic and sped toward Santa Monica Boulevard. She talked nonstop, animatedly, on a cell phone, with no idea I was following as she rolled through the stop sign at Elevado and ran the one at Carmelita. Without signaling, she hung a risky left turn on Santa Monica and continued east, one hand still grasping the phone. The other steered, and sometimes she removed it to gesticulate and swerved into other lanes. For the most part, motorists kept their distance from her, until another young woman in a Porsche Boxster honked and flipped her off.

Kayla ignored her, kept gabbing, weaved her way to Canon Drive, drove south, and parked in the service alley behind the Umberto hair salon. A valet held open the driver's door, and Kayla sprang out wearing a lacy black midriff top, black leather pants, and high-heeled boots. On her head was a silver lamé baseball cap. Her blond ponytail protruded through the adjusting band.

No tip for the valet, just a smile. Someone had told her that was enough.

She entered the salon with a bounce in her step.

♦

"Two-hundred-dollar haircut," said Milo. "Ah, youth."

We were in the Seville, and I was driving east on Olympic, toward Mary Lou Koppel's office.

I said, "You reach the boys who were in the accident?"

"Both of them, and they back up what the Quicks told us. Gavin was in the back, sandwiched between them. When the car hit the mountain, they were belted and got jostled from side to side. But the impact squeezed Gavin forward, and he hit his head on the driver's seat. He shot out like a banana out of a peel, one described it. Both said Gavin was a good guy but that he'd changed big-time. Stopped being social, withdrew from them. I asked if he'd slowed down mentally, and they hesitated. Not wanting to put him down. When I persisted they admitted he'd dulled. Just wasn't the same guy."

"Anything about obsessive behavior?"

"No, but they hadn't seen him for a while. They were pretty shook-up about his being murdered. Neither had any clue who'd want to hurt him, and they didn't know about any blonde he'd dated other than Kayla. Who one of them called 'a spoiled little witch.' "

"The anonymous blonde," I said.

"I called the TV stations," he said, "asked if they'd run the death shot. They said no, too scary, but if I got an artist's rendition that toned it down, they might. If airtime permitted. I sent a copy of the photo to one of our sketchers, we'll see. Maybe the papers would run the actual photo. Grant the poor kid her fifteen seconds of fame."

"Too scary," I said. "Are they watching the same tube I am?"

He laughed. "The media talk about public service, but they're out to sell commercial time. Alex, it was like pitching a story to some showbiz asshole. What's in it for *memememe*—okay, here we are, why don't you circle around to the back, see if Mary Lou's Mercedes is there?"

◆

It wasn't, but we parked anyway and went into the building.

The door to the Pacifica-West Psychological Services suite was unlocked. This time, the waiting room wasn't empty. A tall woman in her forties paced and wrung her hands. She wore a gray leotard set, white athletic socks, pink Nikes, had long legs, a tiny upper body, short, black, feathered hair combed forward. Her eyes were blue and sunken and pouched and too bright, her face was glossy and raw, the color of canned salmon. Skin flaked around her hairline and ears; recent skin-peel. Her expression said she was used to being mistreated but was learning to resent it. She ignored us and continued pacing.

All three call buttons were red.

Drs. Gull, Koppel, and Larsen healing souls.

Milo said, "I wonder when her session ends."

The black-haired woman kept walking, and said, "If you're talking about Dr. K, take a number. My appointment was supposed to start twenty minutes ago." She crossed the office twice, picked at her scalp, stopped to investigate the magazines on a table. Selecting *Modern Health,* she leafed through the issue, kept it folded at her side as she paced some more. "Twenty-*three* minutes. She'd better have an emergency."

Milo said, "She's usually pretty punctual."

The woman stopped and turned. Her face was stretched tight yet drawn. Fear scalded her eyes, as if she'd stared at an eclipse. "You're not patients."

"We're not?" said Milo, keeping his voice light.

"No, no, no, no. You look like—why are you here?"

He shrugged, unbuttoned his jacket. "We're just waiting to talk to Dr. Koppel, ma'a—"

"Well, you can't!" the woman shouted. "I'm next! I need to see her!"

Milo glanced at me. Begging for help.

"Absolutely," I said. "It's your time. We'll leave, come back later."

"No!" she said. "I mean . . . you don't have to, I don't own this place, I'm not entitled to assert myself at that level." She blinked back tears. "I just want to have my time. My own time, that's not overly narcissistic, is it?"

"Not at all."

"My ex-husband claims I'm an incurable narcissist."

"Exes," I said.

She stared at me, probing for sincerity. I must have passed because she smiled. Said, "It's okay for you to sit down."

We did.

◆

The waiting room remained silent for another fifteen minutes. For the first five, the woman read her magazine. Then she introduced herself as Bridget. Returned her eyes to the pages, but her heart wasn't in it. A pulse throbbed in her temple, conspicuous enough for me to see from across the room. Racing. Her hands clasped and unclasped, and her head bobbed from the magazine to the red buttons. Finally, she said, "I don't understand!"

I said, "Let's call her. Her service will pick up, and maybe they can tell us if she's got an emergency."

"Yes," said Bridget. "Yes, that's a good plan."

Milo whipped out his phone, Bridget rattled off the number, and he punched it. What a team.

He said, "Dr. Koppel, please ... Mr. Sturgis, she knows me ... what's that? You're sure? 'Cause I'm right here in her waiting room, and her session light's on ..."

He clicked off.

Bridget said, "What, what?"

"Her service says she didn't check in this morning the way she usually does, and they have no idea where she is. She had two early patients before her radio interview, missed them, too."

Bridget cried out: "Damn her! That's *fucking* narcissistic!"

Snatching her purse, she raced to the door, swung it open, slammed it behind her. The silence she left behind was sour.

"I think," said Milo, "that I prefer my job to yours."

◆

Five minutes later, he was pounding the door to the inner offices. A muffled man's voice said what might have been, "Hold on!" and the door opened a crack. The eyes that looked out at us were pale brown and down-slanted behind octagonal bifocals. Analytic. Not amused.

"What's going on?" Well-modulated voice,

tinged by a Nordic inflection. What I could see of his face was smooth and ruddy, the chin melting into soft flesh. A chin coated by a clipped, gray-blond goatee. Centering the beard was a prim, narrow mouth.

"Police," said Milo. "We're looking for Dr. Koppel."

"Police? So you pound the door?" Calm voice—almost amused, despite the irritation.

"You're—"

"Dr. Larsen. I'm in the midst of seeing a patient and would prefer that you leave. Why are you looking for Mary Lou?"

"I'd rather not discuss that, sir."

Albin Larsen blinked. "Suit yourself." He began to close the door. Milo caught it.

"Officer—"

"Her session light is on," said Milo, "but she's not in."

The door opened wider, and Larsen stepped out. He was five-ten, in his mid-fifties, upholstered by an extra fifteen pounds, wore his whitening hair in a longish crew cut. A green, hand-crocheted, sleeveless vest sheathed a pale blue button-down shirt. His khakis were pressed and pleated, his bubble-topped brown shoes polished glossy.

He took a long moment to look us over. "Not in? How would you know that?"

Milo recounted his conversation with the service operator.

"Ah," said Larsen. He smiled. "That doesn't mean anything. Dr. Koppel could have been called in to the office because of a patient crisis and simply neglected to check with her service."

"A crisis here in the office?"

"Our profession is rife with crisis."

"Frequently?"

"Frequently enough," said Larsen. "Now I suggest that the best way for us to deal with this situation is for you to leave your card, and I'll make sure—"

"Have you seen her today, Doctor?"

"I wouldn't have. I've been booked clear through since 8 A.M. So is Franco—Dr. Gull. We all have very full schedules and try to stagger our patients in order to avoid a log-jam in the waiting room." Larsen tugged at his shirtsleeve, exposed a pink-gold vintage Rolex. "In fact, my next appointment is in ten minutes, and I've left a patient waiting in my office, which is grossly unfair and unprofessional. So kindly leave your card, and—"

Milo said, "Why don't we check to see if Dr. Koppel's in her office?"

Albin Larsen began to fold his arms over his chest but stopped himself. "That would be inappropriate."

"Otherwise, I'm afraid we're going to have to wait right here, Dr. Larsen."

Larsen's prim mouth got even smaller. "I believe that if you pause to reflect, sir, you'll find you are being heavy-handed."

"No doubt," said Milo. He sat down and picked up the copy of *Modern Health* discarded by the face-peeled woman.

Larsen turned to me, as if hoping for reason. I looked at the carpet.

"Very well," he said, "I'll go check."

He stepped back into the inner hallway and shut the door. Seconds later, he returned, expressionless.

"She's not there. I don't understand it, however I'm sure there's an explanation. Now, really, I must return to my patient. If you insist on staying here, please don't create a commotion."

CHAPTER

15

"Now that," said Milo, as we left the building, "is what I call a shrink. Unflappable, soft-spoken, analyzing every-thing."

"I don't qualify?"

"You, my friend, are an aberration."

"Too flappable?"

"Too damn human. Let's check out Dr. K's residence. Have time?"

"Sure," I said. "Let's see how the real shrinks live."

◆

Motor vehicle records put Mary Lou Koppel's address on McConnell Drive, in Cheviot Hills.

I drove west, past Century City and south to Pico, continued half a mile past Rancho Park and the radar gun of a stone-faced motorcycle cop. Milo waved at the officer, but he didn't return the gesture. McConnell was a lovely street, hilly and winding and, unlike the horticulturally regimented arteries of Beverly Hills, graced by an adventurous mix of street trees.

Koppel's house was a two-story brick Tudor set high on a knoll above thirty stone steps. The steep driveway would have been a challenge for a car with a puny engine. No sign of the Mercedes, but the garage door was closed.

Milo said, "Maybe she was more scared of two murders in her practice than she let on and decided to take a little vacation."

"With no advance notice to her patients?"

"Fear can do that to you." He eyed the climb. "Okay, pass the pitons and let's start the climb. How're your CPR skills?"

◆

He trudged up first, muttering, "At least there's a view," and I followed two steps behind. He was huffing and gasping by the time we got to the top.

"With . . . this," he panted, "she . . . doesn't need . . . a . . . *damnhomegym*."

Up close, the house was beautifully kept, windows sparkling, copper gutters spotless, carved oak door freshly varnished. Plantings of ferns and elephant ear and papyrus and white roses softened the used-brick front. A stone pot of mixed herbs bathed the covered entrance in fragrance. A multitrunk jacaranda formed the centerpiece of the tiny, perfect lawn. Between its branches was an eastern panorama: the L.A. basin and the San Gabriel Mountains beyond. Despite the smog blanket, staggering. As Milo rang the bell, I stared out at miles of terrain and thought what I always think: way too big for one city.

No one answered. He tried again, knocked, said, "With her car gone, no big surprise, but let's be thorough."

We walked around the left side of the house to a small square of backyard dominated by a lap pool and more thick planting. High ficus hedging on three sides prevented scrutiny by the neighbors. The pool was gray-bottomed and immaculate. A covered patio covered a brick barbecue with a built-in chimney, outdoor furniture, potted flowers. A hummingbird feeder dangled from a crossbeam, and, off in a corner, a miniature fountain—a bamboo spout tipping into a tiny barrel—burbled prettily.

The rear wall was a bank of French doors. Three sets were blocked by drapes. One wasn't and Milo went over and peered in.

"Oh my," he said.

I went over to have a look.

The back room was set up with white leather sofas, glass side tables, an oak-and-granite wet bar, and a five-foot-wide plasma TV with accompanying stereo gizmos. The TV was tuned to a game show. Ecstatic contestants jumped as if on trampolines. Great color and definition.

Off to the left side, Mary Lou Koppel slumped on one of the sofas, facing us, her back to the screen. Her limbs were splayed, and her head was thrown back, mouth gaping, eyes staring at the vaulted ceiling.

Staring sightlessly. Something long and silver protruded from her chest, and her color belonged to nothing living.

All around her, white leather was blotched rusty red.

◆

We remained outside as Milo called in the techies, the coroner, and two black-and-whites for sentry work. In twenty minutes, the scene was bustling.

The coroner was an Asian woman who spoke little English and slipped away without conferring. The coroner's investigator, a heavy, gray-mustachioed man named Arnold Mattingly, emerged and said, "Cho says she's all yours, Milo."

Milo frowned. "She's gone?"

"She's busier than we'll ever be," said Mattingly. "Lots of bodies piled up at the morgue."

"She give you any prelim?"

"Looks like stabbed in the chest with a letter opener, shot through the head. I know you like to draw your own DB chart, but if you want a copy of mine, I'll xerox it."

"Thanks, Arnie. Which came first, the stabbing or the shooting?"

"Not for me to guess, and Cho isn't talking much today." Mattingly cupped his hand but kept his voice loud. "Her husband left her."

"Shame," said Milo.

"Nice lady," said Mattingly. "It really is. Anyway, you want to know my opinion, there was mucho blood around the knife wound. Copious, as they say. And just a little tiny trickle around the bullet hole, more plasma than red stuff."

"Her heart was pumping hard when she got stabbed."

"If I was a betting man," said Mattingly.

"Small-caliber gun?"

"From the looks of it. Koppel, she's that psychologist, right?"

"You know her, Arnie?"

"My wife listens to her when she's on the radio. Says she talks common sense. I say if it's that common, why do people have to pay her?" He shook his head. "The wife'll have a fit when I tell her—it's okay to tell her, right?"

"Go for it," said Milo. "Call the networks for all I care. Any other ideas?"

Mattingly said, "What, this is guess day?"

"It's a crappy day. I'm open to suggestions."

"Humble civil servant like me." Mattingly scratched his head. "My guess would be her line of work, maybe she got on the wrong side of some crazy person." He seemed to notice me for the first time. "That make sense, Doc?"

"Perfect sense."

Mattingly grinned. "That's what I love about my job. I get to make sense. Then when I get home, I'm an idiot." He collected his gear and left.

I said, "Call the networks. Maybe this is the hook you need."

◆

It took a while for the techies to finish printing the house, searching for shoe imprints, blood or other body fluids in remote rooms, signs of forced entry or struggle.

No prints on the letter opener. Nothing else revelatory except for the obvious fact that the opener, antique, bone-handled, with a sterling silver shaft, had come from the desk set in Mary Lou Koppel's home office.

When the house cleared, Milo began the demeaning rummage that murder victims undergo.

A search of the medicine cabinet in Koppel's private bathroom produced the usual toiletries along with birth control pills, a diaphragm and condoms ("Careful gal"), OTC allergy medicine, a salve for yeast infections, Tylenol, Advil, Pepto-Bismol, and physician samples of the sleeping pill Ambien.

"All that advice for everyone else, and she has trouble sleeping," said Milo. "Something on her mind?"

I shrugged.

Her bedroom was a cozy, soft-edged study in sage green and salmon. The quilted spread on the bed was tucked tight, the room perfectly composed.

Milo rifled through a closet filled with red and black. In dresser drawers he found sleepwear that ranged from sensible flannel to skimpy pieces from the Hustler Emporium. He held up a pair of crotchless panties in faux leopard skin.

"You don't buy this for yourself. Wonder who her love interest is."

At the bottom of the underwear drawer, he found a silver vibrator nestled in a velvet bag.

"All kinds of love," he muttered.

I hadn't liked Mary Lou Koppel much, but exposing the archaeology of her life was depressing.

We left the bedroom and headed back to the office so that Milo could sift through her papers. It didn't take long for things to get interesting.

◆

Like the rest of the house, the study was tidy. A squared stack of papers sat atop the dainty French revival desk, weighed down by a red crystal paperweight shaped like a rose. Just off center, next to a gilded leather blotter and below the sterling desk set from which the murder weapon had been lifted.

Milo attacked the drawers first, found Mary Lou Koppel's financial records and tax forms and a stack of correspondence from people who'd tuned in to her media interviews and had strong opinions, pro and con.

Those he bundled together and stashed in an evidence envelope.

He said, "She declared 260 grand a year from treating patients, another 60 from public appearances and investments. Not too shabby."

Court documents in a bottom drawer summarized a divorce twenty-two years ago.

"The husband was some guy named Edward Michael Koppel," he said, running his

finger along lines of print. "At the time the papers were filed he was a law student at the
U. . . . irreconcilable differences, splitting of
assets . . . the marriage lasted less than two
years, no kids . . . onward."

He returned to the desktop, removed the
rose-shaped paperweight, took hold of the
paper stack.

On top was Gavin Quick's chart.

CHAPTER

16

Thin chart.

It didn't take Milo long to finish reading it, and when he did his jaw was tight and his shoulders were bunched.

He thrust it at me.

Mary Lou Koppel had written out a detailed intake for her treatment of Gavin Quick, but her subsequent notes were sketchy.

The intake said enough.

Gavin hadn't come to her because of posttraumatic stress due to his accident. He'd been assigned to therapy by an Orange County judge. Alternative sentencing after being convicted four months ago of stalking a Tustin woman named Beth Gallegos.

Gallegos had been an occupational therapist at St. John's Hospital, where she'd treated Gavin after his injury. According to Koppel's notes, Gavin had become pathologically attached to her, leading Gallegos to transfer his care to another therapist. Gavin persisted in his attempts to date her, phoning her at home, sometimes two dozen times a night, then extending his attempts to early-morning wake-up calls in which he wept and proclaimed his love for her.

He wrote Beth Gallegos long amorous notes and mailed them with gifts of jewelry and perfume. For every day of one manic week, he had two dozen roses delivered to St. John's.

When Beth Gallegos quit and took a job at a rehabilitation clinic in Long Beach, Gavin managed to find her, and his overtures resumed.

Knowing about his head injury, Gallegos was loath to prosecute, but when he showed up at her apartment in the middle of the night, banged on the door, and insisted she let him in, she called the police. Gavin was arrested for disturbing the peace, but the cops told Gallegos if she wanted a more serious charge, she needed to get a restraining order.

She bargained with Gavin's parents: If he ceased, she'd drop the issue.

Gavin agreed, but a week later the phone calls started up again. Beth Gallegos obtained the order, and when Gavin violated it by waiting in the parking lot at the Long Beach clinic, he was busted for felony stalking.

Because of his accident, he was allowed to plead down to a misdemeanor harassment charge contingent upon seeking psychiatric help. His attorney requested and was granted the opportunity to suggest a therapist. With no objection from the D.A., the court assented, and Gavin was referred to Franco Gull, Ph.D.

Koppel noted that she'd informed the court of the transfer from Gull to her.

Covering the legal bases.

"Pt. has poor insight," she wrote, at the end of the intake. *"Fails to see what he did wrong. Possib. Rel. to head injury. Tx will emphasize insight and respect for personal boundaries."*

I gave the file back to Milo.

He was cracking his knuckles, and his thick, black eyebrows dipped toward anger-compressed eyes.

"Nice," he said. "No one thinks to tell me."

"The Quicks wouldn't want Gavin's memory fouled. Given that and the trauma of Gavin's murder, I wouldn't be surprised if they 'forgot.' "

"Yeah, yeah, yeah, but the goddamn Orange County D.A.? The goddamn court? Goddamn Dr. Mary Lou? The kid gets killed, and no one thinks to tell me he got weird less than half a year ago and made someone very, very unhappy?"

"The murder didn't hit the news."

"I've sent teletypes and requests for info on the blonde to every local jurisdiction, including Tustin PD, and Gavin's name is all over it. No doubt it's sitting in some goddamn in-basket."

He tried to crack more knuckles, produced silence. "If the public only knew . . . okay, the kid was a stalker, it's a whole new game."

"How would that relate to Koppel's murder?" I said. "Or Flora Newsome?"

"Hell if I know!" he shouted.

I kept quiet.

"Sorry," he said. "Koppel probably died because of something she knew about Gavin. What that is, I don't have a clue, but it's got to be that. In terms of Newsome, it's looking like Lorraine was right, and I made too much of the similarities between the cases, not enough of the differences."

He bagged the file, paged through the rest of the stack, muttered, "Bills, subscription forms, junk," and replaced it on the desk.

"I actually volunteered for this," he said.

I thought: *You need the challenge.* Said nothing.

"For now," he said, "Newsome stays Lorraine's problem; I'm sticking to my boy Gavin. And all the complications he's wrought. The crazy little bastard."

CHAPTER

17

Mary Lou Koppel's murder hit the news in the usual way: lots of heat, no light, a bit of filler for the papers, a few paragraphs for the perky scripts read by bright-eyed TV smilers who fancied themselves journalists. Lacking much in the way of forensic details, the newsfolk made much of the victim's incursion into their territory. The adjectives "savvy" and "media-smart" were bandied about with the usual relish reserved for clichés.

By the next day, the story was dead.

Milo went through channels and asked LAPD's communications office to get the blond girl's face some media exposure. The hook he presented was the possibility of a bigger story than two kids getting shot up on Mulholland: the link between those killings and Koppel's. The PR cops questioned his grounds for that claim, said no way would TV stations run a morgue shot of a genuine dead person, said they were swamped with all kinds of requests for exposure from other detectives, promised they'd look into it.

I got to his office shortly after he did, sat there as he struggled out of his jacket, which seemed to be strangling him. The effort left his tie askew and shirt untucked. He sat on the edge of his desk, read a message slip, punched an extension on his desk phone. "Sean? Come in."

I said, "Anything new on Koppel?"

"Oh. Hi. Coroner estimates time of death some time last night or early morning. No forced entry, no reports of strange vehicles in the neighborhood."

"What about the gunshot?"

"The neighbors to the north are in Europe. To the south is a woman in her nineties under the care of a nurse. The nurse hears fine, but they both sleep in the old lady's room, and there's a humidifier and an air filter blowing, which blocks out anything short of a nuclear blast." He laughed. "It's like the gods are conspiring. You have any fresh insights?"

Before I could answer, a tall, red-haired man in his late twenties knocked on the door frame. He wore a four-button gray suit, dark blue shirt, dark blue tie. Doc Martens on his feet. His hair was cut short, and freckles speckled his brow and cheeks. He was loose-limbed and built like a point guard, had the rounded, baby-faced look you see on some redheads.

"Hey," said Milo.

"Lieutenant." Small salute.

"Alex, this is Detective Sean Binchy. Sean, Dr. Alex Delaware, our psych consultant."

Binchy remained in the doorway and extended his hand. The room was small enough for us to shake that way.

"Sean's gonna be helping me on Koppel." To Binchy: "Any news on her family?"

"Both parents are dead, Lieut. I found an aunt in Fairfield, Connecticut, but she hadn't seen Dr. Koppel in years. Quote-unquote: 'After Mary Lou moved to California, she wanted nothing to do with any of us.' She did say the family would probably pay for the funeral, send them the bill."

"No one's coming out?"

Sean Binchy shook his head. "They're pretty much detached from her. Kind of sad. In terms of the ex-husband, he's here. In L.A. I mean. But he's not a lawyer. He's into real estate." He pulled out a notepad. "Encino. I left a message, but so far he hasn't gotten back. I thought I'd do more on the neighborhood canvass near Dr. Koppel's house, then try again."

"Sounds good," said Milo.

"Anything else you need, Lieut?"

"No, finishing the canvass is a good idea. Still nothing from the neighbors?"

"Sorry, no," said Binchy. "Seems like it was a quiet night in Cheviot Hills."

"Okay, Sean. Thanks. *Sayonara*."

"See you, Loot. Nice to meet you, Doc."

When Binchy was gone, Milo said, "His former occupation was, get this: bass player in a ska band. Then he got born-again and decided being a cop was the way he'd serve the Lord. He cut his hair and let his pierces close up and scored in the top ten percent of his academy class. This is the new blue generation."

"He seems like a nice kid," I said.

"He's smart enough, maybe a little on the concrete side—A to B to C. We'll see if he learns how to be creative." He grinned. " 'Loot.' Too much TV . . . so far he hasn't brought up the born-again stuff, but I can't help feel one day he's going to try to save me. Bottom line is I can't juggle Gavin and the blonde and Koppel all by myself, and he's a good worker ant . . . so, any thoughts since yesterday?"

"Koppel brought Gavin's chart home, had it at the top of her stack," I said. "She brushed off two murders in her practice as a statistical quirk, but it bothered her, and she went back to review her notes. The fact that Newsome's chart *wasn't* there means she was probably telling the truth about shredding it."

"Not a lot of notes on Gavin to review."

"Maybe the intake was enough. In it, she detailed Gavin's legal problems. What if she tied his murder to the Gallegos stalking? Came up with a suspect, voiced her suspicions to someone, and got killed for her efforts?"

"She voiced her suspicion directly to the

bad guy? She'd be stupid enough to confront him?"

"She might have if he was her patient," I
said. "If she suspected someone in her
caseload, she'd be reluctant to violate confidentiality and go straight to you."

"Back to the nut-in-the-waiting-room
theory."

"It's also possible that she wasn't sure,
just suspicious. So she discussed it with
him."

"Foolhardy," he said.

"Therapy's a lopsided relationship. Despite
all the talk of a partnership, the patient's
needy and dependent, and the therapist has
wisdom to grant. It's easy to overestimate
your personal power. Mary Lou was a strong
personality to begin with. And she got
caught up in the media game, convinced
herself she was an expert on everything.
Maybe she got overconfident, felt she could
convince him to give himself up."

"Talk about an ego trip, if she succeeded."

"Psychologist solves multiple murders," I
said. "Talk about public relations."

He thought about that for a long time.
"One of her patients is a very bad guy."

"No forced entry," I said. "Someone she knew and let into the house. It's worth looking into."

"I can't get hold of her patient records."

"Her partners might know something."

"They're shrinks, too, Alex. Same confidentiality restriction."

"I'm not sure of the legal issues; but if the bad guy isn't officially their patient, they might be okay talking about him in general terms."

"Sounds like legal precedent to me," he said. "What the hell, it's worth a shot." He phoned information, got numbers for Drs. Larsen and Gull, and left messages to call him.

I said, "How's it going with the prints from Koppel's house?"

"There are so damn many, the print guys are figuring at least a week. One thing they did tell me: not a single print near the body. At least a ten-foot radius had been wiped clean. A psych patient who's meticulous. Not an overt nutcase, right?"

"Not even close to nuts," I said.

He flipped open the murder book that had been opened on Mary Lou Koppel. "Ballistics faxed a report this morning. The .22

used to shoot her was similar but not identical to either the Gavin Quick or the Flora Newsome guns. Even discounting Flora, we've got two separate weapons for two murders. This is some guy with easy access to cheapies, knows his way around the street."

"An experienced con," I said. "The kind Flora Newsome could've met on the job."

"Would a guy like that go into therapy?"

"If he had to. Look at Gavin Quick."

His eyes widened. "Alternative sentencing. Someone who *had* to get shrunk. And that gives me a way to get around the goddamn confidentiality. Go through court records, see if any judges assigned any other patients to Koppel."

He slumped. "Huge job."

"Narrow it down to a year or two and put your worker ant on it."

"I will," he said. "I will definitely do that. It's also time to talk to Mr. and Mrs. Quick again, find out about their boy's problem, if he harassed anyone else. So far all I get is their answering machine. I called the D.A. who prosecuted Gavin and the defense attorney. No help at all from them, just another case. I also recontacted Gavin's two friends from the accident, and they had no idea he stalked Beth Gallegos or anyone else. On the intake Koppel did for the court, she said Gavin's obsession could be related to brain damage. What do you think?"

"Another form of obsessive behavior," I said. "Sure, it could be consistent with a prefrontal injury. The other thing to consider is that the vindictive boyfriend wasn't the blonde's. He's Beth Gallegos's beau. What if Gavin broke the terms of his probation and resumed stalking?"

"So the guy stalks Gavin in return, offs him and the blonde? And Koppel?"

"No accounting for passion," I said.

"Okay," he said, "let's visit the object of Gavin's passion."

◆

Phone work revealed that Beth Gallegos had switched jobs again, from the Long Beach clinic to a private educational therapy firm in Westwood.

"Westwood's close to Beverly Hills," I said, as we drove there. "If Gavin was still stalking her, I doubt she'd have chanced it."

"Let's find out."

◆

Beth Gallegos was gorgeous. That did nothing to explain Gavin's obsession—stalking is psychopathology, and plain people are victimized as often as lookers—it was simply a fact.

Petite and black-haired and dusky-skinned, she wore a pale blue uniform cut for blandness that couldn't conceal her tiny waist, flaring hips, and bountiful breasts. Her eyes were amber, her lashes long and curling. Twenty-seven years old, she wore no makeup and looked eighteen. A clean, fresh eighteen. Her nails were unpolished and clipped short. The black hair, sleek and wavy, was tied back in a ponytail and fastened by a rubber band.

Aiming for low-key. Her perfect-oval face and cameo features and lush body rendered the effort useless.

She was uncomfortable talking to us in the lobby of the educational service, and we took the elevator down to the ground-floor coffee shop. A young waitress approached us with a smile, but even though Milo smiled back, something in his greeting wiped the joy from her face.

Beth Gallegos ordered tea, and Milo and I had Cokes. When the order came, he pressed a bill into the waitress's palm. She left quickly and never reappeared.

Gallegos had been edgy since we'd shown up, and Milo tried to put her at ease with chitchat about her job. The outfit she worked for was called Comprehensive Rehab and specialized in stroke victims. Her job was to help patients regain fine motor skills. She found the challenge satisfying.

Milo said, "Sounds like it would be."

Gallegos fumbled with her teacup and avoided our eyes.

"Let's talk about Gavin Quick," said Milo. "Have you heard what happened to him?"

"Yes. I read it in the paper. It was horrible. I cried." She had a slightly nasal, little-girl voice and narrow hands with smooth fingers. A diamond chip ring banded the third finger of her left hand.

More than a boyfriend.

"You cried," said Milo.

"I did. I felt terrible. Despite what Gavin put me through. Because I *knew* what he'd been through. Knew it was the CHI making him do it."

Milo blinked.

"Closed head injury," I said.

Beth Gallegos nodded and spooned sugar into her tea but didn't drink. "CHIs are weird that way. Sometimes nothing shows up on scans, but people change drastically. I'm sure Gavin wouldn't have done those things if he hadn't been injured."

"You've had other brain-damaged stalkers?" said Milo.

Gallegos's hand flew to her mouth. "No, God forbid I should ever go through that more than once. I'm just saying the brain controls everything, and when it's compromised, you get problems. That's why I did everything I could to avoid making it a criminal situation for Gavin." Her eyes got wet.

"The way I see it, ma'am, he left you no choice."

"That's what everyone told me."

"Who's everyone?"

"My family."

"Your family local?"

"No," she said. "My parents live in Germany. My father's a captain in the Army. At first, I didn't tell them what was going on because I knew how my dad would react."

"How's that?"

"For sure he'd have gotten himself a

leave, flown right over, and had a stern talk with Gavin. Once he did find out, I had a hard time convincing him not to do exactly that. That's part of what led me to file charges. I had to assure Dad I was taking care of myself. But I had to do it, no matter what. It was just getting too intense, and Gavin obviously needed help."

"You never told your family, but they found out."

"My sister told them. She lives in Tucson and I confided in her and made her promise not to tell." She smiled. "Of course, she didn't listen to me. Which I understand, I'm not mad. We're close, she had my best interests at heart."

"Anyone else tell you to file charges?"

"What do you mean?"

Milo looked at her ring.

Beth Gallegos said, "He wasn't my fiancé, then. Actually, we started dating right before I filed charges."

Milo tried to put warmth in his smile. "What's the lucky young man's name?"

"Anson Conniff."

"When's the big day?"

"Fall." Gallegos's dark eyes picked up

some wattage. "Lieutenant, why all these questions about me and my family?"

"I need to tie up loose ends."

"Loose ends? Lieutenant, please don't get me involved. I really can't go through it again—please."

Raising her voice. The coffee shop was nearly empty, but the few patrons present turned to stare. Milo glared at them until they turned away.

"Go through what, ma'am?"

Gallegos whimpered and wiped her eyes. "Legal stuff, the courts—I never want to see an affidavit again. Please keep me out of it."

"I'm not out to cause you grief, Ms. Gallegos, but I do need to talk to anyone Gavin had conflict with."

Gallegos shook her head. "There was no conflict. I never yelled at Gavin, never complained. It's just that the problem got out of hand. He needed to deal with it."

"Did he stop?" I said.

"Yes."

"Completely?"

"Completely."

Her eyes danced to one side. I said, "You never heard from him again?"

She picked at her napkin, shredded the

corners, created a small pile of confetti that she collected and placed on her saucer.

"It was basically over," she said. "It was over." Her voice shook.

Milo said, "Beth, you're obviously a good person. That means you're also a very poor liar."

Gallegos glanced at the coffee shop door, as if plotting her escape.

Milo said, "What happened?"

"It was just once," she said. "A month ago. Not really a problem call, a nothing call, that's why I never told anyone."

"Where'd he find you?"

"Here. At the office. I was between patients, and the secretary handed me the phone. He told her he was a friend. She has no idea about my . . . history with Gavin. When I heard his voice I . . . it made my heart pound, and I broke into a sweat. But he was . . . okay. Nothing weird. He said he was sorry for what he'd done, wanted to apologize. Then he told me he'd met someone and was getting his life together, and he hoped I'd forgive him. I said I already had, and that was that."

"You figure he was telling the truth?" said Milo. "About meeting someone."

"He sounded sincere," she said. "I told him congratulations, I was happy for him." She exhaled. "He sounded more . . . mature. Settled."

"Did he tell you about the person he'd met?"

"No. He sounded happy."

"He's happy, he doesn't bug you."

"That, too," she said, "but at the time what I thought was, 'Gavin's finally getting it together.' " She touched the handle of her teacup, swirled the bag. "I never disliked him, Lieutenant. All I ever felt for him was pity. And fear, when things got really intense. But I was happy things were working out for him."

I said, "Anson's probably happy, too."

"I didn't tell Anson about the call."

"Too upsetting."

"He's been through enough with me," she said. "We just started dating when the stalking began. It's not a great way to start a relationship."

Milo said, "Anson must've been pretty upset."

"Wouldn't anyone be?" Gallegos's eyes got clearer. "You're not going to talk to him, are you?"

"We are, Beth."

"Why?"

"Like I said, anyone who had conflict with Gavin."

"Anson didn't have conflict—please, don't go there—don't draw Anson into this. He'd never hurt Gavin, or anyone else. He's not like that."

"Easygoing?" said Milo.

"Mature. Disciplined. Anson knows how to control himself."

"What kind of work does he do?"

"Work?" said Gallegos.

"His job."

"You're actually going to talk to him?"

"We have to, ma'am."

Beth Gallegos placed her face in her hands and kept it there for several moments. When she revealed herself again, she'd gone pale. "I'm so, so sorry Gavin got killed. But I really can't stand any more of this. When Gavin had his trial I was subpoenaed; it was horrible."

"Testifying was rough."

"*Being* there was rough. The people you see in the halls. The smells, the waiting. I waited an entire day and never was called to testify. Thank God. It really wasn't much of a trial, Gavin admitted what he'd done. Later, he and his parents walked right past me and his mother looked at me as if I was the guilty one. I didn't even tell Anson I was going, didn't want him to lose a day's work." Her attention shifted to the left. She bit her lip. "No, that's not the real reason. I didn't want the case to . . . pollute my relationship. I want Anson to see me as someone strong. Please let us be."

Milo said, "Beth, I have no interest in adding stress to your life. And there's no reason to believe you—or Anson—*will* be involved any further. But this is a homicide investigation, and I wouldn't be doing my job if I didn't talk to him."

"Okay," Gallegos said, barely audible. "I understand . . . stuff happens."

"What's Anson's address?"

"We live together. At his place. Ogden Drive, near Beverly. But he won't be there, he's working."

"Where?"

"He teaches martial arts," she said. "Karate, tae kwan do, kickboxing. He was a regional kickboxing champ back in Florida, just got hired by a dojo near where we live. Wilshire near Crescent Heights. He also does youth work. On Sunday, for a ministry in Bell Gardens. We're both Christians, met at a church mixer. We're getting married in September."

"Congratulations."

"He's a great guy," said Gallegos. "He loves me and gives me my space."

CHAPTER

18

I drove east, toward Anson Coniff's dojo.

Milo said, "Gavin had found someone to rock his world."

"At least he saw it that way."

"If we're talking about the blonde, he was seeing straight. Why can't I find out who the hell she is?"

A moment later: "A martial arts instructor. Maybe you can show off your whatchamacallit—those karate dances—"

"Katas," I said. "It's been years, I'm out of shape."

"You make it to black belt?"

"Brown."

"Why'd you stop?"

"Not angry enough."

"I thought martial arts helped control anger."

"Martial arts is like fire," I said. "You can cook or burn."

"Well let's see if Mr. Conniff's the smoldering type."

STEADFAST MARTIAL ARTS AND SELF-DEFENSE

One large room, high-ceilinged and mirrored, floored with bright blue exercise mats. Years ago, I'd taken karate from a Czech Jew who'd learned to defend himself during the Nazi era. I had lost interest, lost my skills. But walking into the dojo, smelling the sweat and the discipline, brought back memories and I found myself mentally reviewing the poses and the movements.

Anson Conniff was five-four, maybe 130, with a boyish face, a toned body, and long, lank, light brown hair highlighted gold at the tips.

Surfer-dude, slightly miniaturized. He wore white karate togs, a black belt, spoke in a loud, crisp voice to a dozen beginners, all women. An older, white-haired Asian informed us the class would end in ten minutes and asked us to stand to one side.

Conniff ran the women through a half dozen more poses, then released them. They dabbed their brows, collected their gym bags, and headed out the door as we approached.

Conniff smiled. "Can I help you, gentlemen?"

Milo flashed the badge, and the smile disintegrated.

"Police? What about?"

"Gavin Quick."

"Him," said Conniff. "Beth read about him in the paper and told me." He laughed.

"Something funny, Mr. Conniff?"

"Not his death, I'd never laugh at that. It's just funny that you'd be talking to me about it—kind of like a movie script. But I guess you're just doing your job."

Conniff flipped hair out of his face.

Milo said, "Why's that?"

"Because the idea of my killing anyone—hurting anyone—is absurd. I'm a Christian, and that makes me prolife and antideath."

"Oh," said Milo. "I thought you might be laughing about Gavin Quick being dead. Because of what he did to Beth."

The height disparity between Milo and Conniff was conspicuous. Karate and other martial arts teach you how to use an opponent's size to your advantage, but pure conversation put Conniff at a disadvantage. He tried to draw himself up.

"That's really absurd, sir. Gavin tormented Beth, but I'd never gloat about him or anyone else dying. I've seen way too much dying ever to gloat."

"The Army?" said Milo.

"Growing up, sir. My brother was born with lung disease and passed away when he was nine. This was back in Des Moines, Iowa. Most of those nine years were taken up by Bradley going in and out of the hospital. I was three years older and ended up spending a lot of time at hospitals. I saw someone die once, the actual process. A man, not that old, brought into the emergency room for some kind of seizure. The doctors thought he'd stabilized and sent him up to the ward, for observation before discharge. The orderlies took him on a gurney in one of those big patient elevators, and my parents and I just happened to be riding in the same elevator at the same time because we'd gone down to X-ray with Bradley. The man on the gurney was joking, being friendly, then he just stopped talking, gave this sudden *stare* off into nowhere, then his head flopped to the side and the color just drained from his face. The orderlies began pounding his chest. My mother slapped her hand over my eyes so I couldn't see, and my father started talking nonstop, keeping up a patter, so I couldn't hear. Baseball, he talked about baseball. By the time we got off the elevator, everyone was quiet."

Conniff smiled. "I guess I'm just not very death-oriented."

"As opposed to?"

"People who are."

"You're protection-oriented," said Milo.

Conniff motioned around the dojo. "This? It's a job."

Milo said, "Where were you last Monday night?"

"Not killing Gavin Quick." Conniff relaxed his posture.

"In view of the topic, you're being kind of lighthearted, sir."

"How should I be? Mournful? That would be dishonest." Conniff tightened his black belt and widened the space between his feet. "I mourn Gavin Quick in the sense that I mourn the loss of any human life, but I'm not going to tell you I cared for him. He put Beth through incredible misery. But Beth insisted on dealing with it in her own way, and she was right. The stalking stopped. I had no reason to want to hurt him."

"Her own way," said Milo.

"Avoiding him," said Conniff. "Going through the legal system. I wanted to confront Gavin—on a verbal level. I thought a man-to-man talk might convince him. Beth said no, and I respected her wishes."

"Man-to-man."

Conniff rubbed his palms along the sides of his tunic. His hands were small and callused. "Yes, I can get protective. I love Beth. But I didn't hurt Gavin Quick. I'd have no reason to."

"Where were you Monday?"

"With Beth. We stayed in. Even if you don't trust me, you should trust Beth. She's all about forgiveness, operates at a high level, spiritually."

"What'd you have for dinner?" said Milo.

"Who remembers . . . let's see, Monday, so it was probably leftovers. Sunday we barbecued steaks and had a lot of leftovers . . . yeah, definitely, leftover steak. I cut it up and sautéed it with peppers and onions, did a stir-fry. Beth cooked up some rice. Yeah, for sure. We stayed in."

"Ever been in psychotherapy, Mr. Conniff?"

"Why is that your business?"

"Covering bases," said Milo.

"Well, I find the question kind of intrusive."

"Sorry, sir, but—"

"I'll answer it anyway," said Conniff. "My entire family went into therapy after Bradley died. We all saw a wonderful man named the Reverend Dr. Bill Kehoe, and I talked to him by myself a few times, as well. He was the pastor of our church and a fully qualified clinical psychologist. He saved us from despair. Is there anything else you'd like to know?"

"That's the only time you had therapy," said Milo.

"Yes, Lieutenant. It took a while—a long while—to stop feeling guilty about Bradley's dying and my surviving, but I got there. Life's darned good, nowadays."

Milo reached into his pocket and brought out the death shot of the blonde. "Ever see this girl?"

Conniff studied the picture. "Nope. But I

know the look. Pure dead. That's the look that flavored my childhood. Who is she?"

"Someone who died alongside Gavin Quick."

"Sad," said Conniff. "There are always sad things in this world. The key is to push past all that and lead a spiritual life."

◆

Back in the car, Milo ran Conniff's name through the data banks. Two parking tickets.

"No con, but he's a strange one, no?"

"Tightly wound," I said.

"The type to clean up carefully."

"He says he was with Beth."

"I'll ask Beth," he said.

"Her say-so will be enough?"

"Like he said, she operates at a high level."

◆

A call from the car produced the same story from Beth Gallegos.

Steak stir-fry.

We returned to the station where Milo found a faxed artist's rendering of the dead girl and a message to call Community Relations.

"Look at this," he said. "Michelangelo's rolling in his crypt."

The drawing was sketchy, lacking in character, useless. He crumpled and tossed it, phoned CR downtown, listened, hung up, grinding his teeth.

"This city, everything's a goddamn audition. They talked to the papers, and the papers aren't interested. Maybe it's even true."

"I can call Ned Biondi. He retired from the *Times* a few years ago, but he'd know who to talk to."

"Now that the PR idiots have given me an official 'no,' I can't just go off and hot-dog. But maybe in a few days, if we still can't ID her." He peered at the Timex, muttered, "How's your time and your intestinal fortitude?"

"A visit to the Quicks?" I said. "Sure."

"You do tarot readings too?"

CHAPTER

19

"T hat *girl*," said Sheila Quick. "She was hired to *help* Gavin, so instead she goes and gets him into *trouble*."

Her living room looked the same, but drawn drapes turned it funereal, and the space had gone stale. The cigarette box from which Jerome Quick had lifted his smokes was empty. Sheila Quick wore a black cotton robe with a zipper up the front. Her ash hair was turbaned by a black silk scarf. Her face was tight and white and old, and she wore pink mules. Above the slippers, her feet were knobby and blue-veined.

She said, "Unbelievable."

Milo said, "What is, ma'am?"

"What she did to him."

"You see Gavin's arrest as Beth Gallegos's fault."

"Of course I do! Do you know how Gav met her? She was a therapist at Saint John's, was supposed to be helping Gav get back his dexterity. She *knew* what he'd been through! She should've been more *understanding*!"

Milo and I said nothing.

"Listen," said Sheila Quick, "if she was so concerned about her safety, why'd she take so long to complain? And then what does she do? Goes straight for the police, dials 911 like it's some big-deal emergency when all Gav did was knock on her door—I know she said he pounded but no one else heard any pounding and Gav told me he just knocked and I believe my son!"

"You don't think she should've called 911."

"I think if she was so convinced there was a problem, she had ample opportunity to come to us. Why didn't she? All she had to do was call and let us know she thought Gavin was a little . . . eager. We'd have talked to him. Why'd she let this alleged problem linger if it was so bad? You're professionals. Does that make sense to *you*?"

Milo said, "She never got in touch with you beforehand."

"Never, not once. See what I mean?"

Milo nodded.

"And then all of a sudden Gav's arrested and we have to hire a lawyer and go through all that rigamarole." Her smile was sickly. "Of course, in the end they dismissed it. Obviously, it was nothing."

Gavin had pled to a misdemeanor and been sentenced to therapy.

Sheila Quick said, "Lieutenant, I certainly hope you don't think what happened to my Gav was related to anything he *did*. Or anyone he knew."

"It couldn't be anyone he knew?"

"Of course not, we know only nice people. And Gavin ..." She began to cry. "Gavin, after the accident, he didn't have anyone in his life except his father and me and his sister."

"No friends," I said.

"That's the point!" she said, pleased, as if she'd solved a difficult puzzle. "It was no one he knew because he really didn't know anyone. I've been thinking a lot about it, Lieutenant, and I'm certain my baby just happened to be in the wrong place at the wrong time."

"A stranger," said Milo.

"Look at September 11. Did any of those people know the pigs who killed them? It's exactly like that—evil's out there and sometimes it bites you and now the Quick family's been bitten."

She sprang up, raced to the kitchen, came back with a plate of Oreos.

"Eat," she ordered.

Milo took a cookie and finished it in two bites, passed the plate to me. I placed it on a side table.

"So tell me," said Sheila Quick. "What progress have you made?"

Milo brushed crumbs from his trousers to his hand, searched for somewhere to put them.

"Just drop it all on the rug, Lieutenant. I clean every day. Sometimes twice a day. What else is there to do around here? Jerry's already back at work, doing his businessman thing. I envy that about him."

"Being able to concentrate?" I said.

"Being able to cut himself off. It's a male thing, right? You men cut yourselves off and go out and hunt and prowl and make deals and do whatever it is you think you're sup- posed to do, and we women are stuck wait- ing for you as if you're some kind of con- quering heroes."

"Mrs. Quick," said Milo, "you're not go- ing to like this question, but I have to ask it anyway. Did Gavin ever run into any problems with women other than Beth Gallegos?"

Sheila Quick's hands closed into fists. "No, and the very fact you're suggesting it—I tell you that's just so . . . distorted— shortsighted." She ripped the scarf-turban from her head and began kneading the fab- ric. Her hair was elaborately pinned, com- pressed tightly to her skull. White roots showed through the blond.

Milo said, "I'm sorry, but I need to—"

"You need to, you need to—what you need to do is find the madman who killed my son."

"The young lady he was with, ma'am. We still haven't been able to identify her."

Sheila got up and snatched the plate of cookies from where I'd placed them. She returned to the kitchen, swung the door closed, stayed in there.

"As predicted," said Milo, "a pretty scene.

I know she's gone through hell but ten to one she was a harpy before."

Minutes passed.

He said, "I'd better go in there and finish up with her. Be kind to yourself and stay here."

Just as he rose, the kitchen door swung open, and Sheila Quick stomped through. She'd unpinned and brushed her hair but applied no makeup. Milo sat back down. She stopped directly in front of us, placed her hands on her hips.

"Is there anything else?"

"The girl Gavin was wi—"

"Don't know her, never seen her, can't change that. No one in the family knows her, including my daughter."

"You asked Kelly."

"I called and asked her if Gavin was dating anyone, and she said she hadn't heard that."

"Were the two of them close?"

"Of course. Kelly's my bright one, she knows her way around."

I said, "Any plans for her to come back?"

"No. Why should she? She's got a life. Even though I don't."

She stared at me. "Gavin was a good human being. A handsome human being, of course girls liked him. Which is why that Gallegos woman is so off base. Gavin didn't need to chase some little . . . nurse type."

"When did he and Kayla Bartell stop dating?"

"Don't know," she snapped. "Why don't you ask her? The . . . she hasn't even been by to see me. Not once. Not a condolence note." A pink mule tapped the carpet. "Are we finished?"

Milo said, "You've heard about Dr. Koppel."

"She got murdered," said Sheila Quick. "I read about it yesterday."

Matter-of-fact, no emotion.

"Any thoughts about that, Mrs. Quick?"

"It's terrible," she said. "Everyone's getting murdered. What a city—I'm thirsty. Would you like something to drink?"

"No, thanks, ma'am. Let me toss a few names at you. Please tell me if any of them are familiar. Anson Conniff."

"No. Who's he?"

"Flora Newsome?"

"No."

"Brian Van Dyne, Roy Nichols?"

"No, no, *no*. Who *are* these people?"

"Not important," said Milo. "Nothing you need to worry about. Thanks for your time."

"Time," said Sheila Quick. "I've got too much of that."

20

Sheila Quick turned her back on us, and we saw ourselves out.

Just before we reached the car, Milo's cell phone beeped. He took the call, big hand concealing the little blue gizmo. "Sturgis . . . oh, hi. As a matter of fact, yes we are . . . right here, at the house . . . yes . . . that so? . . . where's that? When? Sure, that would be fine. Thank you, ma'am, see you soon."

He snapped the phone shut. "That was Eileen Paxton, Sheila's 'baby sister.' She's in Beverly Hills for a meeting, was planning to visit sis, drove by, saw us go in, and decided to wait until we were finished. She'd like to talk."

"About what?"

" 'Family issues' is how she put it. She's a few blocks away, on Bedford, some Italian place, corner of Brighton."

"Time for tiramisu," I said.

He touched his gut and grimaced. "Even I have limits."

"How disillusioning."

◆

The Italian place was named Pagano and it featured three wobbly outdoor tables that blocked most of its share of the sidewalk. Eileen Paxton sat at one of them, wearing a slim-cut black pantsuit and backless high-heeled sandals and sipping a café latte. She saw us, smiled, wiggled a pinkie. Her hair was trimmed shorter than a few days ago, tinted a couple of shades lighter, and her makeup was more intense. She wore diamond stud earrings and a jade necklace, looked as if she was celebrating something.

She said, "I'm so glad we could get together."

Passersby brushed us. Milo edged closer to her, and said, "Here or inside?"

"Oh, here. I like the rhythm of the city."

This particular city was barely a village, a

precious display of conspicuous wealth. The rhythm was set by power-walking pedestrians and oversized engines belching toxins. Milo and I sat down and ordered espresso from an overly moussed waiter with drugged eyes. Eileen Paxton looked content, as if this was a quiet, restful place for *al fresco* dining.

She said, "How did my sister seem to you?"

Milo punted to me.

I said, "She looked a bit depressed."

"What you need to know is that's not all because of what happened to Gavin. Sheila's got long-standing psychological problems."

"Long-standing depression?"

"Depression, anxiety, difficulty coping, you name it. She's always been moody and high-strung. I'm the baby, but I always took care of her. When she married Jerry, I had my concerns."

"About the marriage?"

"About Sheila being able to handle marriage," she said. She turned her head quickly, flashed teeth at Drug-eyes. "Gio, could I have some of those lovely little pistachio biscotti? Thank you, you're a true dear." Back to us: "To Sheila's credit, she worked at her marriage and seemed to do okay. Even though Jerry's no prize."

"He's got problems, too?"

Her squint was furious. "Jerry's sexually predatory. Hits on anything with a vagina and, for all I know, anything with anything else. He hit on me. I've never told Sheila, it would've destroyed her and the marriage, and I didn't want that on my conscience."

But you're telling us.

I said, "When did this happen?"

"A month after they were married. Barely back from their honeymoon. I was also married, and the four of us spent a weekend in Arrowhead—my first husband's family owned a place on the lake, great place with a double dock. Everything was rolling along nicely until one day Sheila went down for a nap—she runs out of steam easily—and my then-hubby had to go to town on business—he was an investment banker. That left just Jerry and me. I went down to sun on the dock in my bikini, and a few minutes later, Jerry came by. We weren't alone ten minutes before he made his move. And I'm not talking subtle. Hand down the bikini bottom." She clawed her hand, made a swooping motion. "He does *not* have a gentle touch."

The plate of hard cookies arrived along with our espressos. Eileen Paxton patted the waiter's hand, selected a crescent, broke it in half, nibbled the tip.

"What did you do?" I said.

"I yanked Jerry's goddamn hand out of there, told him what I'd do to his balls if he ever tried that again. He's despised me ever since, and the feeling's mutual. Not just because of that. Because of what he does to my sister."

"What does he do?"

"He's cheated on her consistently throughout the marriage."

I didn't answer.

She said, "Trust me, I know the bum. All those business trips, doing God knows what. The looks he gives me when we're alone. Gives other women—the girls he hires as secretaries."

"What about them?"

"Sluts. They're supposed to be doing secretarial work, but don't look as if they know how to type. He goes off doing his thing, doing God knows what, and Sheila basically lives alone. She has no friends, no social network. Which is the way it was when we were growing up. I always had a huge social circle. Sheila had trouble relating."

I said, "Doing God knows what. Sheila said he was a metals dealer."

"So I've heard," Paxton said airily. She chewed on a biscotti.

"You have doubts?"

"He must do something, the bills get paid. Yes, he travels around trading aluminum, whatever. But when my husband—my new one—tried to talk to him about investing, Jerry wasn't interested. And Ted's a fabulous broker, someone who could help Jerry. My sense is Jerry isn't great at what he does, has to hustle just to keep his head above. He moves his office every few years, travels all the time."

"Hires sluts as secretaries."

She hesitated. "Maybe I was being a little harsh. I just know what he did to me on the dock that day. And the way his eyes rove."

I said, "You're thinking this could be related to Gavin."

"I want you guys to have all the facts, and I know no one else will give them to you. The family's screwed up, and Gavin was a weirdo. I know Sheila and Jerry are going to tell you he was just a regular kid before the accident, but that's not the way it was. Gavin had problems."

"What kinds of problems?"

Eileen Paxton rubbed the biscotti against her top teeth, as if caressing the enamel. Her tongue snaked out and tickled the pastry, then she took a hard bite and chewed slowly.

"I wouldn't be telling you this except I don't want you misled."

"We appreciate that, ma'am," said Milo.

"Well, good," said Paxton. "Because I do feel uncomfortable, divulging family issues." She sipped latte like a cautious cat, licked foam from her upper lip.

"What kinds of problems did Gavin have?" I said.

"Like father, like son."

"He was sexually predatory?"

"That sounds too harsh," she said. "Gavin hadn't developed into a predator. Yet. But he was . . . okay, there's no reason not to tell you: Last year, Gavin ran into some legal problems over a woman."

"Beth Gallegos," said Milo.

Paxton's face slackened with disappointment. "So you know."

"It came up recently, ma'am. In fact, we were just talking about it to your sister."

"You're serious? Sheila must have gone bonkers. She blamed the victim, right?"

"Exactly, ma'am."

"That's always been her way of dealing with stress," said Paxton. "My poor sister lives on another planet—well, yes, that was part of what I was going to tell you. But that was only Gavin's most serious problem, there have been others."

"Other women he stalked?"

"I know of at least one girl he harassed, and my guess would be more. Because that kind of behavior's a pattern, right?"

"Sure," said Milo. "Who's the other victim?"

"Gavin had a girlfriend—some rich kid from the Flats, I only met her once, skinny little blond thing with a nose like a hawk. I found her kind of snotty. Her father's a prominent jingle writer. Gavin got sexually aggressive with her, and she dumped him."

"How do you know about this, ma'am?"

"Because Gavin told me."

"Gavin talked to you about his personal issues?"

"From time to time." Paxton smiled and caressed her own neck. "The young, hip aunt. He liked the fact that I'm in the industry, more in touch with pop culture than his parents. We'd chat from time to time. The time he told me about Little Miss Beverly Hills—I think her name was Katya, something like that—we were all out to dinner—right up the block at Il Principe, the food's divine."

"I'll have to try it," said Milo. "So this was a family dinner?"

"Gavin, Sheila, and I. Jerry was out of town. As usual."

"How long ago?"

"Um, I'd say half a year, maybe more. Anyway, there we were enjoying the fabulous food—they cook sea bass in a wood oven, make their own pasta from scratch—and all of a sudden, Sheila wasn't feeling well—another typical Sheila thing, she can't enjoy anything, not even a good meal, without suffering—and she ran to the little girls' room and stayed there for a while. Gavin started talking to me, he'd been looking kind of tense all night. Finally, I pried it out of him. He'd lost his girlfriend because she wasn't interested in sex. He called her a 'compulsive virgin.' "

She propped the chewed-down biscotti between her index fingers. Rolled it. Placed it on her plate. "I asked him what had happened, and he told me. While he was telling it, he really worked himself up. It was clear he was angry and frustrated."

"About losing the relationship."

"No, that was the thing. He said he couldn't care less about having a girlfriend, it was not getting *sex* that griped him. It really made him angry."

"This was after the accident."

"Shortly after—maybe it was eight months ago. But Gavin was always easily frustrated. As a little boy he threw all kinds of tantrums."

"Excitable," I said. "And now he was all worked up about not getting sex."

"He talked about sex as if it was his *right*. Said he and the girl, Katya, had been going together on and off since high school, it was about time she put out. Like there was a schedule you adhered to. Then he said everyone else was 'fucking themselves blind,' the whole world was one big fuckfest swimming in jizz and he deserved to swim, too, and she could just go to hell, he'd find someone else."

"Lots of anger," I said.

"He always had a bad temper. It got worse after the accident. It was like his emotional barometer was off—he just did or said what was on his mind. I mean, I'm his aunt and he's talking about *jizz* in a booth at Il Principe. I was mortified. Important people dine at that place."

"Gavin was talking loud?"

"His voice kept rising, and I had to keep telling him to lower it. I tried to reason with him, told him women weren't machines, they needed to be cared for, sex could be fun, but it had to be mutual. He listened, actually seemed to be taking it in. Then he slid over in the booth, and said, 'Eileen, thanks. You're awesome.' Then he grabbed my breast in one hand, the back of my head with the other, and tried to shove his tongue down my throat—Gio? A refill, please."

◆

Milo pressed her for more on Gavin's sex life and the family, but once she'd gotten past the basic hatred, there was nothing. He steered the conversation to Gavin's tabloid fantasies.

"That," she said, "is another thing he was impressed with—my work in the industry. He kept asking me to hook him up with some celebrity parties, so he could observe." She laughed. "As if I'd help him dig dirt on my friends."

"What was his angle?"

"Unearthing filth and selling it to the tabs. He saw it as his journalistic debut, he was going to make his mark as a journalist. I told him the tabs were trash and full of lies, but he wouldn't hear it. He claimed they were more honest than the establishment press because they were open about their goals."

"Filth."

She nodded. "After the accident, Gavin saw the world as one big ball of filth."

I said, "Did he make any progress toward being a journalist?"

"Like take a course or get an internship?" said Paxton. "Not to my knowledge. I'd doubt it. He really wasn't in any shape to go back to school or hold down a job. Too flighty—he was drifting. Dropping out, sleeping in till noon, turning his room into a pigsty. I can't blame him, I'm sure his brain was messed up. But Sheila didn't even try to set limits. And Jerry, of course, was always gone."

"Gavin did go into therapy."

"Because the courts forced him to."

"Did he tell you who his therapist was?"

"Jerry did. Dr. Koppel. Like it was some big deal." She frowned.

"You know her?"

"I've heard her on the radio, and I have to say I'm not impressed. All she does is preach morality to idiots who phone in. Why not just go to church?"

Using the present tense. Milo and I looked at each other.

She said, "What?"

"Dr. Koppel was murdered."

Paxton's face went white. *"What? When?"*

"Couple of days ago."

"My God—why don't I know that—was it on the news?"

"There was an article in yesterday's paper."

"I never read the paper," she said. "Except *Calendar*. Murdered, omigod. Are you saying it had something to do with Gavin?"

"No, ma'am."

"But she—could it be coincidence?"

"Your sister didn't seem impressed by that."

"My sister's crazy. Do you have any idea who killed her?"

Milo shook his head.

"Horrible, horrible," she said. "You think there's a chance it couldn't be related to Gavin?"

"We don't know, ma'am."

"Oh, boy." Paxton stayed serious for a while. Ate her biscotti and grinned. Back to coquettish. "Now you're playing hard to get, Lieutenant."

"Not really, ma'am."

"Well . . . I hope this has been helpful. I've got to go."

"One more question, ma'am. Do you remember that picture I showed you of the girl who died with Gavin?"

"Yes, of course. And I told you I'd never seen her before, and that was true."

"Gavin talked to you about wanting to find a new girl. He told other people he'd succeeded."

"What other people?"

"Let's leave it at other people."

"Mr. Inscrutable Detective," said Paxton. She brushed her knee against Milo's. "A new girl, huh? In Gavin's mind that could've meant anything. Someone he decided to pursue, whether or not she wanted it. Someone he'd seen on TV."

"The girl I showed you was real," said Milo. "And she was in Gavin's car, up on Mulholland, late at night."

"Okay," she said, annoyed. "So he found someone. Everyone finds someone eventually. Look what *happened* to her."

◆

She made sure Milo picked up the tab and flounced away on backless shoes.

"What a piece of work," said Milo. "What a family. So what was her reason for talking to us? Dissing the Quicks?"

"She despises them," I said, "but that doesn't discount her information."

"Gavin's inappropriate sexual behavior? Yeah, he's sounding nuttier by the day."

"If she's right about Jerome Quick, Gavin had a role model. Gavin may have started off with a certain view of women, and the accident weakened his inhibitions further. What intrigues me is the blonde. Gavin had problems approaching women, came on way too strong. Yet an attractive young woman was willing to get intimate with him. A young woman in five-hundred-dollar shoes whom no one's reported missing."

"A pro," he said. "Got to be."

"Severe frustration could lead a boy to buy sex. A Beverly Hills boy might have a decent budget. Especially with a father who sanctioned it. I know she hasn't shown up in any Vice files, but a relative rookie lucky enough not to get busted wouldn't. If she worked on her own, there'd be no one to miss her. If she worked for someone else, they might not want to go on record."

"A father who sanctioned it," he said. "Dad slips Gavin serious dough to get seriously laid?"

"And maybe," I said, "Dad knew where to send him."

◆

Jerome Quick's metals-trading firm was a few miles east of Beverly Hills, on Wilshire near La Brea, on the third floor of a shopworn four-story building wedged between taller structures.

A sign in the empty lobby listed several

units for lease. Most of the tenants were businesses with names that told you little about what they did. Quick's office was on the second floor, midway down a poorly lit linoleum-floored hall. A savory but dis-comforting odor—beef stew just past its prime—permeated the walls.

Quick didn't keep much of an office: A small, mostly empty reception area fronted an office marked PRIVATE. The carpeting was brown, stomped glossy, the walls cheap woodite paneling. The receptionist sat be-hind a cheap woodite desk. She was young and thin, pretty but hard-looking, with ran-domly chopped hair tinted electric blue at the tips. Her makeup was thick and grayish, her lipstick, anoxic gray-blue. Curving bright azure nails were an inch long. She wore a tight white sweater over leather-look black vinyl pants and chewed gum. In front of her was a copy of *Buzz Magazine*. The lack of other periodicals or chairs and her surprise at our presence said visitors were infrequent.

The sight of Milo's badge raised a pen-ciled eyebrow, but the pulse in her neck was slow and steady.

She said, "Mr. Quick's out of town," in a surprisingly sultry voice.

"Where?" said Milo.

She wiggled her shoulders. "San Diego."

"He travel a lot?"

"All the time."

"Nice and quiet for you."

"Uh-huh." The blue nails tapped the magazine. No computer or typewriter in sight.

Milo said, "You're not surprised the police want to talk to him."

She shrugged. "Sure I am."

"Is it the first time the police have wanted to talk to him?"

"I've only been working here for a couple of months."

"Cops been here before?" said Milo.

"Nope."

Milo showed her the photo of the blonde. She blinked hard, turned away.

"You know her?"

"Is she dead?"

"Very."

"Don't know her."

"She's the girl who died with Gavin Quick."

"Oh."

"You do know about Gavin."

"Yeah. Of course."

"Sad," said Milo.

"I didn't really *know* him," she said. "Very sad." She turned the corners of her mouth down. Trying to mean it. Her brown eyes were flat. "Who did it?"

"That's what we're trying to find out, Ms. . . ."

"Angie."

"Gavin come in here?"

"Once in a while."

"How often, Angie?"

"Not often."

Milo unbuttoned his jacket and edged closer to her desk. "How long have you been working here?"

"Three and a half months."

"In three and half months, how many times did you see Gavin Quick?"

"Hmm . . . maybe three times. Could be four, but probably three."

"What did Gavin do when he was here?"

"Went in to see Jerry—Mr. Quick. Sometimes they'd go out."

"For lunch?"

"I guess."

"Was it lunchtime?"

"I think it was."

"What'd you think of Gavin, Angie?"

"He seemed like an okay guy."

"No problems?"

She licked her lips. "No."

"No problems at all? He was always a gentleman."

"What do you mean?" she said.

"We've heard," said Milo, "that Gavin could get pretty enthusiastic. Overly enthusiastic."

No reply.

"Overly enthusiastic with women, Angie."

She placed a hand on the copy of *Buzz*. As if preparing to take an oath. *I swear on all that is hip . . .*

"I never saw that. He was polite."

"Polite," said Milo. "And by the way, what *is* your last name?"

"Paul."

"Angie Paul."

"Yup."

"So Mr. Quick travels a lot."

"All the time."

"Must get boring, just sitting around."

"It's okay." She flexed her shoulders again.

Milo sidled closer to the desk. The top bit into his thigh. "Angie, did Gavin ever hit on you?"

"Why would he do that?"

"You're an attractive woman."

"Thanks," she said, without inflection. "He was always polite."

"Where's the boss off to?"

"Somewhere in San Diego. He didn't say."

"He doesn't tell you where to find him?"

"He calls in."

"Leaving you all by yourself," said Milo.

"I like it," she said. "Nice and quiet."

◆

Before we left, Milo took down her North Hollywood address and phone number and driver's license registration. Driving back to the station, he ran her through the data banks. Three years ago, Angela May Paul had been arrested for marijuana possession.

"Paxton said Quick hired sluts for secretaries," he said. "I don't know if ol' Angie would qualify for that, but he's sure not tapping the executive roster. That office of his, pretty downscale, huh?"

"Keeping the overhead low," I said. "Eileen said he's no tycoon."

"She said he was hustling . . . think Angie was telling the truth about not knowing the blonde? I thought she reacted a bit to the photo, though with that stone face it was hard to tell."

"She blinked hard when you showed it to her," I said, "but it is a death shot."

"The blonde," he said. "Jimmy Choo and Armani perfume. Maybe ol' Jerry provided well for Junior."

He checked his phone for messages, grunted, hung up.

"Drs. Larsen and Gull returned my call. They'd prefer to meet me away from the office, suggested Roxbury Park, tomorrow, 1 P.M. The picnic area on the west side, they go there for lunch from time to time. You up for some grass and trees and chewing the fat with a couple of colleagues? Should I bring a picnic basket?"

"Grass and trees sounds okay but forget the niceties."

CHAPTER
21

Alex, I'm glad I caught you."

It'd been months since I'd heard Robin's voice, and it threw me. No rapid heartbeat; I was pleased about that.

I said. "Hi, how've you been?"

"Well. You?"

"Great."

So civil.

"Alex, I'm calling for a favor, but if you can't do it, please just say so."

"What is it?"

"Tim was just asked to fly to Aspen to work with Udo Pisano—the tenor. There's a concert tomorrow, and the guy's voice is freezing up. They want Tim there yesterday, are flying him on a chartered jet. I've never been to Aspen and would like to go along. We're talking one, maybe two nights. Would you be able to babysit Spike? You know how he is with kenneling."

"Sure," I said, "if Spike can handle being here."

A few years back, on a sweltering summer day, a little French bulldog had made his way across the murderous traffic of Sunset Boulevard and up into the Glen. He wandered onto my property, gasping, stumbling, dangerously dehydrated. I watered and fed him, searched for his owner. She turned out to be an old woman dying in a Holmby Hills manor. Her sole heir, a daughter, was allergic to dogs.

He'd been saddled with an unwieldy pedigree moniker; I renamed him Spike and learned about kibble. He reacted to his new surroundings with élan, promptly fell in love with Robin, and began viewing me as competition.

When Robin and I broke up, custody wasn't an issue. She got him, his leash, his food bowls, the short hairs he shed all over the furniture, his snoring, snuffling, arrogant table manners. I was awarded an echoing house.

I considered finding a dog of my own, had never gotten around to it. I didn't see Spike much because I didn't see Robin much. He'd taken ownership of the small house in Venice that she shared with Tim Plachette, and his regard for Tim seemed no higher than for me.

Robin said, "Thanks so much, I'm sure he'll be fine. Down deep he loves you."

"Must be extremely deep. When do you want to bring him over?"

"The plane leaves from Santa Monica as soon as we're ready, so I was thinking soon."

"Come on over."

◆

This is not your typical dog.

His flat face implies as much frog DNA as canine heritage, his ears are oversized, upright, batlike, and they flex and pivot and fold in response to a wide range of emotions. He doesn't take up much more space than a Pomeranian but manages to pack twenty-six pounds into that cubic area, most of it lead-bone and rippling muscle, clothed in a black brindle coat. His neck is twenty-one and three-quarter inches around, and his knobby head is three hand-breadths wide. His huge brown eyes shine with confidence and he allows himself the barest, patronizing interest in the lives of others. His worldview is simple: Life is a cabaret, and it's all about him.

When I used to take him out alone, women flocked. "Oh, that's the most beautiful ugly dog I've ever seen!" was the operative phrase.

This afternoon, he had as much interest in leaving Robin's side as in snarfing a bowl of lint.

I held out a chew stick. He shot Robin a mournful gaze. She sighed and stooped. "It'll be fine, handsome."

The Saran-wrapped nugget of hamburger I'd concealed in my shirt pocket perked his radar and brought him over, but once he gobbled it, he raced back and hid behind Robin's legs. Great legs.

She said, "Look at this, he's guilt-tripping me."

"The joys of parenthood."

Spike nuzzled her jeans. Tight jeans above suede boots. She wore a black silk T-shirt under a tapestry vest. Her auburn curls were loose, her face was scrubbed and fresh. Those big, liquid brown eyes. The clean sweep of jaw and thin, straight nose.

Those lips; the oversized incisors.

I said, "Let me take him, and you go. He'll fuss, then he'll be fine."

"You're right," she said. She took Spike's face in both her hands. "Listen, you rascal. Daddy will take good care of you, you know that."

What did she call Tim? Stepdaddy?

Spike's trapdoor mouth dropped open, teeth flashed, a purplish tongue flapped.

Beseeching the heavens, he bayed.

I swooped him into my arms, held his taut little body tight against my chest as he sniveled and writhed and hyperventilated. It was like restraining a bowling ball with legs.

"Oh dear," said Robin.

I said, *Bon voyage, Rob."

She hesitated, headed for her truck, changed her mind, and came back. Throwing her arm around my shoulder, she kissed Spike full on the snout.

She was kissing me on the cheek just as Allison drove up in her black Jaguar XJS.

◆

The convertible top was down and her black hair blew like something out of a crème rinse commercial. She wore blue-tinted sunglasses and cream-colored knits with an aqua scarf. Glints punctuated her ears, neck, fingers, wrists; Allison is unafraid of adornment.

She switched off the engine and Robin's arm dropped. Spike tried to leap out of my arms and reacted to his failure with a heart-wrenching howl.

"Hey, everyone," said Allison.

"Hi," said Robin, smiling.

Spike tried his *I'm-strangling-do-the-Heimlich* bit.

"Well, look who's here." Allison patted Spike's head, then she kissed my lips. Robin backed away a few steps.

Spike froze; his head shifted from woman to woman.

It can get like that, buddy.

He moaned.

◆

After Robin drove away, I trailed Allison up the stairs to the terrace, carrying a still-shuddering dog. When we reached the landing, she looked at me—no, at him. Touched his whiskered flews tentatively. "Look at this little guy. I forget how cute he is."

Spike licked her hand.

"You are very, very *cute!*"

Spike began panting heavily, and she petted him some more. He wriggled, twisted his head back and managed to make eye contact with me.

A knowing look, rich with triumph.

Moments later, he was lying at Allison's feet, nibbling on his second chew stick in as many minutes, damning my approach with a jaundiced eye.

Some guys have all the luck.

◆

Mary Lou Koppel's murder had shaken Allison, and that seemed to be why she'd dropped by. As I made coffee for both of us, she pressed for details.

I told her the little I knew.

"So it could be a patient," she said.

"At this point anything's possible."

Her hands were tight around her mug.

I said, "You're upset."

"Not on a personal level." She took a sip. "I have had patients—mostly husbands of patients—who made me uneasy. But that was mostly years ago, when I was taking more referrals from agencies . . . I guess Mary Lou's death hits close to home. Thinking we know what we're doing and maybe we get overconfident. It's not just me. I've gotten calls from three other psychologists who just wanted to talk about it."

"People who knew Mary Lou?"

"People who know I'm seeing you and thought they could get some inside information. Don't worry, I was discreet."

"What was on their minds?"

"Our line of work, the unpredictablity of human beings. I guess they want to convince themselves that Mary Lou was different, and that's why it happened to her."

I said, "They're hoping she ticked off some talk-show nut, and it had nothing to do with her practice."

"Bingo. But from what you're telling me, it *could* be a patient. Someone who met the Quick boy in the waiting room."

"Given the Quick boy's impulsiveness—his behavior with women—the suspect pool has grown beyond the waiting room."

"But Mary Lou's murder," she said. "It has to be something related to her work."

"Any idea about gaining access to her patient files?" I said. "I can't figure out a way to get around confidentiality."

She thought about that. "Not without some kind of clear and present danger—documentation of a threat."

"There was nothing like that in Gavin's chart. And if she was threatened by anyone, she didn't let on to me or Milo. We've got a meeting with her partners tomorrow."

"Gull and Larsen."

"Know them?" I said.

"I've said hi to both of them but nothing more."

"Any impressions?"

"Gull comes across very smooth—very much the Beverly Hills shrink. Larsen's more the academic type."

"Gull was Gavin's initial therapist," I said. "It didn't work out, and Gavin was transferred to Koppel. Now that Gavin's dead, maybe he can tell us why."

"What a troubled kid," she said. "The stalking, putting the make on his aunt."

"If the aunt's to be believed, the family's beyond dysfunctional."

She drank more coffee, took my hand and held it. "At least you and I will never be out of work."

"Neither will Milo."

Spike rolled on his back and began pumping his stumpy legs.

"He looks like an upended turtle," she said. "What are you doing, cutie? Practicing for the upside-down bike race?"

"That's the signal to scratch his belly," I said.

She grinned and complied. "Thanks for decoding, I'm not fluent in dog."

She stopped scratching and made a move for her coffee mug. Spike protested, and she bent down again.

I said, "One-trial learning. Consider yourself conditioned."

She laughed, took the mug, managed to sip and rub. Spike burped, then purred like a cat. Allison cracked up. "He's a sound effects machine."

"He's got all sorts of talents."

"How long's he staying?"

"Couple of days." I told her about Robin's call.

"That was very nice of you."

"It's the least I could do," I said. "It was supposed to be joint custody, but he voted against it."

"Well, that was foolish on his part. I'm

sure you were a great father." She sat up and touched my face and ran a finger over my lips.

Spike sprang to his feet and barked.

"Here we go," I said. To Spike: "Cool it, clown."

"Ooh, stern," said Allison. "You do stern pretty well, my love. I've never seen it before."

"He brings it out in me."

"I always wanted a dog," she said. "You know my mother. Way too neat for hair on the carpet. And Dad was always away on business. I did have a salamander once. It crawled out of its tank and hid under my bed and dried up. When I found it, it looked like a piece of beef jerky."

"Poor neglected child," I said.

"Yes, it was a tragic childhood—though, to be honest, I wasn't very attached to Sally. Wet and slimy discourages bonding, don't you think? But something like this." She rubbed Spike's head. "This I could see."

"It gets complicated," I said.

"How so?"

"I'll show you."

I got up, stood behind her, rubbed her

neck and kissed it. Waited for Spike to go bonkers.

He stared. Defiant. Did nothing.

Her top was V-necked and I slipped my hand under it. She said, "Umm. As long as I'm here . . ."

"So you didn't just come to talk about Mary Lou."

"I did, but so what?" she said. I pinched her nipple lightly, and she leaned back in her chair and sucked in her breath and let it out in a soft laugh. She reached behind and ran her hand along my flank. "You have time?"

I glanced over at Spike. Impassive.

I took Allison by the hand, walked her to the bedroom. Spike trotted ten steps behind us. I closed the door. Silence. Back when it was Robin and me, he'd complained incessantly.

I drew the drapes, undressed Allison, got out of my own clothes. We stood belly to belly, blood rushing, cool flesh warming. I cupped Allison's rear. Her hands were all over me.

Still no complaints from the other side of the door as I carried her to the bed.

We embraced and touched and kissed and I forgot about anything but Allison.

It wasn't till I entered her that the scratching and mewling began.

Allison heard it right away. Lying there, her hands on my arms, her legs propped high on my back, she opened her blue eyes wide.

We began moving together.

The commotion on the other side of the door got louder.

"Oh," she said, still rocking. "See . . . what . . . you . . . mean."

I didn't stop, and neither did she.

Spike kept it up.

To no avail.

When I awoke the next morning at 6 A.M., Allison was next to me, and Spike lay curled on the floor, at the foot of the bed. She'd let him in. For the next two days, he wouldn't even be faking civil.

I left her sleeping and took him outside to do his business. The morning was moist and gray and oddly fragrant. Mustaches of haze coiled down from the mountains. The trees were black sentries. Too early for the birds.

I watched him waddle around the yard, sniffing and searching. He nuzzled a garden snail, decided escargot was an element of his Gallic heritage that he preferred to forget, and disappeared behind a bush. As I stood there in my bathrobe, shivering, head clearing, I wondered who'd been threatened to the point of murder by Gavin Quick and Mary Lou Koppel. Or maybe there was no threat at all, and this was all about pleasure killing.

Then I recalled Gavin's journalistic fantasies, and my questions took off in a different direction.

At breakfast, I said nothing about the murders to Allison. By eight-thirty she'd left for her office, and I was doing some work around the house. Spike remained still in front of the cold TV. He's always been a devotee of the blank screen; maybe he's got something there. I headed for my office and cleared paper. Spike padded in and stared until I got up, went to the kitchen, and fetched him a scrap of turkey. That kept him happy for the rest of the morning, and by 10 A.M. he was sleeping in the kitchen.

When Milo called soon after and asked me to pick him up at noon for the meeting with Drs. Gull and Larsen, I was glad to hear his voice.

◆

I idled the Seville in front of the station. Milo was late to come down, and I was warned twice by uniforms not to loiter. Milo's name meant nothing to the second cop, who threatened to ticket. I drove around the block a couple of times and found Milo waiting by the curb.

"Sorry. Sean Binchy grabbed me as I was leaving."

He closed his eyes and put his head back. His clothes were rumpled, and I wondered when he'd last slept.

I took side streets to Ohio, aimed the Seville east, fought the snarl at Sepulveda, and continued to Overland, where I could finally outpace a skateboard.

Roxbury Park was fifteen minutes away, on Olympic, less than a mile west of Mary Lou Koppel's office. Even closer to the Quick house on Camden Drive. I considered the constricted world that had become Gavin's after his accident. Until he'd driven a pretty blond girl up to Mulholland Drive.

Milo opened his eyes. "I like this chauffering stuff. You ever put in for mileage, the department takes a big hit."

"Saint Alex. What did Binchy want?"

"He found a neighbor of Koppel's, some

kid living seven houses up McConnell, who spotted a van cruising the street the night of the murder. Kid was coming home late, around 2 A.M., and the van passed him, heading north, away from Koppel's house and toward his. He locked his doors, stayed in his car, watched it turn around and return. Going really slowly, like the driver was looking for an address. The kid waited until the taillights had disappeared for a while. He can't say if the van parked or just drove out of sight, but it didn't make another pass."

"Vigilant kid," I said.

"There was a follow-home mugging over on the other side of Motor a few weeks ago, and his parents made a big deal about being observant."

"Two o'clock fits the coroner's estimate. Any look at the driver?"

"Too dark. Kid thought maybe the windows were tinted."

"How old a kid?"

"Seventeen. Binchy says he's an honor student at Harvard-Westlake, seems solid. He's into cars, too, was pretty sure the van was a Ford Aerostar. Black or gray or navy blue, no customization he could spot. He didn't get a peek at the plate, that would be too much to hope for. It's not much, but if we turn up some suspect with an Aerostar, it'll be a nice bit of something."

"Any progress getting access to Koppel's files?"

"I asked three ADAs, and each told me the same thing. Without overt violent behavior or threats by a specific patient against a specific person, forget it."

"Maybe there's another way to learn about Gavin's private life," I said. "He fancied himself a budding journalist, and journalists take notes."

"Oh, man." He sat up, pressed the dashboard with both hands, as if protecting himself from falling forward. "That sty he called a room. All that paper piled up, maybe he wrote something down. And I never checked. Shit."

"It was only a suggestion—"

"The night we notified Sheila Quick, she showed us the room. I felt bad for her, seeing how embarrassed she was. I never bothered to toss." He dug his thumbs into his temples. "Oh, that was brilliant."

"That night we notified Sheila," I said, "it presented as a lover's lane sex murder. No one suspected Gavin might've played a role in his own death. We still don't know that he did."

"Yeah, yeah, I appreciate the therapy, Alex, but the fact is, I should've tossed the damn room right away. Maybe I'm losing it . . . I have to write things down or they leak outta my brain. Okay, no more whining. Proactive, proactive. After Gull and Larsen, I head back to the Quick house. Mrs. Q's gonna love my excavating her dead boy's personal effects." He grimaced. "Hopefully, she didn't throw stuff out."

"I think it'll be a while before she has the energy to face the job."

"The life she leads," he said, softly. "I looked into her hubby's background. Ol' Jerome has earned himself one ticket for speeding and one for failure to make a complete stop. He's not known to our Vice unit or any other I talked to, including Santa Monica and West Hollywood. So if he hired call girls for himself or Gavin, he did it carefully. I ran him through a few search engines and his name comes up once. Reunion of Vietnam vets five years ago, in Scranton, Pennsylvania."

At Century Park East, I stopped at a red light. A few blocks later, I passed the college-sized campus that was Beverly Hills High. Then a block-long stretch of green, clean, and orderly park, with that Potemkin village *rightness* that characterizes Beverly Hills's public areas.

Milo said, "Ready to be collegial? Should I tell them who you are?"

"No, keep it low-key. I'll just listen."

"Ever the observer. Probably a good idea. Okay, turn here on Roxbury, keep going till you get to the south side of the park, and circle around. They said they'll be waiting in the picnic area, off the Spalding side alley on the western edge. Near where the kids and the mommies play."

◆

Albin Larsen and a larger, dark-haired man in a black suit sat at a wooden table just inside the green iron fencing that marked the western border of the park. One of six tables, all shaded by a grove of old Chinese elms. Beverly Hills treats its trees like show poodles, and the elms had been clipped into towering green umbrellas. The psychologists had chosen a spot just north of a sand pit, where toddlers frolicked under the watchful eyes of mothers and maids. Their backs were to the children.

I found a parking slot facing the green fence. Most of the others were taken up by SUVs and vans. The exception was a pair of Mercedes 190s, both deep gray, positioned next to each other. Same cars I'd seen in the parking lot of Koppel's building. Same model as Jerome Quick's.

Milo said, "His and his Benz's."

"They work together but drove here separately," I said.

"Meaning?"

"Meaning let's see."

Larsen and Gull were unaware of our presence and we watched them for a few moments. They sat talking to each other, and eating. Not much conversation, no obvious emotion. Milo said, "Let's go."

When we were ten yards away both men noticed us and put down their plastic forks. Albin Larsen's dress was consistent with what I'd seen the day Mary Lou Koppel had failed to show up at her office: another sweater-vest, this one brown, over a tan linen shirt and a green wool tie. Franco Gull's black suit was finely woven crepe with narrow lapels. Under it he wore a collarless white silk shirt buttoned to the neck. Gold wedding ring, gold watch.

Gull was broad-shouldered and powerful-looking, with a thick neck, a boxer's nose, and a big, rough face that managed to be handsome. His head sported a mass of wavy, iron-flecked black hair. His chin preceded the rest of him by a half inch. Tailored eyebrows arched behind gray-lensed sunglasses, and his skin was rosy.

A bit younger than Larsen—midforties. When Milo and I reached the table, he removed the shades and exposed big, dark eyes. Sad eyes, bottomed by smudgy pouches. They added a couple of years and the suggestion of thoughtfulness.

He was eating take-out Chinese out of the carton. Shrimp swimming in red sauce and fried rice and a side of dwarf spring rolls. Albin Larsen's lunch was mixed green salad heaped in a Styrofoam bowl. Both men sipped canned iced tea.

Larsen said, "Good day," and gave a formal little nod. Gull held out a hand. His fingers were enormous.

Both men were in the shade, but Gull's forehead was beaded with sweat. Spicy shrimp?

Milo and I brushed dust and leaves from the picnic bench and sat down. Larsen resumed eating. Gull smiled with uncertainty.

"Thanks for taking the time, Doctors," said Milo. "Must be tough around the office."

Larsen looked up from his salad. Neither man answered.

"Dr. Koppel's patients," said Milo. "Having to explain to them."

"Yes," said Larsen. "The vulnerability."

Gull said, "Fortunately, we're not talking about a huge number. Unlike physicians, each of us handles only forty, fifty patients at any given time. Albin and I divided up the actives and contacted each one. We're still working on former patients, but it's tough finding them. Mary didn't hold on to her files for longer than a year."

His voice was smooth and soft, but talking seemed to take the wind out of him. He wiped his forehead. The sweat kept coming.

"Is that typical?" said Milo. "Destroying files?"

"It's something each therapist decides independently."

"What about you and Dr. Larsen?"

"I hold on to files for two years. What about you, Albin?"

Larsen said, "It depends, but generally that's about right."

"No official group policy," said Milo.

"We're not an official group," said Larsen. "We share an office suite."

"So what happens to Dr. Koppel's active patients now? In terms of treatment?"

Franco Gull said, "Those who choose to continue with either Albin or me are free to do so. If they prefer a female therapist, we're happy to refer them out."

"Sounds pretty organized," said Milo.

"We need to be. As Albin said, we're dealing with extreme vulnerability. What could be worse for someone needy than to be cast adrift so abruptly?" Gull shook his head and his wavy hair shimmied. "It's a nightmare for them and for us. Unbelievable."

"Dr. Koppel's murder."

Gull's sad eyes tightened. "Are we talking about anything else?"

Albin Larsen speared a tomato but didn't eat it.

"It's a major loss," said Gull. "For her patients, for us, for . . . Mary was vibrant, brilliant, dynamic. She was someone I learned from, Detective. It's hard to comprehend that she's really *gone*."

He glanced at Larsen.

Larsen toyed with a lettuce leaf, and said, "To be snuffed out like that." He wiped his eyes. "We've lost a dear friend."

Franco Gull said, "Do you have any idea who did it?"

Milo placed his elbows on the picnic table. "I know you gentlemen are bound by confidentiality, but a viable threat nullifies that. Are either of you aware of any patient ever making a threat against Dr. Koppel? Any patient who resented her deeply?"

"A patient?" said Gull. "Why would you even think that?"

"I'm thinking anything, Doctor. Covering all bases."

"No," said Gull. "There are no patients like that. Absolutely not." He groped for a napkin, took another swipe at his brow.

Milo glanced at Albin Larsen. Larsen shook his head.

Milo said, "Dr. Koppel dealt with troubled people. It seems a logical place to start."

"Logical in the abstract," said Gull, "but it

doesn't apply to our practice. Mary didn't treat sociopaths."

"Who did she treat?" said Milo.

"People with everyday problems of adjustment," said Gull. "Anxiety, depression, what used to be called neurosis. And basically sound individuals facing choice points."

"Career guidance?"

"All kinds of guidance," said Gull.

"You don't call 'em neurotic anymore, huh?"

"We avoid labeling, Detective. Avoid stigma. Therapy's not treatment in the way a medical procedure is—a doctor doing something to a passive patient. It's contractual. We see ourselves as partners with our patients."

"Doctor and patient working as a team."

"Exactly."

"Problems of adjustment," said Milo. "You're absolutely certain there were no dangerous people in Dr. Koppel's practice."

Albin Larsen said, "Mary would not have enjoyed working with violent individuals."

"And she did only what she enjoyed?"

"Mary was busy. She could choose her patients."

"Why wouldn't she enjoy working with violent people, Dr. Larsen?"

"Mary was committed to nonviolence."

"We all are, Doctor, but that doesn't mean we're insulated from the uglier aspects of life."

Larsen said, "Dr. Koppel was able to insulate herself."

Milo said, "Really?"

"Yes."

"I've heard radio tapes where Dr. Koppel talked about prison reform."

"Ah," said Larsen. "I'm afraid that was my influence. Was I on the tapes, as well?"

"Don't think so, Doctor."

Larsen's mouth got tiny. "It was a topic I got Mary interested in. Not in a clinical sense. She was a socially aware individual, had a human as well as an academic interest in the larger social issues. But when it came to her practice, she concentrated on the everyday problems of everyday people. Women, mostly. And doesn't that say something about the likelihood of her murderer being a patient?"

"Why's that, Dr. Larsen?"

"Criminal violence is usually male-generated."

"You've got an interest in criminal psychology?" said Milo.

"Only as part of the social rubric," said Larsen.

Franco Gull said, "Albin's being modest. He's done terrific things as a human rights advocate."

"From that to private practice," I said.

Larsen glanced at me. "One does what one can in a given time."

Milo said, "Human rights doesn't pay the bills."

Larsen turned to him. "I'm sorry to say, you're correct, Detective."

"So," said Milo, "no psychopaths on Dr. Koppel's patient roster."

A statement, not a question, and neither psychologist responded. Albin Larsen ate a shred of lettuce. Franco Gull examined his gold watch.

Milo whipped out the picture of the blond girl. "Either of you gentlemen recognize her?"

Larsen and Gull examined the death shot. Both shook their heads.

Gull licked his lips. Sweat beaded atop his nose, and he wiped it away with irritation. "Who is she?"

"Was," said Larsen. "She's clearly deceased." To Milo: "Is this related in some way to Mary's murder?"

"Don't know, yet, Doctor."

"Did Mary know this girl?" said Gull.

"Don't know that either, Doctor. So neither of you have seen her around the office."

Gull said, "Never."

Larsen shook his head. Tugged at a button of his sweater-vest. "Detective, is there something we need to know about? In terms of our own safety?"

"Are you worried about your safety?"

"You've just showed us a picture of a dead girl. I assume you feel her death is related to Mary's. What's really going on here?"

Milo put the photo back in his pocket. "All I can advise you is to exercise normal caution. Should either of you come up with a threatening patient—or anyone else from Dr. Koppel's life who seems suspicious—you'd do best to let me know."

He crossed his legs, looked over at the frolicking children. An ice-cream truck cruised through the alley and rang its bell. Some of the kids began pointing and jumping.

Franco Gull said, "Is there anything else? I've got a totally booked afternoon."

"Just a few more questions," said Milo. "About the structure of your partnership with Dr. Koppel."

"Albin told you, it's not a formal partnership," said Gull. "We share office space."

"A purely financial arrangement?"

"Well," said Gull, "I wouldn't reduce it to just that. Mary was our dear friend."

"What happens, now that Dr. Koppel's dead, in terms of the lease?"

Gull stared at him.

Milo said, "I need to ask."

"Albin and I haven't talked about that, Detective. It's all we can do to take care of Mary's patients." He looked at Larsen.

Larsen said, "I'd be in favor of you and I picking up Mary's share of the rent, Franco."

"Sure," said Gull. To us: "It's no big deal. The rent's reasonable, and Mary's share was smaller than ours."

"Why's that?" said Milo.

"Because," said Gull, "she found the building for us, arranged an excellent lease, oversaw the entire renovation."

"Good negotiator," said Milo.

"She was," said Larsen. "Her skills were facilitated by the fact that her ex-husband owns the building."

"Ed Koppel?"

Franco Gull said, "Everyone calls him Sonny."

Milo said, "Renting from the ex."

"Mary and Sonny got along well," said Gull. "The divorce was years ago. Amicable."

"No problems at all?"

"He gave us a *sweetheart* lease, Detective. Doesn't that speak volumes?"

"Guess so," said Milo.

Gull said, "You won't find anyone who knew Mary well who's going to bad-mouth her. She was a fabulous woman. This is really hard for us."

His chin trembled. He put his sunshades back on.

"Gotta be rough," said Milo. "Sorry for your loss."

He made no move to leave.

Larsen said, "Is there anything else?"

"This is just a formality, Doctors, but where was each of you the night Dr. Koppel was killed?"

"I was home," said Gull. "With my wife and kids."

"How many kids?"

"Two."

Out came the notepad. "And where do you live, Doctor?"

"Club Drive."

"Cheviot Hills?"

"Yes."

"So you and Dr. Koppel were neighbors?"

"Mary helped us find the house."

"Through Mr. Koppel?"

"No," said Gull. "As far as I know Sonny's only into commercial. Mary knew we were looking to upgrade. She was taking a walk and noticed the FOR SALE sign and thought it might meet our needs."

"How long ago was that?"

"A year—fourteen months."

"Before that you lived . . ."

"In Studio City," said Gull. "Why is this relevant?"

Milo turned to Larsen. "And you, sir. Where were you that night?"

"Also at home," said Larsen. "I live in an apartment on Harvard Street in Santa Monica, north of Wilshire." He recited the address in a soft, weary voice.

"Live by yourself?"

"I do." Larsen smiled. "I read and went to bed. I'm afraid there's no one to verify that."

Milo smiled back. "What'd you read?"

"Sartre. *Transcendence of the Ego.*"

"Light stuff."

"Sometimes a challenge is good."

"Ain't that the truth," said Milo. "I'll tell you, this *case* is a challenge."

Larsen didn't answer.

Franco Gull checked his watch again. "I really need to head back to the office."

"One more question," said Milo. "I know you can't tell me about any deep dark patient secrets because of ethical restraints. But I do have a question that I think you are allowed to answer. Do any of your patients drive a dark Ford Aerostar minivan? Black, dark blue, maybe gray?"

Above us, the elm canopy rustled and the high, gleeful sounds of childhood play drifted over. The ice-cream truck rang its bell and drove off.

Albin Larsen said, "A patient? No, I've never seen that." His eyes drifted toward Gull.

Franco Gull said, "I agree. No patients I'm aware of drive a car like that. Not that I'd notice. I'm in the office when they park their cars, don't know what any of them drive— unless it comes up in therapy."

His brow was slick with sweat.

Milo scribbled in his pad and closed it. "Thanks, gentlemen. That's all for now."

"There'll be more?" said Gull.

"Depends upon what we find in the way of evidence."

"Fingerprints?" said Gull. "That kind of thing?"

"That kind of thing."

Gull stood so quickly he nearly lost his balance. "Makes sense." Larsen got to his feet, too. Gull was a head taller and a foot and a half broader at the shoulders. High school football, maybe college.

We watched the two of them walk to their Mercedeses.

Milo said, "Now wasn't *that* interesting?"

CHAPTER

23

Sweaty fellow," Milo murmured, as he called DMV.

It didn't take long to get the data. Three vehicles were registered to Franco Arthur Gull on Club Drive. A two-year-old Mercedes, a '63 Corvette, and a 1999 Ford Aerostar.

"Well, well, well."

He pulled the Thomas Guide out of my glove compartment, found a map, and jabbed his index finger. "Gull's house is only a few blocks from Koppel's, so on the face of it, one of his cars in the neighborhood isn't weird. But the witness said the van drove away from his street. Seemed to be looking for something."

I said, "Cruising back and forth at 2 A.M.

isn't neighborly. It's the kind of thing stalkers do."

"A shrink with problems in that area. Wouldn't that be interesting?"

"A shrink the court refers stalkers to. Maybe Gavin found out somehow, and that's why he dropped Gull and switched to Koppel."

"Gull driving by Koppel's house," he said. "She wouldn't have stood for that. Gavin tells her, he's lighting a tinderbox."

"On the other hand," I said.

"What?"

"Three vehicles in the Gull family. The Mercedes for him and a vintage Vette for weekend fun. That leaves the Aerostar for the wife."

"Suspicious wife," he said. "Oh, yeah. Gull and Koppel were having a fling."

"When you talked about evidence, Gull asked about fingerprints. It struck me as out of context. That could be because he knows his prints are in that batch you dusted at Koppel's house."

"More than partners. More than neighbors. She finds him a house close by, all the easier for drop-in fun. Mrs. G suspects and drives by at 2 A.M. Checking up. No wonder the guy's perspiring like a marathon runner."

I said, "You'll find out soon enough. He's got a state license, so his prints are in the system.

He flipped the little blue phone open. "I'll call the techs right now. Meanwhile, let's visit the wife."

"What about excavating Gavin's room?"

"That, too," he said. "but later." Big grin. "All of a sudden, I'm busy."

◆

The Gull residence was a Tudor, not unlike Mary Lou Koppel's, a bit less imposing on a flat lot with no view. Ballpark-quality lawn, the usual luxuriant beds of impatiens, a liquidambar sapling just beginning to turn color, staked in the crater vacated by a larger tree.

The Aerostar van was parked in the driveway. Deep blue. Two bumper stickers: MY CHILD'S AN HONOR STUDENT AT WILD ROSE SCHOOL. And GO LAKERS!

An Hispanic maid answered Milo's knock. He asked for *"La señora, por favor,"* and she said *"Un momento,"* and closed the door. When it opened again, a petite, very slim blond-ponytailed woman in her thirties stood there, looking distracted. Milo's badge changed nothing. She continued to look through us.

White-blond, ice-blue eyes, small bones, beautiful features. Even standing still, she seemed graceful. But dangerously slim; her skin bordered on translucence, and her black velvet sweats bagged. She'd done a fine job with her makeup, but the red rims around her eyes were impossible to conceal.

Milo said, "Mrs. Gull."

"I'm Patty."

"May we come in?"

"Why?"

"This is about a recent crime in the neighborhood."

One slender hand drummed the other. "What," she said, "another mugging in Rancho Park?"

"Something more serious, ma'am. And I'm afraid the victim's someone you know."

"Her," said Patty Gull. Her voice had gone deeper, and any trace of distraction had vanished. Her hands separated, dropped, clamped on her hips. Her lower jaw slung forward. As fine-featured and aquiline as she was, her face took on a mastiff scowl.

"Sure, come in," she said.

◆

The living room was wood-shuttered and paneled in oak stained so dark it was nearly black. The decor looked as if it had been assembled in one day by someone with respect for convention, a tight deadline, and a nervous budget: middling antique copies, equine prints under glass, the kind of still-life paintings you can pick up at sidewalk sales. Further stabs at re-creating manor living were accomplished by a riot of floral chintz, too-shiny brass gewgaws, and artificially distressed surfaces. Just beyond the room was a hallway filled with toys and other child clutter.

Patty Gull perched on the edge of an overstuffed sofa, and we faced her from matching wing chairs. She took hold of a tasseled cushion, held it over her abdomen, like a hot-water bottle.

Milo said, "I noticed your bumper sticker. Someone a Lakers fan?"

"Me," she said. "I used to be a Lakers Girl. Back when I was young and cute."

"Not that long ago—"

"Don't stroke me," said Patty Gull. "I like to think I've held up pretty well, but I'm going to be forty in two years, and I screwed up my body giving my husband two gorgeous children. He pays me back by fucking other women whenever he can."

We said nothing.

She said, "He's a pussy hound, Detective. For that, I could've hooked up with a basketball player. Even one on the bench." Her laughter was brittle. "I was a *good* Lakers Girl, went home after the games, didn't party, held on to my morals. Nice Catholic girl, told to marry well. I married a psychologist, figured I'd be getting some stability." She punched the tasseled pillow. Flung it to one side and hugged herself.

"Mrs. Gull—"

"Patty. I've had it, he's history."

"You're getting divorced?"

"Maybe," she said. "You take stock of your life, and say 'This is what I have to do,' and it seems so obvious. Then you step back and all the complications rain down on you. Kids, money—it's always the woman who gets screwed moneywise. I've stayed out of Franco's business affairs. He could hide everything, and I wouldn't know."

"Have you talked to a lawyer?"

"Not officially. I have a friend who's a lawyer. She was a Lakers Girl, too, but unlike me, she was smart enough to go all the way with her education. I always wanted to get an MBA, do something in the corporate world. Maybe in sports, I love sports. Instead . . ." She threw up her hands. "Why am I telling you this? You're here about her."

"Dr. Koppel."

"*Dr.* Mary Lou *fuck-another-woman's-husband* Koppel. You think Franco killed her?"

Patty Gull examined her fingernails.

"Should I think that, Mrs. Gull?"

"Probably not. The papers said she was shot, and Franco doesn't own a gun, wouldn't have a clue how to use one. Also, he wasn't with her that night. I know because I got up in the middle of the night and drove by her house looking for his car, and it wasn't there."

"What time was this, ma'am?"

"Must've been close to two in the morning. I went to bed at ten, like I always do. Big swinging life and all that. Franco came in before I could fall asleep and we had another fight and he left and I went to sleep. When I woke up and he wasn't there and it was nearly two, I really lost it."

"Because he hadn't come home."

"Because," said Patty Gull, "he wasn't being *penitent*. You're having serious problems and you claim you're penitent and then you have another fight. What do you do? You approach your wife on bended knees and beg her forgiveness. That's the *constructive* thing to do. The caring, *giving* thing. Franco would tell a *patient* to do that. What does *he* do? Stalk out, turn off his car phone, and stay away."

"So you went looking for him."

"Damn straight."

"Figuring Dr. Gull would be with Dr. Koppel."

"Doctor this, Doctor that. You're making it sound like a medical convention. He was *fucking* her. I found them together before." She grabbed for the same pillow, snatched it up, bounced it on a bony knee. "Bastard and bitch didn't even try to be subtle. We live four blocks apart. I mean, rent a room for God's sake, don't soil your own nest."

"You found them at her house."

"You bet."

"When?"

"A month ago. This is *after* Franco promised he'd finally deal with his problem."

"Being a pussy hound."

Hearing her own words repeated seemed to shock her. She said, "Uh, yes. He's always been . . . it's always been difficult. I've been more patient than Mother Teresa, they should *canonize* me. And then I find him with *her*—that was too much—she wasn't even attractive. Now we're talking another level of shoving it in my face."

"How'd you find them?" said Milo.

"Oh, you're going to love this," said Patty Gull. "This is great. Franco gave me the old b.s. about working late. Then he had his answering service call me just before nine to let me know he was still tied up, it would be even later. I knew right away something was up. Franco doesn't see emergency patients. Most of what he does is hand-hold bored Beverly Hills bitches. So I decided to drive over to the office and confront him. Enough is enough, right? So I tell Maria to watch the kids and I start driving to the office and something, I still don't know what it was, makes me take McConnell. 'Cause it's north, it's basically on the way. And I pass her house, and there's his car. Parked in front, parked right in *front*. Is that *gall,* or what?"

"Pretty blatant."

"I parked, ran up those stairs all the way to her backyard, and there they were in the back room. She's got this big-screen TV and on it was a porn video and apparently the bitch and the bastard were feeling playful, decided to imitate whatever filth they were watching."

"Wow," said Milo.

"Wow, indeed. They didn't even bother to lock the door, and I just walked in, walked right past them and they were so into what they were doing that they didn't even hear me. It wasn't until I switched off the TV that they opened their eyes."

She closed her own. Remembering.

"That was delicious," she said. "The expressions on their faces. The way they *looked* at me."

"Shock," said Milo.

"Beyond shock." Patty Gull smiled. "It was like someone from another planet—another galaxy—had landed a UFO in that room. And I just stood there, let them know with my stare that they were busted scum and there was nothing they could do to change that. Then I walked out and drove back home. Twenty minutes later, Franco showed up, looking like he had cancer. I bolted the door and didn't let him in and told him if he tried to trespass, I'd call the police. He left, I knew he would, he always leaves. I didn't see him until the next day. He went to work and was a good little psychologist and came home and tried to talk to me using his psychologist voice. The only reason I let him in was by that time I'd spoken to my friend the lawyer, and she'd slowed me down."

"She advised you not to file."

"I was ready to do it, I really was, but she said life would get really complicated faster than I could imagine. So I allowed the bastard to come home, but he's not allowed to touch me, and I don't talk to him unless the kids are present."

Milo said, "That was a month ago. Between then and the night Dr. Koppel was killed, have you driven past her house?"

"All the time."

"How often?"

"Every other day," said Patty Gull. "At

least. Sometimes every day. It's on my way to go shopping, whatever, so why not? I figure if I do serve Franco, I might as well pile up the evidence. My friend says even with no-fault divorce, the more you can get, the better."

"Have you seen his car there, since?"

"No," she said. "Unfortunately. Maybe they're doing it in the office. Or at some motel."

She clenched her eyes shut.

Milo said, "You do think they continued their affair after you discovered them."

Her eyes flipped open. "That's what Franco does. Fucks and fucks and fucks. He's sick."

"How many other women has he—"

"No," said Patty Gull. "I don't want to go there. Some things are private."

"Were any of them his patients?" said Milo.

"I don't know about that. Franco's business was his domain. That was the deal."

"The deal."

"The marriage deal. I gave up my career and my entire life for him and had kids, and he went out and provided."

"He provide pretty well?"

She waved a languid hand around the dark, floral room. "He did okay."

"Nice place."

"I conceived it myself. I'm thinking of going back and studying decorating."

"Mrs. Gull, in terms of the other women—"

"I said I don't want to go there, okay? What's the difference? I don't know if he fucked his patients. I *do* know he fucked *her*. But he didn't kill the bitch. I told you, he wasn't there that night. And he doesn't have the guts."

"Where was he that night?"

"Some hotel, I forget—ask *him* which one."

"How do you know he was there?"

"Because he called me and left his room number, and I called him back and he was there—the place on Beverly and Pico, used to be a Ramada, I don't know what it is now."

"What'd you guys talk about?"

"Nothing pretty," she said. "Now please leave. I have things to do."

"Don't be offended by this question, ma'am, but where were you—"

"I didn't kill the bitch either. Guns scare me, I've never even touched one. That's one thing Franco and I have in common. We're for outlawing guns, just despise what guns have done to our country. Besides, that night Franco *wasn't* there with her, so why would I bother paying the bitch a visit?"

"You had reason to resent Dr. Koppel. Why not have a chat?"

"At that hour?"

"You were out driving at that hour."

"Five minutes, back and forth," said Patty Gull. "Just to see. I looked for his Benz, didn't see it, drove back home, took an Ambien, and slept like a baby."

Milo said nothing.

"Detective, if resentment was enough of a motive, I'd be killing tons of women, not just her." She laughed, this time with genuine glee. "I'd be one of those serial killers."

◆

Out came the picture of the dead girl. "Know her, ma'am?"

Patty Gull's bravado crumbled. Her mouth opened and her jaw shook. "Is she— she is, isn't she?"

"Yes. Do you know her?"

"No, no, of course not—is she one of Franco's—did he—"

"Right now, we don't know who she is."

"So why are you showing it to me—take it away, it's horrible."

Milo began to comply, but her hand shot out and held the photo in place.

"She looks like me. Not as pretty as I was at that age. But pretty enough, she's a pretty girl." She placed the photo in her lap, continued to stare.

"She *looks* like me. It's *horrible*."

CHAPTER
24

We left Patty Gull sitting in the room she'd decorated.

Outside, Milo said, "Scary lady. Am *I* sweating?"

"She hates her husband but is sure he didn't kill Koppel, provides what she thinks is an alibi. But her not seeing Gull's car at Koppel's the night of the murder says nothing. It's a two-car garage, he could've moved his inside. Especially after being caught once. Or, he made sure to park several blocks away. A third possibility is he checked into the hotel and took a cab."

"Hell," he said, "he could've walked, it's a mile and a half." We headed for the car. "If he did call a taxi, I can find out. Gull interests you, the way he does me?"

"He's smart enough to cover his tracks the way our boy's been doing. And even if Patty's exaggerating, his record with women is interesting. Also, he and Gavin didn't get along. What if it was more than poor therapeutic rapport? What if Gavin learned something that made him a threat to Gull?"

"Sleeping with a patient," he said. "Somehow Gavin finds out about it—hanging around the office, being obsessive. He talked about uncovering scandal, now he found one. But then why would Gull kill Koppel? They were lovers."

"Maybe her indiscretions didn't extend to murder. She figured out what had happened to Gavin and threatened to turn Gull in. Or the affair was no longer useful to Gull. Or both."

"You're talking about one cold guy."

"Not that cold," I said. "He sweats easily. I'm talking about a guy who experiences anxiety but still loves taking risks. Someone who sleeps with another woman four blocks from his house, gets busted, and possibly goes back for more."

"Mary Lou threatening to turn him in . . . she sure wasn't forthcoming when I spoke to her. Then again, maybe Gull hadn't broken it off with her, yet. If he did it a few days later, he'd have two scorned women to deal with . . . what do you think about Patty's seeing a resemblance in the dead girl?"

"It didn't strike me," I said. "I saw it as Patty having ego problems, but maybe she's onto something."

"Gull murdering the old lady symbolically? Right from the beginning you saw this as a symbolic deal."

"If Gull's our guy, it could also tie in with Flora Newsome. She was Mary Lou Koppel's patient, so Gull would have had opportunity to see her. Combine Flora's feelings of sexual inadequacy, Gull's view of himself as a cocksman and the prestige of his position, and you've got fertile ground for an easy seduction."

"Gull does her, then kills her. His lover's patient, talk about taking risks."

"By the time Flora was killed, she was dating Brian Van Dyne. Maybe Dr. Gull doesn't take well to rejection. By a patient or a lover."

"Evil shrink," he said. "All that sweating. Someone that calculating, you'd think he could keep it under control."

"It's one thing to be cool when you're calling the shots, be it seduction or murder," I said. "Setting up the scene, choreographing, dominating because you've picked submissive partners. Being investigated by the police changes all that. All of a sudden, he's placed in the one-down position."

"My charm intimidates him?"

"Something like that."

"So the best bet is come on strong with the bastard, bulldoze over him."

"You got it," I said. "Method acting."

"The curtain rises," he said. "Let's boogie."

◆

We drove to Franco Gull's office building, parked in an empty slot next to Gull's Mercedes, and headed for the rear door. A janitor was vacuuming the ground-floor carpeting. All six doors to the Charitable Planning suite were closed, and the corridor smelled of inactivity and that same popcorn fragrance.

That same feeling of disuse, and I said so to Milo.

Milo hadn't taken his eye off the janitor. Now, he went over to the guy. Skinny guy, midthirties, with the burnished skin of the hard-drinking homeless, a three-day stubble, lank brown hair, scared-rabbit eyes. He wore a UC Berkeley sweatshirt over baggy gray sweatpants and filthy sneakers. His fingernails were black at the edges. He kept his head down and pushed the vacuum cleaner, trying to pretend a big, hefty detective wasn't heading his way.

Milo moved in that surprising, quick way he can muster, bending and flicking off the machine. When he straightened, he'd pushed closer, and his smile was all the man could see. "Hey."

No answer.

"Quiet afternoon down here on the ground floor."

The man licked his lips. Very scared rabbit. "Yeah," he finally said.

"What's Charitable Planning all about?"

"Beats me." The man had a whiny, congested voice, the kind that makes everything sound evasive. His shoulders rose and fell, rose again, and remained bunched up tight around his scrawny neck. Broken blood vessels explored his nose and cheeks. His lips were cracked and dry, and tattoos snaked their way up his wrist.

Milo glanced at them, and the man tried to slide his hand back into his sleeve.

"UC Berkeley, huh?"

The man didn't answer.

"Alma mater?"

Headshake.

"Work here long?"

"A while."

"How long's a while?"

"Ah . . . mebbe a . . . month, two."

"Maybe."

"I do a bunch of buildings for the owner."

"Mr. Koppel."

"Yeah."

"Ever see anyone actually work at Charitable Planning?"

"Ah . . . ah . . ."

"That a tough question?" said Milo. "Required you to think?"

"I . . . ah . . . I want to answer right."

"Truthful or right?"

"Truthful."

Milo took hold of the man's right wrist, slid the sleeve of the sweatshirt up a scrawny forearm. Grimy skin was specked with discs of scar tissue, most of it concentrated in the crook. The tattoos were blue-black sparked with intermittent red blotches, clearly homemade. Poorly rendered naked women with oversized breasts. A dull-eyed snake with dripping fangs.

Milo said, "Get these at UC Berkeley?"

"Nope."

"What's your real alma mater? San Quentin or Chico?"

The man licked his lips again. "Neither."

"Where'd you do your time?"

"Mostly County."

"County, here?"

"Here, around."

"So you're a short-term guy."

"Yeah."

"What's your specialty?"

"Drugs, but I'm clean."

"Meaning burglary and shoplifting and larceny."

The man placed one hand on the stalk of the vacuum cleaner. "Never any larceny."

"Any assaults or other bad stuff?" said Milo. "You know I'm gonna find out."

"One time," said the man, "I did a battery

thing. But the other guy started it, and they paroled me early."

"Weapon of choice?"

"It was his knife. I took it away from him. It was an accident, mostly."

"Mostly," said Milo. "You cut him bad?"

"He lived."

"How about you show me some ID?"

"I do something wrong?"

"Perish the thought, *amigo.* Just being thorough—you know why we're here, right?"

The man shrugged.

"Why're we here, *amigo*?"

"What happened to the lady doc upstairs."

"You don't know her name?"

"Dr. Koppel," said the man. "The ex-wife. They got along good."

"Lovey-dovey," said Milo.

"No, I . . . uh . . . Mr. Koppel always said just give her what she wants."

"What she wants?"

"If there's a problem. In the building. He said we should fix it fast, give her what she wants."

"He doesn't do that for all his tenants?"

The man was silent.

"So you're trying to tell me not to suspect Mr. Koppel for killing his ex because they were still buddies."

"No, I . . . uh . . . I don't know nothing about nothing." The man rolled his sweatshirt sleeve down his arm.

"Any ideas about who did kill Dr. Koppel?"

"Didn't know her, didn't hardly never see her."

"Except to fix things for her."

"No," protested the man. "I don't do that stuff, I call the plumbers, whatever, and they fix it. I'm just here to clean. Mostly I do Mr. Koppel's buildings in the Valley."

"But today, you're on this side of the hill."

"I go where they tell me."

"They."

"Mr. Koppel's company. They got properties all over."

"Who told you to come here, today?"

"Mr. Koppel's secretary. One of them. Heather. I can give you the number, you can check it out."

"Maybe I will," said Milo. "Now, how about some ID?"

The man fished in a front pant pocket and fished out a wad of bills secured by a rubber band. He slipped off the band, thumbed through the money—grubby singles and fives—and drew out a California identification card.

"Roland Nelson Kristof," said Milo. "This your current address, Roland?"

"Yeah."

Milo scanned the card. "Sixth Street . . . this is right past Alvarado, right?"

"Yeah."

"Lots of halfway houses there. That your situation?"

"Yeah."

"So you still paroling."

"Yeah."

"How'd you get the job with Mr. Koppel?"

"My PO got it for me."

"Who's that?"

"Mr. Hacker."

"Downtown office?"

"Yeah."

Milo gave him back his ID. "I'm going to run you through, Roland. Because a halfway-house guy working a building where someone got murdered is something I need to check out. I find out you lied to me, I pay a visit to your crib, and you know I'm gonna discover something that busts your parole, you know I am. So if there's something you wanna tell me, now's the time."

"There's nothing," said Kristof.

"You never had problems with women? No bad behavior in that department?"

"Never," said Kristof. Until then his delivery had been flat, mechanical. Now a hint of outrage had crept in.

"Never," said Milo.

"Never, not once. I been a junkie since I was fourteen. I don't hurt no one."

"Still on the junk though."

"I'm getting older, it's getting better."

"What is?"

"The hunger," said Kristof. "Days are getting shorter."

"How's your sex life, Roland?"

"Ain't got none." Kristof's declaration was free of regret, almost cheerful.

"You sound happy about that."

"Yeah, I am," said Kristof. "You know what dope does to all that."

"No drive," said Milo.

"Zactly." Kristof smiled wearily, flashing intermittent, brown teeth. "Something else not to worry about."

◆

Milo copied down his address and allowed him to resume vacuuming.

As we climbed the stairs to Pacifica-West Psychological Services and the roar of the vacuum cleaner faded, he said, "That's one habitual con."

I said, "Criminal burnout. Get to a certain age, and it's too pooped to pop."

"Wanna guess how old he is?"

"Fifty?"

"Thirty-eight."

◆

No one sat in the waiting room. Dr. Larsen's session light was off. Dr. Gull's shone red.

"It's three-forty," I said. "If he does the forty-five-minute hour, he'll be out shortly."

"I love your profession," said Milo. "Imagine if surgeons could do that. Cutting out three-quarters of the appendix and billing."

"Hey," I said, "we use the time to chart and to reflect."

"Or if you're Dr. Gull, to put back all the stuff you swept off your desk when you decided to reflectively hump your patient all over it."

"Cynical."

"Thank you."

At three-forty-six the door to the waiting room opened and a flushed, attractive woman in her forties backed out, still chattering to Franco Gull.

He was close behind her, holding her by the elbow. When he saw us, he dropped his hand. The woman sensed his tension, and her cheeks pinkened.

I waited for Gull to start sweating, but he recovered his composure and ushered the woman toward the door, saying, "Next week, then."

The woman was brunette and well padded, swimming in a sea of gray cashmere. She brushed at her hair, favored us with a brittle smile, and left.

Gull said, "Again? Now what?"

Milo said, "We met your wife."

Long silence. "I see."

Milo smiled.

Gull said, "Patty's going through a rough patch. She'll be fine."

"She didn't sound fine."

Gull smoothed back his hair. "Why don't you come in? I'm free for the next hour."

"Or at least forty-five minutes of it," said Milo, under his breath.

Gull didn't hear. He'd turned and was striding toward the trio of inner offices. Albin Larsen's and Mary Lou Koppel's doors were closed.

Gull's was open. He stopped before entering.

"My wife—has got problems."

"Bet she does," said Milo. "Maybe she could use some therapy."

CHAPTER

25

Gull's office was two-thirds the size of Mary Lou Koppel's and set up surprisingly simply. No bird's-eye maple paneling, just beige paint on the walls. Thin, beige carpeting blurred the room's boundaries. Off-white leather couches and armchairs were loosely arranged. Koppel had displayed crystal eggs and Indian pottery. Franco Gull's sole nod to decoration were cheaply framed photographic prints of animals and their young.

I found myself sniffing for the aroma of sex, smelled only a syrupy mélange of perfumes.

Gull sprawled on a sofa and invited us to sit. Before our butts hit the leather, he said,

"The thing you need to know about Patty is that she's dealing with some very serious issues."

"Marital infidelity?" said Milo.

Gull's lips produced a pained semicolon. "Her problems go way beyond that. Her father was extremely abusive."

"Ah," said Milo. "Ah" was a running joke between us. The old therapist's dodge. He turned his head so Gull couldn't see him wink. "All this talk about Mrs. Gull. Guess wives don't get confidentiality."

Gull's eyes sparked. A fleck of moisture appeared from under the shade of a wavy, salt-and-pepper forelock.

I'd been right: Losing the power rule played havoc with his adrenals.

"I'm telling you about Patty because you need to put her in context."

"Meaning I shouldn't believe anything she tells me."

"That depends on what she told you."

"For one thing," said Milo, "she thinks you didn't kill Dr. Koppel."

Gull had been primed to protest. He regrouped, shifted position. "There you go, even someone who's not feeling kindly toward me knows I'd never do anything like that. I don't even own a—"

"You hate guns," said Milo. "She told us that, too."

"Guns are an abomination."

"Mrs. Gull feels she's provided you with an alibi for the night Dr. Koppel was killed."

"There you go," Gull repeated, sitting a bit straighter.

"Yeah, I'm going strong," said Milo. "The thing is, Doctor, what your wife considers an alibi, we don't."

"*What?* Oh, come on, you've got to be kidding." Sweat beads popped at Gull's hairline. "Why would I need an alibi?"

"Don't you want to know what Mrs. Gull told us?"

"Not really." Theatrical sigh, then: "Fine, tell me."

"Mrs. Gull drove by Dr. Koppel's house around 2 A.M., searching for your car. She didn't see it—"

"She did that?" said Gull. "How . . . sad. As I told you, Patty's got serious trust issues."

"You blame her?" said Milo.

"Why did you speak to Patty in the first

place? Why would you even consider something so far-fetched—"

"Let's get back to the alibi, Doctor. Your car not being parked on McConnell. That really doesn't mean much. You could've parked somewhere else in the neighborhood. Or taken a cab from the hotel you stayed at—which was . . . ?"

Gull didn't answer.

"Dr. Gull?"

"This is my personal life, Detective."

"Not any longer, sir."

"Why?" said Gull. "Why are you doing this?"

Out came Milo's pad. "Which hotel, sir? We'll find out anyway."

"Oh, for Christ's sake. The Crowne Plaza."

"Pico and Beverly Drive."

Gull nodded.

"You stay there often?"

"Why would I?"

"It's close to your office, for when you and the missus have a spat."

"We don't have *spats* that often."

Milo's pencil tapped the pad. "Same question, Doctor."

"I've lost track of your questions."

"Do you stay there often?"

"Occasionally."

"When your wife throws you out."

Gull flushed. His hands tightened. His fists were enormous. "My marital issues are of no concern to—"

"What I'm getting at," said Milo, "is do they know you at the Crowne Plaza?"

"I don't know . . . those places."

"What about them?"

"Businesslike, anonymous. It's not exactly the wayfarer's inn," said Gull. "And I'm really not there that often."

"How often is not that often?" said Milo.

"I couldn't quantify."

"Your credit card records could."

"My—this is absolutely—"

"You don't consider the hotel a home away from home? Being so close to the office."

"I don't need a home—I paid cash."

"Why?"

"It seemed simpler."

"For when you bring women there."

Gull shook his head. "This is ridiculous."

"Ever bring Dr. Koppel there?"

"*No.*"

"No need to, I guess," said Milo. "What

with her living so close to the office. And to your house. Make a stopover after work, then continue on to the missus and kids."

Gull's brow was slick and pale. "I don't see what your point is—"

"How far would you say it is, from the office to Dr. Koppel's? A mile?"

Gull rolled his shoulders. "Closer to two."

"Think so?"

"All the way up Pico to Motor and then south to Cheviot."

"Let's split the difference," said Milo. "Mile and a half."

Gull shook his head. "I really think it's closer to two."

"Sounds like maybe you've clocked it, Doctor."

"No," said Gull. "I'm just—forget it. This is pointless."

"You look in pretty good shape, Doctor. Work out?"

"I've got a treadmill at home."

"A little mile and a half walk on a cool June night wouldn't challenge you, would it?"

"That never happened."

"You never walked from the Crowne Plaza to Dr. Koppel's house."

"Never."

"The night she was killed," said Milo. "Where were you?"

"At the hotel."

"Did you call up for food?"

"No, I had dinner before I checked in."

"Where?"

"My house."

"Before the tiff."

"Yes," said Gull. He knuckled an eye. Sleeved his brow.

"You stayed in the hotel all night," said Milo.

Gull rubbed his jaw. "I rented a movie. That'll be on record."

"What time?"

"Elevenish. Check."

"I will," said Milo, "but all that proves is you pushed a button on your remote, not that you stayed to watch."

Gull stared at him. "This is absurd, I didn't kill Mary."

"What was the title of the movie?"

Gull looked away and didn't answer.

"Doctor?"

"It was an adult film. I don't remember the title."

"I guess," said Milo, "it wouldn't help asking you to recap the plot."

Gull managed a sickly smile.

Milo said, "When did you see Dr. Koppel last?"

"That afternoon," said Gull. "Both of us were walking patients out to the waiting room, and we said hi. That was the last time."

"No tryst later that evening?"

"No. That was over."

"What was?"

"Mary and I."

"Who broke it off?"

"It was mutual," said Gull.

"Because?"

"Because it was the right thing to do."

Milo flipped his pad open, scanned his notes. "Alternatively," he said, "if you didn't walk to her house, you could've called a cab."

"I didn't."

"It can be verified, Doctor."

"Verify to your heart's content."

Milo slapped the pad shut. Gull gave a

start and wiped his brow with his sleeve again.

"Doctor, why did Gavin Quick dump you as a therapist?"

"He didn't *dump* me. I transferred him to Mary."

"Why?"

"That's confidential."

"No it's not," barked Milo. "Gavin lost his privilege when someone shot him. Why'd he *transfer* away from you, Doctor?"

Gull's arms had gone rigid, and his palms pressed against the seat cushions, as if bracing himself for takeoff.

"I'm not going to talk to you anymore," he said. "Not without a lawyer."

"You're aware of how that makes you look."

"I assert my rights, and it makes me look bad?"

"If you've got nothing to hide, why have concern about rights?"

"Because," said Gull, "I don't want to live in a police state. With *all* that implies." He forced a smile. Perspiration glazed his face and his neck. "Did you know, Detective, that of all the professions who joined the Nazi party, the police were the most enthusiastic recruits?"

"Really? I heard it was doctors."

Gull's smile faltered. He burned some calories restoring it. "That's it. Not another word." He drew a finger across his lips.

"Sure," said Milo, rising. "No sweat."

CHAPTER
26

A s we left Gull's office, he got on the phone.

Out in the hallway, Milo said, "Lawyering up."

I said, "What did it was your question about Gavin transferring to Koppel."

"Some deep dark secret," he said. "Something that makes him look bad."

"I wonder how much the Quicks know."

"If they know, why didn't they tell me?"

"Maybe it also reflected poorly on Gavin."

"What, Gavin found out the guy supposed to help him with his stalking problem had outstalked him, so he decided to expose him? Why wouldn't his parents talk about that? And how does Koppel figure in?"

"I don't know," I said. "But everything seems to connect to this place."

"I'll have Binchy do a loose surveillance on Gull. See if I can get another baby D on it, too."

"Loose?"

"This ain't TV, unlimited gizmos and manpower. I'll be lucky to get two shifts a day."

We descended the stairs to the ground floor. He said, "So, how effective do you think my leaning on him was?"

"He's lawyering up," I said.

"And would an innocent guy do that? Yeah, I got to him . . . I really wanna know why Gavin left him."

"The neurologist who sent Gavin to Gull might know something about it. Specialists need to stroke their referral sources, so Gull would have offered some kind of explanation."

"Singh," he said. He whipped out his pad, flipped pages. "Leonard Singh, over at St. John's. You mind doing the doctor-to-doctor bit?"

"Not at all."

"Also, if you're still up for calling Ned Biondi, to try to get the blonde's picture in the papers, go ahead."

He handed me a sealed envelope stamped PHOTO, DO NOT BEND. "Here's your chance to be an 'anonymous source.' "

I ran a finger across my lips.

We reached the bottom of the stairs. Roland Kristof and his vacuum cleaner were no longer in sight, and Milo gazed down the empty corridor.

"Ghost town," he said. " 'Charitable Planning.' You picking up *eau de* scam?"

"At the very least *eau de* shadow corporation," I said. "You hassled Kristof. What about him bugged you?"

"He gave off *eau de* con in waves, and my nose is always sensitive to that."

"I thought it might be more than that."

"Like what?"

"A parolee hired by Koppel's ex, working in the building where three murder victims spent some time. Flora Newsome's job at the parole office. Before Koppel got killed, we were surmising about an ex-con."

"Flora again," he said, and resumed walking.

When we got outside, I said, "It doesn't bother you?"

"What?"

"Sonny Koppel hiring a junkie parolee for

building maintenance. The whole con connection?"

"Everything bothers me." When we reached the car, he said, "In terms of Flora, what we were surmising about was her *sleeping* with a con. She mighta slummed, Alex, but I don't see her getting anywhere near a burnout like Kristof."

"So maybe Kristof's not the only parolee on Koppel's payroll. Maybe Koppel's found himself a source of cheap labor. Mary Lou was into prison rehab. There could be some connection."

"Larsen says he gave her the idea."

"Larsen was disappointed we didn't hear him on the interview tapes. Everyone's got an ego."

"Even shrinks?"

"Especially shrinks."

He tried to pull the car door open. I hadn't unlocked the Seville, his arm strained, and he grunted. By the time I'd turned the key, he'd wandered back toward the alley.

When he returned, he said, "It's time to meet Mr. Sonny Koppel. Something *else* that shoulda been done right away. Woman gets killed, go straight for the ex, it's goddamned Detection 101."

"You're dealing with three cases that point in all directions."

He threw up his hands and laughed. "Supportive therapy again."

"Reality."

"If I wanted reality, I wouldn't live in L.A."

◆

As we drove off, he sank into silence. I crossed Olympic, and he announced he'd face Sheila Quick alone for the toss of Gavin's room. I dropped him at the station and returned home. Spike was waiting for me at the door, looking forlorn.

That was new. Generally, his game was nonchalance: remaining in the service porch when I came home, waiting me out when walk time approached, feigning sleep until I lifted his limp body and set four paws on the ground.

"Hey, guy."

He snorted, shook a drizzle of saliva my way, licked my hand.

"Lonely, huh?"

His head dropped, but his eyes remained fixed on me. One ear twitched.

"Really lonely."

He gazed upward and let out a low, hoarse moan.

"Hey," I said, bending on one knee and ruffling his neck, "she'll be home tomorrow."

In the old days, I'd have added, *I miss her, too*.

Spike snuffled and rolled over. I scratched his belly. "How about some exercise?"

He snapped to attention. Pant, pant.

I had an old leash stored in my office closet, and by the time I brought it back he was jumping and yelping and scraping at the door.

"Nice to be appreciated," I said.

He stopped fussing. His expression said, Don't get carried away.

◆

His stubby little legs and attenuated palate could handle a half mile up the Glen and back. Not bad for a ten-year-old pooch—in bulldog years, he was well past retirement. When we returned, he was famished and parched, and I filled his bowls.

While he ate, I called the most current number I had for Ned Biondi. Ned had retired as a senior writer for the *Times* years ago, talked about moving to Oregon, so when I got a no-longer-in-service message, I wasn't surprised. I tried Oregon information, but he wasn't listed.

I'd treated Ned's daughter years ago, a brilliant girl with too-high standards who'd starved herself and nearly died. I supposed the fact that Ned hadn't bothered to leave his forwarding was encouraging. The family didn't need me anymore. How old would Anne Marie be, now—nearly thirty. Over the years, Ned had phoned to fill me in and I knew she'd gotten married, had a child, was still waffling about a career.

The information always came from Ned. I'd never achieved much rapport with his wife, who'd barely spoken to me during therapy. Once treatment was over, Anne Marie didn't speak to me either, not even to return follow-up calls. I mentioned it once to Ned, and he grew apologetic and embarassed, so I dropped it. A year after discharge, Anne Marie wrote me an elegant letter of thanks on pink, perfume-scented stationery. The tone was gracious, the message clear: *I'm okay. Back off.*

No way could I call her to locate Ned. Someone at the paper would know where he was.

As I started to punch in the *Times*'s main number, call waiting clicked in.

Allison said, "Hi, baby."

"Hey."

"How's your day been?"

"Not bad," I said. "Yours?"

"The usual . . . do you have a minute?"

"Something wrong?"

"No, no. I was just—yesterday, when I came by—Alex, you know I like Robin, we've always gotten along. But when I drove up . . . seeing you two . . ."

"I know what it looked like, but she was just thanking me for taking Spike."

"I know." Her laugh was flimsy. "I called to tell you I know. Because maybe I let out a little jealous vibe. I was a little bugged. Seeing her kissing you."

"Chastely," I said. "On the cheek."

She laughed again, then grew silent.

"Ally?"

"I couldn't ascertain the site," she said. "All I saw was two people who . . . you looked like a *couple*—you looked *comfortable* with each other. That's when it hit me. All the history you have with her. There's nothing wrong with that. I just started contrasting it with—it just seems as if we're a ways off from that . . ."

"Allison—"

"I know, I know, I'm being neurotic and insecure," she said. "I'm allowed to do that, once in a while, right?"

"Sure you are, honey, but in this case it's not warranted. The only reason she was there was to hand off Spike. Period."

"Just a peck on the cheek."

"That's it."

"I don't want you to think I've turned into some possessive, paranoid chick—oh, listen to me."

"Hey," I said, "if the situation were reversed, I'd react the same way. Robin has no interest in me, she's happy with Tim. And I'm thrilled to be with *you*."

"I'm your main squeeze."

"You are."

"Okay, I got my self-esteem injection," she said. "Sorry for bugging you in the middle of the day."

"You're my girl, Dr. Gwynn. I find you smooching some dude, it won't be a pretty sight."

"Right. You, Mr. Civilized."

"Don't test me."

She laughed, this time with heart. "I can't believe I made this call. The last thing I want is to be possessive." Her voice caught.

"Sometimes," I said, "it's nice to be possessed."

"It is . . . okay, no more Ms. Mawkish. I've got three more patients coming and each needs to perceive me as all-knowing. Then, it's over to the hospice."

"Any free time at all?"

"I wish. The hospice is having a potluck dinner for all the volunteers, so I'm eating there. The only breathing time I have is right now, last-minute cancellation. What I *should* be doing is charting and returning calls, not whining to you."

"I'll be over in twenty."

"What?" she said.

"I'm coming over. I want to see you."

"Alex, my next patient's due in forty. The drive, alone, will eat up—"

"I want to kiss you," I said. "That won't take long."

"Alex, I appreciate what you're trying to do, but I'm okay; you don't have to indulge my—"

"This is for me. I'm going to be in the neighborhood, anyway. Talking to a doctor at St. John's." Though I hadn't made the appointment.

"Baby," she said, "I can assure you that whatever it was that tweaked my anxiety has passed."

"I want to see you," I said.

Dead air.

"Ally?"

"I want to see you, too."

◆

While driving to Santa Monica, I got Dr. Leonard Singh's number from Information, found out he was on rounds, would be back in an hour. I told his secretary I'd be stopping by and hung up before she could ask why.

When I reached Allison's office building, she was waiting out on the sidewalk, dressed in a sky-blue cashmere cowl neck sweater and a long, wine-colored skirt, drinking something from a cardboard cup and kicking the heel of one boot. Her black hair was tied back with a clip, and she looked young and nervous.

I swung into the no parking zone in front and she got in the passenger seat. The cup gave off coffee and vanilla fumes.

I leaned over, cupped her chin in my hand, kissed it.

She said, "I want lips," and drew me close.

We connected for a long time. When we broke, she said, "I have staked my claim. Want a sip?"

"I don't do girlie coffee."

"Ha." She has a soft, sweet voice, and her attempt at a growl made me smile. "That, my darling, is the primeval sound of the alpha female!"

I eyed the cardboard cup. "Alpha females drink that?"

She glanced down at the beige fluid. "In the postfeminist age one can be simultaneously girlie and strong."

"Okay," I said. "What's next? You drag me into your cave?"

"I wish." She removed the clip, shook her hair loose, pushed thick, black strands behind one ear. Her skin was milk white, and I touched the faint, blue veins that collected at her jawline.

She said, "Alpha female, who'm I kidding? I mewl, and you hurry over. My professional advice is don't encourage that kind of dependent behavior, Alex."

"What's your nonprofessional advice?"

She took my hand. The minutes ticked away, too hurried.

She said, "Does 'not a bad day' mean you've made some progress on Mary Lou?"

I told her about Patty and Franco Gull.

"Is Gull really a suspect?"

"Milo's looking at him pretty closely."

"Murderous shrink. There's another PR coup for our profession."

"You told me Gull came across slick. Do you recall anything else about him?"

She thought about it. "He just impressed me as really into image. The way he carried himself, the clothes, the hair. I'm certainly not surprised he's promiscuous. He had that swagger—physical confidence, like someone who developed charisma early."

"I was thinking high school jock."

"That would fit," she said. "If it turned out he slept with his patients, I wouldn't be shocked either."

"Why not?"

"It's just a feeling."

"But you never actually heard anything to that effect."

"Never heard anything about him except that he was Mary Lou's partner. Maybe that

colored my judgment. Because of her repu-
tation. For being expensive and publicity-
hungry. To me, Gull came across the same
way."

"Albin Larsen doesn't," I said.

"He's more of a professor."

"Apparently he's some sort of human
rights advocate. Maybe they brought him
into the group for respectability. When we
interviewed him and Gull, Gull was sweating
and Larsen seemed to be holding his
tongue. As if he found Gull a bit . . . dis-
tasteful."

"It doesn't sound as if Mary Lou and Gull
were very discreet about their affair," she
said. "So maybe Larsen knew." She shook
her head. "Leaving his car parked in front of
her house. I'm enough of a shrink to think
accidents are pretty rare. My sense is they
both wanted Gull's wife to find out. Pretty
cruel."

I said, "Maybe Koppel saw herself as an
alpha female."

"A true alpha wouldn't need to steal
someone else's man," she said. She
glanced at the dash clock. "I've got five
minutes."

"Shucks."

"So what happens to the practice now that Mary Lou's gone?"

"Gull and Larsen say they'll take any patients who want to continue with them and refer the rest out."

"If even a small percentage of her patients transfer, that could be quite an income boost."

I stared at her. "You see a *profit* motive, here?"

"I agree with you, there's dominance and anger at play and probably some sexual overtones. But profit would a nice side benefit. And if Gull's your murderer, it would fit. What would be more intoxicating to a psychopath than eliminating someone he once possessed sexually and looting her business? It's basic warfare."

Coins of color spotted her ivory cheeks. Robin had always been repelled by these kinds of discussions.

"You," I said, "are an interesting girl."

She said, "Interesting but weird, huh? You drop by for some romance, and I'm analyzing at warp speed."

Before I could answer, she kissed me full on the lips, sat back suddenly.

"On the other hand," she said, "analyzing

is what they sent us to school for. Gotta go. Call me soon."

◆

Dr. Leonard Singh was tall and slightly stooped, with nutmeg skin and clear, amber eyes. He wore an exquisite Italian suit—navy blue overlaid with a faint red windowpane check—a yellow spread-collar shirt, a glistening red tie with matching pocket foulard, and a jet-black turban. His beard was full and gray, his mustache Kiplingesque.

He was surprised to see me in his waiting room, even more surprised when I told him why I was there. But no guardedness; he invited me into the cramped, green space that served as his hospital office. Three spotless white coats hung from a wooden rack. A glass jar of peppermint sticks was wedged between two stacks of medical charts. His medical degree was from Yale, his accent by way of Texas.

"Dr. Gull," he said. "No, I don't really know him."

"You referred Gavin Quick to him."

Singh smiled and crossed his legs. "Here's the way that happened. The boy came to me through the ER. I was one of two neurologists on call, just about to go off service, but someone I've worked with asked me to do the consult."

Jerome Quick had given me a name. The family doctor, a golfing buddy . . .

"Dr. Silver," I said.

"That's right," said Singh. "So I saw the boy, agreed to follow him, did what I could. Given the situation."

"Closed-head injury, nothing obvious on the CAT scan."

Singh nodded and reached for the candy jar. "Care for some late-afternoon sucrose?"

"No thanks."

"Suit yourself, they're good." He pulled out a peppermint stick, bit off a section, crunched, chewed slowly. "Cases like that, you're almost hoping for something blatant on the CAT. You're don't actually want to see tissue damage, because those situations are usually more severe. It's just you want to know what the insult to the brain is, want to have something to tell the family."

"Gavin's situation was ambiguous," I said.

"The problem with a case like Gavin's is you just know he's going to have problems, but you can't tell the family exactly what's going to happen or if it's going to be permanent. When I found out he'd been murdered, I thought, 'Oh my, there's a tragedy.' I called and left a message with his folks, but no one's returned it."

"They're pretty torn up. Any thoughts about the murder?"

"Thoughts? As in who mighta done it? No."

"Gavin's symptoms had persisted for ten months," I said.

"Not a good sign," said Singh. "On top of that, all his symptoms were behavioral. Psychiatric stuff. We cellular types prefer something concrete—a nice solid ataxia, something edematous that we can shrink down and feel heroic about. Once we veer off into your field, we start to feel at loose ends."

He took another bite of peppermint stick. "I did what I could for the boy. Which consisted of monitoring him to make sure I wasn't missing something, then I prescribed a little occupational therapy."

"He had fine motor problems?"

"Nope," said Singh. "This was more supportive in nature. We knew he'd experienced some cognitive loss and personality change. I thought some sort of psychological support was called for, but when I suggested a psych consult to the parents, they didn't want to hear about it. Neither did Gavin. So I backed off and offered O.T., figuring maybe that would be more palatable to them. It was, but unfortunately . . . you know about Gavin's experiences with his therapist."

"Beth Gallegos."

"Nice gal. He tormented her."

"Have you seen that before in CHI cases?"

"You can certainly have obsessive changes, but no, I can't say I've seen anyone turn into a stalker." Singh nibbled the broken edge of the peppermint stick.

"So the family was resistant to psychotherapy," I said.

"*Highly* resistant." Singh smiled, sadly. "I got the impression this was a family big on appearances. Dr. Silver said so, too. Though he didn't know them well."

"Really," I said. "I got the impression he was a family friend."

"Barry? No, not at all. Barry's an OB-

GYN, he'd only recently started treating the mother for premenopausal symptoms."

Jerome Quick had lied about Silver being a golfing buddy. A small lie, but why?

I said, "So what was your connection to Dr. Gull?"

"I don't have one," said Singh. "After Gavin got into trouble because of what he did to Beth, the father called me, saying the boy had been arrested and that the court down in Santa Ana was going to lock him up unless they could show sort of mitigating circumstances. What he wanted from me was a letter stating that the boy's behavior was a clear result of his accident. If that wasn't enough, he wanted me to testify for Gavin."

Singh finished the peppermint stick. "I have to tell you, I was of two minds on that. I hate going to court, I didn't know that I could say all that and be truthful. Beth Gallegos was one of our best O.T.s, a really super gal, and I felt terrible about what happened to her. I had to wonder if letting Gavin off the hook completely was the best thing for anyone. The boy clearly had serious problems, so maybe he needed to learn a lesson. On the other hand, this was jail we were talking about and he *had* experienced a cerebral insult and he *was* my patient. I decided to call the district attorney who was prosecuting the case, and she told me it being a first offense, they weren't gonna throw the book at him. She said if I referred him to a psychiatrist or a psychologist, that would work for her. I asked a couple of the psych guys who attend here, but they all felt it would be a conflict of interest because they knew Beth. Before I could make more calls, Mr. Quick phoned me and said he'd found a good psychologist, right there in Beverly Hills, real close to the house. He said that was important because he didn't want Gavin going too far afield."

"Mr. Quick asked to be referred to Dr. Gull," I said.

"He asked to be referred to Dr. *Koppel,* but she punted and sent him to Dr. Gull. I had my secretary call up and check Dr. Gull's credentials, and everything was in order. I called Dr. Gull, and he seemed like a nice fellow, so I wrote the letter."

He smoothed his tie. The amber eyes

were sharp. "So tell me, was there some problem with that? 'Cause my name's on that referral letter, and if there are going to be problems, I'd sure like to know."

"I can't think of anything that would reflect on you."

Singh said, "That sounds upsettingly vague."

"I'm sorry," I said, "but it's too soon to be more specific. I'll be sure to let you know if that changes."

Singh touched his turban. "Much obliged."

"Were you aware that Gavin didn't stick with Gull?"

"Really?" said Singh.

"No one told you."

"The only communication I got was from Gull. A week in, he called, thanked me, said everything was going fine. Never heard from him again. What happened?"

"Gavin didn't get along with Gull and was transferred to Dr. Koppel."

"Guess she found time for him. Poor Gavin. Whatever he did to Beth, the boy had it rough. Well, if there's nothing else, I've got a ton of paperwork."

He walked me out.

I thanked him for his time, and said, "Dallas?"

"Houston. Born and bred; my daddy was a heart transplant surgeon on Denton Cooley's team." He smiled. "Cowboys and Indians, and all that good stuff."

CHAPTER

27

I got home just after five, tried the *Times* human resources office, found out it was closed. I tried to recall the names of colleagues Ned Biondi had mentioned and came up with one, Don Zeltin, like Ned, once a reporter, now a columnist. I phoned the paper's switchboard, asked for him, got patched through.

"Zeltin," said a gruff voice.

I started to explain who I was and that I wanted to get in touch with Ned.

"Sounds complicated," said Zeltin. "You could be some nut."

"I could be but I'm not. If you don't mind calling Ned—"

"Maybe Ned didn't leave you a number because he doesn't want to hear from you."

"Would calling him and asking be a huge imposition? It's important."

"Psychologist, huh? My ex-wife decided she was going to be a psychologist. Back when she was still my wife. I've got three friends in the same boat. Wife talks about going back to shrink school, get on the horn to your divorce lawyer."

I laughed.

He said, "It's not funny. Actually, it is. She ended up dropping out, and now she lives in Vegas and sells clothes at a crappy boutique. Okay, what the hell, I'll call Ned. Give me your name again."

◆

I looked up Franco Gull in my American Psychological Association directory. He'd gone to college at the University of Kansas, Lawrence. Double major: psychology and business. His move to Berkeley for grad school had been delayed by two years playing semipro baseball at a farm club in Fresno. Not the kind of thing generally listed in the APA book; Gull had been proud of his athletic stint.

Charismatic at a young age, sure about his physicality.

Gull had no academic appointments, had conducted no research since grad school that he cared to specify. His areas of interest were "interpersonal relations" and "insight-oriented therapy." From what I could tell, he'd gone straight from a postdoc at UC Riverside into private practice with Mary Lou Koppel.

While I had the book in front of me, I checked out Albin Larsen. His bio was considerably longer and more impressive. Undergraduate work at Stockholm University, followed by a one-year fellowship in public policy at Cambridge, back to Sweden for a doctorate at Göteborg University and an assistant professorship in the Social Sciences Institute at that same institution. His areas of interest were cultural factors in psychological assessment, the integration of social and clinical psychology, the application of psychological research to conflict resolution, and the appraisal and treatment of war-related trauma and stress. He'd done relief work in Rwanda and Kenya, consulted to Amnesty International, Doctors Without Borders, the

Human Rights Beacon Symposium, World Focus on Prisoners' Rights, and a child welfare subcommittee of the United Nations. Though he'd lived in the U.S. for eight years and had earned a California license shortly after arriving, he'd maintained an academic appointment at Göteborg.

Substantive fellow. Would Koppel and Gull's shenanigans have offended him?

I got on the computer, logged on to the California Board of Psychology website and checked the list of disciplinary actions. Nothing on Gull or Larsen. Whatever Gull's transgressions had been, they'd remained private.

Which might very well be the point.

Had Gavin learned something that made him a threat to Gull?

Was the secret something to do with the Quick family? Why had Jerome Quick lied about Barry Silver being a golfing buddy? Why hadn't he told us that he, himself, had spearheaded the referral?

Did Quick have some kind of prior relationship with Koppel or Gull? Some specific reason he wanted Gavin under the group's care?

If so, he wasn't saying, and now Gavin was dead.

And so was his therapist.

I turned it over a couple of times, produced nothing but a headache, broke for a cup of coffee, found the machine empty, and was loading it when Ned Biondi called.

"Doc," he said. "Sorry for not keeping in touch, but I just moved, and the boxes aren't even unpacked."

"Oregon?"

"The other direction. Got myself a great little apartment on Coronado Island. Dinky little place because everything's so expensive, but what do I need, one guy."

I said, "It's pretty out there."

"Got a view of the bay, the bridge. Norma and I got divorced. To be accurate, I divorced her. Last year."

"Sorry to hear about it."

"Don't be, I should've done it years ago. She's a mean woman, terrible mother—you remember how she wouldn't give you the time of day, wouldn't participate in Anne Marie's treatment?"

"I do."

"Ice queen," he spit. "As far as I'm concerned she was a big part of Anne Marie's problem, I should've recognized it sooner. You probably saw it, but you couldn't come out and say that, right? 'Go divorce your wife, Ned.' You'd have said that, I'd have fired you. But you'd have been right."

"How's Anne Marie?"

"Mostly good," he said. "Not always great. She has her moods, but most of the time, good. That husband of hers is okay, and they just had a third kid. Career-wise, she never got it together, but she says she loves being a mom and why shouldn't I believe her? She's a terrific mom, the kids love her, Bob loves her. Do you know what made me realize I needed to divorce Norma?"

"What?"

"I decided to quit smoking. Finally got serious about it. So what does Norma do? Tries to talk me out of it, I'm talking a pitched battle. *She* didn't want to quit because smoking was something we did together—cigarettes and coffee in the morning, reading the paper. Taking walks and puffing away like the cancer fiends we were. She actually accused me of abandoning her by wanting to quit. I stuck to my guns, and she went ballistic. So I sat back and thought, 'Dummy, she doesn't care if you get sick or die, she just wants what she wants, it's all about her.' Thirty-five years too late, but what the hell, I'm here, and she moved to New York to write a novel and I'm wearing the patch and have worked myself down to seven Winstons a day."

"Congratulations."

"Thanks. So what can I do for you?"

I told him about the photo of the blond girl.

He said, "I'll make a call, but I'm sorry to say I can't promise you, Doc. The paper's not about public service—if it ever was. It's about peddling ad space, and that means going for the hook. From what you're telling me there's no juicy angle to this one."

"A double killing?" I said. "Two kids up on Mulholland?"

"Unfortunately L.A.'s more of a company town than it ever was, and juice means a Hollywood tie-in. Give me a klepto starlet boosting scanties on Rodeo, and I'll guarantee you lots of print inches. Two kids on Mulholland is tragic, but it ain't man bites dog."

"How about this for a hook: The police

didn't want to release the photo because it was too early in the investigation, but an anonymous source supplied it to the *Times*."

"Hmm," he said. "Maybe the editors will go for that, they've got a reflexive dislike of authority. Anytime they can show they're not in lockstep with LAPD it makes them feel the muckrackers they wish they were . . . okay, I'll try. By the way, is it true?"

"LAPD Communications didn't want to release it because they thought it lacked a hook."

He laughed. "Everyone's in showbiz. I'll call and get back to you. Anything more you can tell me about this girl?"

"Nothing," I said. "That's the problem."

"I'll see what I can do, Doc. Good talking to you—as long as I've got you, let me ask you something. Do you believe that study that came out, said guys do better married than single?"

"Depends on the guy," I said. "And the marriage."

"Exactly," he said. "You hit it on the head."

◆

Soon after I hung up, Milo called, and I told him Biondi would try to get the photo in.

"Thanks. Some of the prints came in from Koppel's house, and sure enough, Gull's are all over the place. Along with a bunch of others we can't identify. One we could tag was some guy who showed up in the system because of an assault record, turns out he works for a heating and air-conditioning company, did a service call a month ago. His latents were on the furnace and nowhere else, so that fits. The assault was punching a guy in a bar."

"Like Roy Nichols," I said.

"Lots of anger out there. If people only knew who they let into their homes."

"Do Gull's prints mean much?" I said. "Given his relationship with Koppel?"

"That's what he'd say. What his lawyer would say. He hired a B.H. mouthpiece, by the way. Don't know him, but one of the guys here does. Not high-powered, more like medium-powered."

"Meaning Gull's not that scared?"

"He's scared enough to lawyer up," he said. "Maybe he doesn't know better. Or couldn't afford better. He's got his baby Benz and his Vette, but he's not really rich, right? Even with a hefty fee, you guys are limited by the hours you work."

"Interesting you should bring that up," I said. I told him what Allison had said about profit motive.

"Kill Koppel and steal her patients . . . smart girl, Allison . . . I'd sure like to get into Gull's finances but can't see a way to do it yet."

"How'd it go with Gavin's room?"

"It didn't," he said. "No one home, I'll try tomorrow."

"I spoke to Dr. Singh." I recapped the interview.

"Jerry Quick lied," he said. "What was the point of that?"

"Good question."

"It's time to pay Mom and Dad a closer look. Meanwhile, I've been trying to arrange an appointment with Mr. Edward Koppel, but I can't get past his receptionist."

"The old tycoon shuffle?" I said.

"Seems to be. I figure the best thing's to drop in tomorrow morning. Early, say eight-thirty, maybe catch him before his day gets too tycoonish. You up for that?"

"Want me to drive?"

"What do you think?"

◆

He came by the next morning just before eight, marched into my kitchen, drank coffee and ate two bagels standing at the counter, and said, "Ready?"

I drove over the Glen into the Valley, then east, across Sepulveda, into the heart of Encino.

This was Boomtown Valley, high-rises shining like chrome in the morning sun, traffic jams worthy of downtown, the flavors of money and boosterism comingling easily. But Edward Koppel's office was located in a straggler from an earlier age: a shopworn, two-story stucco box on Ventura just past Balboa, stuck between a used-car lot crammed with secondhand Jaguars, Ferraris, and Rollses, and a storefront Mideastern restaurant.

Behind the building was a small, outdoor parking lot accessible through an alley, with most of the spaces marked RESERVED. Entrance was through a glass door. Identical setup to the building that housed Mary Lou Koppel's group, and I said so.

Milo said, "Here I was thinking some big-time executive suite setup. Maybe Koppel specializes in small buildings he can rent out easily. Why don't you park at the far end, over there."

He directed me to a spot where we could observe every vehicle that arrived. Over the next half hour, four vehicles did. Two compacts driven by young women, a bottled water delivery truck, and a faded green, ten-year-old Buick that disgorged a sloppy-looking, heavyset man wearing wrinkled pants and an oversized brown polo shirt. He carried a brown paper bag and looked half-asleep as he stumbled up the stairs.

Ten more minutes brought two more Toyotas bearing secretarial types. Soon after, the heavy man exited, and drove off, minus his sack.

"What was that?" I said. "A literal bagman?"

Milo frowned, read the face of his Timex, didn't answer.

Half an hour after we'd arrived, we were still sitting there. Milo seemed fine, eyes alive under half-closed, hooded lids, but I was getting itchy. I said, "Looks like Mr. K keeps tycoon's hours."

"Let's pay his office a visit."

◆

The ground floor of the building was divided into three offices: Landmark Realty, SK Development, and Koppel Enterprises. Above were a travel agency, a general contractor, and a secretarial service.

Milo tried the doorknob to Koppel Enterprises and Landmark Realty, found them locked. But SK Development was open for business.

We walked into a large, bright, open area, sectioned into cubicles by waist-high partitions. All four of the young women we'd seen in the parking lot sat at computers typing briskly. Three wore headsets.

At the rear was a door marked PRIVATE. Milo strode past the secretarial pool and tried it. Also locked. The sole typist without a headset got up and walked over to him. Midtwenties, pleasantly plain, she had short dark hair, freckles, and an easy smile, wore a tan cotton-poly pantsuit.

"Can I help you?"

"We're looking for Mr. Koppel."

"Sonny?" she said. "You just missed him."

"What's he look like?"

She glanced around, moved in close, cupped her hand over her mouth. "Kind of chubby. He was wearing a brown polo."

"Drives an old Buick?"

"That's him. Are you guys the police or something?"

Milo showed her the badge.

"Wow."

"Your name, ma'am?"

"Cheryl Bogard." She looked back at the other women. They continued typing.

"They taking dictation on those head-sets?" said Milo.

"Oh, no," said Bogard. "They're listening to music. Sonny has multiple CD tracks set up so they can listen to what they want."

"Good boss."

"The best."

"So, Cheryl Bogard, what do you guys do here?"

"Help take care of Sonny's properties. So how come *you* guys are here? Did one of the buildings get broken into?"

"Does that happen often?"

"You know how it is," she said. "With as many properties as Sonny owns, something's always happening somewhere."

"Real estate empire," said Milo.

"He's got a lot of stuff." Adding happily: "Keeps all of us busy. So where was the break-in this time?"

"Not important," said Milo. "So that was the boss. He didn't stay long."

"He just picked up some papers." She smiled. "Not what you were expecting, huh?"

Milo shook his head.

"You know what they say, Officer. Appearances can be deceiving."

"When's he coming back?"

"Hard to say. He's out on the road a lot. He's got properties in four counties, so that means lots of traveling. We kid him, say he should get himself a nice car, he can sure afford it. But he loves his Buick. Showing off isn't Sonny's thing."

"Low-key."

"He's a real nice guy."

"Could you call him for us?"

"Sorry," she said. "Sonny doesn't use a cell phone in the car. He's kind of old-fashioned, says he doesn't like being disturbed when he's thinking and also, it's not safe talking and driving."

"Safety-conscious," said Milo.

"He's a pretty careful guy. Is there any message you'd like me to give him? About which building had the break-in?"

"Thanks, but it would be better if we spoke directly."

"Okay," said Bogard. "I'll tell him you were here."

"No idea at all when he'll be back?"

"If I had to guess, I'd say late afternoon. If he comes back at all. You never know, with Sonny."

Milo gave her a card, and said, "In case we don't catch him today, please have him call."

"Sure." Cheryl Bogard returned to her cubicle, placed the card in front of her, looked up, and waved.

Milo started to leave, then changed his mind, went over to her, said something, listened to her reply.

As we stepped out into the hall, I said, "What did you ask her?"

"What was in the bag." He rubbed the side of his nose. "Tootsie Rolls, M&Ms, Almond Joy. Ol' Sonny brings candy for the girls. She said they were all watching their weight, ate very little of it. He finishes off what's left."

A block up from Sonny Koppel's corporate headquarters was a coffee shop with a forties-era starship poised for takeoff atop an aqua metal roof. Milo and I sat at the empty counter, sucked in the aroma of eggs crackling in grease, and ordered coffee from a waitress old enough to be our mother.

He cell-phoned DMV. The address on Edward Albert Koppel's driver's license was the building we'd just visited. He'd registered four cars: the Buick, a five-year-old Cutlass, a seven-year-old Chevy, and an eleven-year-old Dodge.

"Buys American," I said.

"You saw him," he said. "You figure Mary Lou would go for a guy like that?"

"They were married years ago, when he was in law school," I said. "Maybe he looked different."

"The Candy Man . . . his secretary sure seemed wholesome." He gulped down his coffee, drummed his fingers on the counter. "Kindly boss, noble patriot, all-around unpretentious guy . . . if it seems too good to be true, it probably is, right? Ready to go?"

"Where to?"

"You're going home, and I'm back to the Quicks' for that toss of Gavin's room. Did you have a chance to check the psych licensing board on Franco Gull?"

"Clean," I said.

"That so? Well, maybe Gavin didn't think so, and look what happened to him."

◆

It was two days before I heard from him again. Ned Biondi hadn't called, and my thoughts had drifted away from murders.

Robin came by and picked up Spike. Despite the two days of bonding, he reverted to instant disdain for me at the sight of her Ford pickup. Running to Robin as she crouched in the driveway, leaping into her arms, making her laugh.

She thanked me for babysitting and handed me a small blue gift box.

"Not necessary."

"I appreciate the help, Alex."

"How was Aspen?"

"Mean-looking men with bubble blond arm candy, lots of dead animal pelts, the most beautiful mountains I've ever seen." She played with an earring. Spike sat obediently at her feet.

"Anyway," she said.

When she moved in to kiss my cheek, I pretended not to notice, and pivoted in a way that made me unavailable.

I heard the truck door close. Robin was at the wheel, looking puzzled as she started up the engine.

I waved.

She returned the wave, hesitantly. Spike began licking her face, and she drove away.

I opened the blue box. Sterling cuff links, shaped like tiny guitars.

◆

When Milo finally called, I was getting out of the shower. "Mr. and Mrs. Quick appear to have taken a vacation. The house is locked up tight. Her van's there, but his car isn't, and a neighbor said she saw them loading suitcases."

"Taking some time off," I said.

"I need to get into that room. I called the sister—Paxton—but she hasn't gotten back to me yet. Onward to Mr. Sonny Koppel. He may drive old cars and dress like a slob, but it's not due to poverty. Guy has title to over two hundred parcels of real estate. Commercial and residential rentals, four counties, just like his girl said."

"Definitely a tycoon," I said.

"He's also got all sorts of holding companies and limited corporations as shields. It's taken me this long to winnow through the basics. This guy's big-time, Alex, and from what I can tell he likes to partner with the government."

"Federal?"

"Federal, state, county. A lot of his holdings seem to be cofinanced by public funds. We're talking low-cost housing projects, senior citizen residences, landmark buildings, assisted care. And guess what: halfway houses for parolees. Including the one on Sixth Street where Roland Kristof crashes.

The state legislature says we have to pay for the board and care of felonious individuals, and Koppel's cleaning up."

"Public-spirited," I said.

"It's a great arrangement. Find some building or construction project that's eligible for bond money or a grant, split your costs with John Q, take all the income. In terms of Koppel's background, all I can find is that he did his undergrad work and law school at the U. But he never practiced, and I can't locate any record of his taking the bar. Somehow he got bankrolled and built up an empire."

"Is the office building where Pacifica practices a government deal?"

"Doesn't seem to be," he said. "But not because it's in Beverly Hoohah. Koppel owns two B.H. properties—a senior residence hotel on Crescent Drive and a shopping center on La Cienega—that were financed with tax bucks. The hotel qualifies for an HUD gift and the strip mall got a FEMA grant because the stores that stood there before were earthquake-damaged."

"He knows how to work the system," I said.

"He works it well. The only time his name

appears on court documents is when he sues someone or someone sues him. Mostly the former—back-rent and eviction cases. Once in a while he gets tagged with a slip-and-fall by a tenant. Sometimes he settles, sometimes he fights. When he fights, he wins. He distributes his business among eight different law firms, all downtown, all white-shoe. But get this: He doesn't even live in a house, let alone a mansion. His primary residence—and it was hard to find—is an apartment on Maple Drive in Beverly Hills. Which sounds nice, but it's not one of the fancy condos, just an old building, kind of shabby, six units. One of Koppel's limited partnerships owns the place, and Koppel lives in a two-bedroom at the back. The manager doesn't even know her tenant's really her boss, because she referred to Koppel as 'the heavy guy, real quiet' and said the owners were some Persians who lived in Brentwood. On several of his rentals, Koppel hires a couple named Fahrizad to serve as his front."

"Elusive fellow," I said.

"Let's challenge that."

◆

Sonny Koppel's stretch of Maple Drive lay between Beverly Boulevard and Civic Center Drive. Mixed-use neighborhood, the west side filled by a granite-clad behemoth that served as Mercedes Benz headquarters, a high-profile, extravagantly landscaped office complex that catered to entertainment lawyers and film agents, and construction dust from a fulminating highrise.

Across the street were two-story apartment buildings, souvenirs of the postwar building boom. Koppel's was one of the dingiest examples, an off-gray traditional with a cheap composite roof. Three upstairs units, three down, a scratchy lawn, struggling shrubs.

Koppel's Buick was parked in back, squeezed into one of the half dozen slots in the open carport. We cruised and found each of Koppel's other cars parked within two blocks, each with Beverly Hills street parking permits that were up-to-date.

An Olds, a Chevy, a Dodge. Gray, gray, dark green. Lots of dust on the first two. The Dodge had been washed recently. I idled the Seville as Milo got out and examined each vehicle. Empty.

I parked, and we headed for Koppel's building.

◆

Sonny Koppel answered the door palming popcorn out of a chartreuse plastic bowl. The fragrance brought to mind the theater-lobby smell of Pacifica's building. Before Milo had his badge out, Koppel nodded as if he'd been expecting us and beckoned us in. He wore a royal blue U. sweatshirt over plaid pajama bottoms and fuzzy brown slippers.

Five-eight, 270 at least, with a melon gut and thinning reddish brown hair that frizzed above a high, glossy pate. He hadn't shaved in a couple of days, and his stubble looked like dandruff. Saggy blue eyes, pendulous lips, short, thick limbs, beefy hands with stubby nails.

Behind him, an old nineteen-inch RCA TV blared financial news from a cable station. Koppel lowered the volume.

"My girls told me you were by," he said, in a sleepy basso. "It's about Mary, right? I was wondering if you'd get in touch—here, sit, sit."

He stopped to study a stock quotation on

the tube, switched off the set, cleared a massive pile of newspapers off a plaid sofa, and brought them over to a metal-legged dinette table. Four red vinyl chairs ringed the table. Hardback ledgers filled two of them. Half the table surface was taken up by more ledgers and legal pads, pens, pencils, a hand calculator, cans of Diet 7-Up, snack bags of assorted carbohydrates.

The apartment was basic: white walls, low ceilings, a front space that served as the living room–eating area, a kitchenette, the bathroom and bedrooms beyond a stucco arch. Nothing on the walls. The kitchen was cluttered but clean. A few feet from the counter, a PC setup was perched on a rolling cart. Aquarium screen saver. An air conditioner rattled.

Sonny Koppel said, "Can I offer you guys something to drink?"

"No, thanks."

"You sure?"

"Positive."

Koppel's soft, bulky shoulders rose and fell. He sighed, sank into a green tweed La-Z-Boy recliner, kept the chair upright.

Milo and I took the plaid sofa.

"So," said Koppel, "what can I do for you?"

"First off," said Milo, "is there anything you can tell us about your ex-wife that could help us solve her murder?"

"I wish there was. Mary was a remarkable person—attractive, really smart." Koppel ran a hand over his scalp. Instead of settling, his hair picked up static and coiled as if alive. The room was dim and he was backlit with fluorescence from the kitchen and the hair became a halo. Sad-looking, pajama-bottomed guy with an aura.

"You're thinking," he said, "how did someone like her ever hook up with someone like me."

His lips curled like miniature beef roulades, approximating amusement. "When Mary and I met I didn't look like this. Back then I was more shortstop than sumo. Actually, I was a pretty decent jock, got a baseball scholarship to the U., had Major League fantasies."

He paused, as if inviting comment. When none followed, he said, "Then I ripped a hamstring and found out I had to actually study to get out of there."

One hand dipped into the popcorn bowl.

Koppel gathered a full scoop and transferred the kernels to his mouth.

Milo said, "You met Dr. Koppel when you were in law school?"

"I was in law school, and she was in grad school. We met at the rec center, she was swimming, and I was reading. I tried to pick her up, but she blew me off." He touched his abdomen as if it ached. "The second time I tried, she agreed to go out for coffee, and we hit it off great. We got married a year later and divorced two years after that."

"Problems?" said Milo.

"Everyone's got them," said Koppel. "What's the cliché—we grew apart? Part of the problem was time. Between her dissertation and my classes, we never saw each other. The *main* problem was I screwed up. Had an affair with a woman in my class. To make it worse, a married woman, so two families got messed up. Mary let me down easy, she just wanted a clean break. Stupidest thing I ever did."

"Cheating on her?"

"Letting her go. Then again, she probably would have broken it off, even if I had been faithful."

"Why's that?"

"I was kind of at loose ends back then," said Koppel. "No goals. Only reason I went to law school was because I didn't know what else to do. Mary was just the opposite: focused, put-together. She has"—He winced—"had a powerful persona. Charisma. I couldn't have kept up."

"Sounds like you're selling yourself short," said Milo.

Koppel looked genuinely surprised. "No, I don't think so."

"I've done some background on you, sir, and you're one of the biggest landlords in Southern California."

Koppel waved a thick hand. "That's just playing Monopoly."

"You've played well."

"I've been lucky." Koppel smiled. "I was lucky to be a loser."

"A loser?"

"I nearly flunked out of law school, then I chickened out of taking the bar. Started experiencing anxiety attacks about taking it that put me in the ER a couple of times. One of those pseudo–heart attack things? By then Mary and I were having our problems, but she helped me through it. Deep-breathing exercises, having me imagine relaxing scenes. It worked and the attacks stopped and Mary expected me to take the bar. I showed up early, looked around the room, walked out, and that was it. That bothered Mary more than my cheating on her. Soon after, she filed."

Koppel's hand waved again, this time limply. "Couple months after that, my mother died and left me an apartment building in the Valley, so all of a sudden I was a landlord. A year later, I sold that property, used the profit and a bank loan to invest in a bigger building. I did that for a few years—flipping and trading up. Real estate was booming, and I made out okay."

He shrugged, ate more popcorn.

Milo said, "You're a modest man, Mr. Koppel."

"I know what I am and what I'm not." Koppel turned his head to the side, as if recoiling from insight. His jowls quivered. "Do you have any idea who murdered Mary?"

"No, sir. Do you?"

"Me? No, of course not."

"She was murdered in her home," said Milo. "No signs of forced entry."

"You're saying someone she knew?" said Koppel.

"Any candidates, sir?"

"I wasn't privy to Mary's social life."

"How much contact did you and she have?"

"We stayed friendly, and I kept up my spousal support."

"How much support?"

"It evolved," said Koppel. "Immediately after the divorce, she got nothing except the furniture in our apartment because we were both starving students. When I started to earn a decent income, she called and asked for support. We agreed on a figure and over the years I've increased it."

"At her request?"

"Sometimes. Other times, I decided to share some of my good luck."

"Keep the ex happy," said Milo.

Koppel didn't answer.

"Sir, how much were you paying her at the time of her death?"

"Twenty-five thousand a month."

"Generous."

"It seemed fair," said Koppel. "She stuck with me when I needed her. Helping through those panic attacks even after I cheated on her. That deserves something."

Milo said, "Twenty-five thousand a month.

I went through her bank records, never saw any back-and-forth on that level."

"You wouldn't," said Koppel. "Mary lived off her practice and re-invested what I gave her."

"In what?"

"We're partnered on some of my properties."

"She let you hold on to what you owed her and put it back in properties."

"Mary did very well partnering with me."

"Who gets her share of the partnered properties now that she's dead?"

Koppel's fingers grazed the rim of the popcorn bowl. "That would depend on Mary's will."

"I haven't found a will, and no executors have come forth."

"That wouldn't surprise me," said Koppel. "For years I've been telling her to do some estate planning. Between her practice and the properties, she was building up a comfortable estate. You'd think she'd have listened, being so organized about everything else. But she was resistant. My opinion is she didn't want to think about death. Her parents died pretty young, and sometimes she had premonitions."

"About dying young?"

"About dying before her time." Tears beaded Koppel's lower eyelashes. The rest of his stubbled face was impassive.

"She have those premonitions recently?"

Koppel said, "I don't know. I'm talking back when we were married."

Milo said, "Assuming there's no will, what happens to her real estate holdings?"

"If there are no creditors or heirs," said Koppel, "they'd revert to me. A hundred percent in the case of the ones whose mortgages I carry—I own a little financing company, allows me to keep things in-house. Those that are bank-financed, I'd have the choice of paying off Mary's share or selling."

"One way or the other, you'd get everything."

"Yes, I would."

Milo crossed his legs.

Koppel emitted a deep, rumbling laugh.

"Something funny, sir?"

"The implication," said Koppel. "I suppose there's a logic to it, Lieutenant, but do the math: Mary Lou's holdings net out to . . . I'd say one and a half, maybe two million dollars, depending on the real estate market. I grant you that isn't chicken feed.

Eventually, she could've retired nicely. But to me, a sum like that isn't significant . . . you say you've looked into my holdings?"

"Two million's a drop in the bucket," said Milo.

"That sounds ostentatious," said Koppel, "but it's true. A couple of million wouldn't make any difference."

"During good times," said Milo.

"Times *are* good," said Koppel. "Times are *always* good."

"No business problems?"

"With business, there are always problems. The key is to see them as challenges." Koppel placed the popcorn bowl between his knees. "What makes it easier for me is I have no interest in acquiring material goods. I do real estate because it seems to be what I'm good at. Since I don't need much—without the burden of *stuff*—I've always got free cash. Meaning there's no such thing as a bad market. Prices go down, I buy. They go up, I sell."

"Life is good," said Milo.

"I'd like to get back into shape physically, and I'm upset about Mary. But when I step back and assess, yes, I have a lot to be thankful for."

"Tell me about the halfway houses you own, sir."

Koppel blinked. "You really have been doing your research."

"I ran into an ex-con vacuuming Dr. Koppel's building and I got curious."

"Oh," said Koppel. "Well, I hire a lot of those guys for custodial work. When they show up, they do a good job."

"They give you attendance problems?"

"No worse than anyone else."

"What about pilferage problems?"

"Same answer, people are people. Over the years, I've lost a few tools, some furniture, but that goes with the territory."

"Your secretary said properties get broken into."

"From time to time," said Koppel. "Not the halfway houses, though. What's to take from there?"

"You recruit your own tenants as janitors?"

"I get recommendations from the halfway-house managers. They send me guys they think are reliable." Koppel lifted the popcorn bowl.

"How'd you get into the parolee business?"

"I'm in the real estate business. A handful of my properties are halfway houses."

"How'd you get into that, sir?"

"I'd never have done it on my own. I'm a bleeding heart liberal but only to a point. It was Mary's idea. Actually, I was pretty wary, but she won me over."

"How'd she come up with the idea?"

"I think Dr. Larsen suggested it—one of her partners. Have you talked to him yet?"

Milo nodded.

"He's an expert on prison reform," said Koppel. "He got Mary into it, and she was all afire. She said she wanted to do more than build up equity, she wanted her investments to do some social good."

"The halfway houses are the properties she partners with you?"

"We're also together on some conventional rentals."

"Pretty idealistic."

"When Mary believed in something, she got very focused."

"But you tried to un-focus her."

Koppel lifted a leg in order to cross it, changed his mind, and planted a heavy foot on the carpet. "I approached the issue like a businessman, let's look at the assets and debits. Mary did her homework, showed me the subsidies the state was offering and I had to admit the figures looked good. Even so, I was concerned about tenant damage, so I'd look at the crowd you're talking about. I also told her I could get equal or better subsidies on what seemed to be safer investments—senior citizen housing, historic properties, where, if you respected the integrity of the structure, you could get three *separate* funding sources."

His eyes had dried, and he was talking faster. In his element.

Milo said, "Mary convinced you."

"Mary said the tenants would be more reliable, not less, because they weren't paying rent so they had no incentive to leave. On top of that, the state mandated supervision by parole officers and provided in-house managers and security guards. She had to work on me for a while, but I agreed to give it a try. Smartest thing I ever did."

"Good deal?"

"The funding's ironclad—long-term state grants that get renewed easily—and the properties can be had dirt cheap because they're always in fringe areas. You're not going to stick a building full of criminals in

Bel Air, right? So there are no NIMBYs, no zoning problems, and once you get past financing the part the state doesn't cover, the rents are great. And listen to this: On a square-footage basis, the income's close to Beverly Hills, because you're not talking multiroom apartments, it's all single rooms. And as opposed to a senior citizen situation where the tenancy-terminating event is death so your occupancy is uncertain, you go in knowing the tenants are there on a short-term deal but they're always going to be replenished."

"No shortage of bad guys."

"Doesn't seem to be," said Koppel. "And turns out there are *fewer* repairs. The bathrooms are all communal, so the plumbing's centralized, there are no kitchens in the rooms, all the tenants get is hot plates. And their use is restricted to certain hours. There's some paperwork, but nothing I haven't seen before. And, let's face it, the state wants you to be a success."

"Define 'success.' "

"The residents stay put and don't roam out in the community to hurt or kill someone."

"Where do I sign?" said Milo.

Koppel smiled. "I should've known listening to Mary would never lead me wrong." He shifted his bulk in the recliner. "Now she's gone. I can't believe it—is there anything else I can tell you?"

"Back to the halfway houses, sir. Great deal notwithstanding, have you ever had any problems with tenant violence?"

"Not to my knowledge. But I wouldn't know."

"Why not?"

"All that's handled in-house," said Koppel. "I'm not a warden. I just own the building, and the state runs it. Why, do you think one of those lowlifes killed Mary?"

"There's no evidence of that," said Milo. "Just covering all bases." He opened his pad. "What's Charitable Planning all about?"

"My foundation," said Koppel. "I give away ten percent a year. Of after-tax income."

"We've been in the building a few times and never saw any activity on the ground floor."

"That's because there isn't much. Twice a month, I go in and write checks to worthy causes. It takes a while because the solicitations come in constantly, everything really piles up."

"An entire ground-floor suite for you to write checks? That's Beverly Hills space, Mr. Koppel. Why don't you rent it out?"

"I had a deal, last year, for a tenant to take the whole floor. An online brokerage. You know what happened to the market. The deal fell through. I was planning to subdivide—rent most of it out and leave a small office for Charitable Planning. But Mary asked me to put a hold on that until she and Larsen and Gull could decide if they wanted it."

"Why would they want it?"

"To expand their practice. They were talking about doing group therapy, needed larger rooms. The only space I use is a small office, the rest is empty. Mary was supposed to tell me in a week or so."

"Group therapy," I said.

"From a business standpoint, I thought it was a smart idea. Treat the max number of patients in the shortest time. I joked with Mary that it had sure taken her a long time to figure it out." Koppel smiled. "She said, 'Sonny, you're the moneyman, and I'm the healer. Let's stick to what we know."

He tugged the side of his mouth, ate some popcorn.

Milo showed him the picture of the dead girl.

Koppel chewed faster, swallowed hard. "Who's that?"

"Someone else who got killed."

"Someone else? Related to Mary?"

"Don't know, sir."

"You're saying what happend was *part* of something . . . that it wasn't just Mary?"

Milo shrugged.

"What's really going on, Lieutenant?"

"That's all I can tell you, sir. Does the name Flora Newsome mean anything to you?"

Koppel shook his head. Glanced at the photo. "That's her?"

"What about Gavin Quick?"

"I know a Quick," said Koppel, "but not Gavin."

"Who do you know?"

"Jerry Quick—Jerome Quick. He's one of my tenants. Who's Gavin? His son? The one who had the accident?"

"You know about the accident."

"Jerry told me about it, said his son was

having some emotional problems. I referred him to Mary."

"How long has Mr. Quick been your tenant?"

"Four months." He frowned.

"Good tenant?" said Milo.

"He pays his rent, but not always on a timely basis. I felt a little . . . used. Especially after I listened to his problems and gave him a referral. I've had to pay Jerry a few visits." He smiled. "That's not what it sounds like—no goons with baseball bats, we just talked, and, eventually, he paid."

"Why would I assume goons with baseball bats, sir?"

Koppel flushed. "You wouldn't. So what's with Gavin?"

"He's deceased."

"Murdered also?"

"Yes, sir."

"My God—what's the connection to Mary?"

"All we know at this time was that Gavin was her patient, and they're both dead."

"My God," Koppel repeated. "There's a lot you can't tell me."

"Is there something more you could tell us, sir?"

Koppel considered that. "I wish there was. Mary and I—we rarely spoke, except when there was a business issue. Even then, there was little to talk about. I set up our partnership so she didn't have to be hands-on. She had her practice, she didn't need to be distracted. Because properties can be demanding. To make them work you have to give them attention like children. I'm on the road all the time."

"All those cars," said Milo.

"I know, I know, it probably seems eccentric, but I need to have reliable transportation . . . Jerry's son? He was young, right? Just a kid."

"He was twenty."

Koppel's face had turned an unhealthy color—bologna left too long in the fridge. "You can't tell me anything?"

"The truth is, we don't know much ourselves."

"Quick's son . . . the girl you showed me—Flora—was she a patient of Mary's, as well?"

"The girl we showed you hasn't been identified yet, so I don't know if she was one of Dr. Koppel's patients. The files are confidential, we can't get in there."

"All those questions you asked me," said Koppel, "about the halfway houses. Are you saying you suspect one of my—one of those tenants had something to do with something really horrible? If you do, please tell me. I really need to know if you do."

"Do you think that's a possibility, sir?"

"How would I have a *clue*?" Koppel bellowed. One of his hands moved spasmodically, knocked against the popcorn bowl, sent it flying.

Yellow rain. When it settled, Koppel was covered with kernels and husks and dust.

He stared at us, breathing heavily. Milo went into the kitchen and unrolled a paper towel from a wooden spool. He came back and began brushing Koppel off. Koppel snatched the paper away and flailed at himself. When he finally stopped, yellow grit clung to his sweatshirt and his pajamas.

He sat there, staring at us, still panting.

Milo said, "What else can you tell us about Jerome Quick?"

Koppel didn't answer.

"Sir?"

"I'm sorry. For losing my temper. But you're freaking me out. First Mary, now Jerry Quick's son. That girl."

Milo repeated his question.

"He didn't pay his rent on time, that's it. His excuse was the up-and-down nature of his business. He trades metals, makes deals on scrap. Once in a while he has a windfall that carries him for a while; other times, he loses money. To me it sounded more like gambling than business. Had I known, I never would have rented to him."

"He didn't tell you?"

"He came to me through a leasing agent. In the past they'd been reliable," said Koppel. "It's not as if his rent is prohibitive. I keep all my rents reasonable, want the turnover low."

He looked down and picked stray bits of popcorn from his pajamas. Dropped the first few into the bowl. Ate the rest.

"His son. Poor Jerry. Guess I'll need to cut him some slack." Suddenly, he stood with surprising grace, brushed himself off some more, sat back down.

"What kind of emotional problems did Jerry Quick describe?"

"He didn't get specific. At first I wasn't sure I even believed him. He brought it up when we were having one of our rent discussions. Second month's rent, and he's already twenty days late. I dropped by to talk about it, and he gave me a sob story about how he'd been cheated out of a deal, lost big, and now on top of it his kid was having psychological problems."

"Which he didn't specify."

"I wasn't interested. Figured he was just trying to make me feel sorry for him. The way the referral came about is I called his bluff, said, 'If that's the case, why don't you get him some help?' and he said, 'Yeah, I need to do that.' And I said, 'My ex-wife's a psychologist, and her office is close to your house. You want her number?' He said sure, and I gave it to him. Like I said, I thought it was a dodge. So he actually followed through."

Milo nodded. "How's he been with the rent since then?"

"Chronically late."

"Dr. Koppel never told you about the referral?"

"She'd *never* do that," said Koppel. "Confidentiality, she was big on that. The whole time we were married she never talked about patients. That's another thing I admired about her. Her ethics."

"Mr. Koppel," said Milo, "where were you the night your ex-wife was murdered?"

"You're kidding."

"No, sir."

"Where was I? I was here."

"Alone?"

"Don't rub it in," said Koppel. "That night . . . let's see, that night I think I ran into Mrs. Cohen, the art teacher—in the front unit. Both of us were taking out the garbage. Are you going to ask her? If you do, could you please not mention that I'm her landlord?"

"It's a secret?" said Milo.

"I like to keep a low profile. That way I can come home and relax and not have tenants calling me up for repairs."

"A private home would accomplish that."

"Yeah, yeah, I'm eccentric," said Koppel. "The problem with a house is too much maintenance, and my whole life's about that. Also, I don't need the space."

"Not a lot of stuff."

"What's so sane about accumulating stuff?"

"So you were here all night, sir?"

"Like I always am. Unless I'm on the road."

"How often are you on the road?"

"One, two days a week."

"Where do you stay?"

"Motels. I like Best Western. But I was home that night."

Milo got up. "Thank you, sir."

"You're welcome," said Koppel, tweezing popcorn from his clothes.

The sensitive tycoon," said Milo, when we were back on the sidewalk. "You buying it?"

"I think when it comes to money he'd be something to reckon with. You're not going to check with Mrs. Cohen, the art teacher?"

"What, to verify his alibi? All she saw was him taking out the garbage. Five minutes out of a whole evening, big deal."

"You see him as a suspect?"

"He's landlord to a bunch of cons, and he was shelling out twenty-five grand a month to Koppel. Now that she's dead, not only do the payments stop, he gets all her real estate. That's a hell of a lot of motive. Also, he goes on about being an efficient businessman but keeps an entire floor of a Beverly Hills building vacant. I'd love to get in there, find out what Charitable Planning is really all about."

"Group therapy," I said. "If Sonny was really as enamored of Mary as he made out, I can see him holding the space vacant for her."

"What, you don't see him as a potential bad guy?"

"The way you lay it out, he definitely belongs on the radar screen. But what motive would he have for killing Gavin and the blonde?"

He didn't answer. We headed for my car.

I said, "How's the surveillance on Gull going?"

"He goes to work, returns home. I'm sure his lawyer told him to keep a clean nose."

"The lie about Gavin's referral could be Jerry Quick wanting to hide the fact that he got Mary Lou's name from Sonny. Because if we interviewed Sonny, we'd know he's a deadbeat tenant. Having it come from a physician makes it sound a lot more respectable."

"I guess," he said. "But his kid was killed, you'd think he'd want to be forthcoming."

"Another thing," I said, "is that Sonny sent Gavin directly to Mary Lou, but Gull ended up with the case anyway. Then it *reverted* to Mary. Sonny may be involved somehow, but I can't shake the notion that Gavin's death was connected to his treatment. Same for Flora Newsome. We're talking two patients and their therapist, all dead."

"All skewered," he said. "Someone they all knew. Or who knew them. But maybe nothing to do with the treatment. Some con sent over by Sonny to clean the building spotted them and decided to play. Some real psychopath who's worked the system and passed himself along as a nonviolent parolee. I'll ask Sonny for a list of maintenance guys, see who pops up. Meanwhile, let's go over to the Quick house, again. Maybe Jerry and Sheila returned from wherever it was they went, and I can have a go at Gavin's mess."

◆

I took Gregory Drive all the way to Camden. As we pulled up to the Quick house, Milo said, "Same as before: her car's here, his isn't. Don't bother getting out, this probably won't take long."

He sprang out of the Seville, trotted to the front door, rang the bell. Tapped his foot. Rang again. Shook his head and was about to leave when the door swung halfway open.

I caught a glimpse of Sheila Quick's drawn face.

Milo talked to her. Turned to me. Mouthed, "Come in."

◆

"We were at my sister's house in Westlake Village," she said. Her hair was turbaned by a blue towel, and she wore a quilted beige robe patterned with butterflies and clematis vines. Stains on the robe. Her face was drawn and chalky, eyes stripped of illusion.

"You and your husband?" said Milo.

"Jerry wanted to get away for a couple days." She spoke slowly, slurred, worked hard at forming words. I'd guessed tranquilizers, then I smelled her breath. Lots of wintergreen but not enough to mask the alcohol.

The three of us were standing in her dining room. The space felt heavy, smothering. Where light hit the furniture it exposed a coating of dust.

"Your husband wanted to get away," said Milo.

"From the stress." Sheila Quick's lips curled in distaste.

I said, "You didn't want to go?"

"Eileen," she said. "She thinks her house is the greatest . . . that paddle tennis court of hers. As far as she's concerned why *wouldn't* I want to go?"

She looked to me for confirmation. I nodded.

"Jerry," she said. "Whatever Jerry wants, Jerry gets. You know what I think?"

"What?"

"I think Jerry wanted to stick *me* there. So he *stuck* me there. And went on his merry way."

"He didn't stay at Eileen's."

"I was supposed to be happy because Eileen has a pool and that paddle tennis court. It's not even a full tennis court, it's half of that." She took hold of my sleeve. "We were going to build a pool, Gavin liked to swim."

She threw up her hands. "I hate chlorine. It makes me itch. Why would I be happy just 'cause there's a pool? I wanted Jerry to bring me back. Finally, he called, and I *told* him to bring me back." Woozy smile. "So, here I am."

"Where's Jerry?" I said.

"Working. Somewhere."

"Out of town?"

She nodded. "As usul—usuizul . . . it's funny."

"What is?"

"Jerry hates Eileen. But wanted to stick me in her house so he could Godknowswhat . . . It wasn't right."

She ticked her fingers, talked in a singsong. "Eileen has *her* house, I have *my* house."

"You like your privacy," I said.

"I don't like her pool. It itches. I don't play paddle tennis. She and her husband go to work, I'm left there with all the . . . all the *quiet*. What am I supposed to *do* all day? But Jerry . . . Eileen asked me last week to come over, and Jerry told her forget it. Then he changed his mind. What's *that* all about? I'll tell you what it's about."

But she didn't.

Milo said, "Where's Mr. Quick currently traveling?"

"Who knows? Who knows where he goes? He's like a bird." She waved her hands. "Bye-bye birdie, flew the coop. I stay here. I never leave here, this is my house. Jerry doesn't call. He doesn't want to hear from me."

She squeezed my arm. "It's in . . . consistenant. One day, she's a stuck-up bitch who thinks her shit is perfume. Unquote. Next day he's driving me there and going back to clean up Gavin's room, then he's off. Doing his thing. His thingamjig."

"He cleaned Gavin's room," said Milo.

"He sure *did*! You know what *I* think? I think *that* was it."

"What was?"

"He knew I'd get mad if he cleaned up Gavin's room, so he snuck around me."

"He cleaned the room while you were at Eileen's."

"It was a mess," said Sheila Quick. "We have no disagreement on that, no question about it being a mess. A big. Fat. Mess. Gavin used to be neater, then he had an accident." She let go of my sleeve, swayed, held on to a chair for balance. "Did I tell you about that?"

I said, "Why do you think Jerry decided to clean up the mess?"

"Ask *him*." Smile. "Except you can't.

'Cause he's not here. He's *never* here. I'm *always* here."

The cords of her neck tightened. "I didn't want him to clean Gav's room. I would've gotten mad, I *loved* the mess. It was *Gav's* mess, what was the *rush*?"

She buried her face in her hands and began sobbing. I guided her to a sofa.

Milo went up the stairs.

◆

He came down ten minutes later. I'd gone into the kitchen, found a coffeemaker half-filled with lukewarm coffee, warmed it in the microwave, and brought it to Sheila Quick, guessing on nondairy creamer and one packet of artificial sweetener. Dirty dishes filled the sink. The counters were grimy. Not far from the machine was a nearly empty bottle of Tanqueray gin and a tube of Binaca breath spray.

I held the cup as she drank. Her mouth was still trembling and she dribbled and I wiped her chin.

She glanced up at me. "You're nice. Good-looking, too."

Milo strode into the living room. "Ma'am, I recall a computer in Gavin's room."

"Yes, you do."

"Where is it?"

"Jerry took it, said he was donating it to Beverly Vista School."

"What about Gavin's papers?"

"He boxed everything up and took it out to the garbage."

"Garbage was picked up when?"

"Tomorrow."

He left.

Sheila Quick said, "*He's* in a hurry."

I said, "Jerry was really eager to clean Gavin's room."

"Eager beaver. Eager, eager beaver."

I nodded.

"He said we needed to face reality," said Sheila Quick. "It must've been me. Crying too much, getting on his nerves crying all the time. I don't do anything for him."

I thought she meant the attraction was gone, but she went on: "I don't *want* to do anything for him. He comes home from work, wants his dinner, maybe I open a can. He says, 'Let's go out.' I say no. Why should I *want* to go out? Why should I *want* that?"

I said, "There's nothing for you outside of this house."

"That's *right*. You understand." To no one: "He *understands*."

Milo returned, looking grim.

She patted my shoulder, and said, "He understands."

"He's a very understanding guy," said Milo.

Sheila Quick said, "Jerry cleaned up so I would face reality. My fucking ducking husband *doesn't* get it. He shouldn't have done it without asking me! There were things I wanted to keep." She brightened. "Is it all out there—in the alley? In the garbage Dumpster?"

Milo said, "I'm sorry, ma'am. Your Dumpster's empty."

"Bastard," she said. "For what he did, he should be . . . it was wrong. Who cares where he is? Who the hell *cares*?"

"Has he called?"

"He left a message last night. I was sleeping. I sleep a lot. I erased it. What's he going to tell me? That he misses me? I know he's with some whore. When he travels he's always with whores. Know how I know?"

"How, ma'am?"

"Condoms," she said. "I find condoms in his luggage. He has me unpack, leaves them there, wants me to know." Sick smile. "Doesn't bother me—makes me . . . happy."

"His going to prostitutes?"

"Sure," she said. "Better them than me."

◆

We got a little more coffee in her, but her voice remained thick. I wondered how long it had taken her to work the gin bottle down.

She yawned. "I need to take a nap."

"Sure, ma'am," said Milo. "Just a few more questions, please."

"Please?" She unraveled the towel turban and tossed it on the floor. "Okay, since you said *please*."

"Who referred you to Dr. Koppel?"

"Dr. Silver."

"Your obstetrician?"

Her eyes closed, and her head lurched forward, then froze in place.

"I'm tired."

"Dr. Barry Silver?" said Milo. "Your gynecologist?"

"Uh-huh."

"Did Dr. Silver give you the referral personally?"

"He gave it to Jerry, Jerry called him.

Jerry said he was smart—can I *sleep*, please?"

"One more thing, ma'am. Gavin's room was cleaned out, but I noticed his clothes were still in the closet."

"Jerry was probably gonna take those, too, and give 'em away. Those really pretty Ralph Lauren shirts I bought Gav for Christmas. Gav loved to go shopping with me because Jerry's so cheap. We went to all the stores. Gap, Banana Republic, Saks . . . Barneys. Sometimes we went on Rodeo Drive when they had the end-of-season sales. I got Gav a Valentino sports jacket on Rodeo, better than anything Jerry has. Jerry prolly woulda given Gav's clothes away, but he didn't have time."

Her hands balled into fists. "Jerry can *fuck* himself if he thinks I'll give up Gav's clothes."

◆

We helped her up the stairs and into a master bedroom turned to night by blackout drapes. Rumpled tissues and night shades and two small airline liquor bottles on the nightstand. Bourbon and Scotch. A quarter inch of water floated in a crystal highball glass.

Milo tucked her in and she smiled up at him and licked chapped lips. "Nighty-night."

"One more question, ma'am. Who's your husband's accountant?"

"Gene Marr. With an H."

"Maher?" said Milo.

She started to answer, gave up, closed her eyes.

By the time we were out of the room, she was snoring.

◆

Before we exited the house, Milo brought me to Gavin's room. The same pale blue walls, stripped. The queen bed made up with a deep blue comforter. Gavin's bookcase held a few softcovers and magazines, and two model airplanes. The carpeting was dingy.

The closet was filled with jackets, slacks, shirts, coats.

"Nice wardrobe," I said. "Jerry didn't take the papers out to the garbage. He made sure no one would see them."

Milo nodded and pointed to the stairs.

◆

As we drove away, he said, "Bastard knows why his son was killed, and he's trying to hide it."

He found Quick's business number in his notes, phoned, waited, snapped the phone shut. "Not even a machine."

"He travels and gives blue-nailed Angie the secretary time off."

"Angie of the petty but very definite criminal record. Quick's starting to smell like something more than a grieving dad."

"His landlord hires troubled souls, and so does he," I said. "Maybe compassion's contagious. Or Sonny sent him Angela Paul, as well."

"Sonny the fixer? Get you a medical referral, invest your money."

"Maybe Quick was into him for more than back rent."

"His own kid, and he doesn't say a word."

"Maybe it's more than knowing," I said. "What if he's implicated?"

"Wouldn't that be pretty."

"What'd you find in Gavin's pockets?"

"Who says I found anything?"

"Those questions about Gavin's clothing.

You didn't need ten minutes to flip through a few books and pockets."

He slapped a slow three-four beat on the dashboard with one big palm. "Bastard took the computer—should I even bother calling Beverly Vista school to see if he donated it?"

Without waiting for an answer, he made the call, hung up grinning with rage. "First they've heard about it. You wanna know what I think? Gavin found out about something dirty going on in that building—something to do with Koppel and Charitable Planning and *Daddy*. The kid fancied himself an investigative reporter and figured he'd got himself a nice little scandal. Brain-damaged, but he kept some sort of records. And his old man destroyed them. My damn fault, I shoulda gone through that room first thing."

"What'd you find in the closet?" I said.

He opened to the center of his pad and showed me something sandwiched there, encased in a plastic evidence bag.

Wrinkled sheet of paper the size of an index card. Miniature lined paper, from a pad not unlike Milo's. Numbers written in blue ink. Cramped, smudged. A wavering col-

umn of seven-digit number-letter combina-
tions.

"License plate numbers?"

"That would be my guess," said Milo.
"Stupid kid was *surveilling*."

30

Milo said, "Drop me back at the station. Gonna run these numbers, then head over to the Hall of Records, see if I can find any other link between Jerry Quick and Sonny beyond tenancy. If I leave soon, I can make it downtown in time."

"Want me to take you straight there?"

"No, this is gonna be tedious, I'll do it alone. I also want to talk to Quick's accountant. Luckily CPAs don't get confidentiality. Any word from the *Times* on running the picture?"

"Not yet."

"If your pal Biondi doesn't come through, I'm having a chitchat with my habitually unresponsive *capitan*. He hates seeing my face, so maybe I can promise not to surface for another year if he goes over the heads of those losers in Community Relations and gets someone to push the media. With all the deceit on this one I don't need a victim I can't identify."

"I'll try Ned again."

"Good," he said. "Thanks. Let me know, either way."

◆

I phoned Coronado Island.

Ned Biondi said, "No one called you? Jesus. I'm sorry, Doc. I thought it was worked out. Okay, let me see what's going on, I'll get back to you ASAP."

An hour later, the phone rang.

"Mr. Delaware?" Plummy, theatrical baritone. Every syllable, foreplay.

"Speaking."

"This is Jack Mc*Tell*. From the Los Angeles *Times*. You've got a picture you'd like us to *run*."

"Picture of a homicide victim," I said. "An LAPD detective would like it run, but his superiors don't think it's got enough of a hook for you."

"Well," he said, "I certainly can't *promise* anything."

"Should I bring it by?"

"If you *choose*."

◆

Times headquarters was on First Street, in a massive gray stone building that studded the heart of downtown. I got stuck in freeway mucus, trolled for parking, finally scored a space in an overpriced stacked lot five blocks away.

Three security guards patrolled the *Times*'s massive, echoing lobby. They let several people pass but stopped me. Two of the uniforms made a show of staring me down as the third called up to Jack McTell's office, barked my name into the phone, hung up, and told me to wait. Ten minutes later, a young, crew-cut woman in a black sweater and jeans and hiking boots emerged from the elevator. She looked around, saw me, and headed my way.

"You're the person with the picture?" A *Times* badge said Jennifer Duff. Her left eyebrow was pierced by a tiny steel barbell.

"This is for Mr. McTell."

She held out her hand, and I gave her the

envelope. She took it delicately, between thumb and forefinger, as if it was tainted, turned her back, and left.

I blew another twenty minutes waiting for the parking lot attendant to move six other cars and free the Seville. I used the time to leave Milo a message that the *Times* had the photo, and it was up to the editors' good graces. By now, he was downtown, too, reading microfiche at the Hall of Records, just a couple of blocks away.

Cars were queued up at the 101 on-ramp, so I took Olympic Boulevard west. Avoiding another jam wasn't all of it. That route took me past Mary Lou Koppel's office building.

I made it to Palm Drive by three-thirty, hooked a left, and swung around into the back alley. Gull's and Larsen's Mercedeses were there, along with a few other late-model luxury cars. Next to the handicapped slot, a copper-colored van was stationed. A white stick-on sign on its flanks read:

THRIFTY CARPET AND DRAPERY CLEANING

A Pico address near La Brea. A 323 number.

The rear glass doors had been propped

open with a wooden triangle. I parked and got out.

The corridor smelled like stale laundry. The polyester beneath my feet seeped and made little sucking sounds. At the far end of the hall, a man pushed an industrial shampooer in lazy circles.

Two doors of the Charitable Planning suite were propped open the same way. Mechanical groan from inside. I had a look.

Another man, short, stocky, Hispanic, wearing rumpled gray work clothes, guided an identical machine over the thin, blue indoor-outdoor felt that covered Charitable's floor. His back was to me, and the din overrode my footsteps.

To the right was a small office. A swivel chair had been lifted and placed atop a scarred steel desk. Off in the corner was a rollaway typing table that hosted an IBM Selectric. On the desktop, next to the chair, were five rubber-banded bundles of mail.

I checked out return addresses. United Way, Campaign for Literacy, the Thanksgiving Fund, the Firefighters Ball. I flipped through all the bundles.

Everyone wanted Sonny Koppel's money.

The rest of the suite was one enormous

room with high, horizontal windows covered by cheap nylon drapes. Empty save for a couple of dozen folding chairs stacked against the wall. The Hispanic man flicked off the machine, straightened slowly, as if in pain, ran his hand through his hair, reached into his pocket for a cigarette, and lit up. Still with his back to me.

He smoked, was careful to drop the ash in his cupped hands.

I said, "Hi."

He turned. Surprise, but no con wariness. He looked at his cigarette. Blinked. Shrugged. *"No permisa?"*

"Doesn't bother me," I said.

Resigned smile. No hardness around his eyes, no sloppy tattoos. *"Usted no es el patron?"*

You're not the boss?

"No," I said. "Not today."

"Hokay." He laughed and smoked. "Mebbe tomorrow."

"I'm thinking of renting the space."

Blank stare.

I pointed to the wet carpet. "Nice job— *muy limpia.*"

"Gracias."

I left wondering what he'd cleaned up.

◆

Sonny Koppel had been truthful about Charitable Planning, but what did that mean? Perhaps parceling out partial truths was a strategic defense.

All that B.H. square footage left vacant in case Mary Lou needed it.

If Milo was right about Gavin hanging around, spying, writing down license numbers, what had the boy seen?

Empty room. Two dozen folding chairs.

What more did you need for group therapy?

Had the sessions already begun?

What had gone *on* in there?

◆

I drove a block away, pulled to the curb, and thought more about Gavin Quick.

Brain-damaged, but he'd managed to hold on to his secrets.

Or maybe he hadn't. Perhaps he'd confided in his father, and that's why Jerry Quick had cleaned out his room.

Now Quick was traveling, after stashing his wife at her sister's. Business as usual, or was he on the run because he *knew*?

Eileen Paxton said Quick hired sluts as secretaries. The secretary I'd met had a dope bust and nails too long for typing.

House in Beverly Hills, but a shadow life?

Gavin had been murdered alongside a blond girl whom no one cared enough about to call in missing. All along, I'd wondered if she was a pro. Jerry and Gavin were both sexually aggressive.

Had the blonde been a gift from father to son? Another referral by Sonny Koppel?

Angie Paul claimed not to know her. Milo had noticed her blinking. I'd explained it away as a reaction to death.

The blonde.

Gavin's type. Two miles north, in the high-priced spread, lived a blond girl who knew Gavin before his accident. A girl we still hadn't spoken to.

The last time I'd followed Kayla Bartell she'd driven to a midday hair appointment. That meant she wasn't holding down a nine-to-five job.

Rich girl with plenty of leisure time? Maybe she'd spare me some.

◆

The Bartell mansion was lifeless as a mortuary behind its white iron security blanket. A white Bentley Mulsanne with rear plates that read MEW ZIK was parked in the circular drive, but no sign of Kayla's red Cherokee.

I continued to Sunset. Cars whizzed by both sides of the median strip, and I waited for a lull to hook right and retrace to the turnaround. It took a while. Just as I swung onto the boulevard, I caught a glimpse of red in my side mirror.

Probably nothing. I got back on Camden anyway.

◆

The Jeep was parked in front of the house.

I drove six houses down and parked, figuring I'd give it half an hour.

Eighteen minutes later, Kayla, dressed in white but carrying a big black bag, exited the house, got in the red SUV, waited until the gates slid open, and sped past me.

◆

Exact same path she'd taken the last time. Santa Monica west to Canon Drive. More pampering at Umberto?

But this time, she passed the salon and continued two blocks down to a Rite Aid pharmacy.

First hair, now makeup? Wouldn't a girl like that buy her cosmetics at a boutique?

Watching her for five minutes gave me my answer, but it wasn't what I expected.

◆

She went straight for the nail polish. I stood on the end of the aisle as she studied a rack of small bottles. The white outfit was a midriff T-shirt that advertised her tan tummy, over white ostrich-skin lowriders and open white sandals with orange plastic heels. Her long hair was tucked into a white denim cap that she wore at a jaunty tilt. Big white plastic earrings. She bounced on her heels a couple of times, seemed to settle down as she peered at the polish.

Big decision; her pretty face creased. Finally, she chose a vermillion bottle and dropped it in her shopping basket. Then so fast that I almost missed it, two other bottles were slipped into the big black handbag—same bag I'd seen that first night, oversized, embroidered with roses.

Not a good match for the white-white

duds, but something that size did have its utility.

She moved up the aisle to the eyeliners. One in the basket, two in the purse. Brazen, not even a cautionary look. The store was quiet, poorly staffed. If surveillance cameras were operating, I couldn't see them.

I hung back, pretended to browse mouthwash, strolled to the next aisle, sauntered back, keeping my head down. Now she was over by the lipstick. Same routine.

She moved through the store that way for ten minutes, concentrating on small articles. Dental floss, contact lens cleaning solution, aspirin, candy. Boosting double the amount of whatever she put in her basket.

I bought a ten-pack of gum, was behind her when she checked out.

She walked cheerfully to her Cherokee, swinging her bag and wiggling her tight little butt. I managed to get to the SUV first, slipped out from the front of the vehicle, and took hold of the black bag.

She said, "What the—" then she recognized me.

"Cop." She nearly choked on the word.

It seemed a poor time for full disclosure. I said, "You've got a little problem, Kayla."

Green-gray eyes widened. Glossy lips parted as she contemplated a reply. Such a pretty girl, despite the hook nose. Such empty eyes.

She said, "I was doing research. For a term paper."

"What was the subject?"

"You know." She glanced off to one side, cocked a hip, tried to work up a smile.

I said, "Where do you go to school?"

"Santa Monica College."

"When?"

"What do you mean?"

"It's late June. School's out."

"Maybe I'm in summer session."

"Are you?"

No answer.

"What's your major?"

She stared at the asphalt, raised her head, chanced eye contact. "Design . . . um . . . and psychology."

"Psychology," I said. "So you know the name for this."

"For what?"

I took the bag from her, pulled out a bottle of contact lens solution, some shrink-wrapped Tylenol and Passionate Peach lip gloss. "For this, Kayla."

She pointed to the Tylenol. "I get head-aches."

"You've got a big one now."

Her eyes darted around the parking lot. "I don't want someone to see me."

"That's the least of your problems."

"Please," she said. "C'mon."

"We need to talk, Kayla."

"C'mon," she repeated. Arched her back. Removed her beret and tossed her hair and let loose a blond storm.

She blinked twice. Batted her lashes and did something silly with her head. Golden hair shimmered. "C'mon," she said, nearly whispering. "I can fix it."

"How?"

Slowly spreading smile. "I'll blow you," she said. "Like you've never been blown before."

I took her car keys, positioned her behind the wheel of her Jeep and ordered her not to move as I slid in on the passenger side. Keeping my door open an inch. Her car was her territory. Hopefully the open door would insulate me from a kidnapping charge if the truth ever got out.

She jammed the beret back on her head. Carelessly; golden strands leaked out.

"Please," she said, staring out the windshield. Her middy blouse rode up. Rapid breathing pulsed her flat belly.

I let the silence sink in. Cars drove in and out of the Rite Aid lot. Tinted windows afforded us privacy.

I wondered if she'd cry.

She pouted. "I don't know why you won't just let me do it—I'll make you feel real good, *and* I'll return the stuff. Okay?"

Sonny Koppel had talked about stuff being a burden.

I said, "Here's what we'll do. You'll return everything and promise never to do it again. But first, you'll talk to me about Gavin Quick. If you're honest and open and tell me everything you know about him, we'll call it even."

She turned quickly and gawked at me. Her hawk nose was powdered. Beneath the film I saw delicate freckles. The gray-green eyes had turned calculating.

She said, "That's it?"

"That's it."

She laughed. "Cool. I wasn't really into giving you head. Speaking of *Gavin*."

"That was Gavin's thing?"

"Wham *bam* was Gavin's thing. Even for a

young guy, he was fast. Even if he came twice in a row. I mean they all start out that way, but you can train them. Not Gavin. The twenty-second man. So I stopped."

"Stopped having sex with him."

"It was never sex," she said. "That's the point."

"What was?"

"Being with him felt like . . . playing basketball. He shoots, he scores, he zips up, you go out for coffee."

"That why you broke up?"

"We didn't break *up,* because we weren't like *going* together, you know?"

"What was your relationship?"

"We knew each other. For years. From Beverly, we had classes together. Then he went to college to do what*ever,* and I decided to study design. It's better at SMC than at some university, you know."

"SMC's strong on design?"

"For sure. You can just do it and not mess with all that other stuff."

"Like psychology," I said.

She grinned. "You caught me. Again. That research story was pretty lame, huh?"

"Beyond lame."

"Yeah," she said. "I should've prepared something better. How'd you catch me?"

"You weren't exactly subtle."

"I never got caught before."

"Been doing it for a while," I said.

She started to reply, shut her mouth.

"Kayla?"

"I thought you weren't going to bother me about that if I told you about Gavin."

"You brought it up."

"I did?"

I nodded.

"Oh," she said. "Well, then I effed up. Let's stick to Gavin. Which I didn't. Stick to him, you know?" She laughed. Stopped and placed a finger across her lips. Spanked her hand. "*Bad* Kayla. I shouldn't be doing that."

"Doing what?"

"Laughing at him, his being dead and all."

"Any idea who killed him?" I said.

"Nope."

"A girl was found with him. Blond, about your size—"

"Skankadoo," she said.

"You know her?"

"I've seen her. He like showed her *off* to me. As *if*. My friend Ellie said she looked like me, but I was like get a refund on your *LASIK*, girl. Then Ellie was like, 'Not like a twin, Kayle, like just a little. Like if you had a rough night.' " She shook her head. "No way; that thing was trailer-trash skankplasm. But then I thought maybe Gavin, being brain-damaged and all, liked her because he thought she *did* look like me. Because he couldn't have me, and she was like sloppy seconds, you know?"

"When did he show her off to you?"

"After I told him no more quickie-city."

"After the accident?"

"*Way* after," she said. "This was like— couple of months ago? I thought he'd stopped bugging me 'cause I hadn't heard from him in a while, but then he started calling me again. I expected him to like break down and beg, you know? Because he *claimed* he was really into me. But he just called and wanted to hang out. So that proves he was lying, he really *wasn't* into me. Right?"

"Unusual for Gavin," I said.

"What do you mean?"

"Giving up so easily. I've heard he could be pretty persistent."

"After the accident he got really weird that

way. Started calling me again, like twenty times a day. Dropping over, bugging my dad." Faint smile. "I guess he did end up begging. Then he stopped."

Because he was stalking Beth Gallegos. I said, "So he wanted to hang out."

"He wanted to go somewhere and park and put his cock in my mouth. I felt sorry for him, so I did it once. But never again."

"No more speed-record sex," I said.

"You're making me sound mean," she said, pulling at loose strands and trying to stuff them back in the beret. Unsuccessful, she yanked off the hat and began kneading it.

"You should apologize," she said.

"For what?"

"Saying I'm mean and a slut."

"You said you felt sorry for Gavin—"

"Exactly. I was being nice. After the accident he got kind of . . . I don't want to say retarded because it sounds so mean, but really, that's what it was. So I felt sorry for him and wanted to help him."

"Makes sense," I said.

"It does," she agreed.

"So Gavin slowed down intellectually."

"Like before, he could be obnoxious, but

he was smart. But now—it was . . ." She probed her cheek with her tongue. "I want to say pathetic."

"Sounds like it was."

"Huh?"

"Pathetic."

"Yeah, exactly, like it really *was*."

"The time you went out with him—"

"It was only once. I felt sorry for him."

"Where'd you park?"

"Up on Mulholland?" Her mouth froze in a tiny O. "That was where—omigod."

"Was that a regular spot for you and Gavin? Back in the old days?"

"Sometimes." She started crying. "That could've been me."

"Tell me about the blond girl," I said.

She wiped her eyes, smiled. "Too bleached out, you could see her roots."

"Where'd you meet her?"

"I never met her, like actually hanging out. Me and Ellie went to a movie and later we went to Kate Mantolini for the vegetable plate. Sometimes Jerry Seinfeld goes there."

Her eyes drifted out a side window, switched direction, and focused on a parking sign. "I hope I don't go past the validation time."

I said, "You and Ellie at Kate Mantolini."

"Yeah," she said. "We were like into our veggies and in comes Gavin with this skank. I'm talking Ross-Dress-for-Less blouse and a skirt up to her you-know-what." Her eyes dropped to her sandals. "She did have cool shoes. Black, open-backed. Very Naomi Campbell."

"Jimmy Choo," I said.

"How'd you know?"

"She was wearing them the night she was murdered."

"They were cool shoes. I figured she boosted them." She chuckled. "Just *kidding!*"

"So Gavin walked in with her—"

"And pretended not to see me so I pretended not to see *him*. Then he had to walk past us to get to his booth and he pretended to all of a sudden spot me and be all like surprised, like, hey-it's-you, Kayla."

"What did you do?" I said.

"I waited until he came right up to the table, I mean right up, so like no way could you ignore it."

"Then what?"

"Then I said, 'Hey, Gav,' and he wiggles his finger and the skank comes over and she's like 'who are you?' Like she's got it all goin' on. Which she *doesn't*. And Gavin's like this is . . . whatever her name was. And Skanky just stands there in her Jimmy's like she's the star of an E! True Hollywood Story or something."

"You don't remember her name?"

"Nope."

"Try."

"It's not like I was listening."

"Try," I said.

"It's important?"

"It is."

"Why?"

"Because she's dead."

"Hmm." She flipped her upper lip with her index finger, let it snap down against her teeth. Repeated it several times, making little ploppy noises. Squished the beret and watched the soft fabric pulsate amoebically as it regained its shape.

"Kayla?" I said.

"I'm thinking," she said. "I guess I'd like to say Chris. Or Christa. Something Chris-sy."

"Any last name?"

"No," she said. "Definitely not. Gavin

never mentioned a last name. This wasn't like some big introduction. Gavin was like 'I don't *need* you, look what *I've* got.' "

"He said that?"

"No, but you could just tell. Later, he came up and said how cool she was."

"Later when?"

"When Skanky went to the bathroom and left him alone. She was in there a long time, I'm thinking dope—she *looked* like a doper. Real skinny. There was no way anyone could think she looked like me. But Gavin . . ." She crossed her eyes and tapped her forehead.

"She left him alone, and he came to your table."

"Yeah, and Ellie was like 'Who's your new *lay-dee,* Gav?' And Gavin's like, 'Christa—I think it was Christa, something like that, maybe Crystal. And Ellie's like, 'Pretty cute, Gav.' But not meaning it, dissing him, you know? And I'm not saying a thing, I'm working on my steamed spinach, which is the coolest part of the vegetable plate. Then Gavin gives this sick smile and moves away from Ellie and he bends down and whispers in my ear, 'She does it all, Kayla. Endlessly.' And I'm like 'More like endlessly boring and endlessly preemie' but I just think it, I don't say it. Because Gavin wasn't normal anymore, it would've been like dissing a retard. Also, because by that time he'd moved back to his booth. Like he didn't care what I had to say."

I said, "What else can you tell me about Christa?"

"Maybe it was Crystal," she said. "I'm thinking Crystal's more right."

"She never said a word to you?"

"No, but Gavin did. Actually, he said more than what I just told you."

I waited.

"It was mean, I really don't want to remember."

"It's important, Kayla."

She sighed. "Okay, okay. When he bent down and whispered in my ear, was like how great she was, he also said, 'She's a dancer, Kayla. *She's* got all the moves.' Like I don't. You know what it really means, right?"

"What?" I said.

"Get real," she said. "A dancer means a stripper. They all call themselves dancers. She was skank-spread on a croissant."

"You know any strippers?"

"Me? No way. But she had that . . . the

way she stood, the way she . . . she was like look at my body, it's the greatest body, I love my body, I'll take off my clothes for a mixed green salad."

"Easy morals," I said.

"Which is stupid," she said. "The way it is with guys, you want 'em to respect you, you got to hold something back."

"What can you tell me about Gavin's home life?"

"Like his parents?"

"Yes."

"His mom's nuts, and his father's a horn-dog. Probably where Gav gets it."

"The old man make a move on you?"

"Yuk," she said. "No way. You just hear things."

"About what?"

"About who's sleeping around."

"Jerome Quick was sleeping around?"

"That's what Gavin said."

"He told you?"

"He was like bragging," she said. "Like, my dad's a stud, and so am I."

"This was after the accident?"

"No," she said. "Before. When Gavin was still talking like a normal person."

"You say his mother's nuts."

"Everyone knows that. She was never at school stuff, you'd never even see her out in her backyard, she'd be all up in her bedroom, drinking, sleeping. At least Gavin's dad came to school stuff."

"Gavin was closer to him."

She stared at me, as if I'd posed the question in a foreign language.

I said, "Did Gavin ever tell you about his career plans?"

"Like what job he wanted?"

"Yes."

"Before the accident he wanted to be a rich businessman. Afterward, he talked about writing."

"Writing what?"

"He didn't say on what." She laughed. "As if."

"Did he ever talk to you about being suspicious of anyone?"

"Huh?" she said. "Like some spy thing?"

"Like that," I said.

"No. Can I get going. Pu-leeze? I'm supposed to meet Ellie over at Il Fornaio, and I don't want to go over the parking limit. Paying for parking sucks."

"So does paying for cosmetics," I said.

"Hey," she said, "I thought that was over with."

"What else can you tell me about Gavin?"

"Nothing. He was out of my life, running with skanks—you think that's why he was killed? Running with bad people?"

"Maybe," I said.

"There you go," she said. "It pays to be good."

CHAPTER
31

I had her go into the pharmacy and get a shopping bag. Dumping the stolen goods in the bag, I said, "Leave it inside the door."

Sudden, bone-white pallor flashed through her makeup. "Don't make me go in there. Please."

She placed a hand on my sleeve. No seductiveness; her knuckles were white.

"Okay," I said. "But you have to promise to be good."

"I do. Can I go? Ellie's waiting."

◆

Gavin had bragged to Kayla about all the sex he was getting from the blonde. Maybe that was trying to one-up the old girlfriend. But it also fit the call girl theory.

Christa or Crystal. I tried Milo again. His cell remained switched off.

Listening to Kayla Bartell, learning about the sad stumble that had been Gavin Quick's life, had sapped my energy. Allison and I were due to meet for dinner at seven, and I resolved to push all of it out of my head.

I pretty much stuck to that, but by evening's end, I found myself talking to Allison about the Quick family's meltdown, wrong turns and bad luck, the death of intimacy.

An unnamed girl in a stainless-steel drawer, body stitched back together and relegated to cold storage.

Like the therapist she was, Allison mostly listened, and that kept me going. I knew I was being morose but didn't want to stop talking. As I pulled up to her house, my own voice hurt my ears.

"Sorry," I said. "What a fun guy."

She said, "Why don't you sleep over?"

"You want more of this?"

"I'd like you to stay the night."

"I've never known you to be a masochist."

She shrugged and played with my index

finger. "I like seeing you first thing in the morning. You always look really happy to see me, and there's no one else I can say that about."

♦

We went straight to her bedroom, got undressed, shared a chaste, closed-mouth kiss, slipped easily into sleep. I woke up three times in the middle of the night, twice to think discouraging thoughts and once because I felt myself being jostled. I forced my eyes open, saw Allison hovering over me, breasts dangling, grasping a corner of the comforter and looking none too awake herself.

I said something that would've been "Huh?" had my tongue been working.

"You were . . . covered up," she said, groggily. "I didn't see you moving, wanted to . . . check."

"M'fine."

"Guh . . . night."

♦

Morning light seared my eyelids. I left Allison sleeping, went into her kitchen, took in the paper, searched for a picture of the dead girl, didn't find it. Allison had morning patients and would be up soon, so I got to work on breakfast.

Moments later, she shuffled in sniffing the air, wearing an oversized khaki T-shirt and fluffy slippers, face creased by bed wrinkles, hair topknotted carelessly.

"Eggs," she said, rubbing her eyes. "Y'sleep okay?"

"Perfectly."

"Me too." She yawned. "Did I snore?"

"No," I lied.

"Sank like a stone," she said. "Boom."

No memory of waking up to make sure I was okay. She'd cared about me in her dreams.

◆

I was back home for fifteen minutes when Milo phoned from his car. His breathing was harsh, as if he'd run uphill. "I tried reaching you at nine."

"Spent the night at Allison's."

"Good for you," he said. "What's your schedule like today?"

"Open. I might have a first name on the blond girl. Crystal or Christa."

"How'd you find *that* out?"

"Kayla Bartell. It's a bit of a story—"

"Tell me when I get there, I'm already at Sepulveda and Wilshire. The pooch still bunking with you?"

"No, he's gone."

"Okay, then, I'll eat this beef jerky myself."

◆

He entered the house wearing a sad gray suit, mud brown shirt, gray poly tie, and chewing on the thickest rope of dehydrated meat I'd ever seen.

"What is that?" I said. "Python jerky?"

"Buffalo, low-fat, low-salt. Special deal at Trader Joe's." His hair was flat, and his eyes were red. We went into the kitchen.

"Tell me the story."

I recounted my talk with Kayla.

He said, "Little klepto, huh? And you played bad cop. Nice work."

"It was probably illegal."

"It was a chat between two adults." He twisted the knot of his tie. "Got any coffee left?"

"Didn't make any."

"No prob, I'm wired, anyway . . . Christa or Crystal. Why'd Kayla peg her for a stripper?"

"Because Gavin said she was a dancer," I said.

"Well," he said, "name a girl Crystal and what's more likely? That she'll get a Ph.D. in biomechanics, or end up shaking her tail for tips?" He removed his jacket and tossed it over a chair. Since he'd arrived, the air was turbulent.

"Kayla also said she looked like a doper."

"The coroner found nothing in her system. What about the *Times*?"

"They run on their own schedule," I said. "Why'd you ask about mine?"

He took a sheet of paper from his jacket pocket and handed it to me. Typed list.

1. 1999 Ford Explorer. Bennett A. Hacker, 48, Franklin Avenue, Hollywood.
2. 1995 Lincoln sedan. Raymond R. Degussa, 41, post office box in Venice.
3. 2001 Mercedes Benz sedan, Albin Larsen, 56, Santa Monica.
4. 1995 Mercedes Benz sedan, Jerome A. Quick, 48, Beverly Hills.

"DMV data from Gavin's list," he said.

"Gavin copied down his father's license number?"

"Weird, no? Could it be a brain damage thing? Do you guys have a name for it?"

"Overinclusiveness . . . But something else jumps out at me. Quick's car is listed last. You'd think spotting his father's car would have caught Gavin's attention first."

"Unless he listed the cars in order of arrival, and Daddy arrived last."

"Good point," I said. "So what are you thinking, some sort of meeting?"

He nodded. "Quick and Albin Larsen and the other two. The big question is why was Gavin surveilling Daddy? It smells to me like Daddy was up to no good, and that's why he cleaned out Gavin's room—getting rid of any evidence his kid mighta come up with. Then he left town—his kid's just been murdered, and he's off traveling again, leaving the wife alone, doing business. It smells *ripe*, Alex. The mistake ol' Jerry made was not clearing out Gavin's clothes."

He picked up the list, refolded it, put it back in his pocket. "It's not much. But to my mind, it changes everything. Let me tell you about the other guys on the list."

I said, "The con cleaning the building—Kristof—said his parole officer was named Hacker."

He sat down at the kitchen table. "I'm impressed. Yeah, he's a PO working out of the downtown office, and Raymond Degussa's one of his former clients. Major client, string of arrests for assault, larceny, extortion, armed robbery, dope. Degussa beat a bunch of raps, pleaded out others, did some county time, finally got tagged for fifteen years on a strong-arm robbery beef. San Quentin, time shaved for good behavior, and he seems to have behaved himself during parole, checked in with Hacker regularly, got free and clear two years ago. I called over to Q and spoke with an assistant warden who's relatively new to the job and didn't know Degussa. What she dug up for me was that he was a dominant con, no gang membership, but he never got victimized. They figured him for a supplier of some kind because he always had cigarettes and candy. He was also a suspect in at least two inmate murders, but there was no evidence."

"Career bad guy," I said. "Two suspected murders, and he got time shaved for good behavior?"

"Without evidence he did. Prison administrators have their own agenda: They're always overcrowded, want to move guys out. And wonder of wonders, Degussa appears to be rehabilitated. Not a single brush with the law since being off parole."

"A friendly parole officer would help that," I said. "Successful rehabilitation. Albin Larsen would like that. Maybe Degussa was one of his pet projects. Or Mary Lou Koppel's. What weapon was used in those prison murders?"

"A blade; in prison it's always a blade."

"Any impaling?"

"Nothing about that in his file."

"Degussa went away on a strong-arm robbery," I said. "Any weapon at all?"

"Just intimidation."

"Did Bennett Hacker spend any time at any of those satellite offices?"

"Flora Newsome," he said.

"She worked in parole. It seems awfully coincidental."

"Yeah . . . I didn't want to ask too much. If Hacker's dirty, I don't want him to know I'm snooping around. But I'll do what I can to sniff behind the scenes."

He drummed the table. "I'm getting that feeling—the stew is starting to simmer. But everything's still at arm's length—like I'm cooking in someone else's kitchen."

He got up, paced the room, tugged at his tie. "The way I see it, Gavin convinced himself he was gonna be some kind of investigative reporter, was nosing around in his dad's affairs. Or, he'd noticed funny goings-on at the therapy building, first. Started doing some serious surveillance, took notes."

"A psychologist, a parole officer, and a con," I said. "Without Jerry Quick, it could just be some sort of treatment arrangement."

"*Precissimoso.* Jerry being there takes it in a whole other direction. Jerry's a womanizing hustler who hires someone like Angie Paul for his front gal. He's also Sonny Koppel's tenant. And Sonny's Mary Lou's business partner in the halfway houses, the moneyman. The one who referred Jerry to Mary Lou in the first place."

"Have you found any business dealings between Sonny and Quick?"

"Not a damn thing. And I dug deep, yesterday *and* early today."

He slouched over to the fridge, returned drinking pink grapefruit juice from a carton. "Can't find a speck of *dirt* on ol' Sonny. No slumlord problems, no criminal complaints, no one in Organized Crime has ever heard of him. So far he's coming across as exactly what he claims to be: a guy who owns a lot of properties. He was also being straight about giving away big bucks. Franchise Tax Board says Charitable Planning is on the up-and-up as a tax-exempt foundation. Sonny files his papers on time and donates at least a million every year."

"To whom?"

"The poor, the sick, the halting. Every worthy disease, plus Save the Bay, Nourish the Trees, Coddle the Spotted Owl, whatever."

"Saint Sonny," I said.

"If it looks too good to be true . . . I don't know what that meeting was about, but the only thing that makes sense is they're all involved in something shady. Maybe Sonny got a hook into Jerry Quick because Quick's always cash shy. But I still can't figure out what use Quick would be to him. Putting that aside for the moment, what kind of scam could a bunch of shrinks pull off that would make big bucks?"

"The first thing that comes to mind," I said, "is basic fraud—overbilling insurance or the state. The easiest target would be the state—some kind of government contract. Sonny would know how to work that angle. He gets the government to finance his halfway houses and his senior citizen housing. He claims the halfway houses were Mary Lou and Larsen's idea. Maybe that's true, but if owning halfways helped plug Sonny into a subsidized treatment plan, that would appeal to his business sense."

"Therapy for cons," he said.

"A built-in supply of patients. Patients they could bill for whether or not they treated them because who's going to complain?"

"Sonny and Mary Lou and Larsen. And Gavin saw some kind of staff meeting."

"Gavin didn't copy down Gull's license number," I said. "So maybe Gull missed the meeting. Or he wasn't involved. He's got personal problems, and he sweats too much. If I were setting up a slick criminal enterprise, I'd view him as a poor risk."

"I'd still like to know why Gavin ditched him as a therapist." He paced some more. "For a guy like Sonny to get involved in a scam, it would have to be big money."

"Maybe not," I said. "Sonny claims he's

not into accumulating stuff. That seems to be true, meaning he's turned on by the game—the *process* of making money."

"Soaking the government."

"Or Sonny did figure out a way to make some serious money. He claims he was holding the ground floor open until Koppel and the others decided about group therapy. If they were setting up some sort of parolee treatment that brought in big bucks, that would justify leaving the Charitable Planning suite vacant. I got into the space, yesterday. They were cleaning the carpets, and I was able to walk in. Empty, except for a small office for Sonny and a big room with some folding chairs. Why would Sonny need chairs if all he did was come in and sign checks? But they'd be useful if some-one checked and you were claiming to be running groups. Of course if the person checking was your pal, you wouldn't need to put up much of a front."

"Bennett Hacker," he said. "There's some deal with the parole board, and Hacker's the overseer."

"A guy in Hacker's position could also sup-ply names in return for kickback. And Raymond Degussa, being a wily, dominant con—someone who pulled off robberies using intimidation alone—could convince the patients to cooperate."

"Headshrinking for parolees," he said. "Something like that could really bring in serious money?"

"If there were enough parolees," I said. "Let's do the math. Private practice group therapy can run between fifty and a hundred bucks an hour. Medi-Cal reimburses for much less—fifteen, twenty. But there are all sorts of other things you can bill Medi-Cal for. Individual treatment, initial intakes, follow-ups, testing, case conferences—"

"Case conferences. As in getting together, after hours, at the building. How much does Medi-Cal pay for that?"

"Thirty-six bucks for thirty minutes. If these people have hooked on to some supplemental program that adds to the Medi-Cal billing—something Sonny wangled—the fee could be substantially higher. But let's be conservative and assume the core is group therapy at twenty dollars per patient per session. I saw at least two dozen folding chairs. If they're running groups of twenty—or claiming to be—each group session would bring in four hundred bucks an hour. Running six groups a day five times a week would bring in twelve thousand dollars. That alone would be six hundred grand a year. Add more patients, toss in additional fees, and it could get interesting. Especially if you're not really doing any work."

"Millions," he said.

"It's not inconceivable."

"Each con gets daily group therapy . . . how many groups could you justify for a single patient?"

"If you've set up an immersion model, you could treat him all day."

"What, like that deal where you sat all day and some guy yelled at you for being weak-willed and wouldn't let you pee?"

"Est, Synanon," I said. "There's plenty of precedent, particularly with substance abuse. A case could be made for immersion for cons, because the aim would be large-scale change on several dimensions. The answer to an inquiring skeptic would be that it was still cheaper than keeping them in prison. And that if it really straightened them out, it was a giant money *saver*."

"Mary Lou and her rehab kick," he said. "Going on the radio—she and Larsen." He laughed. "The government pays to shrink bad guys. I'm in the wrong business. So are you, for that matter."

I said, "How many parolees live in Sonny's halfway houses?"

"Three houses? I'd guess a couple of hundred."

"Think about the income if everyone got on the rolls."

"Hundred bucks a week per con—five grand a year. A million bucks for group therapy alone."

"Plus other charges."

"The only problem is, Alex, a couple of shrinks doing all that billing would be physically impossible."

"So they use assistants—peer counselors. And they flat out lie, bill for sessions that never take place."

"Peer counselors," he said. "Meaning other cons? Yeah, that's the rage, ain't it? Ex-gangbangers become facilitators, junkies go the drug-counseling route. That's where a guy like Degussa would fit in . . . scumbags doing therapy. That's legal?"

"Everything depends how the contract's written," I said. "And a guy like Sonny would know how to get a juicy government contract."

"All those billable hours," he said. "The place would be jumping. But it's not."

"Maybe that discrepancy occurred to Gavin."

"Brain-damaged ace reporter ferrets out fraud," he said. He drank juice, put the carton down, wiped his lips with his sleeve. "All you need is a room and some chairs to make a million. Yeah, it's a fat scam, but Sonny gives away a million a year. Why would he mess with this? The game?"

"Maybe something else," I said.

"What's that?"

"Making Mary Lou happy."

"She didn't end up too happy," he said.

"Maybe something went wrong."

"So they were cleaning the carpet. The day after we spoke to Sonny. Who was doing it, scuzzbags like Roland Kristof?"

"Didn't appear to be," I said. I gave him the name of the company, and he copied it down.

"A rehab scam," he said. "But we're back to the same question: Where does Jerry Quick fit in?"

"That office of his," I said. "Not much business goes on there."

"A front."

"Maybe his real job's working for Sonny."

He frowned. "This whole scenario, it makes Quick more than just a sleazy bastard. It means he knows why his son was killed and instead of telling us, he cleans out the room."

"That could've been fear," I said. "First Gavin, then Mary Lou Koppel. That's why Quick left town. When you called the office, no one answered. Maybe Quick told Angie to take some time off."

"He splits . . . leaves his wife behind . . . because they don't get along anyway. He doesn't give a damn about her."

"That would also explain the daughter—Kelly—not coming home after Gavin's death. Quick wants her out of the way."

"The scam crumbling . . . if it really exists."

"A scam would explain Flora Newsome, too. While she was working in the parole office, she learned something she shouldn't have. Maybe Mary Lou got greedy and wanted a bigger cut. Or Gavin's getting killed changed her perspective."

"What, she suddenly developed moral fiber?"

"Money games are one thing, murder's

another. Perhaps Koppel panicked and wanted out. Or she tried to lean on Sonny."

He got up again, circled the room a couple of times. "There's another possible angle on Flora, Alex. She could've been in on the scam, flagging files of incoming parolees, passing along names."

"Could be," I said, thinking about Evelyn Newsome, living on memories, trying to put her life together.

He stared out the kitchen window for a long time. "Career criminal, parole officer, shady metals dealer. And Professor Larsen, the human rights dude. We've been focusing on Gull, haven't paid much attention to Larsen."

He drained the juice carton, let out a long, windy sigh. "I've got an appointment with Jerry Quick's CPA in Brentwood. Then I'd better start doing detail work on Degussa and Hacker, find out, among other things, if either of them interfaced with Flora's satellite office."

He snapped the case shut and saluted. "All this still leaves Crystal, the mystery blonde."

"Gavin's girl," I said. "He confided in her.

Or he didn't, and she just happened to be in the wrong place."

"So you've changed your mind, she wasn't the primary target."

"Flexibility is the hallmark of maturity."

He grinned. "Seeing as your schedule's open, should you choose to accept the mission . . ."

"What?"

"Scholarly research. Excavate every goddamn thing you can about Albin Larsen and the others. Look for the kind of easy government money we're guessing about. State, local, Fed, private. Something with poor oversight that would be easy to pad."

"Sounds like a typical grant," I said.

"So young, yet so cynical. So, do we have a deal?"

"A deal implies reciprocity," I said.

"Virtue, m'lad, is its own reward."

32

Virtue took its sweet time paying off.

Jerome Quick's name pulled up no hits. Neither did Raymond Degussa's or Bennett A. Hacker's.

Edward "Sonny" Koppel was a man of means, but his public profile was low: twenty references in all, sixteen noting Koppel's charitable contributions. Most of those consisted of Koppel's name on donor lists. When he was identified at all it was as an "investor and philanthropist." No photos accompanied any of the citations.

Albin Larsen was a good deal more cybervisible. For the last decade, he'd balanced the practice of psychology with delivering lectures on the role of psychology in social activism in his native Sweden as well as in France, Holland, Belgium, Canada, and Kenya. His name popped up sixty-three times.

That kind of travel conflicted with doing long-term therapy; then again, it was easier to maintain a patient load when you weren't actually seeing your patients.

I began slogging through the hits. Larsen's connections to Africa went beyond giving speeches; he'd been a U.N. observer in Rwanda during the genocide that had seen eight hundred thousand Tutsis exterminated and had consulted to the subsequent war crimes tribunal.

Some of the citations were repetitive, but the thirty I examined were all more of the same: Larsen doing good works.

Not the profile of a swindler or a murderer. Before reaching the end, I shifted gears and started searching for psychotherapy programs for parolees and other ex-cons, found surprisingly few. No government projects in California, other than a state-funded truck-driving school for recently released felons. That one had earned a bit of scrutiny when one of its graduates, tanked up on meth, had crashed his big rig into a restaurant in Lodi. But I found no sign the grant had been terminated.

Everything else I came up with was academic—a smattering of social scientists espousing theories and playing with numbers. When treatments for criminals did exist they tended to be outside the therapy mainstream. A group in Baldwin Park promoted meditation and "attitudinal healing" for ex-cons, and one in Laguna trumpeted the power of arts and crafts. Martial arts, tai chi specifically, was the treatment of choice for an organization in San Diego, and there was no shortage of religious groups touting techniques of moral change.

I phoned the State Department of Health, endured nearly an hour of voice mail and on-hold stupor before speaking to a jaded woman who informed me that she hadn't heard of any treatment groups for parolees but that if one existed, they wouldn't know about it, the Department of Corrections would. Another forty minutes of telephonic torment by the Corrections switchboard, as I was shunted from menu to menu. I started pressing "0" like a man possessed, finally reached an operator and was told that the office was closed.

Four-fifteen. My tax dollars working over-time.

I returned to the last dozen citations on Albin Larsen. A few more speeches, then a joint statement issued by Larsen and a U.N. commissioner named Alphonse Almogardi, in Lagos, Nigeria, promising that the United Nations would do everything in its power to bring the perpetrators of the Rwandan genocide to justice.

Links attached to that one connected me to an African public affairs website. The big story took place in Kigali, the Rwandan capital: a June 2002 march by thirty-five hundred genocide survivors branding the International Criminal Tribunal a farce. During the eight years since the tribunal's establishment, only seven war crimes trials had been convened, all of low-level military officers. As the years ground on, witnesses died or disappeared. Those who persisted had endured threats and harassment. Accused butchers grew wealthy as their defense attorneys kicked back shares of tribunal-financed legal fees.

More damaging was the accusation that the tribunal judges were actively conspiring to delay the trials of big-ticket mass murderers because of fears that hearings in open court would reveal the complicity of U.N. personnel in the genocide.

From the safety of her office in Dublin, a tribunal registrar named Maria Robertson responded by scolding the survivors for their "incendiary language" and cautioned against "instigating a cycle of violence." Speaking in Lagos, consultant Professor Albin Larsen stressed the complexity of the situation and advised patience.

The nineteenth hit also emanated from the Nigerian capital, and it gave me pause: description of a program called Sentries for Justice, aimed at helping steer young African men away from lives of crime.

The group, staffed by European volunteers, functioned by *"offering synergistic alternatives to prison that engender efficacious rehabilitation and attitudinal shifting through a holistic emphasis upon the interplay between socially altruistic behavior and communal social norms set into place during the pre-Colonial era but disrupted by colonialism."* Services offered included parenting education, jobs skills training, drug and alcohol counseling, crisis intervention, and something called "cultural demarginalization." Synergy was illustrated by the use of Sentries buses, driven by Sentries alumni, for transporting criminal detainees to court. Most of the volunteers had Scandinavian names, and Albin Larsen was listed as a senior consultant.

I printed the citation, and moved to the last few hits. More speeches by Larsen, then the final reference, posted three weeks ago: calendar of events at a Santa Monica bookstore named The Pen Is Mightier. A Harvard professor named George Issa Qumdis was scheduled to deliver a speech on the Middle East, and Albin Larsen would be there to introduce him.

The speech was tonight, in four hours. Professor Larsen was a busy man.

I scanned the Sentries for Justice citation for buzzwords and keyed them into several search engines. "Syngerstic alternatives," "efficacious rehabilitation," "attitudinal shifting" "demarginalization" and the like pulled up lots of academic verbiage but nothing useful.

It was 5:30 P.M. when I pushed away from the computer, and I had nothing much to show.

I made some coffee, munched on a bagel,

and drank, thinking and looking out my kitchen window at a graying sky. I realized I'd been seduced by the cheap trick that was cyberresearch and decided to do it the old-fashioned way.

◆

Olivia Brickerman and I had worked together at Western Pediatric Hospital, she as a supervising social worker, I as a fledgling psychologist. Twenty years my senior, she'd seen herself as my surrogate mother. I hadn't minded one bit because she'd been a benevolent mother, down to home cooking and a cheerfully nosy interest in my love life.

Her husband, an international chess grand master, had written the Final Moves column for the *Times*. He'd since passed on, and Olivia had dealt with her loss by plunging herself back into work, taking a series of short-lived, well-paying state consultantships, then easing into a position at the genteel old school across town where I was nominally a med school professor.

Olivia knew more about grantsmanship and the way government operated than anyone else I'd ever met.

At five-forty, she was still at her desk. "Alex, darling."

"Olivia, darling."

"So nice to hear from you. How's life?"

"Life is good," I said. "How about you?"

"Still kicking. So, how's the new one working out?"

"She's working out great."

"Makes sense," she said. "Both of you in the same profession, lots of common ground. Which isn't to say I have anything against Robin. I love her, she's lovely. So's the new one—that hair, those eyes. No surprise there, a good-looking guy like you. Get yourself a new dog?"

"Not yet."

"A dog is good," she said. "I love my Rudy."

Rudy was a walleyed, shaggy mutt with a lust for deli meat. "Rudy rocks," I said.

"He's smarter than most people."

Last time I'd spoken to her—three or four months ago—she'd sprained an ankle.

"How's the leg?" I said. "Back to jogging yet?"

"Hah! Can't get back to a place you've never been. Truthfully, the leg's still a little gammy; I should take off weight. But thank

God. The latest thing is, I'm on blood thinners."

"You all right?"

"Well," she said, "I've got thinner blood. Unfortunately, nothing else got thin. So what can I do for you, darling?"

I told her.

"Department of Corrections," she said. "Haven't had much to do with those yokels in a long time. Not since I consulted to Sybil Brand. Back then they had some state grants for therapy, but that was all for inside the prison, helping inmates with kids learn to be good mothers. Good idea, but the oversight was pathetic. Never heard about an outside project such as you're describing."

"It may not exist," I said.

"And you're asking about this because . . ."

"Because it may relate to some murders."

"Some murders," she said. "Ugly stuff?"

"Very ugly."

"You and Milo . . . how's he doing, by the way?"

"Working hard."

"He'll always be doing that," she said. "Well, I'm sorry nothing comes to mind but just because I haven't heard about it, doesn't mean it doesn't exist. I've been teaching, have kind of lost touch with the divine world of public monies . . . what you're describing could be a pilot study, let me fire up my Mac and see . . . okay, here goes, click click click . . . can't seem to find any pilot post-prison rehab therapy studies from NIH or HHS or . . . the state . . . maybe it's private . . . no, nothing on that list, either. So maybe it was approved as a full-term grant, not a pilot."

I said, "You might want to check under 'Sentries for Justice,' and if that doesn't work, I've got some other buzzwords for you."

"Give them to me."

" 'Synergy,' 'demarginalization,' 'attitudinal shifting,' 'holistic interplay—' "

"That sound you're hearing in the background is Mr. Orwell groaning."

I laughed. Waited. Listened to Olivia humming and muttering to herself.

"Nothing," she said, finally. "Not on any databases I can find. But not everything makes it into the computer in a timely fashion, there are good, old-fashioned printed lists. I don't keep them here, have to go over to the main office. Which is locked for the night . . . give me some time, darling, and I'll see what I can do."

"Thanks, Olivia."

"You're more than welcome. Come over sometime, Alex. Bring Allison. Is she a vegetarian or something like that?"

"On the contrary."

"Oh, lucky you," she said. "Then definitely bring her over. I'll marinate some skirt steaks, my skirt steaks are famous. You bring Allison and some wine. I could use some adorable people in the house."

◆

Six-thirty. Milo called me from his desk.

"Jerry Quick's CPA was cagey, but I managed to get a few things out of him. First of all, I got a clear impression Quick is not a big-money client. Secondly, Quick's income comes in spurts, he's got no regular income coming in, just whatever deals he can close, and the CPA never sees the checks, just writes down what Jerry tells him. His main gripe was that Jerry's income was unstable, so establishing estimated tax was a hassle."

"Not a big-money client," I said. "How's he's been doing recently?"

"Couldn't get the guy to spill specifics, but he did say Quick was late to pay his bill."

"Same thing Sonny Koppel complained about, so maybe Quick's living on the edge. House in Beverly Hills, a Mercedes, albeit one that's a few years old. Appearances are important. Toss in Gavin's medical bills, and there'd be pressure."

"Sure," he said. "It would explain Quick getting into something iffy and lucrative. But what it doesn't explain is why would Sonny and the others *want* him involved? Guy's a middling *metals* dealer. What could he offer?"

"Guns are metal."

"From therapy to guns? A burgeoning crime syndicate?"

"It's just what came to mind," I said. "Dealers like to deal. Quick travels around buying scrap. Don't police departments scrap confiscated weapons?"

"Yeah," he said. "Anything's possible, but there's still nothing to connect Quick or anyone to therapy mischief, let alone arms mischief. And I still can't locate the bastard. I got hold of his home phone records, but there're no calls to any airlines. No travel-related stuff of any kind. Couldn't find any business phone, so I asked Sheila about it. She said he uses prepaid cells. Which is just what you'd do if your business was shady. Meanwhile, Sheila still has no idea where he is. So maybe you were right and he is on the lam."

"How's she taking that?"

"She was pretty soused but did sound a little scared. As in maybe this is more than just another of Jerry's business trips. When she sobers up, it'll be worse; lucidity can be a bitch. I also bopped over to Quick's office. Closed, no sign of Angie Blue-Nails, mail's piled up in front of the door, all junk solicitations."

"Maybe his important mail goes somewhere else."

"That would not shock me," he said. "I phoned Angie's apartment in North Hollywood. No answer. On the other fronts, Mr. Raymond Degussa works as a bouncer at a club in East Hollywood. Petra doesn't know him, but she checked Hollywood files, and Degussa's name came up on a patrol call. Hassle at the club, Degussa got into it with an unruly patron, patron called the cops, showed them a shiner, claimed Degussa threatened to kill him. But there were no witnesses, and the complainant was stoned and hostile and obnoxious, so no charge."

"Death threats," I said. "Sweet guy."

"I'm sure he mans the velvet rope with tact and diplomacy. Other than that one incident, he's kept his nose clean. Here's something juicier: Bennett Hacker, our probably errant PO, did circulate through some of the satellites, including the one where Flora Newsome temped, but he was only there two weeks."

"That's long enough," I said. "How's your schedule tonight—say in an hour?"

I told him about Albin Larsen's appearance at the bookstore. "We could drop by to observe, have a chance to see Larsen in another context. Unless you think that would alarm Larsen."

"Another context," he said. "Not a bad idea. In terms of alarming Larsen, we've got a cover story. We wanted to talk to him about Mary Lou and Gull and with his being such a busy little shrink and our not wanting to disrupt his practice, we figured this would be the best way."

"In addition to being a cover, it would

make him think the focus is still on his partner. Is Binchy still watching Gull?"

"Yes. Gull's keeping a low profile . . . little bookstore jaunt tonight . . . sure, let's do it."

I gave him the address.

He said, "Let's meet, say half a block east, corner of Sixth. Arrive a little early—seven-fifteen."

"Scoping out the scene?"

"Hey," he said, "no cheap seats for us."

33

I got to Broadway and Sixth at 7:10. Traffic was lazy. The sky was hammered tin.

Evenings are inevitably cool in Santa Monica; tonight marine winds whipped the June air frigid. Winds rich with kelp and rot, the metallic-sweet promise of rain. A couple of homeless guys pushed shopping carts up the boulevard. One muttered and sped past me. The other took the dollar I offered, and said, "Hey, man. You have a better year, okay?"

"You, too," I said.

"Me? I had a great year," he said, indignant. He wore a salmon-colored cashmere sport coat, stained and frayed, that had once belonged to a large, rich man. "I beat the shit out of Mike Tyson in Vegas. Took his woman and made her my bitch."

"Good for you."

"It was *reeeel* good." He flashed a gap-toothed grin, leaned into the breeze, and shoved on.

A moment later, Milo rounded Sixth and strode toward me. He'd changed at the station, wore baggy jeans and an old, oatmeal-colored turtleneck that added unneeded bulk. Desert boots clopped the sidewalk. He'd folded something stiff and shiny into his hair, and it spiked in places.

"Kind of authorial," I said. "One of those Irish poets." To me he still looked like a cop.

"Now all I need is to write a damn book. So, who wrote the one tonight?"

"A Harvard professor. George Issa something, the Middle East."

We began walking toward the store. "Issa Qumdis."

"You know him?" I said.

"Heard the name."

"I'm impressed."

"Hey," he said. "I read the papers. Even when they don't run photos of dead girls. Speaking of which, I hit the clubs, trying to locate Christa/Crystal. But tonight, we intellectualize—here we are. Looks like college days, huh?"

His college had been Indiana U. Most of what I knew about his student years had to do with being in the closet.

We stood outside the bookstore as he inspected the facade. The Pen Is Mightier was a half-width storefront, glass above salt-eaten brick, with signage reminiscent of a Grateful Dead poster. Most of the blackened window was papered with flyers and announcements. Tonight's reading was heralded by a sheet of paper headlined "Prof. George I. Qumdis Reveals The Truth Behind Zionist Imperialism." Next to that was the sticker of a boutique coffee brand, the legend "Java Inside!" and a B rating from the health department.

"B," said Milo, "means a permissible level of rodent droppings. I'd stay away from the muffins."

No coffee or muffin smells inside, just the must of old, wet news pulp. Where the walls weren't hidden by rough pine bookshelves, they were exposed block. Bookcases on wheels were arranged haphazardly at the center. Pocked vinyl floors were the color of too-old custard. A twenty-foot ceiling was spaghettied by ductwork and ladders—not library rollers on rails, just foldable, aluminum ladders—supplied for those willing to climb their way to erudition.

A heavyset, long-haired Asian kid sat behind the register, nose buried in something bound in plain brown wrappers. A sign behind him said NO SMOKING, but he puffed on an Indian herbal stick. Another sign said READING IN BACK over a pointing hand. The clerk ignored us as we filed past and began squeezing through the choppy maze created by the portable cases.

The book spines I could make out covered a host of isms. Titles shouted back in the hoarse adolescence of dime-store revolution. Milo scanned and frowned a lot. We ended up in a small, dark clearing at the rear of the store, set with thirty or so red plastic folding chairs that faced a lectern. Empty chairs. On the rear wall was a sign that said BATHROOMS (UNISEX).

No one but us.

For all his talk of good seats, Milo remained on his feet, retreating until he was back in the bookcase maze, positioning himself at a slant.

Perfect vantage spot. We could watch and remain out of view.

"It's good we're early," I whispered. "Big crush and all that."

He glanced over at the seats. "All those folding chairs. You could do group therapy."

◆

For the next ten minutes no one showed up, and we passed the time browsing. Milo seemed distracted, then his face loosened and took on a meditative cast. I browsed and by the time the first people began trickling in, I'd received a quick education on 1. How to build homemade bombs, 2. How to farm hydroponically, 3. Vandalism in the service of the greater good, and 4. The ethical virtues of Leon Trotsky.

The audience dispersed itself among the chairs. A dozen or so people, divided into what seemed to be two groups: twentyish, pierced-and-branded, dreadlocked rage hobbyists in expensive shredded duds, and sixtyish couples swathed in earth tones, the women helmeted by severe gray bobs, the men frizzy-bearded and shadowed by cloth caps.

The exception was a thickset, wavy-haired guy in his fifties, wearing a navy pea coat buttoned to the neck and crumpled houndstooth pants, who positioned himself front row center. His jaw was a stubbled shelf. He wore black-rimmed glasses, had wide shoulders and serious thighs, and looked as if he'd just finished organizing dockworkers. He sat stiffly, folded his arms across a barrel chest, scowled at the lectern.

Milo studied him, and his eyes slitted.

"What?" I whispered.

"Angry fellow up in front."

"Probably not unusual for this crowd."

"Sure," he said. "Lots to be angry about. It's comfier and cozier in fucking North Korea."

◆

Seven-forty, forty-five, fifty. No sign of Albin Larsen or the speaker or a bookstore staffer. Quiet audience. Everyone just sitting and waiting.

Just before eight, Larsen entered the room with a tall, dignified-looking man wearing a glen plaid, suede-elbowed hacking jacket, brown flannel trousers, and shiny peanut-butter-colored demiboots. I'd expected someone Mideastern, but Professor George Issa Qumdis had the ruddy complexion and magesterial bearing of an Oxford don. I put him at fifty-five to sixty, a comfortably lived middle age. His longish salt-and-pepper hair curled over the collar of a crisp white shirt. His rep tie probably meant something. Haughty nose, hollow cheeks, thin lips. He half turned his back on the audience and glanced at an index card.

Albin Larsen stepped up to the lectern and began talking in a low voice. No niceties, no thanking the audience. Right into the topic.

Israeli oppression of the Palestinian people.

Larsen spoke fluently with minimal inflection, smiling wryly as he noted the "profound historical irony" of Jews, the victims of oppression, becoming the world's greatest extant oppressors.

"How odd, how sad," intoned Larsen, "that the victims of the Nazis have adopted Nazi tactics."

Murmurs of assent from the audience. Milo's face was expressionless. His eyes shifted from Larsen to the audience and back.

Larsen's manner stayed low-key but his rhetoric poured out hot and vindictive. Each time he uttered the word "Zionism" his eyes fluttered. The audience began warming to the topic, nodding harder.

Except for the burly guy in the pea coat. His hands had dropped to his knees and he was rocking very slightly in his front-center seat. Head canted away from the lectern. I caught a clear view of his profile. Tight jaw, clenched eyes.

Milo studied him some more, and his own mandible tensed.

Larsen went on a while longer, finally indicated George Issa Qumdis with an expansive wave, took out a sheet of paper, and offered morsels from the professor's academic résumé. When he finished, Issa Qumdis walked to the podium. Just as he began to speak, footsteps behind Milo and me made both of us turn.

A man had entered our aisle. Midthirties, black, well groomed, very tall, wearing a well-cut gray suit over a charcoal shirt buttoned to the neck. He saw us, smiled apologetically, retreated.

Milo watched him edge away and hook a

quick right turn. The black man never reappeared and Milo's hands began to flex.

Why all the tension? This was a lecture at a bookstore. Maybe too much work with too little outcome. Or his instincts were sharper than mine.

Professor George Issa Qumdis unbuttoned his jacket, smoothed back his hair, smiled at the crowd, cracked a joke about being accustomed to lecturing at Harvard, where the audience hadn't reached puberty. A few chuckles from the audience. The guy in the pea coat began rocking again. One of his hands reached behind his head and scratched vigorously.

Issa Qumdis said, "The truth—the inalienable truth—is that Zionism is the most repugnant doctrine of all, in a world rife with malignant dogma. Think of Zionism as the pernicious anemia of modern civilization."

One of the pierced-and-brandeds snickered into his girlfriend's ear.

Issa Qumdis warmed to his topic, branding Jews who moved to Israel "nothing less than war criminals. Each and every one is deserving of death." Pause. "I would shoot them myself."

Silence.

Even for this audience that was strong stuff.

Issa Qumdis smiled and smoothed his lapel, and said, "Have I offended someone? I certainly hope so. Complacence is the enemy of truth and as a scholar, truth is my catechism. Yes, I'm talking about jihad. An American jihad, where—"

He stopped, openmouthed.

The guy in the pea coat had shot to his feet, and shouted, "Fuck you, Nazi!" as he fooled with the buttons of his coat.

Milo was already moving toward him as Pea Coat whipped out a gun, a big black gun, and fired straight at Issa Qumdis's chest.

Issa Qumdis's snowy white shirt turned to crimson. He stood there, wide-eyed. Reached down and touched himself and came away with a red, sticky thumb.

"You pathetic fascist," he burbled.

Still on his feet. Breathing fast, but breathing. No loss of balance. No death pallor.

Red rivulets wormed down his shirtfront and filthied the edges of his jacket.

Besmirched, but alive and healthy.

The man in the pea coat fired again, and

Issa Qumdis's face became a crimson mask. Issa Qumdis cried out, wiped frantically at his face. Albin Larsen sat in his chair, amazed, immobile.

"Oh my God," someone said.

"That's *pig's* blood!" yelled the man in the pea coat. "You Arab *pig*-fucker!" He charged toward Issa Qumdis, tripped, fell, righted himself.

Issa Qumdis, blinded by blood, kept swiping at his eyes.

Pea Coat raised his weapon. Black plastic paint gun. Shrieking, "Fascist!" a woman in the second row, one of the gray-hairs, shot to her feet and grabbed for the weapon. Pea Coat tried to shake her off. She clawed and scratched and got hold of his sleeve and hung on.

Milo hurried to the front, zigzagging through the makeshift aisles, dodging chairs, as the woman's companion, a bald, weak-chinned man wearing granny glasses and a red CCCP sweatshirt jumped up and began rabbit-punching the back of Pea Coat's neck. Pea Coat struck back at him, caught him on the shoulder, and the man fell back on his rear.

Issa Qumdis had cleared his eyes, now,

was staring at the melee. Albin Larsen stood behind him, stunned, as he handed Issa Qumdis a handkerchief and led him toward the back of the store.

By the time Milo reached the fracas, another gray-hair had joined in and Pea Coat had been pounded to the ground. The woman who'd fought for the paint gun had finally gotten hold of it. She aimed downward, shot a torrent of blood at Pea Coat but he kicked her and her aim shifted and she hit her companion instead, reddening his jeans.

"Shit!" he cried out. A flush captured his face. He began kicking viciously at Pea Coat's prone body.

Milo yanked him away. Pea Coat struggled to his feet, took a roundhouse swing at Granny Glasses, missed, and lost his balance again. Issa Qumdis and Larsen had slipped into the unisex bathroom.

The woman aimed the paint gun again, but Milo pressed down on her arm and the weapon dribbled onto the floor.

"Who're you?" she exclaimed.

A couple of pierced-and-brandeds stood. I rushed over just as someone shouted,

"Get the fascist!" and the crowd erupted into shouts and curses.

Milo grabbed Pea Coat's sleeve and dragged him toward the back door.

The young men marched forward and got within arm's length of Milo. Milo stopped the bigger one with a quick, hard squeeze of bare biceps. The man's eyes fluttered.

Milo said, "It's under control, *compadres*. Go away."

No badge-flash. His tone froze them.

I got the rear door open, and Milo shoved Pea Coat out into the briny, night air.

As the door swung shut slowly, I looked back. Most of the onlookers had remained in their seats.

A few feet behind the folding chairs, half-concealed by bookshelves—tucked in his own vantage point—stood the tall, thin black man in the good gray suit and the charcoal shirt.

◆

Behind the store was a service alley, blackened by night. Milo propelled Pea Coat westward, walking fast, shoving the man when he faltered. Pea Coat began cursing and struggling, and Milo did something to his shoulder blade that made him squeal.

"Let go of me, you commie bastard!"

"Shut up," said Milo.

"You—"

"I'm the police, idiot."

Pea Coat tried to stop short. Milo kicked at his heel, and the man jerked forward involuntarily.

"Police . . . *state,*" he said. His voice was thick and raspy, words punching out between shallow breaths. "So you're a fascist, not a commie."

"Another moron heard from." Milo spotted a parked car a few yards up, shoved Pea Coat to it, pushed him up against the trunk. Jerking one of the man's arms behind his back, he got his cuffs free, snapped them around the man's wrist, twisted the other arm, and completed the task.

Since Pea Coat had aimed his paint gun till now, no more than five minutes had passed.

The man said, "Antisemitic—"

"Keep your mouth shut and your head down."

Milo frisked him thoroughly, came up with a wallet and a key ring.

The man said, "I know exactly how much is in there, so if you're—"

Milo's finger landed atop Pea Coat's shoulder blade. The memory of the first touch made the man break off midsentence.

I could hear cars rumble by on Broadway; but for that, the night was still.

Milo inspected the wallet. "There's twenty bucks in here. You know different?"

Silence.

Then: "No."

"Twenty whole dollars," said Milo. "Preparing for a big night on the town, smart guy?"

"He's Hitler," said the man. "That pig. He lies, he's Hitler—"

Milo ignored him and read his driver's license. "Elliot Simons . . . what's this, here . . . Cedars-Sinai ID card—RN . . . you're a nurse?"

"Surgical nurse," said Elliot Simons.

"Great for you," said Milo. "You're a little out of your element, Mr. Simons."

"He's Hitler, he lies, claims to be—"

"Yeah, yeah," said Milo.

"Stop cutting me off, let me finish," said Simons. "He claims to be—"

"He's a fraud," Milo cut in. "Wrote a book,

claiming to be a Palestinian refugee from Jerusalem, but he was born in Italy, is half-English, half-Syrian. There was an exposé on it in one of the Jewish magazines."

I stared at my friend. So did Elliot Simons.

He kept quiet as Milo thumbed through his credit cards. Then: "You've been watching him? Who sent you?"

"Who do you think?" said Milo.

"The government? They finally got smart and put him under surveillance? About time, the man's a traitor, September 11 happens, and the government still can't get it right. How many outrages does it take to get you people on the ball?"

"You see Issa Qumdis as a terrorist."

"You heard him."

Simons had a workingman's face, an ordinary face. Except for his eyes. They blazed with something well beyond anger.

He rattled his cuffs. "Let me out of these."

"How long have you been stalking him?" said Milo.

"I haven't stalked anyone," said Simons. "I read the papers, found out he was spreading his lies, and decided to do something about it. I'm not apologizing for anything, you want to arrest me, go ahead. I'll tell the whole story."

"Which is?"

"The guy's Hitler with a fancy Ivy League degree." Simons's eyes heated further. "My parents were in Auschwitz. I'm not going to stand by and let some fucking Nazi spread big lies."

Milo pointed to the red splotch across the front of the pea coat. "That really pig's blood?"

Simons grinned.

"Where'd you get it?" said Milo.

"East L.A.," said Simons. "One of the slaughterhouses. I took some heparin from work and mixed it in. It's an anticoagulant, I wanted to make sure it was nice and wet."

"Fancy work. Being a surgical nurse and all."

"I'm the best," said Simons. "Could've been a doctor but couldn't afford to go to med school. My dad was always sick, couldn't work, because of what they did to him in the camp. I'm not whining, I do fine. Put four kids through Ivy League colleges. I'm the best. You don't believe me, check me out, the doctors love me. They ask for me because I'm the best."

"You know Dr. Richard Silverman?"

Simons nodded hard and fast. "I know him, he knows me. Magician with a knife—how do *you* know him?"

"I know of him," said Milo.

"Yeah, well," said Simons. "You call and ask Dr. Silverman about Elliot Simons. He knows I'm no nut; when it comes to getting the job done I'm totally focused."

"Tonight you were focused on ruining Issa Qumdis's clothes."

"If only I had a real gun—"

"Don't say more, sir," said Milo. "For your sake, I don't want to hear any threats."

" '*Sir*'," said Simons. "All of a sudden you're turning official?" Another shake of his cuffs. "So what now?"

"Where'd your kids go to school?"

"Three at Columbia, one at Yale. Fuck them," said Simons, spraying spittle. "Not my kids. *Them,* the Nazis and those commies back there who believe all that shit. Fifty years ago they wanted to exterminate us, we survived and thrived and said, 'Fuck you, we're smarter than you.' So *fuck* them. You want to arrest me for standing up for my people, fine. I'll get a lawyer, I'll file suit against the Nazi bastard who kicked me back there and his douche bag Nazi bitch. Then I'll sue that Arab scum and that Swedish prick who's probably fucking him in the ass and throw you in, too."

Breathing hard again.

Milo said, "Why'd you single out Issa Qumdis?"

"He's a Nazi, and he's here."

"Any other reason?"

"That's not reason enough for you?" said Simons. Muttering, *"Goyische kopf."*

"Yeah, I'm a stupid goy," said Milo. "Meanwhile, it's you with blood all over your clothes and your hands in cuffs and all you accomplished back there was to solidify that guy's support."

"Bullshit," said Simons. "They came in as Jew-haters, they'll go out as Jew-haters, but at least they know we're not going to stand by while they try to herd us into the ovens."

He peered at Milo. "You're not Jewish, are you?"

" 'Fraid not."

"What, German?"

"Irish."

"Irish," said Simons, as if he found that baffling. To me: "You Jewish?"

I shook my head.

Back to Milo: "So, what, cops are reading *The Jewish Beacon*?"

"I pick up stuff, here and there."

Simons smiled knowingly. "Okay, so you *are* on a serious surveillance. About time."

"The guy who introduced Issa Qumdis," said Milo. "What about him?"

"What *about* him?"

"What should I know about him?"

"Fucking *Swede*," said Simons. "Another fucking *professor*—my kids had professors at college, I could tell you stories—"

"Let's keep it to Professor Larsen, specifically," said Milo. "What should I know about him?"

"He's with that Nazi, so *he's* probably a Nazi—did you know that the Swedes *claimed* to be neutral during the war, but meanwhile they were doing business with the Nazis? SS soldiers were fucking the Swedish women right and left, having orgies, getting the Swedish women pregnant? Probably half of the supposed Swedes are German. Maybe he's one of them. Larsen. Did you hear what he said in there? I should've shot him, too."

"Stop," said Milo. "You keep talking like that, I've got to take you in."

Simons stared at him. "You're not going to?"

A car drove up the alley, slowed to pass us, continued to Sixth, and turned left.

Milo remained silent.

"What?" said Simons. "What's the deal here?"

"You drive here in your own car?"

"This is L.A., what do you think?"

"Where are you parked?"

"Around the corner."

"Which corner?"

"Sixth," said Simons. "What, you're going to *impound* me?"

"What kind of car?" said Milo.

"Toyota," said Simons. "I'm a nurse, not a goddamn doctor."

◆

Keeping the cuffs on, we walked him to his car. Two vehicles in front of my Seville. Milo's unmarked was across the street.

"Here's the deal," said Milo. "You drive straight home, don't pass Go, don't come back here. Ever. Stay away, and we call it a lesson."

"What's the lesson?" said Simons.

"That it's smart to listen to me."

"What's special about you?"

"I'm a dumb *goy* who knows the score." Milo took hold of Simons's collar, bunched it up around the man's thick neck. Simons's eyes bugged.

He said, "You're—"

"I'm doing you a favor, idiot. A big one. Don't test my good nature."

Simons stared back at him. "You're choking me."

Milo released a millimeter of fabric. "Big favor," he repeated. "Of course, if you prefer, I can arrest you, get you plenty of publicity. Some people will consider you a hero, but I don't think the doctors at Cedars are going to keep asking for you when they find out about your lack of judgment."

"They'll ask," said Simons. "I'm the—"

"You're stupid," said Milo. "You got your clothes full of pig's blood and accomplished zero."

"Those people—"

"Hate your guts and always will, but they're a fringe minority. You want to accomplish something, volunteer at the Holocaust Center, take high school kids on

tour. Don't waste your time on those idiots."
He shrugged. "That's only my opinion. You
disagree, I'll feed your martyrdom fantasies
and stick you in a nice little jail cell with
some other guy who it's a sure bet didn't
get an A in ethnic sensitivity."

Simons chewed his lip. "Life is short. I
want to stand for something."

"That's the point," said Milo. "Survival's
the best damn revenge."

"Who said so?"

"I did."

Simons finally calmed down, and Milo un-
cuffed him. He looked down at his bloody
pea coat, as if noticing the stain for the first
time, plucked at a clean bit of lapel. "This
thing's finished, I can't bring it home to my
wife."

"Good point," said Milo. "Get the hell
outta here." He returned Simons's wallet
and keys and put him in his Toyota. Simons
drove off quickly, sped up to Broadway,
turned right without a signal.

"That," said Milo, "was fun." He checked
out his own clothing.

"Clean," I said. "I already looked."

He walked me to the Seville. Just as we
got there, a voice from behind, mellow, cul-

tured, just loud enough to be audible, said, "Gentlemen? Police gentlemen?"

◆

The tall black man in the gray suit stood on the sidewalk, maybe ten feet away. Hands laced in front. Smiling warmly. Working hard at nonthreatening.

"What?" said Milo, hand trailing down toward his gun.

"Might I talk to you gentlemen, please? About one of the people in there?"

"Who?"

"Albin Larsen," said the man.

"What about him?"

The man talked through his smile. "May we talk somewhere in private?"

"Why?" said Milo.

"The things I have to say, sir. They are not . . . nice. This is not a nice man."

CHAPTER

34

Milo said, "Come forward very slowly, keeping your hands clear. Good, now show me some identification."

The man complied, drew out a shiny black billfold, removed a business card, and held it out. Milo read it, showed it to me.

Heavy stock, white paper, engraved beautifully.

Protais Bumaya

Special Envoy,
Republic of Rwanda
West Coast Consulate
125 Montgomery Street, Suite 840
San Francisco, CA 94104

"Acceptable, sir?" said Bumaya.

"For the time being."

"Thank you, sir. Might I have your name?"

"Sturgis."

Perhaps Bumaya was expecting a warmer introduction, because his smile finally faded. "There's a place—a tavern up the block. Might we convene there?"

"Yeah," said Milo. "Let's convene."

◆

The "tavern" was on the opposite side of Broadway, between Fourth and Fifth, a windowless dive named the Seabreeze, with wishfully Tudor trim and a rough, salt-ravaged door that had once passed for English oak. Remnant of the Santa Monica that had existed between the two population waves that built the beachside city: stodgy Midwestern burghers streaming westward for warmth at the turn of the twentieth century, and, seventy years later, left-leaning social activists taking advantage of the best rent control in California.

In between there'd been the kind of corruption you get when you mix tourists, hustlers, balmy weather, the ocean, but Santa

Monica remained a place molded by self-righteousness.

Milo eyed the Seabreeze's unfriendly facade. "You been here before?"

Bumaya shook his head. "The proximity seemed advantageous."

Milo shoved at the door, and we entered. Long, low, dim room, three crude booths to the left, a wooden bar refinished in glossy acrylic to the right. Eight serious drinkers, gray-haired and gray-faced, bellied up against the vinyl cushion, facing a bartender who looked as if he sampled the wares at regular intervals. Yeast and hops and body odor filled air humid enough for growing ferns. Nine stares as we entered. Frankie Valli on the jukebox let us know we were too good to be true.

We took the farthest booth. The bartender ignored us. Finally, one of the drinkers came over. Paunchy guy in a green polo shirt and gray pants. A little chrome change machine hanging from his belt said he was official.

He looked at Bumaya, scowled. "What'll it be?"

Milo ordered Scotch, and I said, "Me, too."

Protais Bumaya said, "I would like a Boodles and tonic, please."

"We got Gilbeys."

"That will be fine."

Green Shirt smirked. "It better be."

Bumaya watched him waddle off, and said, "Apparently, I have offended someone."

"They probably don't like tall, dark strangers," said Milo.

"Black people?"

"Maybe that, too."

Bumaya smiled. "I had heard this was a progressive city."

"Life's full of surprises," said Milo. "So, what can I do for you, Mr. Bumaya?"

Bumaya started to answer, stopped himself as the drinks arrived. "Thank you, sir," he told Green Shirt.

"Anything else?"

"If you've got some salted peanuts," said Milo. "If not, just a little peace and quiet, friend."

Green Shirt glared at him.

Milo downed his Scotch. "And another of these, too."

Green Shirt took Milo's shot glass, crossed over to the bar, brought back a refill and a bowl of nubby pretzels. "These salty enough?"

Milo ate a pretzel and grunted. "Gonna earn my stroke honestly."

"Huh?"

Milo flashed his wolf's grin. Green Shirt blinked. Backed away. When he'd reclaimed his stool, Milo gulped another pretzel, said, "Yeah, it's a real progressive city."

Protais Bumaya sat there, trying not to show that he was studying us. In the miserly light his skin was the color of a Damson plum. Wide-set almond eyes moved very little. His hands were huge, but his wrists were spindly. Even taller than Milo, six-four or -five. But high-waisted; he sat low in the booth, gave a strangely boyish impression.

The three of us drank for a while without talking. Frankie Valli gave way to Dusty Springfield only wanting to be with us. Bumaya seemed to enjoy his gin and T.

"So," said Milo, "what's with Albin Larsen?"

"A progressive man, Lieutenant Sturgis."

"You know different."

"You were at the bookstore observing him," said Bumaya.

"Who says it was him we were observing?"

"Who, then?" said Bumaya. "George Issa Qumdis gives political speeches all the time. He is a public man. What could a policeman learn from watching him? And that fellow in the Navy jacket. Impulsive, but not a serious criminal."

"That's your diagnosis, huh?"

"He sprays paint," said Bumaya, dismissively. "You questioned and released him. You are a detective, no?"

Milo reread Bumaya's business card. "Special Envoy. If I call this number and ask about you, what are they going to tell me?"

"At this hour, sir, you will get a recorded message instructing you to call during regular business hours. Should you call during business hours, you will encounter another recorded message replete with many choices. Should you make the correct choice, you will eventually find yourself talking to a charming woman named Lucy who is the secretary to Mr. Lloyd MacKenzie, Esquire, an articulate, charming San Francisco attorney who serves as de facto West Coast Consul for my country, the Republic of Rwanda. Mr. MacKenzie, in turn, will inform you that I am a legitimate representative of my country."

Bumaya flashed teeth. "Should you choose to avoid all that, you may simply believe me."

Milo drained his second Scotch. Strong, abrasive stuff; I was working at getting the first shot down.

"Special envoy," he repeated. "You a cop?"

"Not currently."

"But?"

"I have done police work."

"Then cut the bullshit and tell me what you want."

Bumaya's eyes glinted. He wrapped long, manicured fingers around his glass, poked a finger into the drink, pushed the lime wedge around. "I wish for Albin Larsen to get what he deserves."

"Which is?"

"Punishment." Bumaya reached into an inner pocket and produced his shiny black billfold. Flipping it open, he fingered what appeared to be a stitched seam. The stitching parted, exposing a slit. Reaching into the slit, he drew out a tiny white envelope.

Gazing across the table, Bumaya flicked

the edge of the envelope with a shiny fingernail. "How familiar are you with the genocide that ravaged my country in 1994?"

"I know that lots of people died and that the world stood by and watched," said Milo.

"Nearly a million people," said Bumaya. "The most frequently quoted figure is eight hundred thousand, but I believe that to be an underestimate. Revisionists who wish to minimize the horror claim only three hundred thousand were butchered."

"Only," said Milo.

Bumaya nodded. "My belief, backed up by observation and knowledge of specifics, is that when deaths from severe injuries are factored in the final number will be closer to one million, or perhaps even more."

"What does any of that have to do with Albin Larsen?"

"Larsen was in my country during the genocide, working for the United Nations in Kigali, our capital, during the worst of the atrocities. Consulting. A human rights consultant."

"What did that mean, in the context of your country?"

"Whatever Larsen wished it to mean. The

United Nations spends billions of dollars paying the salaries of people who do exactly as they please."

"Not a fan of world bodies, Mr. Bumaya?"

"The United Nations did nothing to stop the genocide in my country. On the contrary, certain individuals on the U.N. payroll played active and passive roles in the mass murders. International bodies have always been good at condemning tragedy after the fact, but staggeringly useless at preventing it."

Bumaya raised his glass and took a long, hard swallow. The small white envelope remained wedged between the fingers of his free hand.

"You're saying Larsen was involved in the genocide?" said Milo. "Are we talking active or passive?"

"Is there a difference?"

"Humor me, sir."

"I do not know, Detective Sturgis," said Bumaya. "Yet." He glanced at the bar.

"Want another?"

"I do but I will decline." Bumaya flicked the white envelope again. "In January of 2002, a man named Laurent Nzabakaza was arrested for complicity in the Rwandan genocide. Prior to that, Nzabakaza had served as administrator of a prison on the outskirts of Kigali. Most of the prisoner were Hutus. When the violence began, Nzabakaza unlocked their cells, armed them with spears and machetes and clubs and whatever firearms he could find, and pointed them at Tutsi homes. It was a family outing; Nzabakaza's wife and teenage sons participated, cheering the murderers on as they raped and hacked. Before all that finally came to light and Nzabakaza was arrested in Geneva, he found himself a new job. Working as an investigator for the International Criminal Tribunal for Rwanda. Albin Larsen helped him obtain that position. Larsen has done the same for other individuals, several of whom have subsequently been identified as genocide suspects."

"The bad guys are working for the court that's supposed to be trying them."

"Imagine Goering or Goebbels being paid by the Munich tribunal."

"Is Larsen some sort of bigwig among the Hutus?"

"Larsen was—is an opportunist. His credentials are impeccable. Doctorate in psychology, a professor both in Sweden and the United States. He has been on the U.N. payroll and that of several humanitarian organizations for over two decades."

"Human rights expert," I said.

Bumaya opened the little white envelope and removed a small color photo that he laid in the middle of the table.

Two smiling boys in white shirts and plaid school ties. Gleaming ebony skin, clear eyes, cropped hair, white teeth. One slightly older than the other; I guessed nine and eleven.

"These lads," said Bumaya, "are Joshua and Samuel Bangwa. At the time this picture was taken they were eight and ten. Joshua was an excellent student who loved science and Samuel, the older boy, was an excellent athlete. Their parents were Seventh Day Adventist elders who taught at a church school in the village of Butare. Shortly after Kigali fell to the Hutu insurgents, Butare was targeted because it had been a primarily Tutsi town. Both of the boys' parents were hacked to death by Laurent Nzabakaza's troops. Their mother was repeatedly raped, pre- and post-mortem. Joshua and Samuel, hidden in a closet and watching through a crack in the door, escaped and were eventually spirited out of Rwanda by an Adventist minister. As crucial witnesses against Nzabakaza, they were taken to Lagos, Nigeria, and put up at a U.N. boarding school that catered to diplomats' children and the offspring of Nigerian government officials. Two weeks after Laurent Nzabakaza was apprehended in Switzerland, the boys failed to show up for breakfast. A search of their room found them in their beds. Their throats had been cut ear to ear. A single stroke of the razor for each child, no wasted energy."

"A pro," said Milo.

Bumaya extracted the lime wedge from his glass, sucked on it, put it back. "The school was a guarded, secure facility, Detective, and there were no signs of forced entry. The case remains unsolved."

"And Albin Larsen—"

"Was a psychological consultant to the school, though seldom on the premises. However, one week before the boys were slaughtered, he arrived in Lagos and took a room in the faculty wing. The alleged reason for his visit was a U.N. site certification.

While he was there, he engaged in other local activities, as well."

"Such as—"

"Allow me to finish. Please," said Bumaya. "It has been learned that Larsen was not due to inspect the school for several months and chose to step up the schedule."

"You think he killed the two kids?" said Milo.

Bumaya's brow creased. "I have learned nothing to indicate that Larsen has ever acted violently. However, he is known to have associated with violent people and to facilitate their actions. What would you, as a detective, say about the following confluence of facts: Larsen's friendship with Laurent Nzabakaza, the threat the boys represented to Nzabakaza, Larsen's unexpected presence at the school."

Milo picked up the photo, studied the smiling faces.

Protais Bumaya said, "I'm certain Larsen hired someone to slaughter those children. Am I able to prove it? Not yet."

"You were sent here to prove it?"

"Among other assignments."

"Such as?"

"Fact-finding."

"Find any facts?" said Milo.

Bumaya sat back and exhaled. "So far, I have not accomplished much. That is why when I saw you observing Larsen I thought, 'Aha, this is my opportunity.' " He flattened his hands on the table. His knuckles were gray. "Would there be any way for you to share information with me?"

"It doesn't work that way."

Long silence.

Bumaya said, "I see."

"What else do you know about Larsen?" said Milo.

"In terms of?"

"What were his other 'local activities.' "

"Professor Larsen is a man of far-reaching interests," said Bumaya, "but for my purposes, they are not relevant."

"I care about my purposes," said Milo.

"He was involved in *programs*." Bumaya uttered the word as if it were a curse. "U.N. sponsored programs, private humanitarian programs. Larsen affixes himself to programs for personal gain."

"Misery pimp," said Milo.

Bumaya smiled faintly. "I have never

heard of that expression. I like it. Yes, that is an apt description."

"Are we talking big money?"

Bumaya's smile stretched wider. "One would think, that with all the paperwork bureaucracies require, someone would ascertain that there are only so many hours in a week."

I said, "Larsen pads his bills."

"Consultant here, consultant there. To believe his vouchers, he is the busiest man in the world."

Milo said, "What kind of programs are we talking about?"

"I am familiar only with those in my country and in Lagos. For the most part, we are talking about schools and welfare societies. At least a dozen. When one examines the paperwork *in toto,* one finds that Larsen was working 150 hours per week."

"Any of those programs involve prison rehabilitation?" said Milo.

Bumaya smiled.

"What?" said Milo.

"Prison work is how Larsen came to know Laurent Nzabakaza. He obtained Lutheran church funding for a psychological training program to help prisoners in Nzabakaza's prison overcome their criminal tendencies. Sentries for Justice. Substantial payments to Nzabakaza helped . . . is the expression, 'grease the runway'?"

"The skids," said Milo. "Grease the skids."

"Ah," said Bumaya. "In any event, the prisoners treated by Sentries for Justice were the exact group armed by Nzabakanza and aimed at Butare. Larsen had already begun an identical program in Lagos, and when the genocide ended his Rwandan activities he began concentrating more on the Nigerian branch."

One big, dark hand closed around his glass. "I believe I will take another drink."

Milo took the glass, went to the bar, brought it back, filled high.

Bumaya drank half. "Thank you . . . Larsen attempted to latch himself onto the Bosnian crisis but failed because of too much competition. Recently, he's expressed considerable interest in the Palestinian issue. Was one of the foreigners who traveled to Jenin to express support for Arafat during the Israeli siege. He supplied the U.N. with stories about the Jenin massacre."

"The one that never occurred," said Milo.

"Yes, a brief, but inflammatory international fraud ensued, and Larsen was paid for his consulting. His entrée to that region is likely because a cousin of his—Torvil Larsen—is an official with UNRWA in Gaza. When international conflict arises, Larsen will always be there to make a few dollars. If he is not stopped."

"You aiming to stop him?" said Milo.

"I," said Bumaya patting his chest, "am a fact-seeker, not a man of action."

Milo looked at the photo of the smiling boys. "Where in L.A. are you staying?"

"At the house of a friend."

Out came Milo's pad. "Name, address, and phone number."

"Is that necessary?"

"Why," said Milo, "would you have a problem telling me?"

Bumaya lowered his eyes. Finished his drink. "I'm staying with Charlotte and David Kabanda." He spelled the surname slowly. "They are physicians, medical residents at the Veterans Hospital in Westwood."

"Address?" said Milo.

"Charlotte and David know me as a university classmate. I studied law. They believe I'm a lawyer."

Milo tapped his pad. "Address."

Bumaya recited an apartment number on Ohio.

"Phone?"

Bumaya rattled off seven digits. "If you call Charlotte and David and divulge what I've told you, they will be confused. They believe I am conducting legal research."

"Their apartment your sole place of residence?" said Milo.

"Yes, Detective."

"You're an envoy but you don't get hotel chits?"

"We are a very poor country, Detective, struggling to reunify. Mr. Lloyd MacKenzie, our de facto consul, serves us at a discount rate. A genuine humanitarian."

Milo said, "What else can you tell me about Larsen?"

"I have told you much."

"Shall I repeat the question?"

"A one-way avenue," said Bumaya.

"Uh-huh."

Bumaya showed two rows of even, pearly teeth. "That is all I have to say about the matter."

"Okay," said Milo, closing the pad.

"Sir," said Bumaya, "it is in both our interests to cooperate."

"Sir," said Milo, "if there's something you need to know, I'll inform you. Meanwhile, be careful. A foreign agent getting involved in an ongoing investigation wouldn't be a good thing."

"Detective, I have no intention of—"

"Then we'll have no problem," said Milo.

Bumaya frowned.

Milo said, "Want another drink? It's on me."

"No," said Bumaya. "No, thank you." The snapshot of the murdered boys remained on the table. He picked it up, placed it back in his snakeskin billfold.

"You pretty good with firearms, Mr. Bumaya? Being a former cop and all that."

"I know how to shoot. However, I am not traveling armed."

"So if I look around your friends' apartment, no guns are going to show up?"

"Not one," said Bumaya. His mouth moved around, covering a swath of emotional territory, until it finally settled on a small, flat smile. "Perhaps I have not made myself clear, Detective Sturgis. My sole purpose is to gather facts and to report back to my superiors."

"All this trouble for Albin Larsen."

"He and others."

"Others here in L.A.?"

"Here, other cities. Other countries." Bumaya's eyes shut and fluttered open. His irises, once clear and inquisitive, had clouded. "I will be doing this for a very long time."

◆

We watched him leave the bar.

Milo said, "Think I was rough on him?"

"A bit."

"I sympathize with the cause, but he's all about his own goals, and I don't need complications. If I can get Larsen off the street, I'll be doing Bumaya and his superiors the biggest favor of all."

"Makes sense," I said.

"Does it?" He frowned. "Those two boys." He looked away, summoned Green Shirt for a third shot.

Green Shirt looked down at me. "You, too?"

I placed my hand atop my glass and shook my head. When Milo's refill arrived, I said, "Bumaya has his own agenda, but what he said firms things up for us. Larsen's got a history of exactly the kind of scam we theorized about. And he uses violence when it suits him."

"The quiet ones," Milo muttered.

"Tonight, when he introduced Issa Qumdis, he had plenty of fire."

"Ideology and profit," he said.

"Misery pimp. I like that."

He drank.

I said, "Just out of curiosity, how do you know so much about Issa Qumdis?"

"What, cops don't read?"

"Never knew you to be political."

He shrugged. "Rick leaves books and magazines around. I pick 'em up. One of them happened to be *The Jewish Beacon,* with the article that claimed Issa Qumdis invented himself."

"Never knew Rick to be political, either."

"He never was. Even gay issues didn't mobilize him." He stretched his neck and winced. "His parents are Holocaust survivors."

After all these years I knew little about Rick. About Milo's life when he closed the door of his little house in West Hollywood.

He said, "They were always getting after him about it."

"The Holocaust?"

He nodded. "They wanted him to be more aware of being Jewish. There was always baggage, the gay thing complicated it. When his folks found out, they freaked out, the Holocaust got all mixed up in it. His mother crying like someone had died. His father yelling at him and telling him he was stupid because now the Nazis would have *two* reasons to gas him."

He drank more Scotch, swirled it around like mouthwash. "He's an only child, it hasn't been easy. What made it better was the passage of time and his parents getting older. Eventually, he and his old man could talk about it."

Something Milo had never experienced before his own father died.

"Then came September 11, and Rick changed," he said. "He took it personally. The fact that Arabs were behind it, the revisionist theories blaming the Jews. All the anti-Semitic swill coming out of Saudi Arabia and Egypt. All of a sudden, Rick got more interested in being Jewish, started reading up on Jewish history, Israel. Started giving money to Zionist causes, subscribing to magazines."

"That you happened to pick up."

"The Issa Qumdis thing caught my eye because the basic point was that the guy was a scamster but that it hadn't impeded his academic career. That always fascinates me. How little reality has to do with the way life plays out—he *was* something, wasn't he? Tenure Personified, that cultured stance, then coming out and saying people should be killed. Pretty damn hateful for a college professor."

"Lots of hatred in academia," I said.

"You've seen that, personally?"

"It's usually more subtle, but you'd be amazed at what goes on at faculty parties when the scholarly set thinks no one's listening."

"Wonder if Issa Qumdis spouts off that way at Harvard. Don't colleges have hate speech regulations?"

"The rules are enforced selectively."

"Whose ox is being gored . . . yeah, it's a sweet world. Enough about that, time to focus on the evil Dr. Larsen. Learn anything about any local scam?"

"Not yet. I asked Olivia to look into it.

Gave her the Sentries program as a lead because I came across it surfing."

"Sentries for Justice . . . Olivia's as good as it gets . . . By the way, Franco Gull finally broke routine and went to a health club. Pumped iron, ignored the ladies, went home. So maybe he knows about the scam and what the stakes are. The guy tends to get emotional. Maybe he can be wedged and cracked open. Make sense?"

"You'd be showing your hand."

"Yeah, but if I don't make any other progress soon, what choice do I have?" He rubbed his face. "Okay, I'll wait till you hear from Olivia, but eventually I'm gonna have to make a decision—" His cell phone beeped, he slapped it against his ear. "Sturgis . . . when? Really. Okay, give me the number."

His pad and pen were still out and he scrawled hastily, clicked the phone shut with a strange smile on his face. "Well, well, well."

"Who was that?"

"Detective Binchy. Obedient lad that he is, he is at his desk wrapping up his paperwork before he sets out for another looksee on Gull. A call just came in for me, and he took it. Sonny Koppel, wanting to talk. He's *dining*. Coffee shop on Pico. I'm invited to drop by."

"That include me?"

"Sure," he said. "I'm including you."

CHAPTER
35

The coffee shop was called Gene's, and it was one of the few bright spots on a dark, quiet block. South side of Pico, just a few yards from the traffic on La Cienega. A short stroll from the eastern border of Milo's district.

It was ten-forty when we got there, and the place was fully lit. Long, skinny room with grubby vinyl floors, a Formica counter, and seven matching tables bleached by high wattage. A sign in front said OPEN TO MIDNIGHT. Inside, two young guys in oversized eyeglasses whispered conspiratorially over coffee, pie, and the bound screenplay placed equidistant between them. An old woman gummed an egg salad sandwich.

Behind her, a muscular man in gray work clothes read old news in the morning paper and worked on a hamburger.

Shrouded in a limp, gray raincoat, Sonny Koppel sat at the counter forking bacon and eggs into his mouth. The counterman ignored Koppel, as he scrubbed a deep fryer. When we approached, he turned briefly then returned to his chore.

Koppel wiped his mouth, got off his stool, and carried his plate, his napkin, and his utensils to a front table. Near the door but away from the other diners. Under his raincoat, he wore mocha brown sweats with white piping. Loosely laced tennis shoes covered smallish, wide feet. He'd shaved recently, had nicked himself several times.

His coffee cup remained behind, and Milo brought it over to the table. The counterman turned, and said, "Anything for you guys?"

"No, thanks."

Koppel was still on his feet when Milo brought the coffee cup over.

"Thanks," he said. "One sec." Returning to the counter, he snagged ketchup and Tabasco sauce. Finally, he pulled out a chair, sat, wiped his lips. Bounced a fork tine against the rim of his plate and smiled at his plate. "Breakfast food. I like it for dinner."

"To each his own," said Milo. "What can we do for you?"

"That photograph—of that girl. Do you still have it with you?"

Milo reached into his jacket pocket, produced the death shot, and handed it to Koppel.

Koppel studied it and nodded. "When you first showed it to me, there was something about it. But I couldn't place it, really had nothing I could tell you, so I said I'd never seen her. I really wasn't sure I had." He licked his lips. "But it stuck in my mind."

"Now you think you know her," said Milo.

"I can't be certain," said Koppel. "If it is her, I only saw her a couple of times—literally. Two times." He glanced at the photo again. "The way she is here, it's hard to say . . ."

"Death'll do that to you."

Koppel swallowed air. Forked a strip of bacon, lost it midair, and watched it land just shy of his plate. He picked it up between his fingers, set it back next to the mound of eggs, kissed the grease on his fingertips.

"Where do you think you might've seen her, Mr. Koppel?" said Milo.

"She might be a girl I saw at Jerry Quick's office. Hanging around with Jerry's secretary."

"Jerry's secretary . . ."

"Angie Paul."

"You know Angie personally?"

"I know her from coming over to talk to Jerry about the rent." Koppel scratched the side of his nose. "You're interested in her, as well? She always made me wonder."

"About what?"

"She didn't seem to do much. She wasn't who I'd pick as a secretary. Then again, she probably didn't have to make much of an impression."

"Why's that?"

"Not much traffic at Jerry's office. I've never seen anyone there but the two of them."

"And possibly this girl?"

"Maybe," said Koppel. "Only maybe."

Milo said, "You don't drop in very often at Mr. Quick's office, but this girl was there twice."

Koppel flushed. "I don't . . . all I'm saying—what do I know? If I wasted your time, I'm sorry."

Milo placed an index finger on a corner of the death shot.

Sonny Koppel said, "This must seem strange to you. First I say I don't know her, then I call you."

Milo smiled.

"I'm just trying to do the right thing, Lieutenant."

"We appreciate that, sir. What else can you tell us about this girl?"

"Just that," said Koppel, peering at the death shot for several more seconds. "It could be her."

"A girl hanging around with Angie in Mr. Quick's front office."

"That was the first time. Two, three months ago. The second time was more recent—six weeks ago. I saw the two of them—her and Angie—as they left the building together. It was lunchtime, I assumed they were going out to lunch."

"Where'd they go to eat?"

"I didn't follow them, Lieutenant. I was there to see Jerry."

"About the rent."

"Yes." Koppel scratched behind his ear.

"I'm getting the feeling that by trying to do what's right I'm complicating my life."

"In what way, sir?"

"Like I said, it must seem funny to you." Koppel pushed the photo toward Milo. "Anyway, that's all I know."

Milo passed the shot from hand to hand, like a three-card monte artist. "Hanging around with Angie."

"Talking. Like girls do."

"Girls just wanna have fun," said Milo.

"They didn't seem to be having fun," said Koppel. "What I mean is they weren't laughing or giggling. In fact, the time I saw them leaving together I figured it for some sort of serious discussion because when they saw me they shut up fast."

"Serious discussion on the way to lunch."

"Maybe they weren't going to eat. I'm assuming because it was lunchtime."

"Did Angie call the other girl by name?"

"No."

"What else can you tell me about her? Physically."

"She wasn't tall—average. Slim. She had a good figure. But she was a bit . . . she didn't look like someone who'd grown up with money."

"Nouveau riche?" said Milo.

"No," said Koppel. "More . . . her clothes were nice but maybe a little too . . . obvious? Like she wanted to be noticed? Maybe she wore a bit too much makeup, I can't really remember—I don't want to tell you things that aren't accurate."

"A little flashy."

Koppel shook his head. "That wasn't it. I don't want to be cruel . . . she looked . . . a little trashy. Like her hair. No hair is that blond naturally, unless you're five years old, right?"

"Sounds like you had a good look at her."

"I noticed her," said Koppel. "She was pretty. And shapely. I'm a guy, you know how it is."

Milo smiled faintly. "Anything else?"

"No, that's it." Koppel picked up his fork. The eggs had hardened. He speared a big clot and shoved it into his mouth. The two guys with the screenplay got up from their table, looking vexed, and left the coffee shop in silence.

Milo said, "Last time we spoke, you mentioned your ex-wife wanting to use the bottom floor of her building for group therapy."

"She was supposed to give me a final answer before she . . . before her death."

"She give you any details about the nature of the therapy?"

"No," said Koppel. "Why would she?"

"No particular reason," said Milo. "Still gathering facts."

"Have you made any progress at all?"

Milo shrugged.

Sonny Koppel said, "Whatever the group therapy thing was, it's not going to happen. Albin Larsen called me yesterday, said it was okay to rent out the bottom floor. Mary was the glue that held them together. With her gone, it wouldn't surprise me if Larsen and Gull tried to break their lease."

"They don't like the building?"

"I'm not sure they'll be willing to take on the financial burden. Mary got a sweetheart rent deal from me. There's no lease, it's month to month."

"You're gonna raise it?"

"Hey," said Koppel, "business is business."

"You have a problem with them?"

"I had very little to do with them. Like I said, Mary held things together. Whenever there was some business to discuss—a repair, whatever—Mary was the one who'd call." Koppel smiled. "I didn't mind. It was a chance for us to talk. Now . . ."

He threw up his hands.

Milo said, "She was the business person, but it was Larsen who got her interested in halfway houses."

"He struck me as an idea guy," said Koppel. "But when it came to the nuts and bolts, it was all Mary."

"Mary and you."

"I had nothing to do with the day-to-day operations. I just know something about real estate."

"Like getting government funding," said Milo.

Koppel nodded. No blink, no tremble, not a single errant muscle.

"Did your ex-wife ever ask for help getting some sort of government funding for the group therapy she planned downstairs?"

"Why would she? What would I know about therapy?"

"You're a savvy person."

"In my limited sphere," said Koppel. "I already told you, Mary never consulted me on professional matters." He twirled his fork. "It's getting to me. Mary's death. Pretty stupid, huh? We hadn't been together for years, how often did we talk, once a month, tops. But I find myself thinking about it. For someone you know to go like that." He caressed his voluminous belly. "This is my second dinner. I do that—add meals—when things pile up."

As if to illustrate, he ingested two bacon strips.

"Mary was a powerful person," he said, between mouthfuls. "It's a big loss."

◆

Milo waltzed around the prison rehab issue, but Koppel wasn't biting. When Koppel called over to the counterman for a double order of rye toast and jelly and tea with honey, we left him opening marmalade packets and returned to the Seville.

Milo said, "So what's his game?"

"Sounding you out. And letting you know he knew nothing about Mary Lou's professional dealings."

"Nudging us closer to the blonde."

"Closer to Jerry Quick," I said. "Deflecting attention from himself."

"A big man who dances fast. Larsen's call

about not needing the space—think they're pulling up the tents?"

"Probably."

"The blonde hanging with Angie. Wonder if it really happened."

"One way to find out," I said.

◆

Angela Paul's last known address was a big-box, fifty-unit apartment complex just west of Laurel Canyon Boulevard and north of Victory, in an undistinguished section of North Hollywood. The freeway was a mile south, near Riverside Drive, but you could still hear it, rumbling, insistent.

The air was ten degrees warmer than back in the city. A sign in front of the complex said two months of free satellite TV was included with new leases and that this was a security building. Security meant card-key subterranean parking and a pair of low-gated entrances. All that had no effect on the litter in the gutters or the splotchy blemishes that stained the facade—painted-over graffiti.

No parking spots. Milo told me to pull into a red zone near the corner, he'd pay for the ticket.

The twin gates meant two groups of mail slots. A. Paul's button was on the north end of the building. Apt 43. No answer. No manager's unit listed. Back to the southern gate.

Apt 1, no name, just *Mgr*.

It was 11:40 P.M. Milo jabbed the button.

I said, "Let's hope for a night owl."

"What's a little sleep deprivation in the service of justice?"

◆

A male voice said, "Yes?"

"Police."

"Hold on."

I said, "He doesn't sound surprised. Maybe the tenants are interesting."

A buzzer sounded, and we pushed through the gate.

The fifty units were arranged in two tiers that looked down on a long, rectangular courtyard that should have held a pool. Instead there was sketchy grass and lawn chairs and a collapsed umbrella. A couple of utility doors on the ground floor were marked TO PARKING LOT. Three satellite dishes rimmed the flat roof. TV sounds washed across the courtyard. Then: music, a smudge of human voice, breaking glass.

The manager's unit was just to the right, and a man stood in the open doorway. Young, short, maybe thirty, with a head shaved clean and a little frizzle of chin beard. He wore gym shorts, a baggy white T-shirt that read WOLF TRAP 2001, and rubber flip-flops.

When we reached him, he said, "I was expecting uniforms."

"You get a lot of uniforms?"

"You know, noise calls and such."

Milo flashed his ID.

"Lieutenant? Is this serious or something?"

"Not yet, Mr . . ."

"Chad Ballou." He extended his hand for a soul-shake, thought better of it, and rotated into the conventional position.

Milo said, "Lots of noise calls?"

Ballou's eyes traced the tiers. "Not more than you'd expect with all these people. I tell the tenants to let me know first if there's a problem, but sometimes they don't. Which is fine, I don't really want to deal with their stuff."

"You manage the units full-time?" said Milo.

Chad Ballou said, "Relatively full-time. My

parents own the place. I'm at CSUN, studying classical guitar. They think I should
study computers. The deal is I do this instead of their just giving me money." He
smiled cheerfully. "So what's up?"

"We're looking for Angela Paul."

Ballou touched his chin growth with his
right hand. His nails were longish and
glossed. Those on his left hand were
clipped short. "Paul . . . Forty-three?"

"That's the one."

"The stripper."

"You know that for a fact?"

"She put it on her lease application," said
Ballou. "Brought in pay stubs from a club to
prove it. My folks wouldn't have approved,
but I said, hey, why not? Her income's better than a lot of the losers who try to get in."
Ballou grinned. "They put me in charge, I
figure it's up to me to decide. Anyway, she's
been no problem, pays her rent. What's the
deal?"

"We want to question her about an ongoing investigation."

"Have you tried her unit?"

"No answer."

"Guess she's out."

"She out a lot?"

"I wouldn't know," said Ballou.

"You have a pretty good view from your place," said Milo.

"When I'm here, I'm mostly practicing or studying. Unless there's a complaint. And she never complained about anything."

"She have visitors?"

"I couldn't tell you that, either. I haven't really seen her much. Forty-three's all the way on the north end, upstairs. She can take the corner staircase down to the parking lot door, go in and out without being noticed."

"So you've never seen her with anyone else?"

"Nothing registers."

Milo showed him the shot of the blond girl.

Ballou's eyes widened. "She looks dead."

"She is."

"Wow—so this is really serious. Is she going to be in trouble—the stripper? All I need is for some big mess that freaks out my parents."

Milo waved the photo. "Never seen her?"

"*Never.* What happened to her?"

"Someone made her dead."

"Jesus . . . you're not going to tell me if I have something to worry about?"

"If Angie Paul's body is lying moldering in her unit, you might."

Chad Ballou blanched. "Shit—you're serious?"

"You mind taking a look?"

"I'll give you the key," said Ballou. "You look."

"Legally," said Milo, "that would pose a problem. You as the manager, have a right to make reasonable inspections. Say, if there's a suspected gas leak, or a circuit goes out. Any maintenance issue."

Ballou stared at him. "Moldering . . . sure, sure—can I just open the door, and you look?"

"Fine."

"Should we do it now?"

"In a sec," said Milo. "First tell me where Ms. Paul does her stripping?"

"That I can do. That I can definitely do."

We followed Ballou into his apartment. Neat, sparse, devoid of character, with a sixty-inch digital TV in the front room along with three classical guitars on stands. The set was tuned to MTV. Heavy metal band, high volume. Ballou turned it down, saying, "I'm eclectic."

In the kitchen, next to the fridge, stood a trio of three-drawer files. Ballou opened the center drawer and fished out a black file folder. He opened it, thumbed, said, "Here we go," and held out a sheet of paper.

Angie Paul's rental application. She'd claimed income of three thousand a month net, and a note in the margin said, "Verified." Under place of employment, she'd listed *"The Hungry Bull Club, W.L.A. branch (Exotic Dancer)."* My eyes dropped to the bottom of the form. Personal references.

1. Rick Savarin (manager, THB)
2. Christina Marsh (coworker)

Christa or Crystal.

I said, "You ever check out her references?"

Ballou said, "She showed me pay stubs."

"What about previous landlords?" said Milo. "Isn't it standard to call them?"

"I think," said Ballou, "that she said she was from out of town."

"Where?"

"Is this going to matter? Oh, man."

Milo said, "Where out of town?"

"I don't remember. She made enough money to handle the rent easily and came up with first, last, and damage deposit. So she stripped, big deal. She's been an okay tenant."

Milo folded the application and put it in his pocket. "Let's have a look at her place."

♦

Angie Paul's unit was similar in dimension to Ballou's. Also neatly kept, with a smaller TV, cheap furniture, cotton throws, a couple of rose-and-kitten prints on the walls. The smell of heavy, musky perfume reached the doorway where I stood near Chad Ballou.

Milo disappeared into the bedroom area. Ballou tapped his foot, and said, "So far, so good?"

I smiled. It didn't comfort him.

A minute later, Milo emerged saying, "Nothing moldering. When Ms. Paul shows up, don't tell her we were here but give me a call." He handed Ballou a card.

"Sure . . . can I lock up?"

"Yup."

The three of us descended the stairs, and

Milo had Ballou point out Angie Paul's parking slot. Empty.

"She still driving a '95 Camaro?"

"Think so," said Ballou. "Yeah, bright blue."

◆

We returned to the Seville. Half past midnight. No parking ticket.

"Lady Luck's smiling down on us," said Milo. "Finally."

I said, "Christina Marsh."

"Yeah, could be."

I started up the engine and he slapped a manic cha-cha beat on the dashboard. Three Scotches and Lord knew how many consecutive work hours, and he was running a mental marathon.

"Good morning," I said.

"You tired?"

"Not a bit."

"Me neither. When's the last time you visited a strip joint?"

"Not for a while."

"I've been to a few," he said. Big grin. "Seen women strip, too."

CHAPTER
36

The Hungry Bull, West L.A. branch, was on Cotner off Olympic, in an industrial zone that smelled like rubber cement. Next to the club was a Rolls-Royce junkyard, husks of once-glorious chassis and auto viscera piled high behind chain-link.

Not much farther was a co-op art gallery where a gifted painter had been strangled to death in a bathroom. The last case Milo and I had worked together. If he was thinking about that, he wasn't showing it.

The club was housed in a windowless hangar painted matte black. Double-quilted chromium doors looked tacked on. A neon sign promised strong drinks and beautiful women.

The industrial setting was perfect: no day-time neighbors with NIMBY fever, no one to complain about the hyperdisco two-four boogie beat punching through black stucco.

The strip joint billed itself as a "gentle-man's club." The parking lot was full of dusty compacts and pickups, and the two dark-haired guys guarding the doors were elephantine and tattooed. Somehow, I doubted we'd find jowly hale-fellows savor-ing cognac and fine cigars amid book-lined, mahogany splendor.

Milo showed his badge to Elephant One and received a bow-and-scrape. "Yessir, what can I do for you?"

"Rick Savarin on tonight?"

The bouncer's cantaloupe face was bi-sected by an old gray knife scar that ran from the middle of his brow, changed direc-tion across the bridge of his nose, mean-dered across his lips, and terminated in the crook of a chin you could lean on for sup-port.

"Yessir. He's in his office. Someone will di-rect you, sir."

"Thanks."

"You're welcome, sir."

Elephant Two, even bigger and sun-glassed, held the door. Immediately inside, yet another giant, this one lanky and long-haired and Caribbean, ushered us to the left, down a short corridor that ended at swinging doors, also quilted, in black vinyl.

The main room's color scheme was black with crimson trim. Three steps led to a sunken pit where intent-looking men ringed a circular stage. Two women danced naked, pulling off some pretty good gymnastic moves, and making love to stainless-steel poles. Both were ultrablond, big-haired, rail-thin, with breasts inflated well past biology. Each wore a red garter on her left thigh. The girl with the sun-ray tattoo bluing her entire back had more cash stuffed in hers.

We reached the black vinyl doors. The lanky giant pointed and pushed them open. He stayed behind as we entered a short vestibule with two unmarked wooden doors and one with an aluminum sign that read MANAGER.

Before Milo could knock, the door opened, and a young man wearing an extravagant black toupee smiled and held out his hand. "Rick Savarin. Come on in."

Savarin had on a soft-draping, powder blue suit with shawl-lapels, black silk T-shirt, blue Gucci loafers with no socks, a gold chain around a too-tan neck. His office was small and functional and smelled like a Shirley Temple. On his desk was a framed photo of a plain-looking woman and a puzzled toddler.

Savarin said, "My sister, back in Iowa. Sit down, make yourselves comfortable. Can I get you guys something to drink?"

"No thanks," said Milo. "You from Iowa, too?"

Savarin smiled. "Long time ago."

"Farm boy?"

"That was a *real* long time ago." Savarin slid behind his desk, sat, wheeled his chair to the wall, braced himself with a loafer on a drawer handle. On the wall were several nude calendars with the Hungry Bull logo and one from a liquor distributor.

"So," he said, tenting his hands. He looked around thirty-five, was well built, with puffy blue eyes and a tense mouth. When the mouth opened, a band of flashy dentition blared forth. Snowy caps. The hairpiece looked borrowed.

Milo said, "Angie Paul."

"Angie?" said Savarin. "She worked here a while back. Her stage name was Angie Blue."

"The nails."

"The nails, the G-string, she drove a blue car. It's a competitive environment, and the girls figure they need something distinctive. In Angie's case a nice rack would've helped, but she convinced herself blue was a big deal." Savarin chuckled. "So what's she been up to?"

"We're looking for her as a person of interest," said Milo. "When did she stop working here?"

"Four months ago."

"Did she quit or was she fired?"

"She quit," said Savarin. "One of the customers—one of her regulars—swept her off her feet."

"Fraternizing with the customers?"

"It's against the rules, and we do our best to enforce it. But the girls who work here aren't exactly into rules."

"Who was the regular?"

"Some middle-aged guy, used to show up

two, three times a week, then we wouldn't see him, then he'd be back."

"To see Angie?"

"Always," said Savarin. "Lucky for her." He passed a hand over his chest. "Some guys like the natural look. With all the silicone and saline I see all day, frankly a girl with a sweet face and a natural rack is a turn-on for me. But most customers?" He shook his head. "Even guys who like natural want *something,* and Angie was pretty near flat. I didn't want to hire her, but she had good hips and a good butt, moved good during her audition. Also, she caught me at a time when I was low on girls."

"This regular really went for her."

"He came only on days when she was dancing, sat right in front, kept his eyes on her nonstop. She started doing her thing for him. He tipped her heavy; I guess they developed a relationship." Savarin scratched his head. "I never saw her do a lap dance for him; that should've tipped me off."

"How so?"

"He had no need for lap because he was getting it after hours."

"Describe this guy."

"Middle-aged, pretty ordinary," said Savarin. "I never learned his name because he always paid cash and sat by himself and one time when I went over to ask if there was anything he needed, he blew me off."

"What'd he say?"

"He just waved his hand, like don't bother me, I'm concentrating. Fine with me, it was his cash. He drank mostly soft stuff but a lot of it. Five, six Cokes a night. With lime. Occasionally he'd want some rum in it."

"Middle-aged," said Milo.

"I'd say fifty. Six feet tall, kind of skinny— kind of slumpy."

"Slumpy."

"Standing bent over, you know? Like something was sitting on his shoulders."

Milo nodded. "What else?"

Savarin said, "Let's see . . . gray hair."

"Gray comb-over?"

Savarin flinched. "I wouldn't call it a comb-over. Not a formal, sprayed-in-place comb-over. This was more like he was shoving what he had to one side and for-getting about it."

"What about his clothes?"

"Casual—sweaters. I can tell you what he drove. Little Baby Benz, black, or maybe gray. Dark. Mr. Businessman. I figured him for money, some guy with an office, a lawyer or something."

"He always come in by himself?"

"Always. Kept to himself, too."

"Angie ever mention his name?"

"I'm thinking," said Savarin. "Maybe Larry? She only mentioned it one time, and that was when she gave her notice. To be honest, I wasn't sorry to see her go."

"Small rack," said Milo.

"That and not the best attitude. Up there—onstage, it's all about putting your-self in a special place. A *giving* place. You've got to convince the clients you care about them. Angie had a sullen thing going on. Some guys dig that, the thrill of the chase, you know? But most of 'em want big smiles, this big welcome. That's what we're all about."

"Welcoming the clientele."

"Hospitality," said Savarin. "When some-one spunkier came along I'd probably have let Angie go. You can teach someone moves, but if they don't want to learn hos-pitality, you can't teach them."

"So she came in here and gave notice and said she was going off with Larry."

"I think it was 'Larry,'" said Savarin. "Don't ask me to swear on it."

"What she say about him?"

"She said she'd gotten a better offer from one of her regulars. Making it sound like she was getting some kind of important job, but I figured he was putting her up on the side."

"Why's that?"

"Guy like that," said Savarin. "Money to burn, she's thirty years younger than him. You don't come in here looking for office managers."

"She said he had an office?"

"Maybe . . . this was months ago."

"Could the regular's name have been 'Jerry'?" said Milo.

Savarin brightened. "You know I think it was. Larry, Jerry . . . who is he?"

"A guy."

"He hurt her?"

Milo shook his head. "What about Christina Marsh?"

"Christi? Friend of Angie's. Referred Angie to us. She quit, too, maybe a month after Angie. Her I *was* sorry to see go. Not huge in the chest department but big enough, and with a real nice shape to them—like pears, you know? Sweet little pink nipples, she didn't have to rouge 'em. Her whole body had this milk-fed thing going on. Limber, too. She could really work the pole."

"Why'd she quit?"

Savarin shook his head. "Her I don't know, she just stopped showing up. I called her once, twice, she didn't return, I moved on." He held out his hands. "This business, pays to be philosophical."

"You have a number for her?"

"Probably somewhere. The owners come in periodically and clear paper, but maybe something's still there."

"Who are the owners?"

"Consortium of Chinese-American businessmen. Lucky guys."

"Business is good," said Milo.

"Business is *great,* wish I had a piece. I get bonuses, though."

"Where's corporate headquarters?" said Milo.

"Monterey Park. The original club is there, it was designed for an Asian clientele. There are seven others besides this one. Ontario, San Bernardino, Riverside. All the way down to San Diego County. My cash flow's among the best."

"Any other owners besides the guys from Monterey Park?"

"Nope."

"Who owns the building?"

Savarin smiled. "Nice little eighty-year-old lady from Palm Springs who inherited from her husband. Grace Baumgarten. She came in one time, watched the girls dance, said she remembered when she could move like that."

"Anyone else involved in the business?"

"Besides employees?"

"Any other owners?"

"No, that's it."

"What about bouncers? Any others besides the guys on tonight?"

"I use some Cal State football players from time to time," said Savarin.

"Ever use a guy named Ray Degussa?"

"Nope. Who's he?"

"A guy."

"Okay, I won't ask," said Savarin. "But *can* I ask why you want to know about Angie and this Jerry guy and Christi? What I mean to say, is it something that could affect business?"

Milo showed him the death shot. Savarin's tan lost some bronze.

"That's Christi. Oh, man. What the hell happened to her?"

"That's what we're trying to find out."

"Christi," said Savarin. "Oh, man. She was basically a nice kid. Not too smart, but nice. Talk about your farm girl. I think she was from Minnesota or someplace. Natural blonde. Oh, man. That's a shame."

"Big shame," said Milo.

"Let me see if I can find you that paperwork."

◆

Out in the vestibule Savarin unlocked one of the unmarked doors on a closet full of boxes and bottles of cleaning fluids. He rummaged through file boxes. It took a while but he came up with a single sheet of pink paper labeled Employee Data that listed a Social Security number and a mailing address for Christina Marsh and nothing else.

Vanowen Boulevard, North Hollywood. Not far from Angie Paul's apartment complex. Christina Marsh had begun working at the club eight months ago, stopped showing up six months later.

Soon after Gavin had begun therapy.

Milo said, "There's no phone number here."

Savarin took a look at the sheet. "Guess not. I think she said she hadn't gotten one yet. Just moved, or something like that."

"From Minnesota."

"I think it was Minnesota. She looked Minnesota, real creamy. Sweet kid."

"Not bright," I said.

"When she filled this out," said Savarin, "it took her a real long time, and she was moving her lips. But she was a great worker."

"Uninhibited," I said.

"She'd squat for a dollar tip, show you everything. But there was nothing . . . foxy about it."

"Sexy but not foxy?"

"Sexy *because* it wasn't foxy," said Savarin. "What I'm trying to say is there was nothing *teasy* about her. It was like fucking the pole and showing everything was just a way to show off what nature gave her. Wholesome, you know? Guys like that."

Milo said, "Did she mention where she worked before?"

Savarin shook his head. "When I saw how she moved, I didn't ask any more questions."

"She have any regulars?"

"No, she wasn't that way, she circulated."

"Unlike Angie."

"Angie knew she couldn't compete physically, so she concentrated on finding one guy, really worked him. Christi was a people person, pulled in max tips. That's why I was surprised when she didn't show up. How long ago was she . . . when did it happen?"

"Couple of weeks ago," said Milo.

"Oh. So she was doing something in between."

"Any idea what?"

"I'd say dancing at another club, but I'd have found out."

"The club grapevine."

Savarin nodded. "It's a small world. Girl moves to the competition, you hear about it."

"Who's the competition?"

Savarin rattled off a list of clubs, and Milo copied them down.

"The girls working tonight," he said. "Any of them know Christi or Angie?"

"Doubt it. None of them have been here longer than a couple of months. Not at this branch, anyway. That's our big thing. We cycle the talent."

I said, "Helps avoid too many 'Jerrys.' "

"Keeps *everything* fresh," said Savarin.

Milo said, "It's a small world. Maybe one of the girls knew Angie or Christi from before."

"You can go backstage and talk to them, but you'd probably be wasting your time."

"Well," said Milo, "I'm no stranger to that."

◆

Backstage was a cluttered corridor crowded with costumes on racks and makeup on tables, bottles of aspirin and Mydol, lotions and hair clips, ambitious wigs on Styrofoam forms. Three girls lounged in robes, smoking. A fourth, slender and dark, sat naked with one leg propped on a table, trimming her pubis with a safety razor. Up close, the pancake makeup caked. Up close the girls looked like teenagers playing dress-down.

None of them knew Angela Paul or Christina Marsh and when Milo showed them the death shot, their eyes grew frightened and wounded. The girl with the razor began to cry.

We muttered some words of comfort and left the club.

◆

The detectives' room was empty. We continued to Milo's office, and he kept the door open and stretched in his chair. It was nearly 2 A.M.

He said, "So what're they doing in Minnesota? Milking the cows? Harvesting wild rice?" He shook his head. "Milk-fed."

I said, "Too early to start calling locals?"

He rubbed his eyes. "Want coffee?"

"No, thanks."

He pulled out the picture of Christi Marsh and stared at it. "Finally, a name." Switching on his computer, he ran her name through NCIC, the local databases. No hits. Not even a driver's license, and her Social Security number pulled up no record of employment.

"Phantom girl," he said.

"If she was freelancing at a cash business," I said. "There'd be no need for record-keeping?"

"A pro, like you suspected. So where'd she meet Angie?"

"Working at a club that doesn't file paper.

Or Angie was hooking, too. The Vice guys didn't know Christi because she was new in town, hadn't gotten caught."

"Minnesota," he said. "I'll start calling there in a couple of hours. Got *lots* of calls to make. Sure you don't want some coffee? I'm gonna have some."

"No sleep for the weary?"

"I got out of the habit." He pushed himself to his feet, slouched away, returned with a Styrofoam cup. Plopping down, he drank, rubbed his eyes some more.

"When's the last time you did sleep?" I said.

"Can't recall. What, you're fading?"

"I'm good for a while longer."

He put his cup down. "It's like there are two parallel things going on, the Jerry Quick side and the Albin Larsen–Sonny Koppel side. I'm having trouble putting them together. Let's start with Jerry: shady guy, sexually inappropriate, uses prepaid phones, travels a lot, allegedly to trade metals but doesn't make much money at it. Doesn't pay his rent on time, chases tail, and doesn't bother to hide it from his wife. When he's in town, he leaves his wife alone at night so he can enjoy his favorite stripper.

Eventually, he hires her away to be his alleged secretary even though her nails are too damn long for typing. Savarin was probably right, Jerry kept Angie on the side, put her in the office as a way to make it look legit. That way, she'd be in proximity if he felt like a little desktop aerobics. Now he's gone, and so is Angie."

"The two of them hiding out together," I said.

"The question is: hiding from what?"

"Things are falling apart, the scam's gone bad. Jerry and Angie know why Gavin was murdered. Know they could be next."

He considered that. "I still can't see any role for Quick in the scam, but who knows what the hell he's really about . . . okay, so maybe he even feels guilty about Gavin, but most of all he doesn't want the truth to come out because that'll point the finger at him as helping cause his kid's death. He cleans out Gavin's room, stashes Sheila at her sister's, plans to go back home and finish the cleanup but gets scared and lams, taking Angie with him. She's got to be freaked out, too—losing her friend, Christi. The girl she and Jerry hooked up with Gavin, to keep Gavin happy."

"Angie didn't seem freaked when we talked to her," I said. "She blinked when you showed her the picture—but that's still pretty cool."

"True," he said. "Cool girl. A pro."

"In terms of Jerry's role in the scam, maybe he worked for Sonny as a fixit guy, some kind of procurer. What if he hired Angie away from the club for more than sex on the side? A hooker/stripper might know some cons, and cons are raw meat for the scam."

"Jerry's a pimp . . . They'd have Bennett Hacker and Ray Degussa to supply cons."

"For all we know," I said, "it was Jerry who put Hacker and Degussa in contact with the others. Degussa is a bouncer, and a guy like Jerry who frequents strip clubs would meet bouncers. Through Degussa, Jerry met Hacker. He introduced the two of them to Sonny Koppel, who just happened to have an interest in some halfway houses."

"Jerry's being Sonny's tenant was a front, and Sonny spun us that yarn about Jerry not paying his rent to snow us."

"And to distance himself from Jerry. An enterprising fellow like Sonny would've seen the opportunity. He's got the halfway houses and, because of Jerry Quick, the contacts. Toss in an ex-wife with an interest in prison reform and her partner, a guy with a twenty-year history of making money off misery, and it would've seemed perfect."

"Meeting of the nasty little minds," he said. "Perfect till it wasn't."

I said, "Gavin's accident started the downward spiral. He underwent personality changes, turned into a stalker, got busted, and needed court-ordered therapy. Sonny could fix that, by sending Gavin to someone who could be counted upon to say the right things to the court. But that good deed came back to bite him, because Gavin started thinking of himself as a muckraker. He snooped and found some serious muck."

Milo closed his eyes, and sat without moving. For a moment I thought he'd fallen asleep. Then he sat up and stared at me, blankly, as if he'd been dreaming.

I said, "You still with me?"

Slow nod.

"Jerry lied to us about the referral, made up the story about Dr. Silver being his golf partner precisely because he wanted to hide his ties to the group. He suggested it was a sex crime. Another attempt to deflect you."

"Dear old Dad," he said. "Claims to be a metals dealer, but he's really a pimp."

"With Gavin's stalking problem, Jerry probably figured he was being a *great* dad by setting him up with Christi. And Gavin seemed happy, bragged to Kayla about his sex life with his new girlfriend. The only trouble was his brain injury continued to skew his thinking. He took down license numbers, including his father's. Someone found out, and that got him and poor Christi Marsh killed. Mary Lou figured it out, and it scared the hell out of her. Bilking the Department of Corrections is one thing, murder's another. Maybe she pressured Sonny and Larsen to drop the whole thing. She knew Sonny carried a torch for her, thought she had him under control. But cornered, Sonny wasn't harmless, at all. And neither was Albin Larsen."

"If Bumaya can be believed about Larsen, we're talking monster."

"Monster with a Ph.D.," I said. "Clever, calculating, dangerous. Mary Lou overvalued her own charisma."

"What about Sheila? In the dark about all of it?"

"Sheila's got serious emotional problems. She and Jerry have been unavailable to each other for years, but he's stuck by her for appearances. Now one kid's out of the house, and the other's dead. Toss in some panic, and it would be the perfect time for him to split."

"Appearances," said Milo. "The house, the Benz, B.H. school district for the kids. Then Gavin gets his cranium shaken up, and it all falls apart. What about the impalement? The sexual angle? For simple executions, shooting would've been enough."

"The impalement's icing on the cake," I said. "Someone who enjoys killing. Someone who's done it before."

"Ray Degussa," he said. He got up, walked to the door, looked up and down the empty corridor, said, "It's quiet," and sat back down. "So Mary scammed but couldn't handle murder?"

"She could've rationalized the scam, told herself they were doing good, just padding the bill a bit. Who was the victim anyway? A corrupt prison bureaucracy."

"It's exactly the line of bullshit an asshole

like Larsen would've fed her." He frowned. "Problem is, this whole house of cards is predicated upon a scam, and we don't even know one exists."

"I'll check with Olivia in a few hours."

"You really think Mary Lou would be foolish enough to threaten Larsen and the others? Would she be blind to the kind of people she was dealing with?"

"Believing your own PR can be very dangerous."

"What about Gull?"

"Either he was involved, or he wasn't."

"I wonder why Gavin fired him."

"Me, too."

"Crazy kid," he said. "Stupid, crazy kid. Crazy family."

"What about the other kid in the family?" I said. "The one who didn't come home after her brother died. Sometimes it's the ones who get away who have the most interesting things to say."

"Kelly, the law student at BU."

"Her first year at law school would be over by now. But she stayed in Boston."

"Another item for the old to-do list. Lots of to-dos. I need to sleep."

"We both do," I said.

He struggled to his feet. The rims of his eyes were scarlet, and his face was gray. "Enough," he said. "Let's get the hell outta here."

37

The phone woke me up. I'd gone to bed at 3:30 A.M.

As my eyes cleared, I focused on the clock. Six hours later.

I grabbed the receiver, fumbled, got hold of it.

"Found it," said Olivia Brickerman. "The key was divergent thinking."

"Morning," I said.

"You sound groggy."

"Long night."

"Poor baby. Want to brush your teeth and call me back?"

I laughed. "No, tell me."

"The problem," she said, "was that I was being too limited, concentrating on awards and grants. As if that's the only way stuff gets funded. Finally, I shifted gears and voila! This thing was *legislated*, Alex. Tacked on as a rider to a tough felony sentencing law. Assemblyman Reynard Bird, D-Oakland—you know him, used to be a Black Panther?"

"Sure."

"Bird got the rider stuck on the bill as part of the old give-and-take. So now you can send bad guys to prison for long periods, but when they get out, they get free therapy."

"Any bad guys?"

"Any paroled felons who ask for treatment get it. Up to a year of individual and/or group for each bad guy, no restriction on hours, and the funding comes straight from Medi-Cal. That's why I couldn't find the money stream. It's a drop in the ocean of general medical payments."

"Sweet deal for felons," I said. "And for providers."

"Sure is, but few providers have taken the state up on it. Either they don't know about it, or they don't want criminals crowding their waiting rooms. Probably the former. Bird never publicized it, and usually he's the first to throw a press conference. I found out his third wife's a psychologist, and guess what: She's running two of the biggest programs in Oakland and Berkeley. Almost all the activity's up north. There's another program in Redwood City, and some groups in Santa Cruz that are run by an eighty-five-year-old shrink who practiced in L.A. and retired. The one you're probably interested in is Pacifica Psychological Services, Beverly Hills, California. Right?"

"How'd you know?"

"It's the only program in Southern Cal."

"Payment straight out of the Medi-Cal cookie jar," I said. "What's the reimbursement level?"

"Wait, there's more, darling. We're talking Medi-Cal *plus*. The bill authorizes surcharges because of an 'exigency' clause. The funds come out of some legislative slush account, but the administration's through Medi-Cal."

"Meaning these are patients your average doctor wouldn't want to treat, so the state provides an incentive. How much of one?"

"Double reimbursement," she said. "Actually a bit more than double. Medi-Cal pays fourteen dollars for group therapy by a

Ph.D., fifteen for an MD. Providers under this bill get thirty-five. The same goes for individual therapy. From twenty an hour to forty-five. Seventy bucks for the initial intake and forty-eight for case conferences."

"Thirty-five an hour for group," I said, recalculating my previous estimates. Lots of zeroes. "Not bad."

"There's no fiscal oversight I can find, just bill the state and collect."

"Any way to find out how much each program has billed?"

"Not for me, but Milo could probably do it," she said. "If he wants to pursue it further, I'd call Sacramento. Ask for Dwight Zevonsky, he's a good guy who investigates fraud."

I copied down the number.

"What's the official name of the program?" I said.

"No name, just Assembly Bill 5678930-CRP-M, Amendment F," she said. "Subtitled 'Psychocultural demarginalization of released offenders.' Which was one of your buzzwords. I found a couple others in the text of the rider. 'Attitudinal shifting,' 'Holistic emphasis.' The individual programs are free to take on their own names. The one in Beverly Hills is called—"

"Sentries for Justice."

"Yes, just like you said. So, what, this has been done before?"

"Oh, yeah," I said.

"Where?"

"You don't want to know."

◆

I found out the name of Assemblyman Reynard Bird's third wife and ran her through the Internet.

Dr. Michelle Harrington-Bird. A tall, Scottish-born redhead in her forties who favored African robes and spoke out frequently about political issues. The assemblyman was in his seventies, a legislative vet known for passionate oration and the ability to fix potholes in his district.

In one of the many photos I found, Harrington-Bird was posed with a group of fellow psychologists that included Albin Larsen. A bunch of therapists hanging out at a convention. Larsen stood next to Harrington-Bird, goateed, bespectacled, wearing a tweed suit over a sweater-vest and looking like Hollywood's incarnation of

Freud. His body language implied no intimacy with the assemblyman's current spouse.

All business. Plenty of incentive for that.

Harrington-Bird had borrowed Larsen's terminology for the wording of the bill. No doubt Larsen had impressed her with descriptions of his human rights work in Africa. I wondered what she'd think about his role in African genocide. About two little boys left in their beds with their throats cut.

I found Larsen and Harrington-Bird paired three more times, as signatories on political ads. After printing what I thought was relevant, I got on the phone.

◆

Milo said, "Oh, man, Olivia. She should run the world."

"She's overqualified," I said. "Now we know the funding's real and that Larsen got in on it early."

"Reynard Bird. Wonder how high this will go."

"There's no evidence Bird or his wife colluded on any scam. Larsen knew her professionally, and they hobnobbed politically. He may have used her, too."

"She's into human rights?"

"She's into petitions. Protesting U.S. involvement in Afghanistan and Iraq, et cetera. Larsen signed the same ads."

He grunted. "So when did the funding start?"

"Year and a half ago. Reimbursements began sixteen months ago. Pacifica was in at the outset."

"Thirty-five bucks for each con-hour," he said. "Even more than we estimated."

"Huge incentive to keep it going. And to cover up when exposure was threatened. If Mary Lou posed any sort of threat, the obvious solution was to eliminate her."

"Bullet and impalement. Speaking of which, here's my contribution to the database. Through some fancy detective footwork, I located a retired guard supervisor at Quentin who actually knew Raymond Degussa. He's certain Degussa was responsible for not two but *three* inmate contract killings and maybe as many as five others. In-house hit man, the gangs hire them to keep their own noses clean. With all that, they just couldn't get any evidence on the asshole. When Degussa wasn't offing people, he did all things that make parole boards salivate. Attended church, served as a pastor's assistant, volunteered to make Christmas toys for ghetto kids, worked as a volunteer library clerk. And get this: He went regularly for counseling. This is a guy who appreciates the value of therapy."

"Bet he does."

"And here's the fun part, Alex: This supervisor, God bless him, told me all the hits featured some kind of impaling and a combination MO, which is unusual for prison killings, mostly it's cut and run. Degussa cut all right—your basic throat and multiple body slashing by shiv. But he followed it up with a coup de grâce through the neck or chest with some sort of pointed object. In a couple of cases, the objects were found: sharpened fountain pen, meat skewer purloined from the prison kitchen. Raymond's definitely our bad guy."

"He has no record of sexual crimes?"

"His sheet's what I told you—larceny, drugs, armed robbery. But those are only the things he gets caught for. Who knows what he does in his spare time? Starting tonight, I'm switching Sean Binchy from surveilling Gull to watching Degussa. I'll be there at the start, to make sure he doesn't get into trouble. Watching a sweating shrink's one thing, this bad boy's another."

"Gull's off the screen?"

"On the contrary. Now that we know the scam's real, we've got something to use against him. Assuming you still see him as the weakest link."

"If you want to lean on someone, he'd be my choice."

"I want *badly* to lean," he said. "A couple more things. The address Christi Marsh gave is a mail drop, big surprise. She only rented the box for two months, and the clerk has no recollection of her. Did you check the paper this morning?"

"Not yet."

"They finally ran the photo. Page thirty-two, at the bottom, along with three sentences asking anyone with knowledge to call me. No calls yet. On the Quick family front, I tracked down sister Kelly. She stayed in Boston to work at a law firm. But she just took a sudden leave of absence, supposedly sick grandmother in Michigan."

"You think she could be well west of Michigan."

"I phoned the house but no answer, have

a call in to Eileen Paxton just in case she got sisterly, again. How about we get together, sooner rather than later, to talk about Franco Gull. I have a few ideas about the fine art of social pressure."

38

F ranco Gull had retained the services of a criminal defense lawyer named Armand Moss. Moss had passed the assignment to an associate, a stunning brunette woman of around forty named Myrna Wimmer.

The meeting was held in Wimmer's office, a glass-lined room on the top floor of an office building on Wilshire near Barrington. It was a glorious day, and the glass served its purpose.

Myrna Wimmer wore a burgundy pantsuit and had flawless ivory skin. Her artfully highlighted wedge cut was glossy and efficient. A Yale law degree was displayed like the icon it was. The photos on her credenza said she had a doting husband and five gorgeous kids. She moved like a dancer, her greeting was warm. Slanted gray eyes under artfully shaped brows could've melted paint.

She said, "For the record, Dr. Gull is here of his own volition and is under no obligation to answer any questions, let alone those deemed inappropriate."

"Yes, ma'am, anything you say," said Milo.

Wimmer regarded him with amusement, turned to Gull, who sat on a club chair near the longest glass wall, feet planted on the carpet, looking drained and thinner. The chair rested on casters, and Gull's movements made it shudder.

He had on a black suit, white mock-turtleneck, oxblood calfskin loafers. Little red clocks on his black socks. A folded linen handkerchief was wadded in one big hand. No sweating, yet, but preparing himself? Or maybe his lawyer had provided the hankie.

Milo took the seat farthest from Gull. I got close.

"Good morning," I said. It was 11 A.M., and the view out Myrna Wimmer's glass walls deserved some serious meditation. I was there for anything but, dressed in my best navy suit, a white pin-collar shirt with French cuffs, and a gold jacquard tie. Last time I'd gone that route someone had mistaken me for a lawyer. The sacrifices we make for the public good.

Two days had passed since Christina Marsh's photo had run in the paper. A couple of schizophrenics had phoned Milo, each with oddly congruent stories about alien abductions, each certain Christina was really from Venus. Comic relief; with the schedule he'd been keeping Milo needed it.

Two nights attempting to surveil Raymond Degussa had gone flat when the bouncer had failed to show up for his club gig. A check at his last-known address revealed it to be eighteen months out-of-date, and now Milo had more to search for.

Before we'd headed for Myrna Wimmer's office, he'd shown me mug shots of Degussa and a DMV photo of Bennett Hacker. Degussa's stats put him at six feet, 198, with multiple tattoos. Long, seamed face, thick neck, strong features, black hair oiled and brushed straight back. In one of the pictures, Degussa wore a thick, drooping mustache. In others he was clean-shaven. Tiny slit eyes projected profound boredom.

Hacker was six-two, 170, with thinning dishwater hair and a chin that fell far short of assertive. He wore a white shirt and tie, smiled faintly for the motor vehicles camera.

According to Medi-Cal investigator Dwight Zevonsky, the PO was a rich man. Both of them were.

Franco Gull hadn't responded to my greeting, so I repeated it.

He said, "Morning."

I kept my suit jacket buttoned, kept my posture authoritative. "Pretty outside," I said. "But that's irrelevant to you."

No answer.

"All that dissonance must be tough, Franco."

Myrna Wimmer said, "Pardon me?"

"Dissonance. When self-image clashes with harsh reality." I scooted closer to Gull. He pressed himself against the back of the armchair. The chair rolled back a couple of inches.

"What is this?" said Wimmer. "I canceled an appointment to hear psychobabble?"

I addressed Gull. "First off, you need to

know that I'm not a police officer, I'm your peer."

Franco Gull's left eye twitched, and he glanced at Wimmer. She said, "What's going on?"

Milo said, "Dr. Delaware's a clinical psychologist. He consults to the department."

Gull glared at me. "You never thought to mention that."

"No reason to," I said. "There is now."

Wimmer folded her arms across her chest. "Well, *this* is different."

"Any problem with that?" said Milo.

She held up a finger. "No one talk, I'm thinking."

"Maybe it'll be more pleasant for your client," said Milo. "No rubber hose, a bit of collegiality."

"That remains to be seen." To me: "What's your angle—first of all, what's your name, again?"

I told her, and she made a show of writing it down. "Okay, *now* what's your angle?"

"Clinical psych." I turned to Gull. "I've been trying to understand how you got into this dismal situation."

Gull looked away and I went on: "I did a little research on you, but that only put more pieces in the puzzle." I edged even closer. Gull tried to wheel backwards, but the casters caught in the carpet.

"Franco—may I call you Franco? Franco, the gap between the person I learned about and what's happening to you now is rather wide."

Gull licked his lips.

Myrna Wimmer laughed. "Oh boy, Psych 101."

I turned to her. "Is that okay with you?"

The question surprised her. "You're asking my opinion?"

"What I mean," I said, "is that if I'm taking the wrong approach—if you've got a better approach to communicating with Dr. Gull, please let me know." Speaking softly, so that she had to cant her head to hear.

She said, "I—just get on with it. I've got another appointment in forty-five minutes."

I turned back to Gull: "You graduated summa cum laude, Phi Beta Kappa from the U. of Kansas in Lawrence. You managed that while playing four years of varsity baseball. Not just run-of-the-mill baseball. In your senior year, you came close to breaking the university's RBI record. I find that more than impressive, Franco. Talk about your well-rounded scholar. Kind of a Grecian ideal, no? You'd know about that, you switched from classics to psychology in your sophomore year."

Myrna Wimmer circled behind her desk and sat down. She looked angry and fascinated.

Franco Gull didn't move or speak.

I said, "Two years in the Minor Leagues and no one there has anything but good things to say about you. Too bad about that hamstring shred."

Gull said, "Things happen." And started to sweat.

I said, "Same goes for Berkeley. We both know how tough it is to get into a place like that, but you were tops on their list. As a grad student, you kept up the good work. Your dissertation supervisor, Professor Albright, is getting on in years, but his memory is pretty sharp. He told me you were a hard worker, your research was substantive, you really knew how to focus on problem-solving. He hoped you'd go into academia—but that's another story."

Gull mopped his neck.

I said, "Then there are all your good works. In addition to all the required clinical hours for your doctorate, you volunteered your services at a home for abused kids. The same year you were writing your dissertation. *That's* impressive. How'd you find the time?"

Gull said, "You do the job."

"You did more than the job, Franco. Lots more. And your research—'Reactions of Latency-aged Girls from Divorced Homes to a Personal Space Challenge.' Good stuff, you got it published in *Clinical and Consulting Psych,* no mean feat for a student. After you graduated, you didn't pursue it. Pity. Your findings were provocative."

Gull said, "Ancient history." He crossed his legs, forced a smile at Wimmer. "Is there a point to this, Myrna?"

Wimmer touched her platinum watch and shrugged.

I said, "Your postdoc supervisor, Dr. Ryan, also remembers you as bright and industrious. That entire year, you never came close to any ethical breach. The odd thing is that she remembers you as exceptionally *respectful* of women."

Gull's lips clamped shut.

I kept silent.

He said, "I still am."

I said, "The year you graduated, academic jobs were tight, and the offers you received were all in the Midwest. Is that why you opted for private practice? How can you keep 'em down on the farm once they've seen Beverly Hills?"

Gull said, "Ever been to Kansas?" He shifted the hankie to his other hand. "I graduated with serious debt. No one gave me a damn thing for free."

"No need to apologize for going into practice," I said. "Who says academics accomplish that much for society?"

"True."

"Take Albin Larsen, for example. Academic appointments on two continents, travels all over the world, touting ideals. But we both know where most of his money comes from."

Gull said, "I have no idea what you're talking about."

I said, "Okay, then, back to this thing with you and women. The promiscuity—the compulsive skirt-chasing. When exactly did it start, Franco? Were you able to fool Dr. Ryan, or was it something that you latched onto when you realized how much power you had as a therapist?"

Gull reddened. "Screw you," he said, wrapping big fingers around the hankie. "Myrna, let's end this."

"Absolutely," said Wimmer. "Gentlemen, we're through."

"No prob," said Milo, genially.

"That was beyond rude," said Gull, getting to his feet.

"It certainly was," said Wimmer.

We remained seated.

She said, "Gentlemen, I've got a busy calendar."

"I understand, ma'am," said Milo. He stood, removed some folded white papers from his pocket. "I'll be as quick as possible enforcing this arrest warrant on Dr. Gull."

Gull had been fooling with the neck of his sweater. His hand dropped as if scalded, and his head snapped back. "What!"

Milo stepped closer to him. "Doctor, this is an arrest war—"

Wimmer said, "What's the charge, Lieutenant?"

"Char-*ges,*" said Milo. "Multiple counts of murder, conspiracy to commit murder, insurance fraud. A few other things. Your client should be—"

Gull's eyes were wild. "What the hell are you talking—"

Wimmer said, "Let me handle this, Franco." To Milo: "Give me that."

Milo handed her the warrant. He'd trolled the D.A.'s Office for an Assistant D.A. willing to issue the paper. Gull's fingerprints all over Mary Lou Koppel's house had helped, as had a call from State Fraud Investigator Dwight Zevonsky. The finishing touch had been a bottle of twenty-five-year-old Glenlivet pressed into the palm of a sixty-year-old hardnose ADA, Eben Marovitch, two months from retirement, whose wife had left him for a psychiatrist.

"Proud of me?" Milo had asked, as we ascended the elevator to Wimmer's office. "Applied psychology and all that."

◆

As Wimmer read the particulars of the warrant, Franco Gull retreated from Milo, keeping his back to the glass. Behind him were gorgeous blue sky and the coppery contours of a sunlit downtown. He stood as still as a piece of sculpture. Life-size sculpture. *California Terror with Panoramic View.*

Wimmer finished reading, returned to the first page, reviewed. Her mouth tightened.

"What, what?" said Franco Gull.

No answer.

"Myrna—"

"Shh, let me finish."

"Finish what? It's ridiculous, it's—"

Wimmer silenced him with an air-chop, completed her perusal, refolded the warrant. "It's patently ridiculous, Franco, but apparently valid."

"What does that mean, Myrna? What the fuck does that *mean*?" The handkerchief was wadded tightly in his hand, and his knuckles were ivory knobs. Sweat trickled from his hairline, but he made no attempt to swab. "Myrna?"

Milo took out his cuffs. The metallic sound made Gull jump.

Myrna Wimmer said, "Oh, please."

Milo said, "You read the charges."

Gull said, "Myrna—"

Wimmer said, "What it means, Franco, is that you'll have to go with them." Disapproval in her voice. As if Gull had disappointed her. "Where will you be booking him, Lieutenant?"

"Charges like these?" said Milo. "Gotta be the main jail."

Gull said, "Jail? Oh, God, no."

Wimmer smiled at Milo. "Could you do me a favor and book him at West L.A.? Save me the drive?"

"*Book* him?" said Gull. "Myrna, how can you just—"

Milo said, "No can do, Counselor, sorry."

Wimmer looked ready to spit.

Gull's eyes had filled with tears. "Myrna, I can't *do* this."

She said, "Does your wife have access to your finances? If so, I'll call her and we'll get to work on bail. If not—"

"Bail? Myrna, this is *insane*—"

"Is that an official diagnosis, Doctor?" said Milo.

"Please," said Gull, backing off some more and pressing against the glass. "You don't know what you're doing, I've never done any of what you say I've done. Please." Sucking in breath. *"Please."*

Milo said, "Turn and place your hands on Ms. Wimmer's desk, Doctor. If you're carrying any weapons or illicit substances, now would be the time to tell me."

"Murder?" Gull was shouting. "What the

hell are you talking about? *Murder?* Are you *insane*?" He opened his hand and the hankie fluttered to the carpet. As he watched it fall, his knees buckled, but he managed to stay upright.

Myrna Wimmer said, "Calm down, Franc—"

"Calm down? Easy for you to say, you're not the one—"

"As your advocate, Franco, I advise you not to say anything—"

"All I'm saying is I never *did* anything, what's wrong with saying I never *did* anything?"

Milo said, "Hands on the desk, please." He began walking toward Gull. "Franco Gull, you have the right to remain silent—"

Gull's powerful physique tensed. He doubled over, began to weep. "Oh, God, how can this be *happening*!"

Myrna Wimmer shot me a *hope-you're-happy* glare.

Milo jangled the cuffs. Gull stepped forward, placed his hands on the desk. Wept some more.

Milo bent one of Gull's arms behind his back and cuffed it. Gull cried out.

"Are you hurting my client?" demanded Wimmer.

"Maybe psychologically," said Milo. "Not too tight, is it, Doctor?"

"God, God," said Gull. "What can I do to *fix* this?"

Milo didn't answer.

"Why are you saying I *killed* someone? Who? *Mary?* That's *crazy,* Mary was my friend, we were—I never would've—"

Milo drew back Gull's other arm.

Gull shouted, "What is it you *want*?!"

I said, "For you to be forthcoming."

"Forthcoming about *what*?"

Myrna said, "Be quiet, Franco."

"What? And let them put *these* on me and take me to *jail*?"

"Franco, I'm sure this will—"

"What *I'm* sure of is I never killed anyone or *conspired* or did *any* of those things!" Gull twisted to make eye contact with me. "What you're doing is unethical. You should be ashamed of yourself."

I said, "Feel free to file a complaint. Though I don't imagine you'll want to."

He said, "What gives you the right to judge me?"

"Forthcoming," I said, "doesn't mean gamesmanship." To Milo: "My opinion is we should wrap up."

Milo placed his hand on Gull's scruff and turned him around and placed a palm in the small of Gull's back. "Time to go to jail, Doctor."

Gull shouted, "Stop! Please! I'll be *forth-coming*. Okay, yes, I *chased* a few skirts. You want to talk about that? *Fine,* I'm ready to *talk* about it. I've got a little *problem,* is that what you wanted to hear? I pleasured women, received pleasure in return, it has nothing to do with jail or *murder* or any other fucking *bullshit* that would send me to jail! And yes, that *is* an official diagnosis, I'm *qualified* to diagnose, I *am* a good psy-chologist, fucking *great* psychologist, all my patients get *better*!"

I said, "Like Gavin Quick?"

Gull said, "He—that—he wasn't really my patient."

"No?"

"I saw him for four, five sessions. It ended."

"Why?"

"Take these things off, and I'll tell you."

"Tell us, now."

Wimmer said, "Franco, my advice to you is to not tell them any—"

Gull said, "The stupid kid didn't want to see me because he found out I was sleeping with a patient. Okay? Happy? I'm humiliated, I am now officially, publicly shitfaced humiliated. But I never *killed* anyone! Take these things off."

Myrna Wimmer said, "I need an Advil."

◆

Milo removed the cuffs and sat Gull in the same armchair.

Gull said, "Can we all calm down and get rational, here?" His face was sodden.

Milo said, "If you continue to show some honesty, we might be able to work something out."

Wimmer said, "I want that on the record."

Milo said, "Sorry, no."

"Then I refuse to have my client—"

"Myrna, stop complicating things, stop being a goddamn *lawyer*!" said Gull. "It's not *your* life!"

Wimmer frowned at him, dry-swallowed the two Advil tablets in her palm. "You've been warned, Franco."

Gull turned to me. "Honesty about what? I told you, I slept with a patient."

"Only one?" I said.

His eyes searched mine. Trying to figure out how much I knew.

"More than one," he said. "But not that many more, and it was always consensual. The stupid kid found out and threw a fit and said he could no longer trust me, he wanted to fire me. Then he threatened to report me. He, of all people."

"What do you mean?" I said.

"The whole reason he was there was to deal with his *own* sexual issues. *He* was a stalker. So who was he to get self-righteous?"

"You don't understand why he'd think you weren't the ideal therapist, Franco?"

"I understand, I understand," said Gull. "It shouldn't have happened, but it did. But he was snooping, it's not as if I flaunted it or anything like that. The point is, the kid was brain-damaged, his mentation was distorted."

"Not thinking straight," I translated for Milo.

"In addition," said Gull, "he was pathologically compulsive—extremely perseverative. Cognitively and behaviorally."

I said, "Once he got hold of something he wouldn't let go."

"Precisely," said Gull. As if that settled it.

"How'd he find out?" I said.

"I told you, by snooping." Gull let out a harsh laugh. "Stalking *me*."

"Where?"

"He hung around the building after his session was over, came back after hours, and waited in his car, out on the street."

"Where on the street?"

"Palm Drive. Out back, behind the parking lot. It didn't register at the time, but later, when he confronted me, I realized he'd been sitting there."

"What kind of car?"

"Mustang."

"Color?"

"Red. Red convertible. But he always kept the top up, and the windows were tinted, so I never saw if anyone was inside."

I said, "That's the car he was killed in."

"Well, I'm sorry about that, that's unfortunate," said Gull. "But I had nothing to do with it."

"He confronted you and threatened to report you."

"You don't kill someone for that."

"What do you kill them for?"

"Nothing. Violence is always wrong." Gull searched for his hankie. I spotted it, on the floor behind him, but didn't let on.

He said, "You don't kill anyone for any reason. I'm a firm believer in nonviolence."

"Make love, not war."

"You're making me sound glib and lecherous. It wasn't like that. Some women need tenderness."

Wimmer's hands clawed.

I said, "So Gavin hung around the building."

"He damn well did."

"How often?"

"Don't know," said Gull. "I caught him once."

"When he caught you."

Silence.

"How did it happen?"

"Are you going to use it against me?"

"Ethical violations are the least of your problems."

"What do you want?"

"Everything you know about everything I ask."

"The Grand Inquisitor," he said. "How can you justify this, professionally?"

"We all make adjustments," I said.

Milo jangled the handcuffs.

Gull said, "Sure. Fine. Let's do it."

"That okay with you?" I asked Wimmer. "Busy schedule and all."

Wimmer hesitated. Gull whined, "Myrna?" She looked at her watch, sighed, sat back in her chair. "Sure, make yourselves comfortable. *Boys.*"

39

Franco Gull said, "I should've followed my instincts, never wanted to treat him."

"Not your type of patient," I said.

He didn't answer.

A few minutes ago, he'd cleared his throat several times, and Milo had suggested to Myrna Wimmer that someone get water for her client. Looking vexed, she phoned for a pitcher and glasses, but when they arrived Gull refused to drink.

Clutching at the smallest choice.

I said, "Why didn't you want to treat Gavin Quick?"

"I don't like adolescents," said Gull. "Too much crisis, too much in flux."

"Add brain damage to that."

"That, too. I hate neuropsych. Boring. Uncreative."

"Brain-damaged adolescent," I said. "Also, he was male."

"I see males."

"Not many."

"How would you know?"

"Am I wrong?"

"I'm not divulging personal information about my patients," said Gull. "No matter what pressure you put on me."

I said, "Ethics and all that."

Gull was silent.

"Gavin watched the building," I said. "How did he find out you were sleeping with a patient?"

Gull winced. "Is this necessary?"

"Very."

"Fine, fine. He was there in the parking lot when we came out."

"You and the patient."

"Yes. A lovely person. I walked her out. It was late, dark, she was my last patient, and I was leaving, too."

"Chivalrous," I said. "What did Gavin see?"

Gull hesitated.

Milo stretched his legs. Myrna Wimmer polished the dial of her watch with her sleeve.

Gull said, "We kissed. Yes, it was stupid to be that open. But who knew anyone was watching? The kid was parked at the curb, for God's sake."

"Nosy," I said.

"You need to understand: This wasn't some exploitative thing. It was loving. Mutual and *loving*. This woman had experienced some severe losses in her life, and she needed comfort."

"Deep comfort," said Milo.

"What I did was wrong. In a formal sense—a normative sense. But the specifics of the situation dictated a certain degree of intimacy."

I said, "Therapeutic kindness."

"If you must know."

Myrna Wimmer picked up a legal pad and pretended to read. She looked as if she'd swallowed a cup of sewage.

Gull turned to me, flushed. "I don't expect you to understand."

I said, "So you did it in the office. On a couch? On the desk?"

"That is vulgar—"

"Your conduct was vulgar."

"I've told you. She was lonely—"

"And had experienced severe losses."

Myrna Wimmer shook her head.

"All right," said Gull. "I'm a bastard. Is that what you want to hear?"

I said, "Back to the beginning: You don't like adolescent males, but you agreed to treat Gavin Quick."

"As a favor to Mary. The referral came to her but she was booked and I'd just discharged a patient—a very successful case, I might add. So I happened to have an open slot. Which is extremely rare."

"Why'd Mary ask you to see Gavin and not Albin Larsen?"

"Albin only works part-time."

"Too busy with good works," I said.

Gull shrugged.

"Did Mary tell you how the referral came to her?"

"Through her ex-husband. He's our landlord, in fact—and Gavin's father was a tenant of his, had mentioned Gavin's legal problems. The actual referral came through a neurologist I'd never heard of. Gavin was claiming brain damage had caused the stalking."

"You don't believe that."

Gull shrugged off the question.

I said, "It doesn't take brain damage to get a guy sexually aggressive."

Gull exhaled. "This is wearying me."

"So sorry."

Wimmer said, "*Is* there anything more?"

I said, "Did you have much contact with Gavin's parents?"

"The father only," said Gull, "and just once. I thought it was unusual, generally it's the mother. I asked the father about it, he said his wife wasn't feeling well."

"What did you learn from Mr. Quick?"

"Not much, I took a quick family intake. He seemed very concerned about his son."

I said, "Initially, Mary had no time for Gavin, but once Gavin fired you, she took over."

"I suppose she made time," said Gull. "As a favor to me."

"So Gavin wouldn't make waves."

Silence.

I said, "What did you give her in return?"

"I agreed to take night call for two months."

Milo said, "Did that include calling on her at night?"

Gull glared at him.

"The questions stands, Doctor."

"Mary was a highly sexual person. She had strong needs, and I was able to fill them. We enjoyed each other. I don't see that as sinful. But in answer to your question: No. Mary and I were perfectly competent at separating our professional and personal lives."

I said, "Who murdered her?"

"I have no idea. From these questions, you obviously think it had something to do with Gavin Quick."

"You don't?"

"I don't think anything."

"A therapist and her patient murdered within days of each other. You've never wondered about it?"

"I wonder," said Gull. "I just don't have answers."

"Any guesses?"

He shook his head.

"The girl murdered alongside Gavin," I said. "Had you ever seen her before?"

"I told you the first time you showed me that picture. No."

"The picture was in yesterday's paper. Bring back any memories?"

"I didn't read yesterday's paper."

"No interest in world affairs."

"Not much," said Gull. "I'm not a political person."

"Unlike Albin Larsen."

"You keep bringing him up."

"So I do." I looked over at Milo. He appeared serene.

Myrna Wimmer moved forward, perching on the edge of her desk chair. Her mouth was set, and her shoulders were tight.

Gull said, "Gavin Quick, now Albin. You're losing me."

I said, "Why did Albin just inform Sonny Koppel that your group had no further interest in leasing the ground floor?"

"No *further* interest? Why would we need the bottom floor? It's already leased, isn't it? Some sort of charitable foundation."

"Charitable Planning."

He nodded.

"What are they about?" I said.

"Don't know."

"You've been neighbors for a while."

"I never see anyone go in there except Sonny Koppel. And that's not very often."

"How often?"

"Once, twice a month. Maybe it's one of his businesses. He owns several."

"Tycoon?"

"Apparently."

"How do you know that?"

"From Mary. She got us the suite through him. Handled all the paperwork on our lease."

"Take-charge gal," I said.

"Mary was a mover. Albin and I are more . . . cerebral. She got us a great deal on the lease because Sonny was still fond of her."

"She told you that?"

"She told me and laughed about it," said Gull.

"Making fun of Sonny."

"To be frank, she didn't think much of him. Mary could be . . . cutting. It wasn't typical of her, but she could get that way."

"And Sonny brought out Mary's cutting side."

"You know exes."

"What exactly did Mary tell you about Sonny?"

"That soon after she'd married him he'd turned into a fat slob. That she'd never found him attractive in the first place but had deluded herself he might be workable. She liked the fact that he was a law student. Then he flunked his bar exam, and she started viewing him as the quintessential loser. Her phrase."

"A loser who became a tycoon."

"That surprised her. She said being rich was wasted on Sonny, he didn't know how to spend money, didn't know how to enjoy life."

"Sounds like the fondness ran one way," I said.

"You think he killed her?"

"Why would we think that?"

"Ex-husband," he said. "Unrequited love. Maybe he found out how Mary really felt about him. Maybe it came to a head."

"Did Mary ever give you any indication that things got hostile between her and Sonny?"

"No, but she wouldn't have mentioned it to me."

"Despite you being friends—despite all that intimacy."

Gull said, "All I can tell you is what happened."

"Do *you* like Sonny Koppel as a suspect?"

"I'm saying given the situation, I'd look into it."

"Instead of looking into you," said Milo.

Gull ground his teeth. "I haven't *killed* anyone."

I said, "How many patients are you carrying, currently?"

The change of subject threw Gull. He sat up, ran his fingers through his hair, shook his head. "I told you, I can't talk about patients."

"I'm not asking for names, just your approximate patient load."

Gull glanced over at Myrna Wimmer. She ignored him.

Milo said, "You fuck them but won't talk about them. Spare me."

"Now wait one—"

"No, *you* wait, Doctor." Milo's voice had taken on that bear growl. "Forthcoming means no more bullshit. The question was how many patients are you seeing, not their quirks or their bra sizes."

Gull's face lost color. "Okay, okay, let me see . . . I work . . . thirty-eight hours a week with regular patients, have another . . . maybe twenty-five who pop in for occasional sessions."

"Tune-ups," said Milo.

"I don't run a garage."

"Sixty-five total," I said.

"That's an estimate."

"Those sixty-five. You'd remember their names."

"Sure."

I pulled a page of computer printout from my jacket and unfolded it on my lap.

"Does the name 'Gayford Woodrow' mean anything to you?"

"No."

"What about 'James Leroy Craig'?"

"Same answer," said Gull.

"Carl Philip Russo," I said. "Ludovico Montez, Daniel Lee Barendo, Schendley Paul, Orlando Jones."

Headshake.

"Roland Kristof, Lamar Royster Collins, Antonio Ortega."

"Who *are* these people?"

"Patients for whom you've billed Medi-Cal a considerable amount over the last sixteen months."

Gull looked stunned. "That's ridiculous. First of all, I don't accept Medi-Cal patients. Second, those are all men, and my patients are almost exclusively women. Third, I'd know if I treated someone."

"And got paid for it."

"This is absolutely psychotic."

I picked up the list and read some more. "Akuno Williams, Salvador Paz, Mattias Soldovar, Juan Jorge Montoya, Juan Eduardo Lunares, Baylor Hawkins, Paul Andrew McCloskey—"

"No, none of them," said Gull. "This is a mistake."

"Never treated any of them? Not once?"

"Not once."

"Don't see any Medi-Cal patients at all."

"Why would I? Reimbursement's pathetic, and I'm booked with solid-paying patients."

"Then why'd you bother to obtain a Medi-Cal billing number?"

"Who says I did?"

I walked over to him and held the printout in front of his eyes. "Is this your signature on an application to be a provider?"

He said, "It looks like—I may have obtained a number, but I never really used it."

"Over the last sixteen months you've received over three hundred thousand dollars in Medi-Cal reiumbursement. Three forty-three and fifty-two cents, to be precise."

He grabbed for the sheet. I whipped it away.

"Let me see that!"

"You received a provider number but didn't *really* use it."

Silence.

I said, "Here's where 'forthcoming' enters the picture."

Gull said, "Fine, fine, I applied to get a number, just . . . to keep all my options open. In case there was a lull, I could fill in the time. But three hundred thou? You're out of your mind!"

"The state payments went to a billing address in Marina Del Rey."

"There you go," he said. "I don't *have* an address in the Marina. Can't remember the last time I *went* to the Marina. Someone obviously screwed up—your so-called *investigation* is screwed up." A smile spread slowly across his lips. "I suggest you do your homework. Both of you."

I said, "No Marina for you? No harbor-front dinners for you and the missus?"

Gull turned to Wimmer. "Do you believe this, Myrna? I've just showed them they're totally off base, and they can't admit it. Are you thinking what I am—a harassment suit."

Wimmer didn't answer.

I rattled the printout. "None of those names mean anything to you?"

"Not a one. Not a *single* one."

"What about this name, then: Sentries for Justice."

Gull stopped smiling. One hand shot up spasmodically and grabbed his upper lip. Twisting. Like a kid playing with a rubber mask.

Sad mask.

"You know that name," I said.

"That," he said. "Oh, boy."

CHAPTER

40

Gull pointed to the water pitcher on Myrna Wimmer's desk. "I think I will have some of that."

Wimmer aimed a cold smile his way. Gull got up and poured himself a glass. Drained it standing near the desk and refilled.

"I need," he said, "to put everything in context."

I said, "Go for it. If Ms. Wimmer's schedule allows."

Wimmer said, "Oh, sure, this is the fun part of my day."

Gull said, "Yes, I did apply for a provider number but only at Mary's and Albin's urging. The two of them were socially aware.

One of the issues they got involved in was penal rehabilitation."

"Who got into it first?"

"I think it was Albin's idea, but Mary began carrying the ball."

"She was the mover."

"Mary," he said, "wasn't the most creative person in the world, but once she put her mind to something, she went full bore. The two of them got the idea of setting up treatment for paroled criminals, in order to fight recidivism. I admired what they were doing but chose to stay out of it."

"Why?" I said.

"As I told you, I was busy enough. And I was skeptical. These people—criminals. They've got entrenched personality disorders. Psychotherapy has never been very effective for that kind of thing."

"Mary and Albin disagreed."

"Especially Mary. She was passionate about it. State money was going to be freed up, it was more than just theory."

"How'd she find that out?"

"One of Albin's political connections—he's involved in a lot of progressive causes—is the wife of a politician from up north. She's a psychologist, too, and she got her husband to pass a bill that authorized psychotherapy on demand for paroled felons. Albin helped her with the wording. He told Mary, she told me."

"But you declined," I said. "Entrenched personality disorders."

"Yes."

"Also, the reimbursement rates couldn't match your private fees."

"I work for a living," said Gull. "I don't see why I should apologize for that."

"What's your hourly fee?"

"Is that relevant?"

"Yes."

"I use a sliding scale. From one-twenty to two hundred per session."

"Medi-Cal pays twenty and restricts the number of sessions."

"Medi-Cal's a joke," said Gull. "Mary said the bill doubled the rates—some sort of political give-and-take. But forty's still a joke. I opted out."

"How'd Mary and Albin react to that?"

"Albin didn't say much. He rarely does. Mary was upset with me, but that didn't last."

Milo said, "Your being intimate friends and all that."

Gull sniffed.

I said, "You declined to participate but obtained a Medi-Cal provider number."

"At Albin's and Mary's behest. They said the state preferred settings with multiple providers, it would look better if all of us were listed. Mary filled out the paperwork and I signed and that was it."

He was sweating heavily now, searched again for his linen hankie. I pulled a tissue out of a box on Wimmer's desk and handed it to him. He wiped his face hastily, and the tissue turned into a little gray sphere.

"You're saying you never actually saw any patients on the program?"

"Basically," he said.

"Basically?"

"I saw a few—very few. At the beginning, just to get the ball rolling."

"How many is a few?"

He removed a pair of tiny-lensed reading glasses from his pocket and began playing with the sidepieces.

"Franco?"

"Three. That's it. And no one with any of the names you mentioned."

"How was it, treating ex-cons?"

"It wasn't a good experience."

"Why not?"

"Two of them were chronically late and when they did show up, they were high on something. It was obvious they were just passing the time."

"Why would they do that?"

"How should I know?"

"Any indication they were getting paid to show up?"

Gull's brows arched. "No one ever mentioned that. Whatever the reason, they weren't motivated. No insight, no desire to acquire any."

"What about the third patient?" I said.

"That one," said Gull, frowning. "That one upset me. He wasn't drunk or stoned, and he talked. Talked plenty. But not about himself. About his girlfriend. What she needed, how he figured to give it to her."

"What did she need?" I said.

Gull folded and unfolded the glasses. "Orgasms. Apparently, she was anorgasmic, and he was determined to fix the problem."

"Did he ask your help with that?"

"No," said Gull, "that's the point, he didn't want anything from me, he thought he knew everything. Very aggressive, very . . . not a pleasant man. Even though he tried to be charming. *Attempted* to speak intelligently."

"He couldn't pull it off."

"Not hardly. Faking it—the typical antisocial charm. If you've had any experience with sociopaths, you'd know what I mean."

"Pretentious," I said.

"Exactly, prototypical antisocial pretentiousness." His body loosened. Pretending we were colleagues having a clinical chat. "Flowery use of language, overly solicitous. *Playing* at being civilized and thinking he was putting one over on me. But his fantasies." He exhaled.

"Sadistic?"

"Dominance, bondage and, yes, I'd say a touch of sadism. He talked incessantly about tying this woman up and making love to her aggressively for as long as it took to force orgasms out of her body. He *didn't* use the term 'making love.' "

"Sexual tough guy," I said.

"His fantasies involved multiple penetration, bondage, foreign objects. I tried to get him to address this woman's needs, suggested that perhaps she needed some tenderness, some intimacy, but he laughed that off. His plan was to quote-unquote 'stick her every which way until she screamed for mercy.' "

He smiled with practiced weariness. Any reticence about discussing patients had vanished. "I, for one, couldn't see what any of that had to do with reducing recidivism, and when he stopped showing up, I told Mary I'd had enough of the program and the people it brought in."

He placed the eyeglasses back in his pocket, laced his hands, and sat forward. "You need to understand: I'd never do anything to hurt Mary. *Never.*"

I said, "So you saw only three Sentries for Justice patients. For how many sessions, total?"

"I believe twelve—certainly not much more than that. I remember thinking that apart from being unpleasant and unproductive, the project was a financial loser. I think the total billable charges didn't even amount to five hundred dollars. That's why your three hundred thousand figure is absurd. And the money didn't come to Marina del Rey, it came to Mary at the office, she cashed the state check and distributed the money to me. You really do need to check your facts, gentlemen."

"Mary was the bursar."

"So to speak. Yes."

Milo removed several sheets of paper from his attache case and passed them to me. I showed Franco Gull a mug shot of Raymond Degussa.

He said, "Yes, that's him. Ray."

"Mr. Dominance."

He nodded. "Did he murder Mary?"

"Why do you ask?"

"Because he impressed me as someone clearly capable of violence. The way he carried himself, the way he sat, walked—like a barely tethered animal." He studied the picture. "Look at those eyes. He made me uncomfortable. I told Mary that. She laughed it off, said there was nothing to worry about."

"The girlfriend he talked about," I said. "Did he mention her name?"

"No, but I saw her. At least I assume it was her."

"You assume?"

"Shortly after Ray had stopped coming to see me, I spotted him with a woman. His arm was around her. He seemed . . . proprietary."

"Where'd you see them?" I said.

"I happened to step out into the waiting

room to get my patient, and the two of them were also sitting there. At first I thought there'd been some kind of scheduling problem, that Ray expected a session. But before I could say anything, Mary came out and the woman went back with her."

"The girlfriend was a patient of Mary's."

"Apparently."

I showed him a shot of Flora Newsome, alive and smiling.

"Yes," he said. "Good Lord, what's this all about?"

"Did you see this woman with Ray Degussa any other times?"

"Once more," said Gull, "as I arrived at the building and they were walking out to the parking lot. It surprised me—the way she looked. Putting a face to the person he'd talked about. A man like that, I'd have expected someone a bit more . . . obvious."

"A bimbo," said Milo.

"This woman was . . . she looked like a bank clerk."

"She was a teacher," I said.

"Was," said Gull. "You're saying . . . God, how far does this *go*?"

"Knowing Degussa was a thug, did you tell Mary his fantasies about her patient?"

"No, I couldn't. Confidentiality. That was one thing we were adamant about. All three of us. Once our doors closed, that was it. No cross-office chitchat about patients."

"You didn't see Degussa as a threat to Flora Newsome?"

"Flora," said Gull. "So that's her name . . . good God." He bounded up, snatched another tissue. "There was nothing to warn anyone about. Nothing that even approached a Tarasoff level. He never said he wanted to hurt her, just that he wanted to make her come."

"Make her scream for mercy," I said.

"I took that as a metaphor."

Milo said, "Him being a poetic type."

"He killed her?" said Gull. "You're saying he actually killed her?"

"Someone did."

"Oh God. This is my worst nightmare."

Milo said, "Hers was worse."

No one spoke for a while, then Gull said, "Did he assault her sexually?"

Milo said, "We'll ask the questions."

"Fine, fine—God, this is draining me, I'm drying up." Gull stood again, poured two glasses of water, and finished both. His face was glossy. Fluid in, fluid out. A man of little substance.

I said, "Who else was involved in Sentries for Justice?"

"Just Mary and Albin."

"What about Ray Degussa?"

"Him? You're saying he was—you know, now that you mention it, he *did* seem to be near the office a lot. After he stopped coming for therapy."

"Where'd he hang out?"

"I'd see him walking up the block, and he'd nod and smile and give a thumbs-up. As if we were friends. I assumed he worked nearby."

"You ever talk to him?"

"Just hi and good-bye."

"A thug nearby, that didn't bother you?"

"Mary and Albin were treating criminals."

"But you assumed Degussa worked nearby."

Gull shrugged. "I really didn't pay much attention to any of it."

"When did the Sentries sessions take place?"

"I assume after hours."

"So as not to upset the regular clientele."

Gull nodded.

"You and Mary and Albin Larsen never discussed specifics?"

"Frankly," said Gull, "I didn't want to know."

"Why not?"

"Criminals. I find them unsavory. I wanted to keep my distance from any . . ."

"Any what?" said Milo.

"Any unpleasantness."

"So you suspected there might be something illegal going on."

Myrna Wimmer said, "Don't answer that. It could be selfincriminating."

Gull said, "But I didn't do anything criminal."

Wimmer glared at him, and he shut his mouth.

Milo said, "Counselor, your client's got an interesting way of blocking out things he doesn't want to deal with. Isn't the point of therapy breaking through all that denial?"

"Lieutenant, from where I'm sitting, my client has proved most cooperative. Do you have any other questions I'd deem acceptable?"

Milo nodded at me, and I showed Gull Bennett Hacker's DMV photo. "What about this man? Ever seen him?"

"I've seen him with Albin a couple of times."

"Where?"

"Over at Roxbury Park, having lunch with Albin. The same spot where you found us. Albin goes there frequently, said it reminds him of parks in Sweden."

"Albin ever introduce you to this man?"

"No. I assumed he was a therapist, as well."

"Why's that?"

"I don't know, really . . . perhaps his demeanor."

"Which was?"

"Quiet, pleasant."

"What about Sonny Koppel?" I said. "What was his role in Sentries for Justice?"

"Sonny? None that I know of."

"Mary never mentioned his being involved?" said Milo.

"The only thing Mary told me was that Sonny owned some properties that she'd convinced him to use as halfway houses, and that's where she and Albin were going to get their patients. She said it made everything easy."

"Ready supply of patients."

"I don't believe her intentions were anything but noble. She felt she could do some good and make money."

"Even at low reimbursement rates."

Gull was silent. Then he said, "Whatever took place, I chose not to participate. I think I deserve some credit for that."

"We'll put a gold star on your chart, Doctor."

I said, "You're saying Sonny wasn't involved."

"I doubt Mary would have included Sonny in anything substantive. He repulsed her. Frankly, Mary was aware of how Sonny felt about her, and she turned it to her advantage. To get a great lease on our suite, to finance her own real estate investments."

"She borrowed money from Sonny?"

"Not loans, gifts. She'd ask for money, and he'd say yes. She joked about it. Said, 'I use every part of the pig except the squeal.' "

Myrna Wimmer's nails clacked against the edge of her desk.

Gull said, "I don't want to paint a negative portrait of Mary. Being married to a man like Sonny couldn't have been easy. Have you met him?"

"We have," I said.

"Can you imagine Mary with someone like that?"

"Why? Was Sonny rough on her?"

"No, nothing like that. Just the opposite." Gull fidgeted.

"What?" I said.

"To be frank, Mary liked things a little . . . she enjoyed being dominated. In a loving way. Once she arrived at a point of trust and intimacy."

"Bondage?"

"No, there were never ropes involved, just physical pressure."

"Holding her down."

"At her request," said Gull.

"Sonny wouldn't do that."

"Sonny *couldn't* do that. She said back when they'd been married, any demand she placed on him to exhibit dominance turned him instantly impotent. Because *he* needed to be dominated. She saw that as part of his general problem—'flabby psyche, flabby body' was the way she termed it."

Gull patted his own midriff. "In my opinion, that's really why she left him. He wouldn't assert himself with her."

"So she used him."

"She said, 'Sonny wants to be controlled, I'm doing him a favor by pulling his strings.' "

"But she never mentioned Sonny being involved in Sentries?"

"All she mentioned was his owning the buildings."

"What about Albin Larsen?" I said. "He and Mary ever develop anything physical?"

Gull looked offended. "I'm *certain* they didn't."

"Why?"

"Albin's not Mary's type."

"Also not dominant?"

"As far as I can tell, Albin's asexual."

Milo said, "Got a monk thing going on?"

"In all the time I've known Albin, he's never expressed any interest in sex or sexual matters. And we've worked together for years."

"Too busy doing good works," I said.

"People channel their drives in various ways," said Gull. "I don't judge. I always have seen Albin as someone who might've been comfortable in a monastic setting. He lives very simply."

"Admirable," said Milo.

Gull said, "About all those names. Are you

saying someone actually claims I treated those men and billed Medi-Cal?"

"The state of California claims."

"Ridiculous. It never happened."

"The paperwork says it did, Doctor."

"Then someone screwed up, or someone's lying. Check my bank accounts—check the money trail or whatever you call it. You won't find any three hundred thousand unaccounted for."

"There are plenty of ways to hide money, Doctor."

"Well, I wouldn't know what they are."

"The paperwork, Doctor—"

"Someone's lying!" Gull shouted.

Milo smiled. "Now who could that be?"

Gull was silent.

I said, "Any theories?"

Myrna Wimmer said, "Be careful here, Franco."

Gull inhaled deeply and let his breath out very slowly. "You're saying Mary and Albin falsified bills in my name and pocketed the money."

Milo said, "You're saying it, Doctor."

Gull swiped at his glassy brow. "I guess I am. And now Mary's dead."

"So she is, Doctor."

Gull sweated profusely and didn't bother to mop it up. "You can't be serious." His voice had changed. Higher register, strained.

I said, "During the same period you ostensibly billed for 340,000 dollars' worth of felon therapy, Mary billed for 380, and Albin Larsen billed 440."

Gull said, *"Albin?"*

I said, "That's the question. Now let's work on the answer."

As we rode the elevator from Wimmer's high-rise to the ground floor, Milo said, "You squeezed him dry, congrats."

"Thanks," I said.

"Not pleased?"

"It needed to be done."

As we pulled out into traffic, he said, "When I hunt and actually bag something, I get hungry. I'm thinking red meat."

"Okay."

"Not up for it?"

"Red meat's fine."

"Had a big breakfast?"

"Had nothing."

"You find playing Grand Inquisitor that repugnant?"

"A little outside my training."

"Hey," he said. "Psychological warfare. In
Vietnam, the Army woulda had you writing
pamphlets."

"Where's the red meat?" I said.

"Okay, change the subject . . . Wilshire,
near the beach, there's a new place that
dry-ages, but if you find the notion of feast-
ing after breaking down another human being repugnant, I understand. Even though
said human being is a self-serving slime-
ball."

"Now that you put it that way."

"Gull may not have been in on the scam
or the killings directly, but I don't buy the
complete-innocent act. I think the deal the
ADA authorized was a gift."

Two-year suspension of Gull's psychology
license in return for full cooperation in all
criminal and civil matters pertaining to . . .

"More than fair," I said. "Let's eat."

◆

The steak house had microbrews on tap
and an adjacent dry-aging room whose picture window faced the boulevard. A family

of tourists stopped to admire sides of beef hanging from gleaming hooks, and Milo took the time to join them. Two little kids pointed and giggled, and the father said, "Cool." The mother opined: "I think it's brutal."

Inside, seated at a back booth, Milo said, "Controlled decay kicks up the taste. Kind of like real life."

I said, "Real life is hard to control."

He clapped my shoulder. "All the more reason to gorge."

Over two mountains of Steak Delmonico, baked potatoes the size of running shoes, and a bottle of red wine, we reviewed what we'd learned from Gull.

Milo said, "Sonny is coming across as a victim, not a bad guy."

"No reason for Gull to lie about that. On the contrary. If there was a way to spread the blame, he'd have done it."

"So maybe Gull doesn't know the inside dope, or Sonny really is just a poor shmuck, hung up over his ex. Who happened to make a lot of money."

"And didn't know how to spend it," I said.

"And out of the goodness of her heart, Mary helped him. *She* sure liked the green stuff, didn't she? Nice lucrative practice, extra bucks from the ex, and she still risks it all going for a scam."

"Maybe it was more than dollar signs," I said. "Maybe it was the thrill of pulling off something illegal. Like we said, she probably rationalized it as penalizing a corrupt system."

He gobbled steak, said, "Interesting woman, our Mary. Cultivates an identity as a professional woman and a dispenser of wisdom, but she had no compunction tapping Sonny for an increased allowance. Top of that, she liked being held down."

"Power's a strange drug. Sometimes people in authority like being controlled sexually."

"Where'd you hear that?"

"I've seen it."

"Oh." He sopped up gravy with a wedge of sourdough. "You believe Gull never talked to Mary about Degussa's fantasies concerning Flora?"

I said, "Even if he didn't, Mary had to have some idea what was going on. Flora came to her for treatment and sexual unresponsiveness, and Mary knew Degussa from the scam. Knew what kind of person he was.

For all we know Degussa *sent* Flora for therapy. To tune her up sexually."

"Brian Van Dyne said Flora had heard Mary on the radio."

"There's a lot Brian Van Dyne wasn't aware of."

"Fiancée with a shadow life," he said. "Flora juggled the two of them?"

"Flora met Degussa while working at the parole office. He put on some of that macho sociopath charm, and she threw Roy Nichols over for someone even tougher. The thrill was forbidden fruit. Then she met Van Dyne and started thinking matrimony, but she didn't want to give up the game."

"A nice, respectable teacher to show off for Mom, rough trade on the side."

"It's possible Flora's murder had nothing to do with the scam," I said. "Her crime scene was a lot bloodier than any of the others, and there was no forced entry. To me it feels like passion and sex gone haywire. When we met Roy Nichols, you wondered about a jealousy motive. Why not apply that to Degussa?"

"Degussa found out about Van Dyne and blew," he said.

"The wrong guy to betray. Toss in Flora's

inability to climax, and you're talking rage fodder. A guy like Ray Degussa would take sexual unresponsiveness as a personal insult."

"Sticking her every which way. That's a goddamn blueprint for what he ended up doing to her. And Mary Koppel never warned her."

"Confidentiality," I said. "She was big on that."

He sawed at his steak, stopped. "So I should take Flora off the scamster list?"

"No evidence she was involved."

"And," he said, "her mom's a nice old lady."

"That, too."

"Confidentiality . . . Mary didn't want to jeopardize the cash flow. Three hundred fifty plus of her own inflated billing, and she and Larsen split another three hundred that came in under Gull's name. That's over half a million each, in addition to what they were earning legitimately. And Mary had an allowance."

"Mary had contempt for Sonny because he didn't know how to live."

"She lived, all right. Until she didn't. The key is finding all that money. Zevonsky's getting the ball rolling on financial subpoenas."

"Knowing about Larsen's African connections might help."

"Here's hoping." He saluted, finishing off a mammoth chunk of steak, chewed slowly, swallowed. "How do you see Mary's murder going down? She makes noise to Larsen, gets threatening, and he dispatches Degussa to finish her off."

"That's exactly what I think."

I refilled my wineglass and took a long swallow. Nice cabernet. The latest from the health mavens was that booze was good for you, if you didn't overdo it.

That was the key: knowing the boundaries.

He said, "It all fits but I'm still short on proof. Can't even get a home address on Degussa. The club he works for pays him cash under the table."

"Try the Marina," I said. "Flora took Van Dyne there for brunch. Maybe because she'd been there with Degussa."

"Bobby J's—yeah, I like that, if she was gaming that would be fun for her. I'll drop by again, flash Degussa's mug."

He hitched his trousers, and we left the

steakhouse. He must've left a huge tip—cop's tip—because the waiter followed us out to the sidewalk, thanked him, and shook his hand.

Milo told him, "Enjoy," and we returned to the unmarked.

"With what we know now," he said, "I should also be able to get some extra personnel for serious surveillance. This is good, Alex. Not anywhere near a slam dunk, but good."

"Nice to see you happy."

"Me? I'm always a ray of sunshine." As if illustrating, he spread his lips in something that might have been a smile and switched on the police radio as he drove. Humming along, atonally, with the dispatcher's droll recital of outrage and misery.

Midway back to the station, he said, "There's still the matter of how Jerry Quick fits into the scam."

"Maybe he doesn't," I said. "Gull knew him only as Gavin's father, and maybe that's the point. Jerry started following *Gavin* around. Because Gavin had been acting strange. Gavin didn't know that and spotted his dad and copied down his license plate.

In Gavin's damaged mind, everyone was part of the conspiracy."

"Gavin was paranoid?"

"Prefrontal damage can do that."

"A concerned father would be helping us, Alex, not destroying evidence and hiding out. Quick's been gone, what—five days. What the hell is *that* all about?"

"Good point," I said.

"Just because Gull wasn't aware of Quick's involvement doesn't mean Quick's a virgin. We've got a guy who hires a stripper as a phony secretary, uses prepaid phone cards, leaves condoms in his luggage to rub salt in wifey's wounds, hits on his sister-in-law, doesn't pay his bills on time. To me that's precisely the kind of tainted citizen who'd love something like Sentries for Justice. I'll buy the concerned dad bit up to a point—the point where Quick supplied Gavin with Christi Marsh. Which got *her* killed, too. Quick knows if it all comes out, he's in big trouble with his family, not to mention the law. So he cuts out and leaves Sheila to fend for herself. This is *not* Ward Cleaver."

"I wonder how Sheila's doing," I said.

"Ever the shrink. Feel free to drop by and

do some therapy. God knows she needs it. Meanwhile, I'm gonna earn the salary the city pays me."

A block later: "Did I thank you for all your help?"

"More than once," I said.

"Good," he said. "Got to be civilized."

CHAPTER

42

South Camden Drive at two in the afternoon was a pretty scene.

Temperate Beverly Hills weather, unfettered by seasons, nice houses, nice cars, nice gardeners mowing nice lawns. Up the block from the Quick house, an elderly man made his way along the sidewalk with the help of twin walkers and a tiny Filipina attendant. As I drove by, he smiled and waved.

Happiness had so little to do with the state of your bones.

The door to the white traditional was open, and Sheila Quick's minivan idled in the driveway, exhaust pipe blowing delicate puffs of smoke that dissipated quickly in the warm, smooth air.

Woman's silhouette in the front passenger seat. I got out and approached the van, found Sheila Quick sitting stiffly, looking hypnotized, her window up.

She didn't notice me and I was about to knock on her window when a young woman came out of the house hefting an oversized blue duffel.

When she saw me she froze.

Tall, slim, dark hair drawn back in a careless ponytail. Pleasant face, less plain than in the family photo. She wore a hooded blue sweatshirt over jeans and white sneakers. Down-slanted eyes, her father's large jaw. His slightly stooped posture, too; it made her look weary. Maybe she was.

"Kelly?"

"Yes?"

"My name's Alex Delaware. I work with the L.A. Police—"

"*With* the police? What does that mean?"

First-year law student, trained to parse? Or she'd chosen the profession because it fit her nature?

I said, "I'm a psychologist who consults

to LAPD. I've been involved in your brother's—"

Hearing "psychologist" she turned her head toward her mother. She said, "I just got in to town, don't know anything about that."

A cheery voice behind me said, "Hi!"

Sheila Quick had rolled down her window and was waving and smiling. "Hello, again!"

Kelly Quick lifted her duffel, came forward, interposed herself between me and her mother.

"He's with the police, Kell."

"I know, Mom." To me: "Excuse me, but we're kind of in a hurry."

"Getting away for a while?"

No answer.

"Where to, Kelly?"

"I'd rather not say."

"Aunt Eileen's?"

"I'd rather not say." Kelly Quick edged past me, to the rear of the van, lifted the hatch, and loaded her duffel. Two large suitcases were already there.

Sheila Quick said, "Still no sign of Jerry! For all I know, he's dead!"

Still cheerful.

"Mom!"

"No need to be dishonest, Kelly. I've had enough dishonesty to last me—"

"*Mo*-ther! *Please!*"

Sheila said, "At least you said 'please.' " To me: "I raised them to be polite."

I said, "Where you heading?"

Kelly Quick got between us, again. "We're in a hurry." Her mouth twisted. "Please."

Sheila Quick said, "This one is smart, nothing wrong with her brain. She was always a great student. Gavin had the charm and the looks, but Kelly had the grades."

Kelly Quick's eyes misted.

I said, "Could we talk, Kelly? Just for a moment?"

Fluttering eyelashes, cock of hip. A hint of the adolescence she'd barely left.

"Fine, but just for a moment."

We walked a few yards past the van. Sheila Quick called out, "Where are you two going?"

"Just one sec, Mom." To me: *"What?"*

"If you're heading to your aunt Eileen's, that'll be easy enough to find out."

"We're not—we can go anywhere we want."

"Of course you can, I'm not here to stop you."

"Then what?"

"Have you heard from your father?"

No answer.

"Kelly, if he's gotten in touch and given you instructions—"

"He hasn't. Okay?"

"I'm sure he instructed you not to talk. I'm sure you think you're helping him out by obeying."

"I don't obey anyone," she said. "I think independently. We need to get going."

"You can't say where?"

"It's not important—it really isn't. My brother was murdered, and my mom . . . she's having problems. I need to take care of her, it's as simple as that."

"What about your dad?"

She looked at the sidewalk.

"Kelly, he could be in serious trouble. The people he's dealing with shouldn't be underestimated."

She raised her eyes but stared past me.

"No one knows better than you about your mother's vulnerability. How long do you think you can take care of her?"

Her head snapped back toward me. "You think you know."

"I'm sure I don't."

"Please," she said, "don't make matters worse."

Tears blurred her eyes. Old eyes in a young face.

I stepped aside, and she returned to the van, got in the driver's seat, locked the door. As she started up the engine, Sheila prattled and gesticulated.

Festive mood. Kelly was grim, hand planted on the wheel. Not going anywhere until I did. I pulled away from the curb.

When I reached the corner, I looked back in my rearview mirror and the van was still there.

◆

Milo was out, so I asked for Detective Sean Binchy.

He said, "So you think Mr. Quick phoned his daughter?"

"That would be my guess."

"So she probably knows where he is. Think I should put a BOLO on the van?"

"I'd check with Milo about that. When will he be back?"

"He didn't say," said Binchy. "Something about going over to the Marina for lunch. I think there was more to it, but that's what he said. Usually he ends up explaining."

◆

An hour later, Milo showed up at my house and explained.

"Had a nice cool drink at Bobby J's," he said, rubbing his gut. "Found a waitress who recalls Flora and Degussa eating there several times. Brunch *and* dinner. She remembered them because she thought they were an odd couple."

"The teacher and the thug."

"She said Degussa flirted with her shamelessly, and Flora just sat there and took it. She also said Degussa ate funny—all hunched over his food, like someone was going to steal it."

"Prison etiquette," I said. "She ever see Flora with Van Dyne?"

"Nope. Either it wasn't on her shift, or ol' Brian didn't make an impression. Extra kudos to you for the Marina lead. I found an address there for Bennett Hacker."

"Thought he lived on Franklin."

"As of seven months ago he's got two addresses, apartment on Franklin, condo on Marina Way. Maybe his weekend getaway."

"Guess what paid for it," I said. "I wonder how much kickback he got from Sentries."

"Total billing was over a million and a quarter during the sixteen-month period, so there'd be enough for everyone. Larsen and Mary could have shot him and Degussa a third and still ended up comfy."

"Maybe that's what they used Gull's phony billings for."

"That's Zevonsky's job to iron out. I'm concentrating on four homicides, meaning when Bennett Hacker leaves the parole office today, he gets tailed. I found a nice, unobtrusive car in the department pool, plan to be downtown in half an hour. Binchy'll be in radio contact. Wanna come along, maybe take pictures if my hands aren't free?"

I said, "Smile and say cheese."

◆

"Nice and unobtrusive" was a dark gray Volvo station wagon with black-tinted windows and an I LOVE L.A. bumper sticker. The interior smelled of tobacco and incense. On the passenger seat was a Polaroid camera and five film cartridges. I placed them on my lap.

"Hot wheels."

"Confiscated from a drug dealer," he said. "Peppier than it looks, he installed a tur-bocharger."

"Drug dealers drive station wagons?"

"Life's full of surprises," he said. "This one was a junior at the U., selling ecstacy to his frat brothers. Daddy's a surgeon, Mommy's a judge. It used to be her car."

As he drove toward downtown, I filled him in on my encounter with Kelly and Sheila Quick.

"The high-achieving kid," he said. "Quick called her home to help out."

"He knows he's in trouble, and he wants his family out of the way. And he needs someone to take care of Sheila."

"Another stash at Eileen Paxton's house?"

"When I mentioned that, Kelly clammed up."

At the next red light, he scanned his notepad for Paxton's numbers and punched in her office. He got her on the phone, talked very little, did plenty of listening, hung up and clicked his teeth together.

"Sheila and Kelly were indeed supposed to show up at her place tonight, but Kelly just called, said there'd been a change of plans, wouldn't specify what they were. Paxton tried arguing with Kelly but Kelly hung up and when Paxton called back, the car phone was switched off. Paxton says Kelly was always stubborn. Says her sister's deteriorating psychologically, she's never seen her this bad. She was just about to call me. Sheila look that bad to you?"

"Pretty fragile," I said. "Everything she thought she had is slipping away. Sean wondered if he should put a Be-on-the-Lookout on the van."

"Sean's been watching too much TV. Sheila and Kelly aren't suspects, they're a couple of scared women. With good reason. A BOLO would put them in the cross hairs, and hell if I'm gonna do that."

He got on the 405, transferred to the 10 East. Two exits later: "Wonder if the Quicks have passports."

"Family escape?" I said. "If Jerry's got enough money saved up, could be."

"Makes me feel sorry for him," he said. "Until I think about all those impaled bodies. For all we know he flew somewhere already and is having wifey and daughter meet him. Or he just cruised across the border to Mexico."

"Wifey and daughter and Angie Paul?" I said.

He clicked his tongue. "Yeah, there would be that little problem . . . I'll have Sean check with the airports and the border patrol, then do another look-see at Angie's place."

He switched to the fast lane, made the call to Binchy at seventy miles per. "Sean, I've got a few tasks for you—really? Think so? Okay, yeah, sure, give it to me." To me: "Could you copy this down?"

I found a gum wrapper in the glove compartment and wrote down the name and the 805 number he recited.

He gave Binchy his orders and hung up. "When it rains, it El Niños. What just might be a solid tip on Christina Marsh just came in. This guy claims he's her brother, saw her picture in the paper. Grad student at UC Santa Barbara, lives in Isla Vista. Once we finish with Hacker, I'll see if it's for real."

◆

California Department of Corrections, Parole Division, Region III, was located on South Broadway near First, in the heart of downtown. We got onto the 110, left the freeway at Fourth Street, drove south and got stuck in gridlock near Second. Milo had me call the parole office and ask for Bennett Hacker.

"Can you sound like a con?"

"Hey," I said, deepening my voice. "Don't crowd me, man."

He laughed. I maneuvered voice mail structured to make me give up, finally ended up talking to a brusque, hurried woman. How many felons would have the patience?

She barked, "You one of his assignments?"

"That's what they tell me," I said.

"Got an appointment?"

"No, but I—"

"You need an appointment. He's not here."

"Oh, man," I said. "Any idea when he'll be back?"

"He left," she said. "Like a minute ago."

I gave up.

◆

Milo cursed. "Three o'clock, and the guy takes off."

"She said a minute ago," I said. "If he

parks outside the building, maybe we can spot him leaving."

Traffic wasn't moving. Then it crawled. And stopped. Four cars in front of us. Downtown shadows turned the sidewalk charcoal.

"What the hell," said Milo, slamming the station wagon into PARK. He got out and looked up and down Broadway. The right lane was closed, blocked by groupings of orange cones. The cones demarcated oblong excavations. The air smelled of asphalt, but no work crew was in sight.

Milo flashed his badge at four startled drivers, got back in, watched them veer to the right, perilously close to the cones. He drove through the parting.

"Power," he said, waving his thanks. "Intoxicating." He coasted another ten feet, found an illegal parking spot next to a cone-surrounded hydrant. Right across from the parole building. The sidewalks were crowded, and no one paid attention.

Seconds later, a husky female parking officer approached, pad in hand. When she reached his window, out came the badge. He talked fast, gave her no chance to speak. She left glowering.

He said, "I'd cast her in a prison movie. The ruthless matron with no heart of gold."

We waited. No sign of Bennett Hacker.

"A minute ago, huh?"

"Maybe there's a rear exit," I said.

"Wouldn't that be sad."

Five more minutes. Big, gray government building, lots of people coming and going.

Three minutes later, Bennett Hacker was disgorged through the front door, in a crush of other civil servants.

◆

He was easy to miss, stepping away from the crowd to light up a cigarette.

But when the view cleared, he was still puffing. Wearing an illfitting gray sport coat over navy chinos, a dark blue shirt, a silver and aqua striped tie. Still smoking, he walked up the block to a hot dog stand.

Milo cruised forward, and I took Hacker's picture. Mouth full of chili dog.

Hacker walked another block, eating and smoking. Unhurried. Not a care in the world.

Following slowly enough so as not to be noticed was a challenge. Traffic either sat still or spurted ahead. Milo broke lots of traffic laws, managed to pull it off. I took

Polaroids when I had a clear shot. The prints revealed the ultimate forgettable man: tall, lanky, unremarkably featured and colored. One noticeable trait: slightly pigeon-toed. It made him seem unsteady, almost drunk.

At the next corner, Hacker finished the chili dog, tossed the greasy paper wrapping at a wastebasket, and missed. He turned without stopping to pick it up.

"There you go," I said. "You can bust him for littering."

"I'm keeping score." Milo edged up to the corner.

Hacker entered an outdoor municipal parking lot.

Milo said, "We stay here and wait till he comes out. We're looking for a '99 Explorer. The reg says black, but that coulda changed."

"He has two addresses, but just one car?"

"Yup."

"He doesn't spend on fancier wheels," I said. "Or clothing. The place in the Marina is his prize."

"Got to be. His crib on Franklin's a dump. One-bedroom walk-up in an old three-story building. I drove by last night, figuring to catch a glimpse of him, maybe with Degussa. No luck. His mailbox is full. Now I know why. He prefers the sea breeze."

♦

The Explorer was black turned to gray by weeks of dirt. Bird shit speckled the top and the hood.

Bennett Hacker avoided the freeway and took side streets west: through the downtown crush to Figueroa, then south to Olympic, past Staples Center, all the way to Robertson. Then a right on Pico, to Motor, southward to Washington, where the avenue dead-ended at the Sony studio lot. Another right turn, and we were heading for the Marina.

A circuitous route; it took nearly an hour. Hacker made no attempts at shortcuts or slick maneuvers. He drove the way he walked. Slow, easy, not even a lane change unless it was essential. He smoked constantly, rolled the window down and flicked butts.

Milo stayed three cars behind him, and there was no sign Hacker noticed. At Palms, Milo phoned Sean Binchy and told him to forget about joining the tail, it wasn't looking complicated. Binchy was mired in bureaucracy and enjoying it: airline records, the border patrol, querying the IRS for Jerome Quick's tax records.

Milo told him, "Glad it's fun for you, Sean."

At Washington, just east of Palawan Way, Bennett Hacker stopped at a 7-Eleven and bought himself a Slurpee, and I took a picture of him sipping through two straws. Still drinking, he got back in the Explorer, turned onto Via Marina and drove right past his apartment. Tossed the empty cup out the window where it bounced along the median.

He continued through the Marina—past Bobby J's and a spate of other harborside restaurants—and pulled into a strip mall on the south end.

Coin Laundromat, liquor store, window grate company, boat outfitters.

HOG TRAIL MOTORCYLE SHOP.

Fat-lettered, Day-Glo banners above the garage entrance said a big sale was going on. Big shiny bikes, many of them chopped and customized, were arranged in a tilting chorus line out in front.

"Here we go," said Milo. "A new toy for our civil servant."

I photographed Hacker entering the shop and kept clicking away when he came out a few moments later talking with another man.

His companion bummed a cigarette. Big, solid guy in a white T-shirt and tight blue jeans. Work boots. His hands and arms and the shirt were grease-stained.

Multiple tattoos, slicked-back dark hair. Raymond Degussa looked heavier and older than his most recent mug shot. He'd grown back his mustache, now graying, and added a soul patch that emphasized a heavy lower lip.

"Well, well," said Milo. "Mr. Ray does have a day job. Probably another cozy cash situation, like the club. No papers filed, no tax returns."

"Look what's on the floor to his right," I said.

Three rolls of black tarpaulin. Neoprene; a shred had been found at Flora Newsome's crime scene.

Milo's jaw set.

"I don't want to push good fortune," I said, "but that window grate company over there has got to keep iron bars in stock. Talk about one-stop shopping."

"Oh, yeah," said Milo. "How about some more pictures?"

Click click click.

Degussa found a rag and wiped his hands. Bennett Hacker talked, and both of them blew smoke that vanished in the beach air. No expression on Degussa's long, hard face.

Then he nodded and grinned and snapped the rag and flicked it ten feet away into a white bucket just past the Neoprene rolls. Two points. This one could shoot.

He peeled off his greasy T-shirt, revealed slab pecs, a hard, protruding belly, bulky hirsute shoulders, arms, and neck, a thick waist softened by love handles. Some definition, but mostly size. Prisons had free weights for bulking up, no fancy toning machines.

Crumpling the shirt, he returned inside the bike shop, came out wearing a short-sleeved black silk shirt that hung loose over the same jeans and boots.

"Untucked," I said. "Wonder if he's armed."

"Wouldn't shock me."

I reloaded the camera and photographed Degussa and Hacker as they got in the Explorer. The SUV hooked an illegal U, returned to Washington, turned south on Inglewood and pulled to the curb just shy of Culver Boulevard, in front of a bar called Winners.

One of those clay-colored, cinder-block masterpieces with a Bud sign in the single fly-specked window and a HAPPY HOUR WELL-DRINKS discount banner above the door.

Milo spotted a space across the street, ten yards north. He hung his own illegal U and parked.

I *click-clicked* the front of the bar.

Milo said, "Too small for us to go in without being noticed, so we just wait."

◆

An hour later, Hacker and Degussa still hadn't emerged. Half an hour in, Milo had chanced a walk down the block and a look-see around the back of the bar.

"The rear exit's bolted. Eventually, they'll have to show at the front."

As we sat there, he checked with Sean

Binchy a couple more times. No record, so far, of Jerome Quick or Angela Paul flying anywhere.

Jerry and Angie.

Gavin and Christi.

Like-father-like-son had spawned a nightmare, and I found myself feeling sympathy for Quick, no matter what else he'd done.

Milo groused, "No record at the Mexican border, but what the hell does that mean? After 9-11, you'd think they'd register every damn car, but they don't, it's still that stupid *random* crap. Leaving a big fat hole for Quick to walk through."

I was about to commiserate when movement in front of Winners caught my eye.

"The party begins," I said.

◆

Hacker and Degussa and two women stood on the sidewalk as their pupils adjusted to the light.

A blonde, a brunette, both in their late thirties. Big hair, heavy in the hips and bust. The blonde wore a black tank top over epidermal jeans. The brunette's tank was red. Backless high-heeled sandals gave them both a mincing, butt-jiggling walk. Alcohol added some wobble.

Faces that had once been pretty had been paved over by bad decisions.

Hacker stopped to light up, and Degussa stretched his arms around both the women. Cupped their breasts. The blonde threw her head back and laughed. The brunette made a playful grab for his groin.

Milo said, "Classy."

The four of them got in the Explorer and returned to Hacker's apartment, entering the subterranean garage through an electric gate.

"Party time," said Milo, "and yet again, I'm not invited."

CHAPTER

43

The building's manager was a man in his sixties named Stan Parks. He wore a short-sleeved white shirt and gray slacks, had thinning hair and a disapproving mouth. A thirty-year-old Caltech engineering diploma hung behind his desk. His office was on the ground floor, next to the elevator, and the rumble of the lift shook the room at random intervals.

He said, "Hacker has no lease, just a month-to-month. He and his roommate."

"Raymond Degussa?"

"Raymond something. Let me check." Parks tapped the keys of a laptop. "Yup, Degussa."

"Did he move in the same time as Hacker?"

"Two months later. Hacker cleared it with me. I told him no subleases, the check had to come from him, no split obligations."

"How are they as tenants?"

"They're okay. Your month-to-months, they're the ones who give you troubles. I prefer leases, but it's not one of the best units, stayed vacant a long time."

"What's wrong with it?"

"There's nothing wrong with it, it's just not one of our best. Not the harbor side, and the way the trees grow at that particular height you can't see much of anything on the other side."

"What trouble has he given you?"

Parks frowned and played with a pencil, stippling three fingertips, then passing the shaft between his fingers. "Look, I'm not just the manager, I'm part owner. So if there's something going on that affects the building, I need to know."

"Who are the other owners, sir?"

"My brothers-in-law, the dentists." The elevator vibrated the room. Parks sat through it, stoic. "I depend on this place. Is there something I should worry about?"

Milo said, "At this point, no. What kind of problems have Hacker and Degussa given you?"

"At this point," said Parks.

"The problems, sir?"

"A few noise complaints at the beginning. I spoke to Hacker, and it stopped."

"What kind of noise?"

"Loud music, voices. Apparently, they bring women in, throw parties."

"Apparently?"

"Mostly I'm sitting in here," said Parks.

"Ever see the women?"

"A couple of times."

"The same women?"

Parks shook his head. "You know."

"Know what, sir?"

"The type."

"What type is that?" said Milo.

"Not exactly . . . high society."

"Party girls."

Parks's eyes rolled. "Hacker pays his rent. I don't get involved in the tenants' personal lives. After those first few complaints, they've been fine."

"What's the rent on their unit?"

"This is a money issue? Some sort of financial crime?"

"The rent, please."

Parks said, "Hacker pays 2200 a month. The unit has two full bedrooms and a den, two baths, and a built-in wet bar. On the harbor side it would be over three thousand."

"The women you saw, would you recognize any of them?"

Parks shook his head. "Everybody minds their own business here. That's the point of the Marina. You get your divorced people, your widowed people. People want their privacy."

Milo said, "Everyone doing their own thing."

"Like you, Lieutenant. You ask all these questions, tell me nothing. You seem pretty good at keeping your business to yourself."

Milo smiled.

Parks smiled back.

Milo asked to see Hacker's parking slot, and Parks took us down to a subgarage that smelled of motor oil and wet cement. Half the slots were empty, but the black Explorer was in place. Milo and I looked through the windows. Food cartons, a windbreaker, maps, loose papers.

Stan Parks said, "Is this about drugs?"

"Why would it be?" said Milo.

"You're examining the car." Parks went over and peered through the windows. "I don't see anything incriminating."

"Where's Mr. Degussa's spot, sir?"

Parks walked us a dozen slots down to a Lincoln Town Car, big, square, the predown-size model. Chrome rims, shiny paint job. Custom job, a heavy, brownish red.

Parks said, "Pretty ugly color, don't you think? Put all that money into restoration and end up with something like that. I keep a few collector cars, no way would I go this color."

"This color" was the precise hue of dry blood.

"Ugly," I said. "What cars do you keep?"

"A '48 Caddy, '62 E-type Jag, a '64 Mini-Cooper. I'm trained as an engineer, do the work myself."

I nodded.

Parks said, "By the way, Degussa also drives a motorcycle, puts it over there." Indicating a section to the right, smaller slots for two-wheelers.

No bikes in sight.

"He pays extra for that," said Parks.

"Wanted it for free, but I told him twenty bucks a month."

"A bargain," said Milo.

Parks shrugged. "It's not one of the better units."

◆

We left the Marina, and Milo asked for the 805 number I'd written down and the name that went with it.

Cody Marsh.

The Volvo was equipped with a hands-off phone system, and Milo plugged his little blue gizmo into it as he drove. He punched in Cody Marsh's number. Two rings and a voice said he was being rerouted to a mobile unit. Two additional rings, and a man said, "Hello?"

"Mr. Marsh?"

"Yes."

"This is Lieutenant Sturgis."

"Oh, hi." Fuzzy reception. "Hold on, let me switch off the radio ... okay, I'm back, thanks for calling. I'm in my car, coming down to L.A. Any way you can see me?"

"Where are you?"

"The 101 Freeway, coming up on ... Balboa. Traffic's not looking great, but I can probably be in West L.A. within half an hour."

"Christina Marsh is your sister?"

"She is . . . was . . . can you find time to see me? I'd really like to find out about her."

"Sure," said Milo. "Meet me at a restaurant near the station. Café Moghul." He spelled the name and recited the address.

Cody Marsh thanked him and cut the connection.

◆

We drove straight to the restaurant, arrived in twenty-five. Cody Marsh was already seated at a corner table drinking milk-laced chai.

Easy to spot; solitary patron.

By the time we stepped through the glass beads, he was on his feet. Looking exactly as if someone had died.

"Mr. Marsh."

"Thanks for seeing me, Lieutenant. When will I be able to see my sister—to identify the body?"

"You're sure you want to go through that, sir?"

"I thought I had to," said Cody Marsh. "Christi has no one else."

He looked to be around thirty, with long, wavy, brown hair parted in the middle, had on a gray shirt under a cracked, brown leather jacket rubbed white at the pressure points, rumpled beige cargo pants, white running shoes. Ruddy square face, thick lips, and tired blue eyes behind horn-rimmed glasses. Five-ten with an incipient beer belly. The only hint of kinship to the dead girl, a dimpled chin.

"Actually, sir," said Milo, "you don't have to do it in person. You can look at a photo."

"Oh," said Marsh. "Okay. Where do I go to see a photo?"

"I've got one right here, sir, but I have to warn you—"

"I'll look at it."

Milo said, "How about we all sit down?"

◆

Cody Marsh stared at the death shot. His eyes closed and opened; he folded his lips inward. "That's Christi." He raised his fist, as if to pound the table, but by the time the arc was completed, the hand had stopped short of contact.

"Dammit."

The pleasant sari-draped woman who ran

the café turned to stare. Milo never talked business to her, but she knew what he did.

He smiled at her, and she resumed folding napkins.

"I'm sorry for your loss, sir."

"Christi," said Cody Marsh. "What *happened*?"

Milo took the photo and put it away. "Your sister was shot while parked in a car on Mulholland Drive, along with a young man."

"Was the young man a friend?"

"Seemed to be," said Milo. "His name was Gavin Quick. Know him?"

Cody Marsh shook his head. "Any idea *why* it happened?"

"That's what we're looking into. So Christi never mentioned Gavin Quick."

"No, but Christi and I weren't . . . in close communication."

The saried woman came over. Milo said, "Just chai, right now, please. I'll probably see you tomorrow for lunch."

"That would be lovely," said the woman. "We'll have the *sag paneer* and the *tandoori* salmon on special."

When she was gone, Cody Marsh said, "Can the . . . can Christi be released? For a funeral?"

"That's up to the coroner's office," said Milo.

"Do you have a number for them?"

"I'll call for you. It'll probably take a few days to get the papers in order."

"Thanks." Marsh *pinged* his teacup with a fingernail. "This is horrible."

"Is there anything you could tell us about your sister that would be helpful, sir?"

Ping ping. "What would you like to know?"

"For starts, when did Christi move to L.A.?"

"I can't say exactly, but she called me about a year ago to tell me she was here."

"You guys hail from Minnesota?"

"Baudette, Minnesota," said Marsh. "Wall-eye Capital of the World. People who some-how find themselves there get their picture taken with Willie Walleye."

"A fish."

"A forty-foot model of a fish. I got out as soon as I could. Did my undergrad at Oregon State, taught grade school for a few years in Portland so I could save up enough money to go to grad school and study history."

"History," Milo repeated.

"Those who forget the past are con-demned, and all that."

I said, "Did your being in Santa Barbara play a role in your sister's coming out to California?"

"It would be nice to say yes," said Marsh, "but I seriously doubt it. The entire year we've seen each other exactly twice. Spoke on the phone maybe three or four times. And we'd been out of contact for a long time well before Christi left Minnesota."

"Those two times," I said.

"Here, in L.A. I was attending symposia and called her. Actually, I called her three times, but once she was busy."

"Busy doing what?" said Milo.

"She didn't say."

"Where'd you meet her?"

"We had dinner at my hotels."

"Which hotels?"

"That's important?" said Marsh.

"Anything could be important, sir."

"You're the expert . . . let's see, one was a Holiday Inn in Pasadena, the other was a Holiday Inn in Westwood. Christi met me in the coffee shop and came dressed totally inappropriately. For an academic meeting, I mean. Not that she was attending meetings, but the . . . the place was teeming with academics."

"And she didn't look academic," said Milo.

"Not hardly."

"Inappropriate how?" I said.

"I really don't want to talk ill of my sister."

"I understand."

Marsh pinged his cup some more. "Both times she wore halter tops with no backs, very, very short skirts, spike heels, lots of makeup." Marsh sighed. "There was faculty all around, people were staring. The first time I let it go, figuring she didn't know what to expect. The second time I said something to her and it was a very tense meal. She cut it short, announced she had to go, and just walked out without saying goodbye. I didn't try to follow her. Afterward, I realized I'd been a prissy jerk, phoned her to apologize, but she didn't return the call. I tried again but by that time her number was inactive. A month later I heard from her, and she didn't mention a thing about walking out. I asked for her new number, but she said she was using prepaid cell phones—disposable, so there was no sense copying down the number. I'd never heard of that."

"She say why she was using prepaids?"

"She said it was simpler. I took that to mean she didn't have enough of a credit history to get a real phone account. Or she had no permanent home."

"Out on the streets?"

"No, I think she was living somewhere, but not in a permanent place. I tried to find out, she refused to tell me. I took that to mean she thought I'd disapprove."

Ping ping. "I probably would've. Christi and I are very different."

I said, "She called you to reconnect."

"She managed to track me down at the History Department, I walk in one day and find a message in my box that my sister called. At first I thought it was a mistake." Cody Marsh winced. "I didn't think of myself as having a sister. Christi and I have the same father but different mothers, and we didn't grow up together. Christi's significantly younger than I—I'm thirty-three and she's . . . was twenty-three. By the time she was old enough to relate to, I was in Oregon, so we really didn't have a relationship."

"Are her parents alive?"

"Our father's dead. And so is *my* mother.

Christi's mother is alive, but she has serious mental problems, has been institutionalized for years."

"How many years?" I said.

"Since Christi was four. Our father was a raging alcoholic. As far as I'm concerned, he killed my mother. Smoking in bed, blind-drunk. My mother was drinking, too, but the cigarette was his. The house went up in flames, he managed to stagger out. Lost an arm and part of his face, but it didn't put a dent in his drinking. I was seven, went to live with my maternal grandparents. Soon after, he met Christi's mom in a bar and started a whole new family."

"Serious mental problems," I said.

"Carlene's schizophrenic," said Marsh. "That's why she hooked up with a one-armed, scar-faced drunk. I'm sure drinking was what they had in common. I'm sure drinking and living with my father didn't help her mental state. I was the lucky one, my grandparents were educated, both teachers, religious. My mother was trained as a social worker. Marrying him was her big rebellion."

"And he raised Christi after her mom was institutionalized?"

"It couldn't have been much of a raising. I don't know the details, I was living in Baudette, and he took Christi over to St. Paul. I heard that she dropped out of high school, but I'm not sure exactly what grade. Later, she went to Duluth with him—he was working on some sort of land crew. Then back to St. Paul. A really bad neighborhood."

Milo said, "Sounds like you kept tabs."

"No," said Marsh. "I heard things from my grandparents. Filtered through their biases." Marsh worked several strands of hair over his face, spread them back, shook his head. "They hated my father, blamed him for my mother's death and everything else that was wrong in the world. They loved recounting his misfortunes in great detail. The slum neighborhoods he was forced to live in, Christi failing in school, dropping out. Christi getting into trouble. We're talking editorializing, not straight reporting. They saw Christi as an extension of him—bad seed. They wanted nothing to do with her. She wasn't their blood. So Christi and I were kept apart."

"What kind of trouble did Christi get into?" I said.

"The usual: drugs, keeping bad company, shoplifting. My grandparents told me she got sent to one of those wilderness camps, then juvenile hall. Part of it was their *schadenfreude*—reveling in someone else's misery. The other part was that deep down they worried about me. Being half-Dad genetically. So they used Dad and Christi as negative examples. They were preaching to the converted because Christi represented everything *I* despised about my roots. The trash side, as my grandparents called it. I was a good student, well behaved, destined for better things. I bought into that. It wasn't until my divorce—" He smiled. "I neglected to mention that somewhere along the way I got married. That lasted nineteen months. Soon after the divorce, both my grandparents died, and I was feeling pretty alone, and I realized I did have a half sib I barely knew and maybe I should stop being a self-righteous jerk. So I tried to get in touch with Christi. Nagged my great-aunt—my grandmother's sister—until she told me Christi was still living in St. Paul, 'doing burlesque.' I phoned a few strip clubs—I was motivated, the whole rebonding fantasy—and finally located the place where Christi worked. She wasn't happy to hear from me, very distant. So I bribed her by wiring her a hundred bucks. After that, she started calling every couple of months. Sometimes to talk, sometimes to ask for more money. That seemed to bother her—having to ask. There was a shy side to her, she'd pretend to be tough but she could be sweet."

Milo said, "She give you any other details about her lifestyle?"

"Just that she was dancing, we never got into details. When she called, it was always from a club, I could hear the music going. Sometimes I thought she might've sounded high. I didn't want to do anything to put distance between us. She liked the fact that I was a teacher. Sometimes she called me 'Teach' instead of my name."

Marsh removed his glasses and wiped them with his napkin. Unshielded, his eyes were small and weak. "Then her calls stopped, and the club said she was gone, no forwarding. I didn't hear from her for over a year, until I got the message in my box at school."

"No idea what she was doing for over a year?"

Marsh shook his head. "She said she'd

made enough from dancing to relax for a while, but I wondered."

"About what?"

"If she'd gotten into other things. I put that out of my head because I had no facts."

"Other things such as . . ."

"Selling herself," said Marsh. "That was another thing my grandparents were always telling me about Christi. She was promiscuous. They used less-kind language. I didn't want to hear it."

He took hold of his cup, managed to get down some chai.

"Christi had learning problems, but I guess one thing she could always count on was her looks. She was an extremely beautiful child. Skinny as a stick when she was little, white-blond hair below her waist. It was never clean or combed and she wore mismatched clothes—Dad didn't have a clue. Sometimes, not often, he'd drop in unannounced. My grandfather would always storm up to his room and not come down. Grandmother called Christi 'the street urchin.' As in, 'Here's the bum and the street urchin come a-knocking. Better Lysol the cups and glasses.' Usually, I'd escape to my room, too. One time, Christi couldn't have been more than four, so I was fourteen, she ran up the stairs, flung my door open, and *threw* herself on me."

Marsh pulled at the skin around his jaw. "Hugging me, tickling me, giggling, an idiot could've seen she was reaching out. But it annoyed me. I yelled at her to stop. Bellowed. And she got off me, stared with this *look* in her eyes. And slunk out. I really crushed her."

His eyes were dry but he wiped them. "I was fourteen, what did I know?"

I said, "What do you know about her life in L.A?"

"In L.A. she didn't ask me for money, I can tell you that." He nudged his teacup aside. "I guess that bothered me. Because of what she might be doing to get by. Was she involved with bad people?"

"Did she imply that?"

Marsh hesitated.

"Sir?"

"She did tell me some wild stories," said Marsh. "The last time we spoke, over the phone—"

Milo said, "How long ago was that?"

"Three, four months."

"What kind of wild stories?"

"More out there than wild," said Marsh. "She talked extremely fast so I wondered if she'd gotten into drugs—amphetamines, cocaine, something that was hyping her up. Or worse, could she be ending up like her mother."

"Tell us about the stories," I said.

"She claimed she was working with secret agencies, doing undercover work, spying on gangsters hooked up with terrorists. Making big money, wearing expensive clothes—expensive shoes, she went on a long time about her shoes. She really wasn't making much sense but I let her go on. Then she just stopped talking, said she had to go, hung up."

He pulled at his hair. "That's the last time we talked."

Milo said, "Secret agencies."

Marsh said, "Like I said, out there."

I said, "And shoes were a big deal to her."

"Spying and wearing good shoes," said Marsh. "She even mentioned a brand, some Chinese thing."

"Jimmy Choo."

"That's the one." Marsh stared at us. "What? It was true?"

"She was wearing Jimmy Choo shoes the night she died."

"Oh, God. And the rest—"

Milo said, "The rest was fantasy."

"Poor Christi," said Marsh. "Fantasy as in mental illness?"

Milo glanced at me.

"No," I said. "She was misled."

"By the person who killed her?"

"It's possible."

Marsh moaned, covered his face with his hand.

We watched his shoulders heave.

"At least," he said, "she wasn't going crazy."

"That's important to you."

"My grandparents—they raised me well, in a pseudo-moral sense. But I came to realize that they weren't moral people. The way they demeaned Christi, her mother. Even Dad. I hated him but I came to realize that everyone deserves grace and charity. Grandmother and Grandfather always said Christi would end up like her mother. Made jokes about it. 'Mad as a loon.' 'Weaving baskets in Bedlam.' This was a *child* they were talking about. My *sister*. I didn't like hearing it but I never objected."

He gathered a handful of hair and twisted it hard enough to pucker the top of his brow.

"They were wrong. That's good."

I said, "Did Christi mention any names of people she was working with in the secret agencies?"

"She said she couldn't. 'This is *covert,* Teach. This is the real mindfucking powerful *mojo,* Teach.' "

Marsh slid his cup closer. "Someone mis-led her . . . who?"

"Can't say anything more at this point, sir," said Milo.

Marsh's smile was resigned, but it warmed up his face. A man comfortable being disappointed. "Running your own covert operation?"

"Something like that."

"Can you at least tell me this: Are you feeling any optimism? About finding out who did it?"

"We're making progress, sir."

"I guess I have to be satisfied with that," said Cody Marsh. "Is there anything else?"

"Not at this point, sir." Milo took his number, and Marsh stood.

"So you'll call the coroner for me? I really want to see my little sister."

◆

We watched him leave.

Milo said, "Secret agent mojo. Think she *coulda* been going off the deep end?"

"I think someone convinced a girl with learning problems that she was playing spy games. Think prepaid phones."

"Jerry Quick."

"He hooked her up with Gavin," I said. "Maybe he decided to give her another assignment: spying on his fellow scamsters. What if he was pulling a con within a con and got discovered and that's why he's on the run?"

"Running Christi as a mole."

"She'd be perfect for the assignment. Undereducated, gullible, low self-esteem, living on the fringe. Growing up with a neglectful alchoholic father, she would've craved an older man's attention. Jerry was an operator who didn't pay his rent on time, but he did drive a Mercedes and he lived in Beverly Hills. To girls like Angie Paul and Christi, he would seem like a sugar daddy."

"Christi would be perfect for something else," he said. "Partying with Hacker and Degussa and bringing Jerry back the info.

Compared to those slatterns we just saw them with, Christi would've been a prize."

The saried woman came over and asked if we needed anything.

"How about some mixed appetizers?" said Milo.

She walked off, beaming.

He said, "Bastard buys her Jimmy Choos."

"And Armani perfume and various other toys," I said.

"Parks claims he wouldn't recognize any of the women Hacker and Degussa partied with, but I could show him Christi's death shot. Problem with that is, he'd freak out and want to evict Hacker and Degussa, so I can't trust him to keep quiet."

A tray of fried things arrived.

"Want some?"

"No thanks."

"All for me, then." He dipped something round into parsley-topped yogurt. "Christi wasn't killed just because she happened to be with Gavin. Her cover got blown—hell, maybe she *was* the target, not Gavin, like we thought at the beginning. That would explain the sexual overtones."

I thought about that. "Degussa impaled

men in prison, and did the same to at least three women. He *didn't* impale Gavin. You could be right, he concentrated his rage on Christi. Even with that scenario, though, Gavin was more than an accidental victim. As Jerry Quick's son, he'd be a target for revenge. Or, Degussa was replaying Flora Newsome."

"What do you mean?"

"The jealousy scenario," I said. "If Degussa had partied with Christi, seeing her make love to Gavin would not have made him happy."

"Degussa was dating Flora," he said. "Christi was a party girl. This asshole picks up floozies in bars, he's not into emotional involvement."

"Maybe he is. Not romantically, but in terms of ownership. You said it yourself: Christi would've been a step up. Young, good-looking, compliant. What if Degussa wanted her to himself? Think about the Mulholland crime scene, the way the bodies were found: Gavin's fly was open and Christi's top was off. Degussa followed them, watched them park, watched them engage in foreplay. If all he was after was a quick execution, he could've stepped in earlier and gotten it over with. Instead, he waited. Watched them. The timing was significant: no consummation. The message was: You may try, but you won't succeed. By shooting Gavin in front of Christi, he demonstrated to her that he was the dominant male. She was shocked, terrified. Maybe she tried to flirt her way out of it. Degussa shot her, too, then had fun with his iron rod."

Milo put his fork down. Looked as if the last thing he wanted to do was eat.

I said, "The more I think about it, the more it makes sense. This is a hypermacho, action-oriented psychopath who doesn't take well to rejection."

He put cash on the table, called Sean Binchy and ordered him to find two other cops and do a careful surveillance on Hacker and Degussa. "Don't lose them, Sean." Hanging up, he rubbed his face. "If you're right about Jerry Quick assigning Christi to Gavin and to Degussa, he used her in ways she couldn't imagine."

He snatched up an appetizer. Gulped it down. Frowned.

"Bad batch?" I said.

"Bad world."

CHAPTER

44

Roxbury Park—4:40 P.M.
The picnic tables. Shade from the Chinese elms and a declining sun turned the redwood the color of old asphalt.

This late in the afternoon, only four children occupied the play area. Two little boys roaring and running wildly, a toddling girl, hand held by her mother, making her way up the stairs of a double-hump slide and whooshing down. Over and over. Another boy, pensive, alone, sitting and scooping sand and letting it trickle through his tiny fingers. Three uniformed maids discussed something with glee and animation. Blue jays squawked and mockingbirds aped them. Traffic from Olympic was distant and hushed.

The ten-year-old ice-cream truck, once white now gray, was parked facing the fence. The truck's flanks were decorated with hand-painted renderings of sugary delights in unlikely colors. An elaborately calligraphic statement of ownership read: GLO-GLO FROZEN DESSERTS, PROP: RAMON HERNANDEZ, COMPTON, CALIFORNIA.

On the front passenger seat was a cooler stocked with juice bars, cream sandwiches, and pop-ups. In case anyone asked.

So far, no one had. The trickle of kids and the lateness of the hour combined to discourage commerce. And the truck's position, too, just out of sight of the play area.

Parked close enough to have a clear view of the picnic tables.

In the driver's seat sat a detective named Sam Diaz, a technical specialist from Parker Center. Thirty-five, compact, mustachioed, Diaz wore a white sweatshirt over baggy white cotton painter's pants. A coin dispenser hung from his waist. In his pocket was a commercial food license identifying him as Ramon Hernandez and a wallet full of small bills. Under the sweatshirt rested his holstered 9 mm.

Jerry-built into the truck's dashboard was forty thousand dollars of long-distance, outdoor recording equipment. The kind National Geographic uses to memorialize birdcalls. The mikes were turned down, and the arias of the jays and mockingbirds were reduced to peeps. So was the noise from the play area: squeaks of high-pitched glee, the murmur of adult voices.

The equipment was hard to spot, unless you got inside the truck and saw all the knobs and the LEDs and the wires that ran under the partition separating the seats from the rear storage area. A talk hole had been cut into the partition, covered by a sliding door, now open. The truck's doors were locked, and its windows were tinted several shades darker than the legal limit. Hasty job, some of the tinting plastic had puckered around the edges. Why anyone would go to the trouble of concealing an ice-cream truck was the obvious question, but no one was asking.

Milo and I sat in back, on two vinyl bench seats borrowed from an impounded Toyota and bolted to the floor. Another hasty job;

the stiff cushions wobbled and squeaked when we moved, and keeping still was driving Milo crazy. He'd finished two ice-cream sandwiches and a peanut-studded drumstick, balled up the wrappers, and tossed them in a corner. Muttering, "Gluttony rules."

Behind the truck was an alley, and beyond that the high-fenced backyards of the pretty view houses on South Spalding Drive. Through a tiny, tinted heart-shaped window cut into one of the truck's rear doors, we could see fifty feet north or south. During the hour we'd been there, eight cars had driven through. No movement from the houses. That was to be expected; this was Beverly Hills.

Bolted to our side of the partition was a small, color TV monitor with a digital readout that ticked off the passage of time. The tint was off: Bright Beverly Hills green had faded to olive, tree trunks were gray, the sky was butter-yellow.

A speaker that hung from a metal hook to the right of the monitor supplied the sound effects.

The only sound, now, was Franco Gull shifting his position on the redwood bench.

He fooled with his hair, gazed off into the distance, studied the top of the table. Working at being disinterested, as he tried to get down some coffee in a Starbucks cup. Big cup, *grande-mega-poobah,* or whatever they called it.

During our second meeting, he'd worked at friendly. Telling me he understood I had good intentions. Letting slip, midway through the interview, that he'd suspected "something wasn't right" with Sentries for Justice, but not knowing what to do about it.

Appreciative of his deal. This was his payment.

The miniature microphone that transmitted his occasional sighs was affixed to the bottom of the picnic table.

Wiring the table was the obvious way to go. Sam Diaz had taken one look at Gull, and said, "The way he sweats, I wire him, he might just go and electrocute himself."

Other than that, Gull's anxiety was no problem. He was supposed to be nervous.

Now, he waited.

We all did.

◆

At five after five, Diaz said, "I've got someone approaching from the Roxbury side—across the bocci field."

A figure—male, anonymous—could be seen in the upper-right quadrant of the monitor. Then lower, larger, as it got closer. As the man approached Gull's park bench, Albin Larsen's form took shape. Today, he wore a wheat-colored sport coat, tan shirt, tan pants. At least that's what I assumed; the monitor dulled it down to off-white.

"That's him," said Milo.

"Mr. Beige," said Diaz. "I coulda used black-and-white."

"Yeah, he's a riot."

When Larsen got close to the bench, he acknowledged Gull with a small nod. Sat down. Said nothing.

Diaz fiddled with a dial and the bird sounds amplified.

Gull said, "Thanks for seeing me, Albin." The speaker turned his voice tinny.

Larsen said, "You sounded upset."

Gull: "I am, Albin."

Larsen crossed his legs and glanced over at the children. Two kids remained. One maid.

Diaz fiddled with another dial, and his

camera zoomed in on Larsen's face. Passive. Impassive.

Diaz backed up, captured both men.

Gull: "The police have been questioning me, Albin."

Larsen: "Really."

Gull: "You don't sound surprised."

Larsen: "I assume it's about Mary."

Gull: "It started out about Mary, but now they're asking questions that confuse me, Albin. About us—our group, our billing."

Silence.

"Albin?"

"Go on," said Larsen.

"About Sentries for *Justice,* Albin."

Milo said, "Guy thinks he's an actor."

I said, "Today, he is."

Albin Larsen still hadn't responded.

We listened to birdcalls, a three-year-old's shout.

Gull said, "Albin?"

Larsen said, "Really."

Gull: *"Really."*

Larsen: "What kinds of questions?"

Gull: "Whose idea was the program, how'd we hear about it, how long has it been going on, did all three of us participate. Then they got personal, and that's

what's bothering me. How much I, personally, billed, could I verify the figures. Did
Mary or you ever talk to me about inten-
tional overbilling. They were really gung ho,
Albin. Fascistic. Sounds to me like they suspect some kind of fraud. Is there something
you and Mary never told me about?"

Silence. Eleven seconds.

Larsen said, "Who asked these questions?"

"The same cops who were by the first
time, along with some idiot from Medi-Cal."

Silence. Gull moved closer to Larsen.
Larsen didn't budge.

Sam Diaz said, "This one's cagey. Bet
he's dry as a bone."

Fourteen seconds; fifteen, sixteen.

Gull: "Is something going on, Albin?
Because if there is, I need to know. *I'm* the
one they're harassing, and I don't know
what to tell them. Is there something I
should know?"

Larsen: "Why would there be?"

Gull: "They—they seem so *sure* of themselves. As if they're really onto something. I
know you and Mary wanted me to see
more Sentries patients, but I told you, I

really wasn't into it. So why would they be bothering *me*? I had nothing to do with the program."

Silence. Nine seconds.

Gull: "Right, Albin?"

Larsen: "Maybe they think you're knowledgeable."

Gull: "I'm not."

Larsen: "Then you should have nothing to worry about."

Gull: "Albin, *is* there something to worry about?"

Larsen: "What did you tell them about your billings?"

Gull: "That I billed for the few patients I saw, and that was it. They were skeptical. I could see it in their faces. Just about came out and called me a liar and said they found what I was telling them hard to believe. Even though it was true—you know that, Albin."

Eleven seconds.

Gull: "Come on, Albin. *Is* there some billing thing I *don't* know about?"

Larsen: "This is really upsetting you."

Gull: "Don't play shrink with me, Albin."

Larsen placed a palm over his heart and smiled faintly.

Gull: "I ask you a straightforward question, and you come back with 'This is really upsetting you.' I've been through the wringer with those fascists, this isn't the time for Rogerian bullshit, Albin."

Sixteen seconds. Then Albin Larsen stood, and Sam Diaz said, "Uh-oh."

Larsen walked several feet away from the table, hands clasped behind his back. Closer to the play area. A professor thinking deep thoughts.

Franco Gull glanced back in the direction of the truck. Helpless expression on his moist face. Looking right at us.

Milo said, "Idiot."

Larsen returned to the table and sat back down. "You're obviously upset, Franco. Mary's death and what it means for us is upsetting."

Gull: "That's the thing, Albin. I get the feeling—from them, the police—that they think Mary's death had something to do with Sentries. I know that's sounds crazy, but if that's what *they* think, who knows where it will lead?"

Four seconds.

Larsen: "Why would they think that?"

Gull: "You tell me. If you know something I should know, you have to tell me, it's only fair. *I'm* on the hot seat—you have no idea how they treat you when they suspect you of something. They phone me incessantly, have me break appointments and come in for interrogations. Have you ever been in a police station, Albin?"

Larsen smiled. "From time to time."

Gull: "Yeah, probably some place in Africa, whatever. But you haven't been a suspect. Let me tell you, it's not fun."

Thirteen seconds.

Gull: "They call it interviewing, but it's interrogation. I swear, Albin, I feel like some character out of a goddamned movie. One of those Kafkaesque things, Hitchcock, everything happens to the unsuspecting fool, and I'm he."

Larsen: "It sounds dreadful."

Gull: "It's *horrendous*. And disruptive—it's starting to affect my work. How the hell am I supposed to concentrate on patients when the next message on my machine could be from them? What if they start shoving paper at me—subpoenas, whatever it is they use. What if they try to comb through my records?"

Larsen: "Did they use the word 'subpoena'?"

Gull: "Who remembers? The point is, they're rooting around like truffle pigs."

Larsen: "Rooting. That's all it is."

Gull: "Albin, I feel I'm not getting through to you." He took hold of Larsen's shoulders. Larsen didn't move, and Gull's hands dropped. "Why are they focusing on Sentries? Tell me the truth: What were you and Mary up to?"

Silence. Six seconds.

Larsen: "We were attempting to inject some compassion into the American criminal justice system."

Gull: "Yeah, yeah, I know all that. I mean nuts and bolts, the billing. It's the billing they're latching onto. They just about came out and said they suspect us of Medi-Cal fraud, Albin. Were you fooling with the billing?"

Larsen: "Why would I do that."

Milo said, "Cagey bastard."

Gull: "I don't know. But they suspect something. Before this thing spins out of control, I need to know if there's any truth to their suspicions. Even if it was some kind of mistake, some paperwork thing. Did you—or Mary—do anything—anything at all—that would give them fuel? Because I think they're after blood, Albin. I really do. I think Mary's death got them thinking in a whole bizarre direction. Obsessive. Like that patient of Mary's who died—you know I treated him. Gavin Quick. Kid was four-plus OCD in addition to all his other problems. I was happy to dump him on Mary but I swear, Albin, dealing with them I started to feel I was being forced into some OCD soap opera. The same questions, over and over and over. As if they're trying to break me down."

Eighteen seconds.

Gull: "You're not saying anything."

Larsen: "I'm listening."

"Fine . . . you know how it is with obsession. The patient gets into something and keeps going at it. Which is okay when you're the therapist and can establish boundaries. But being on the receiving end—these are not sophisticated people, Albin, but they are persistent. They perceive the world in hunter-prey terms and have no respect for our profession. I'm feeling like I'm set up to be the prey, and I don't want that. And I shouldn't think you'd want it, either."

Larsen: "Who would?"

Milo said, "Such empathy."

Sam Diaz said, "If *this* guy was hooked up to the poly, the needles wouldn't even be quivering. Gull, he'd make the machine explode."

Gull waved his hands. Diaz backed the camera several feet farther, establishing postural context.

Larsen just sat there.

Thirty-two seconds of silence passed before Gull said, "I have to say, I'm feeling a little . . . dismissed, Albin. I asked you substantive questions, and you've given me nothing but bland reassurance."

Larsen placed a hand on Gull's shoulder. His voice was gentle. "There's nothing for me to tell you, my friend."

Gull: "Nothing?"

Larsen: "Nothing to be concerned about." Three seconds. "Nothing to lose sleep over."

Gull: "Easy for you to say, you're not the one who's being—"

Larsen: "Would it make you feel better if I spoke to them?"

Gull: "To the police?"

Larsen: "To the police, to the Medi-Cal people. Anyone you like. Would it make you feel better?"

Gull glanced back toward the truck, then he returned his attention to Larsen. Larsen was watching the children, again.

Gull: "Yes, as a matter of fact it would. It would make me feel substantially better, Albin."

Larsen: "Then I will do that."

Six seconds.

Gull: "What will you tell them?"

Larsen: "That nothing . . . untoward has gone on."

Gull: "And that's true?"

Larsen gave Gull's shoulder another pat. "I'm not worried, Franco."

Gull: "You really think you can clear things up."

Larsen: "There's nothing to clear up."

Gull: "Nothing?"

Larsen: "Nothing."

Milo said, "Cold bastard. He's not gonna spill, so much for this."

Sam Diaz's chair squeaked. He said, "Want another drumstick?"

"No, thanks."

"Maybe I'll try one of those orange bars, the vanilla half looks pretty creamy."

On the monitor, Franco Gull ran his hands

through his curls. "Okay, I sure hope so. Thanks, Albin."

He rose to go.

"No, no, no," said Milo. "Stay put, you idiot."

The remaining maid collected her young charges and left.

Larsen stayed Gull with a hand on Gull's cuff. "Let's sit for a while, Franco."

Gull: "Why?"

Larsen: "Enjoy the air. This beautiful park. Enjoy life."

Gull: "You're finished with patients for the day?"

Larsen: "I am, indeed."

Ninety seconds. Neither of them talked.

At a hundred thirty-nine seconds, Sam Diaz said, "Approaching male. From the Roxbury side, again."

Another figure, well in the distance, was crossing the park diagonally, from the east. Striding across the lawn, passing just north of the play area, and continuing into the shadow of the Chinese elms.

Diaz aimed the camera at him, zoomed in.

Good-sized man, broad-shouldered, barrel chest. Blue silk shirt turned teal green by the monitor, worn untucked over blue jeans.

Dark hair combed straight back. Graying mustache, but Raymond Degussa had shaved off his soul patch.

Milo said, "Bad guy, get ready for anything, Sam."

He unsnapped his holster but didn't remove his gun. Unlatching one of the ice-cream truck's rear doors, he got out, closed the door quietly.

I turned back to the monitor. Gull and Larsen remained silent. Gull's back was to Degussa as Degussa made his way over to the picnic table. Larsen saw Degussa, but didn't react.

Then Franco Gull turned, and said, "What's *he* doing here?"

No answer from Larsen.

Gull: "What's going on, Albin—hey, let go of my sleeve, why are you holding me back, let go, what the hell's going on—"

Degussa made a beeline for the table. Was six feet away, reaching under his shirt, when Gull broke free from Larsen's grasp.

Larsen just sat there.

Degussa pulled out a small gun, toylike, pointed it in Gull's direction. Probably a cheap .22, you could throw them away and buy another on the street for chump change.

Five feet from Gull, nice clean target. I thought about Jack Ruby picking off Oswald. Where was Milo?

Gull ducked and shoved Larsen in the path of Degussa's gun and screamed, "Help!" as he dropped to the grass and rolled away. Diaz's camera remained narrowly focused.

Degussa circled around Larsen to get a good shot at Gull. Larsen ducked, helping him along. Gull had tried to get up, but he was caught—legs stuck under the picnic bench, torso twisted.

He placed his hands atop his head, creating a useless shield.

Degussa leaned over the bench.

Aimed.

Crack. The sound of a single pair of hands clapping once.

A hole appeared on Degussa's forehead—black tinted deep brown by the monitor, the same shade as Degussa's customized Lincoln. His mouth dropped open. He frowned. Annoyed.

He lifted his gun arm, still trying to shoot. Let it drop. Tumbled face-first onto the table. The .22 flew out of his hands and landed on the dirt. Albin Larsen dove for it. The man could mobilize when needed.

Sam Diaz said, "Oh, man, I should be out there."

"Where's Milo?"

"Don't see him—I'm calling for backup, then I'm outta here, Doc. You stay inside."

He got on the police radio. I watched Albin Larsen bend and retrieve Degussa's gun. Gull had freed his legs, and he swung them at Larsen, missed, sprang up, turned to run.

Larsen examined the gun, then aimed it, turning his back to the camera.

Crack. Crack. Two bursts of applause. Two holes materialized on the back of Larsen's sport coat, within an inch of each other, just right of the center seam.

Diaz was saying, "Another one just went down, this is Code Three Plus, friend."

Larsen straightened. Stretched his neck, as if plagued by a sudden pinch. The spot on his jacket became a brown stain. His right hand reached back, scratching an itch.

He changed his mind. Rotated, showed the camera a partial profile.

Expressionless. More dreadful applause,

and something puffed in the center of Larsen's neck. At the juncture of ruddy neck flesh with tan shirt.

Larsen reached for that, too. His arms shot out spastically and flopped to his sides.

His body lurched forward, onto the grass.

Gull was twenty feet away, staring, screaming.

Birdsongs on the speaker.

Still life on the monitor.

The Starbucks cup hadn't even moved.

◆

The truck's rear door burst open, and Milo threw himself in.

Ghostly white, breathing hard. "Someone's up there," he panted. "Has to be one of the houses on Spalding, a backyard. Has to be a rifle, I was pinned next to the van."

Diaz returned to the cab, slid the partition open. "Backup's on its way. Gotta be a long-range scope. You okay?"

"Yeah, I'm fine."

Seconds later—seventeen seconds, according to the monitor—came the sirens.

CHAPTER
45

Bennett Hacker folded easily.

Faced with a mountain of evidence compiled by Medi-Cal fraud investigator Dwight Zevonsky—a twenty-nine-year-old with the look of a hippie grad student and the manner of a grand inquisitor—the parole officer traded full disclosure for a guilty plea to fraud and grand larceny that brought him a six-year sentence in a federal prison. Out of California, under protective isolation because Hacker had once been a Barstow patrolman and former cops didn't fare well behind bars, even those who'd befriended cons.

The scam had gone just as we'd theorized: Hacker and Degussa trolling for halfway-house residents whose names could be registered as Sentries patients. Compensating the parolees with small cash payments or drugs, or sometimes nothing at all. At first the cons showed up for sign-in sessions and one follow-up, in the unoccupied suite on the ground floor. Later even that pretext was dropped.

Later, the patient population had stretched beyond the halfway houses, with Degussa charged with finding new recruits.

"Sometimes we used dope, sometimes Ray just scared the junkies," Hacker said. "Ray gives you a look, that can be enough."

He smiled and smoked. Knowing he'd made a good deal. Probably working out six years of angles.

Milo and Zevonsky sat across from him in the interview room. I watched through the one-way mirror. Before being booked, Hacker's contact lenses had been removed, and he'd been issued cheap jail eyeglasses with clear plastic frames. A size too large, they slid down his nose and made his chin appear even skimpier. The gestalt was creepy: malicious nerd in County blues.

Hacker tried to tell the story as if he wasn't a protagonist. Degussa and "his partner" receiving two-thirds of the billings filed under Franco Gull's name—splitting slightly over two hundred thousand dollars during a sixteen-month period.

"Ray was unhappy," said Hacker. "He figured the others were making millions, he should be getting more."

"What did he do about it?" said Milo.

"He was planning to talk to them about it."

"Them," said Zevonsky, "being . . ."

"The shrinks—Koppel and Larsen."

"They were in charge."

"It was all them. They cooked it up, came to me."

"How'd you know them?"

"Koppel used to see me at the halfway house she owned. Checking up on my charges."

"She came to you," said Zevonsky.

"That's right."

"And your job was to . . ."

"Sign my name to some therapy forms. Also, to pinpoint good candidates."

"Meaning?"

"Druggies, losers, guys who wouldn't give problems." Hacker smiled. "She was a businesswoman."

Milo said, "She owned the halfway houses in partnership, with her ex."

"So?"

"What about him?"

"Fat boy? He owned the houses, but he had nothing to do with it."

Zevonsky said, "You're sure you want to go on record saying that?"

"I'm on record because it's true. Why would I lie to you?" Puff puff. "Hell, if I could bring someone else into this, I would. Spread the wealth, do myself some more good."

"Maybe you'd lie just for the fun of it?" said Milo.

"This isn't fun," said Hacker. "This isn't anything near fun."

"What about Jerome Quick?" said Milo.

"Again with that? The only Quick I know is Gavin, and I already told you about him. Who's Jerry, the kid's brother?"

I already told you about him.

Recounting it coldly. Gavin snooping around the building after hours, seeing scruffy men filing in and out for five-minute visits, overhearing things. Conversations about billing.

Gavin, the brain-injured would-be investigative reporter, stumbling upon a real story. And dying because of it.

"Crazy idiot," said Hacker.

"Crazy idiot because he snooped," said Milo.

"And opened up his big yap. He went and told Koppel about his suspicions. During therapy. He'd never seen her with the cons, so I guess he assumed she wasn't in on it. She told Larsen, said she'd handle it. Larsen didn't believe her, had Ray handle it."

Confidentiality.

Milo said, "Who did Gavin see with the cons?"

"Ray and Larsen."

"Aren't you leaving something out?" said Dwight Zevonsky.

Hacker smoked and nodded. "I was occasionally there. Mostly, my job was getting names, making sure the cons were stable."

"Passing out bribes," said Zevonsky.

"Whatever."

Milo said, "Did Koppel know Gavin was going to be whacked?"

"No," said Hacker. "Like I said, she thought she could handle it."

"Larsen didn't believe her."

"Larsen didn't want to wait."

"So he called Ray."

"Ray had done it before."

"Killed for Larsen?"

"No, for himself."

"Who?"

"Guys in prison."

"What about another woman?"

Pause. "Maybe that, too."

"Maybe?" said Milo.

"I don't know for sure. Ray implied it. Said when women put him down they were gonna get stuck with the tab. When he said it, he was playing with a knife. Cleaning his nails."

"Get stuck. He used those words."

"It was a . . . figure of speech with him. When someone went down they were stuck with the tab. Ray could be generous. When we partied, he'd give women whatever they wanted. Long as they didn't disappoint him."

"Disappoint him, how?"

"By not doing what he wanted."

"Bossy fellow," said Milo.

"He could be," said Hacker.

"So Koppel wasn't in on Gavin's murder."

"I told you. No. When she found out, figured out what happened, she went nuts. Threatened to shut the whole thing down. Larsen tried to calm her down, but she was pretty upset. I think what bugged her the most was that one of her patients had been whacked. She took that personally."

"So Ray whacked her, too."

Hacker nodded.

"He told you he was gonna do it. Told you about Gavin, too."

"Uh-uh, no way. If he told me, I would've tried to stop it."

"Being an upright guy and all that," said Milo.

"Hey," said Hacker, winking. "I used to be his PO."

"What about Christina Marsh?"

"She partied with us, a slut, Ray was fucking her. She was a stripper, and he liked her 'cause she was stupid and had a tight body. He bought her expensive stuff."

"Like what?"

"Clothes, perfume. Like I said, Ray could be generous."

"All the money you were making, he could afford to be."

"It ran through his fingers," said Hacker. "Typical con."

"Ray buy Christina shoes?"

"Wouldn't surprise me."

"He liked her."

"He liked what she *did* for him."

"Until . . ."

"Until what?" said Hacker.

"She was also up there on Mulholland, Bennett."

"True," said Hacker.

"This is full disclosure? The deal can be turned around."

Hacker pushed his glasses up his nose. "The deal's already inked."

"You keep twisting things to put yourself out of the picture, we'll tear up the papers and send you over for a 187 prosecution."

"I'm putting myself out of the picture because I wasn't in that picture," said Hacker. "In the Sentries picture, yes. The help-with-the-paperwork picture, yes. But not the up-on-Mulholland picture."

"You knew Ray was going to whack Gavin."

"He never came out and said so."

"He hinted," said Milo. "Said someone was gonna get stuck with the tab."

Hacker hesitated. Nodded.

"He told you about it, afterward."

"Who says?"

"You were roommates."

"We weren't asshole buddies."

Milo mimed tearing up a sheet of paper.

Hacker said, "What he said was, 'I solved our problem.' I didn't ask. Later, a couple of days later, we were getting high in the apartment and he was feeling good and he told me the details. Said it went down easy, the kid was surprised, he didn't put up any resistance."

"Why'd he kill Christina Marsh?"

" 'Cause she was there."

"Any other motivation?"

"He said she irritated him by being with the kid."

"Irritated."

"That's the word he used. Ray had a way . . . using little words for big feelings. I know for a fact that Christi irritated him other times, too, because he told me."

"What'd she do?"

"It's what she didn't do. Not being there when Ray wanted her to be. One time, he scored some high-class coke, wanted to party with her, and she wasn't available. Then she did that again. Said she was busy. Ray didn't like being told no."

"How'd Ray meet Christi?"

"Some bar," said Hacker. "He picked her up."

"A bar where?"

"Playa Del Rey. The Whale Watch. It's a place we went a lot."

"Christi was there," said Milo.

"Right there," said Hacker. "Ripe for the picking—Ray's words."

"You party with her, too?"

Hacker laughed and smoked, shoved his glasses up again, took them off, and said, "I need a smaller size of these."

Milo said, "You party with Christi Marsh, Bennett?"

"Not quite."

"Why's that?"

"Ray wasn't into sharing."

"Ray ever talk about someone named Flora Newsome?"

"Her?" said Hacker, surprised. "Yeah, I knew Flora; she temped at an office where I worked."

"Ray come into that office?"

"Yeah," said Hacker. "As a matter of fact, Ray knew her, too. They dated for a while."

"As a matter of fact," said Milo.

"Why? What's she got to do with any-thing?"

"She got stuck with the check."

Hacker's myopic eyes bugged. "You're kidding."

"You didn't know?"

"I transferred out of that office—it was a satellite—after maybe two weeks. Flora? I liked her. Nice girl, quiet. I thought about dating her myself, but then Ray started with her."

"And Ray didn't like to share."

"He *did* her?"

"Oh, yeah," said Milo.

"Too bad," said Hacker. His voice had dropped; he looked as if he meant it.

"Something bother you, Bennett?"

"What'd she do to piss Ray off?"

"You don't know?"

"I swear I don't."

"You said Ray implied he'd done women."

"Yeah, but like I said he just hinted around—you're saying that was her? Flora? Shit."

"That bother you, Bennett?"

"Sure it does. I liked her. Nice girl. After Ray said he wasn't dating her anymore, I told him maybe I'd give her a try. He got irritated with me, told me sloppy seconds was for losers." Hacker licked his lips. "I thought about doing it anyway, I liked Flora. But you didn't want Ray irritated at you. Was it in the papers?"

"Nope," said Milo. "Small-time story."

"Flora," said Hacker. "Unreal."

"You guys have fun rooming in the Marina?"

"His idea, not mine," said Hacker. "He was supposed to split the rent, so I thought, why not, we'd go our separate ways. He paid one month."

"Don't tell me," said Milo. "You didn't complain."

"Like I said."

"Ray a good roomie?"

"Actually, yes," said Hacker. "Made his bed, vacuumed. You know cons, they can be real neat. I thought it would save me some money. My plan was to own the place, not just rent. My main place is a shit-hole, you saw it. I like the water—you're sure the federal thing is buttoned down? I won't be close to anyone I might've worked with in California? I don't want to be watching my back all the time."

"Buttoned tight."

Hacker smoked, smiled. All thoughts of Flora Newsome vanished.

Milo said, "Something amusing, Bennett?"

"I was thinking," said Hacker. "When the six years are over, I'm gonna be assigned to someone like me."

CHAPTER

46

It would be a long time before Jerry Quick's entire story would be told.

"Maybe never," said Milo.

There was a dash of false hope. A week after I'd seen Kelly Quick and her mother, Kelly made the mistake of using a conventional cell phone, not a prepaid, when she called Rio de Janeiro. Milo had gotten a subpoena for her account, and he traced the call.

"Staybridge Suites Hotel, São Paulo, Brazil."

"Brazil has no extradition treaty with the U.S.," I said.

"Funny thing about that. Quick checked in four days ago with a woman, paid cash, checked out yesterday, no indication where. The registration book lists them as Mr. and Mrs. Jack Schnell, Englewood, New Jersey, and they had passports to prove it. The desk clerk describes it as a May-December thing. Gray-haired guy, younger woman, dark, slim."

"She have blue fingernails?"

"Ka-ching, you get the kewpie doll. Clerk said they looked deeply in love. Clerk said Mr. Schnell bought Mrs. Schnell a string bikini and various other baubles."

I said, "Schnell means 'quick' in German."

"Yeah, I know. Ha-ha-ha."

◆

Mistake number two: A MasterCard belonging to Sheila Quick had been used to rent a room at a Days Inn in Pasadena. Milo and I drove out there, spotted Sheila reading a softcover by the pool, covered by a bulky robe; no string bikini, there. She looked pale and small, and we avoided her and walked up to her room.

Milo's knock was answered by a young female voice. "Yes?"

"Housekeeping."

Kelly Quick opened the door. Saw him,

then me. Said, "Oh, no." She was barefoot, had her hair pinned up, and wore glasses, cutoffs, and an oversized olive drab T-shirt that read US ARMY SPECIAL FORCES. WE GET THE JOB DONE. In her hand was ten pounds of law book.

Milo said, "Hi, Kelly," and showed her his badge.

She said, "I haven't done anything."

"How's the weather in São Paulo?"

She sagged. "I screwed up, should've used a pay phone. He's going to . . ." Her mouth clamped shut.

"Going to what, Ms. Quick?"

Tears filled her eyes. "Going to be disappointed in me."

Milo steered her back into the room. Twin beds, neatly made up. Soda cans and take-out cartons and female clothing all over the place. More law books piled up on a night-stand.

He sat her down on one of the beds. "How's the studying going?"

"It's hard to concentrate."

"Going back in the fall?"

"Who knows."

"No need for this to be difficult, Kelly."

"You think?" she said. "That's a laugh."

"How long are you planning to live this way? Taking care of your mom."

Kelly's dark eyes flashed. "I don't take care of her. She's . . . you can't take care of her, you can just watch her."

"Make sure she doesn't hurt herself."

"Whatever."

I said, "She needs real help, Kelly. And you need to get on with your life."

She glared at me. Foam collected at the corners of her mouth. "You're so damn smart, tell me how to do that."

"Let's call your aunt—"

"Eileen's a bitch."

"She's also an adult, and she lives in California. You need to be back in Boston."

"Whatever." Blink blink.

I said, "We can help you with all that."

"Sure you can."

Milo said, "Where's your dad headed?"

"Uh-uh, screw your help—leave me alone."

"That T-shirt," said Milo. "Dad give it to you?"

No answer.

"I've done some research, Kelly. Found a website where he attended his army reunion. What the site didn't say was that he was in a Special Forces unit. Qualified as a sniper."

Kelly closed her eyes.

Milo said, "I was in Vietnam, myself, know the unit. He was in some pretty hairy situations."

"I wouldn't know."

"I'd bet you would, Kelly. Bet Dad told you plenty."

"Then you'd lose your bet."

"The other thing my research turned up was that no one can seem to find any evidence your dad ever traded metals. We know what he really did for a living, Kelly. His latest freelance was for a gentleman from Africa. He tell you about that? Tell you what he did to pay the bills?"

She turned away from us. "He was a businessman. He supported us."

"So where is he now?"

She shook her head.

"Brazil," said Milo. "With a girl not much older than you."

"He's entitled," Kelly blurted. "He did his best with . . . her. My mom. You don't know what it's like."

"Mom's tough."

"Mom's . . ." She threw up her hands. "She's who she is."

"That's exactly why you shouldn't be forced to be her nurse."

"I'm *not* her nurse; you don't know what you're talking about."

"Look," said Milo, "it's just a matter of time. We're going to dig, and we're going to find out where he got his money and where he keeps it. That happens, any financial support for your mom's going to be turned off."

Kelly faced him. "Why are you doing this? My brother's dead and my mother's sick and he's gone. Don't I deserve a life?"

"You do. You do, indeed."

"Then leave me alone!" she screamed. "Everyone leave me alone!" She lay down on the bed, curled up, scrunched her face, and began pounding the mattress.

Milo gave me a helpless look.

I said, "Let's go."

◆

We stopped at a place on Colorado Boulevard for coffee and theory.

"Protais Bumaya existed," he said. "You saw him, I saw him. But no one's got any record of him entering or leaving the country, and those names he gave us—his supposed friends? Bogus. I never bothered to check. Guy snookered me good."

"He probably tagged along on some kind of diplomatic mission."

He aimed an index finger at me. "Another ka-ching. Matter of fact, last month a trade delegation from Rwanda toured the country. Bumaya's name wasn't on the roster, but what the hell does that mean? Meanwhile, Mr. McKenzie, the erstwhile Rwandan consul in S.F., is charming but not very helpful."

I covered my eyes, then my ears and mouth.

"The techs went over that backyard on Spalding. Owners had been out of town for a month, the gates were locked, but it was easy enough to hop over. Perfect view of the park bench and easy hiding behind a big thatch of banana plants. Wet soil, you'd think there'd be a footprint, but *nada*. Not a single indentation, no shell casings, no cigarette butts."

"Jerry's a pro," I said. "Freelancing for foreign governments. Perfect civilian transition for a restless old Special Forces guy."

"I got B.H. techs to go through his house.

They found gunpowder residue and some iron filings in a locker in the garage but no weapons. Big locker, though, enough for a sizable stash. Rifles, scopes, all the good stuff."

"Bumaya hired Quick to avenge the murdered boys," I said, "and maybe some other people, too. Quick kept a close watch on Larsen, learned about the scam, bided his time. Maybe he was trying to figure out a way to get hold of Larsen's scam money. Like an abduction, where he could force Larsen to give up PIN numbers or foreign account access. He connected Larsen to Mary Lou and Mary Lou to Koppel. Became Sonny's tenant as a way to get closer. Then Gavin had his accident and provided him with another opportunity: He knew Mary Lou was involved in the scam, but he had no beef with her. He chatted up Sonny, got Sonny to refer him to Mary Lou. Sending his kid for therapy would make his presence at the building easy to explain. Mary Lou punted to Gull, but that was no big deal for Jerry. Remember how Gull told us that it was Jerry, not Sheila who brought Gavin in for his first appointment."

"Concerned father," he said. "Special

Forces–trained pro, and he doesn't pay his rent on time."

"Everyone's got their vulnerabilities," I said. "Money was his. Supporting a Beverly Hills lifestyle with intermittent freelance hits could've been a strain. So was feigning respectability and keeping a mistress on the side. A big-bucks payoff would've allowed him some squeeze room. That's why he kept his eye fixed on the scam. Then Gavin messed things up by playing his own little spy game. Copying down license numbers and including his father's. That night, maybe Jerry followed Gavin. Or he was doing his own surveillance and had no idea Gavin had spotted *him*. Maybe Gavin even told him about it, and Jerry explained it away, warned Gavin off. But Gavin was obsessive. He persisted and got killed and Jerry knew why, and now he had another reason to get rid of Larsen. And a second target: Degussa. He cleaned out Gavin's room, to see exactly what Gavin knew, as well as to destroy any link to him. Then he went into hiding."

"Larsen and Degussa. And I led him right to them."

"That bother you?"

"Not one damn bit. You really think Gavin confronted the old man?"

"It's hard to say how much they communicated outside of Jerry trying to get Gavin laid. The first time we met Jerry, he told us he and Gavin were close, but I remember thinking that didn't feel right. He seemed out of touch. The fact that Kelly didn't fly out immediately was also odd. This family's finally come apart, but it was long in the making. Gavin's accident couldn't have been easy for any of them, Jerry included."

"You have sympathy for the guy," he said. "We start looking into his travel schedule, you know we're going to find a whole lot of dead people."

"If they're people like Albin Larsen, I won't be weeping."

He smiled. "Both of us making value judgments."

"It's a human quality."

"You're saying I should not look into his travel records."

"I'm saying Kelly Quick's a nice kid. And what sin did she commit other than to be loyal to her parents?"

"Yeah," he said. "Maybe she'll even go

back to school and become a lawyer. Whatever the hell that means in the greater scope of things."

And that's the last time we spoke about the Quick family.

CHAPTER

47

Friday, 10 A.M. Allison and I were flying to Vegas in eight hours. ("How about nothing wholesome, Alex? How about noise and lights and losing some hard-earned money at the tables?")

I figured to finish some long-neglected paperwork and leave with a clear head.

At 11:14 Milo called, and said, "I need a favor, but if you're jammed, just say so."

"What?"

"Your tone of voice. I'm bugging you."

"What do you need?"

"It took a while to free up Christi Marsh's body for burial. Cody Marsh went back to Minnesota, found a plot, now he's back and is headed over to the morgue. He's got more questions about why she died, wants to meet there. I'd do it, but between all the work on Gavin-Christi–Mary Lou-Flora and a new one—two drug dealers shot in Mar Vista—I'm superjammed."

"When did you pick that one up?"

"Three hours ago," he said. "A nonweird one, don't worry, nothing to bug you about. Bottom line, I really don't have time to deal with ol' Cody and give him the sensitivity he deserves."

"What should he be told?" I said.

"Not the whole truth, that's for sure. Emphasize Christi's good points. I'll leave it up to your wise discretion."

"When will he be at the morgue?"

"In two hours."

"Sure," I said.

"Thanks," he said. "As always."

◆

I drove to Boyle Heights and found a space in the lot that fronted the coroner's office. As I got out of the Seville, an old gray Chevy bumped and smoked into the lot and pulled ponderously into a nearby slot.

Sonny Koppel got out, shielded his eyes from the glare, stared at the sign above the door, and winced. He wore a short-sleeved yellow shirt over rumpled, gray cotton pants and white tennis shoes. His hair was slicked down, and his face bore an unhealthy flush.

He headed for the door. Stopped, saw me, and caught his breath.

"Hi," he said. "What brings you here?"

"Meeting someone."

"Something to do with Mary?"

"No," I said.

"Lots of people dying," he said. "I'm here to claim Mary's body. I've been trying for weeks, have no legal authority because we weren't married anymore. Finally, I cut through the red tape."

"It can be rough."

"Main thing is, I got permission." He sighed. "Mary never said what she'd want in this situation. I figure she'd be happy with cremation."

He looked at me, wanting counsel.

I said, "You'd know."

"Would I?" he said. "I don't think so. I don't think I know much."

"You did your best for her."

"That's nice of you to say."

"I think it's true."

He made puffing noises with his lips. "I hope you're right."

We reached the morgue's glass doors. I held one open for him.

"Thanks," he said. "Have a nice day."

"You, too."

"It's a challenge," he said, "but I'm trying."